Jessica Gilmore d[...]ily holiday. Jessica real[...]rue vocation and procee[...]sing her art: creating a *Dy*[...]and Morten Harket's cheekbones. Writing for Mills & [...]eally is a dream come true!

Married to an extremely patient man, Jessica lives in the beautiful and historic city of York with one daughter, one very fluffy dog, two dog-loathing cats and a goldfish called Bob.

On the rare occasions she is not writing, working, taking her daughter to activities or Tweeting, Jessica likes to plan holidays—and uses her favourite locations in her books. She writes deeply emotional romance with a hint of humour, a splash of sunshine and usually a great deal of delicious food—and equally delicious heroes.

Say hi on Twitter @yrosered or visit sprigmuslin.blogspot.com

Ellie Darkins spent her formative years devouring romance novels, and after completing her English degree decided to make a living from her love of books. As a writer and editor, she finds her work now entails dreaming up romantic proposals, hot dates with alpha males and trips to the past with dashing heroes. When she's not working she can usually be found at her local library or out for a run. You can visit her blog at elliedarkins.com

Cathy Williams is originally from Trinidad, but has lived in England for a number of years. She currently has a house in Warwickshire, which she shares with her husband Richard, her three daughters, Charlotte, Olivia and Emma, and their pet cat, Salem. She adores writing romantic fiction, and would love one of her girls to become a writer—although at the moment she is happy enough if they do their homework and agree not to bicker with one another!

Second Chance at Sea

JESSICA GILMORE
ELLIE DARKINS
CATHY WILLIAMS

MILLS & BOON

First Published in Great Britain 2019
by Mills & Boon, an imprint of HarperCollins*Publishers*
1 London Bridge Street, London, SE1 9GF

SECOND CHANCE AT SEA © 2019 Harlequin Books S. A.

The Return of Mrs Jones © 2014 Jessica Gilmore
Conveniently Engaged to the Boss © 2017 Ellie Darkins
Secrets of a Ruthless Tycoon © 2014 Cathy Williams

ISBN: 978-0-263-27744-9

0819

MIX
Paper from
responsible sources
FSC® C007454

FSC
www.fsc.org

This book is produced from independently certified FSC™
paper to ensure responsible forest management.

For more information visit: www.harpercollins.co.uk/green

Printed and bound in Spain
by CPI, Barcelona

THE RETURN OF MRS JONES

JESSICA GILMORE

For Dan.

Thanks for giving me the time to write
and always believing that I would make it.
I couldn't have done it without you. x

Special thanks must also go to my amazing critique
group, Jane, Julia and Maggie, for three years of pep
talks, brainstorming and patience, to Merilyn for
making writing fun and to Fiona Harper and Jessica
Hart for all their encouragement and support.

CHAPTER ONE

'YOU CAN COME in, you know. Or do you city folk wear coffee patches and bypass the actual drinking process now?'

Lawrie Bennett jumped as the mocking tones jolted her out of her stunned contemplation of the ultra-modern building clinging to the harbour's edge. Turning, half convinced she had conjured up his voice along with her memories, she saw him lounging against the arty driftwood sign, the same crooked smile lurking in familiar blue eyes.

'Jonas?'

No, not a ghost. Subtle changes showed the passage of time: the surfer-blond hair was a little shorter, and a few lines round the eyes added new character to the tanned face.

Embarrassment, guilt, humiliation. Lawrie could take her pick of any of that ugly trio. Being caught hanging around outside her ex-husband's business like a gauche teenager with a crush was bad enough. To have been caught *by* her ex-husband really was a fitting end to what had been a truly terrible few weeks.

Trying to summon up an illusion of control, Lawrie switched on her best social smile—the one that had seen her through numerous meetings and charity balls. But her eyes hadn't got the 'cool and collected' memo, and flicked quickly up and down the lean body facing her.

The black tailored trousers and short-sleeved charcoal shirt were a startling change from the cut-off jeans and band T-shirt uniform of her memories, but the body underneath the sharp lines was as surfer-fit as she remembered. He still looked irritatingly good. And even worse—judging by the smirk that flared briefly in the cool eyes—he was fully aware of both her perusal and approval.

So much for control.

Jonas quirked an eyebrow. 'So, are you…planning to come in?'

How, after all this time, could his voice be so familiar? It was such a long time since she had heard those deep, measured tones tempered with a slight Cornish burr. Yet they sounded like home.

'I was just wondering if I was in the right place,' she said, gesturing at the wood and glass building behind him; so shiny and new, so unfamiliar. 'Everything's different.'

And *that,* Lawrie thought, was the understatement of the century.

'I've made some changes. What do you think?' There was pride in his voice underneath the laid-back drawl.

'Impressive,' she said. And it was. But she missed the peeling, ramshackle old building. The picturesque setting for her first job, her first kiss. Her first love. 'Did you demolish the boathouse?'

Her heart speeded up as she waited for his answer. It mattered, she realised with a shock. She hadn't set foot in the small Cornish village for nine years. Hadn't seen this man for nine years. But it still mattered.

It was her history.

'I had it relocated. It was the start of everything, after all. Demolishing the old girl would have been pretty poor thanks. And we kept the name and brand, of course.'

'Everything?' Was he talking about her? *Get a grip,*

she told herself. Walking down the hill and along the harbour might have sent her spinning back in time, brought all those carefully buried memories abruptly to the surface, but by the look of the building in front of her Jonas had moved on long ago.

'So, are you coming in or not?' He ignored her question, pushing himself off the sign with the languid grace only hours balancing on a board in the rough Cornish sea could achieve. 'The coffee's excellent and the cake is even better. On the house for an ex member of staff, of course.'

Lawrie opened her mouth to refuse, to point out that the building wasn't the only thing to have changed—that, actually, she hadn't touched caffeine or refined sugar in years—but she caught a quizzical gleam in his eye and changed her mind. She wouldn't give him the satisfaction.

Besides, clean living hadn't got her very far, had it? This enforced time out was about new experiences, trying new things. There were worse places to start than a good cup of coffee brewed the way only Jonas could.

'Thank you,' she said instead.

'This way, then.' And Jonas moved to the double glass doors, holding one open for her with exaggerated gallantry. 'And, Lawrie,' he murmured as she walked past him, 'Happy Birthday.'

Lawrie froze. Just half an hour ago she had reached the sad conclusion that you couldn't get more pathetic than spending your thirtieth birthday on your own—not unless you were unemployed, single *and* alone on your thirtieth.

Lawrie was all three.

Adding an encounter with her ex really was the cherry on top of the icing on her non-existent birthday cake. She should have listened to her instincts and stayed indoors and sulked. Damn her conscience for pushing her out to get fresh air and exercise. Both were clearly overrated.

'This is where you say thank you.'

He had moved away from the door and was leading her towards a small table tucked away at the back, clearly at his ease.

'Sorry?' What was he talking about? Maybe she was in some surrealist dream, where conversation made no sense. Any second now she'd be viewing the world in black and white, possibly through the medium of mime.

'I know you've been in the city for a while…' there was an unexpected teasing note in his voice '…but back in the real world when someone wishes you a Happy Birthday it's usual to acknowledge them—often with a thank you.'

For the first time in over a week Lawrie felt the heaviness lift slightly, a lessening of the burden. 'Thank you,' she said with careful emphasis. 'Of course I *might* be trying to forget this particular birthday.'

'Oh, yes, the big three oh.' He laughed as she grimaced. 'It's really no big deal, once you get used to the back ache and the knee twinges.'

'I hoped it might be like the tree falling in the woods—if no one knows it's happening then is it real?'

'*I* know,' he reminded her.

'Thereby foiling my cunning plan.'

A smile curved the corner of his mouth but it didn't reach his eyes. They radiated concern. For her. She didn't need the stab of her conscience to tell her she didn't deserve his concern.

'Well, now it's out in the open you have to celebrate. How about a slice of my signature carrot cake with chocolate icing? Unless, now you're a Londoner, you prefer elaborate cupcakes? Pretty frosting but no real substance?'

Lawrie looked up sharply. Was that some kind of cake metaphor?

'Or would you rather wait till your fiancé joins you?'

And just like that the heaviness engulfed her again. Lawrie searched for the right words, the right tone. 'Hugo and I parted ways. It seemed time for a new beginning.'

'Again?'

There was a lifetime of history in that one word. More than Lawrie could cope with this day, this week. At all.

Coming back had been a mistake. But she had nowhere else to go.

Lawrie hadn't exactly spent the last nine years planning how she'd react if she bumped into her ex-husband, but if she *had* spent time imagining every possible scenario she doubted—short of falling at his feet—that she could have come up with a situation as humiliating as this.

She looked around, desperately searching for a change of subject. 'The café looks amazing.'

It really did. She was standing in an open-plan space, with the driftwood counter along its far end and the blue walls a reminder of the ever-present sea. The real thing was a stunning backdrop framed through dramatic floor-length windows. It was all very stylish—beautiful, even—but once again Lawrie felt a pang of nostalgia for the small, homespun bar she had known.

The season was not yet fully started, but the café was buzzing with mothers and small children, groups of friends and the ubiquitous surfers. There were no menus. The day's choices were chalked up on boards displayed around the spacious room and notices proclaimed the café's values—local, organic and sustainably sourced food.

A flare of pride hit her: *he's done it—he's realised his dreams*. Long before celebrity chefs had made local food trendy Jonas had been evangelical about quality ingredients, sourcing from local farms, and using only free-range eggs in his legendary fry-ups.

'I'm glad you approve. So, what will it be?'

For one second Lawrie wanted to startle him, order something he wouldn't expect. Prove that actually she *had* changed in nine years—changed a lot. But the temptation to sink into the comfort of the past was too much. 'Skinny latte with cinnamon, please. And if you have the carrot cake in…?' She peered up at the menu board, running her eyes over the long list of tasty-looking treats.

'Of course I have it in.'

Jonas turned away to deliver her order, but Lawrie could have sworn she heard him say, 'It *is* your birthday after all.'

She was still there. Jonas tried to keep his concentration on the screen in front of him but all his attention was on the cake-eating occupant at the small table below.

The mezzanine floor that housed his office was situated directly over the kitchens, shielded from the café with blue-tinted glass that gave him privacy whilst allowing him to look out. Some days he was so busy that he completely forgot where he was, and he would look up and notice the chattering people tucking in below in complete surprise. There were bigger offices at his hotel but he preferred it here. Where it had all begun.

'Jonas? Are you listening to me?'

He jumped. 'Of course,' he lied.

'You didn't even hear me come in! Honestly, Jonas, if I want to be ignored I'll stay at home and ask my husband to clean.'

'Sorry, Fliss, I was engrossed in this email.'

Fliss peered over his shoulder. 'I can see why. It's not every day you get offered a million pounds just for letting somebody borrow your bank account, is it?'

Damn spam. 'The spam filter should be picking these up. I was just wondering why it's not working.'

She shot him a sceptical look. 'Delete that and turn your

formidable mind to a real problem for a change. Suzy has been ordered to keep her feet up for the rest of her pregnancy and won't be able to project-manage Wave Fest for us.'

'Pregnancy?' He looked up in shock. 'I didn't know Suzy was expecting.'

'I expect she was keeping it a secret from you, knowing your less than enlightened views on working mothers,' Fliss said drily.

Jonas raised an eyebrow for one long moment, watching her colour with some satisfaction. 'I have no view on working mothers—or on working fathers, for that matter, I just expect my employees to pull their weight at *work*— not be at home with their feet up. Damn! There's only a month to go and we'll never get anyone to take over at this short notice. Fliss, is there any way you can take this on?'

'I don't think so.' The petite redhead was contrite. 'I still have a lot to do with the last café you bought, and if you do take over The Laurels I'll need to start on the rebrand there too. I can help with the PR—I usually do most of that anyway—but I cannot project-manage an entire festival. Suzy has all the information written out and timetabled, so at least all we need is someone to step in and run it.'

Jonas acknowledged the truth of Fliss's statement. Her workload was pretty full-on right now. He pushed his chair back and swivelled round, staring down sightlessly on the room below. 'Think, Fliss—is there anyone, any summer jobber, who's capable of taking this on?'

She stood lost in thought, concentration on her face, then shook her head. 'Nobody springs to mind.'

Jonas grimaced. 'We'll just have to bite the bullet and get a temp in—though that's far from ideal.'

It had been hard enough handing the festival over to Suzy when it and the rest of the business had got too big for him to manage comfortably alone, even with Fliss's support. Letting a stranger loose on such an important event was impossible to imagine.

But he couldn't see another way.

Fliss was obviously thinking along the same lines. 'A temp? That will take at least a week, *and* cost a fortune in agency fees.'

'Bringing outsiders in is never easy, but it looks like we have no choice. You and I will have to keep it all ticking over until we find somebody. We managed the first three, after all...'

She flashed a conspiratorial grin at him. 'Goodness knows how. But we were young and optimistic then—and they were a lot smaller affairs; we are victims of our own success. But, okay, I'll let Dave know I'm working late so he'd better come here for dinner. Again. We were going to come back for Open Mic Night anyway.'

'Great. You drive straight over to Suzy's and go over all those lists and spreadsheets with her. We'll divvy up tasks later. Have another think about anyone internally, and if there really is nobody I'll call a couple of agencies later today.'

A sense of satisfaction ran through him as he made the decision. He was a hands-on boss—too hands-on, some said—but he liked to know exactly how everything was handled, from salad prep to food sourcing. It was his name over the door after all.

Fliss saluted. 'Yes, Boss,' she said, then turned round to leave the room, only to stop with a strangled cry. 'Jonas! Look—in that corner over there.'

'Why exactly are you whispering?' Although he knew exactly what—exactly *who*—she had seen. He cocked an eyebrow at her, aiming for a nonchalance he didn't feel.

Lawrie's unexpected presence was no big deal. He had no intention of letting it become one.

Fliss obviously had other ideas. Her eyes were alight with excitement. 'It's Lawrie. *Look*, Jonas.'

'I know it's Lawrie, but I still don't know why you're whispering. She can't hear you, you know.'

'Of course she can't, but...' Her voice turned accusatory. 'You knew she was here and didn't tell me?'

'It slipped my mind—and it's obviously slipped yours that we were discussing a rather pressing work matter.' His tone was cool. 'Don't you have somewhere to be?'

'Five minutes?' Fliss gave him a pleading look. 'I can't *not* say hello.'

To Jonas's certain knowledge Fliss hadn't seen or spoken to Lawrie in nine years. What difference would a few hours make? But his second-in-command, oldest employee and, despite his best efforts to keep her out, best friend was looking so hopeful he couldn't disappoint her.

He wasn't the only person Lawrie had walked out on.

'Five minutes,' he allowed, adding warningly, 'But, Fliss, we have a lot to do.'

'I know. I'll be quick—thank you.' Fliss rushed from the room, casting him a grateful glance over her shoulder as she did so. Less than a minute later she had arrived at Lawrie's table, falling on her in a breathless heap.

Jonas watched as Fliss sat down at the table. He saw Lawrie look up in slight confusion, her puzzled expression quickly change to one of happiness, and the mobile features light up with enthusiasm as she greeted her friend.

When they both looked up at the office he looked away, despite knowing that they couldn't see through the tinted glass; he had far too much to do to watch them catch up.

Jonas pulled up a report he had commissioned on the

small chain of restaurants in Somerset he was considering taking over and read it.

After ten minutes he was still on the first page.

He glanced over at the window. They were still yakking away. What on earth had they got to talk about for so long?

Typical Lawrie. Turning everything upside down without even trying.

When he had seen her standing outside, looking so uncharacteristically unsure, he had seized the opportunity. As soon as he'd known she was back—heard through the village grapevine that she was here to stay, that she was alone—their moment of meeting had been inevitable. Trengarth was too small for a run-in not to be a certainty, but when it came he'd wanted it to be on his terms.

After all, their parting had been on hers.

Inviting her in had felt like the right thing to do. The mature thing. Maybe he should have left her outside after all.

He looked back at the computer screen and started again on the first line. It was gobbledygook.

Jonas's jaw set in determination. If Fliss had forgotten that she had a lot to do, he hadn't—and he was going to go down there and tell her. Right now.

At first Lawrie hadn't recognised the small redhead hurtling towards her. Nine years ago Fliss had sported a pink bob and multiple piercings and wouldn't have been seen dead in the smart black trousers and blouse she was wearing today, but the generous smile and the mischievous twinkle in the hazel eyes were just the same. After five minutes' excited chatter it was as if they were still teenage waitresses, hanging out after work, although so many things had changed Lawrie could barely keep up.

'You've been working for Jonas all this time?' Try as she

might, she couldn't keep the incredulous tone out of her voice. 'What about acting and RADA?'

'Turns out I am a great amateur.'

Lawrie looked sharply at her but Fliss was still smiling, and there was no hint of disappointment in the candid eyes. 'I am also a great brand and marketing manager—who would have thought it?'

'But you wanted to do so much—had so many plans.'

'I *have* so much! Wait till you meet Dave. He moved here after you left, came for a week's surfing and never left.'

The two girls giggled conspiratorially.

'I have my drama group, and I love my job. I may not have done the travelling or the big city thing, but I have everything I need and want. I'm a lucky girl. But *your* plans sound exciting. New York! I have always wanted to live there—starring on Broadway, of course.'

So she might have made New York sound like a done deal rather than a possibility, but Lawrie had had to salvage pride from somewhere.

She was considering her reply when a shadow fell across the table. Glancing up, she saw a stern-looking Jonas standing there, a frown marring the handsome face. An unexpected flutter pulled at Lawrie's stomach, one she'd thought long dead, and she took a hurried gulp of her coffee, avoiding both his eye and Fliss's sudden speculative gleam.

'I thought you were off to see Suzy?' His attention was all on Fliss.

'I am,' Fliss protested. 'But I have just had a brainwave. How about Lawrie?'

Lawrie's grip tightened on her cup. She could feel her cheeks heating up.

'How about Lawrie, what?' Jonas asked impatiently.

It was odd, being back with the two of them and yet apart, now an outsider. Lawrie took a deep breath and leant back in her chair, affecting a confidence she was far from feeling.

'For Wave Fest, of course. No—listen,' Fliss said, jumping to her feet and grabbing Jonas's arm as he turned dismissively away. 'She's on gardening leave for the rest of the summer.'

'Gardening *what*?' He stopped and looked back at the table, catching Lawrie's eye, a sudden glint of a humour in the stern blue eyes.

She knew exactly what he was thinking—knew that he was remembering her ability to kill every plant with a mixture of forgetful indifference and remorseful overwatering.

'Is this some sort of corporate environmental thing? Time to learn how to garden?'

'No, it's a set period time to serve out your notice away from the office,' Lawrie said, her own eyes warming in response to his and her pulse speeding up as his amused gaze continued to bore into her. 'I'm on paid leave until the end of September.'

'And she's planning to stay in Cornwall most of that time,' Fliss interjected.

'Well, yes. I am. But I'm arranging my next move. I'll be travelling back and forth to London a lot—possibly overseas. What's Wave Fest, anyway?'

'Oh, Lawrie, you remember the festival Jonas and I started, don't you?'

'Actually, Fliss, Lawrie was never at Wave Fest. She was on work placements for the first two.'

The humour had left Jonas's face. It was as if the sun had unexpectedly disappeared behind a cloud. He didn't

say the words she knew he was thinking. She had left before the third.

'I know we're desperate, but Lawrie's a solicitor, not a
project manager—and she knows nothing about festivals.'

'But we need someone organised who can get things
done and she can do that all right. Plus, she's here and
she's available.'

'Fliss, you said yourself that at this time of year organising Wave Fest is a full-time job. If Lawrie's got to sort
out a move—' the sharp blue eyes regarded Lawrie for an
intent moment before flicking away '—she won't be able
to dedicate the time we need to it.'

'Yes, for *me* it would be full time, because I have a
neglected husband and the work of three people to do
anyway, but Lawrie's used to city hours—this will be a
relaxing break for her!'

It was almost amusing, listening to them bicker over
her as if she wasn't there. Lawrie took another sip of her
coffee, letting the words wash over her. After the shock of
the last week it felt nice to be wanted, even if it was for a
small-time job she had no intention of doing.

Suddenly she was aware of an extended silence and
looked up to find two pairs of eyes fixed on her expectantly.

'What?'

'I was just asking why you are on leave?' Jonas said,
with the exaggerated patience of somebody who had asked
a question several times already. 'If "gardening leave"
means you're serving out your notice then you must be
leaving your firm—why?'

The all too familiar sense of panic rose up inside her,
filling her chest with an aching, squeezing tension. None
of this was real. It was some kind of terrible dream and
she would soon wake up and find Hugo snoring beside

her and her pressed suit hung on the wardrobe door opposite, ready for another day at work, doing a job she was darned good at.

'I felt like a change,' she said, choosing her words carefully. 'They were offering good severance deals and I thought, what with turning thirty and everything, that this could be a good opportunity for a new start. After all, it seems silly to specialise in international law and never spend time abroad. I have lots of contacts in New York, so that seems like the logical choice.'

She had repeated the words so often to herself that she almost believed them now.

'That sounds amazing,' breathed Fliss, but Jonas looked more sceptical.

'You deviated from that all-important ten-point plan? Wasn't thirty the year you should have made partner?'

He remembered the plan. Of *course* he remembered it—she had gone over it with him enough, been teased about it enough. *'Lawrie needs to make a plan before we go out for a walk,'* he used to tell people.

She took a deep breath and forced a casual tone into her voice. 'People change, Jonas. I followed the plan for long enough, and it was very successful, but I decided that now I'm single again it might be time to see something of the world and enhance my career at the same time. It's no big deal.'

He raised an eyebrow but didn't pursue the point.

'But you won't be able to start your new job until after September so you *are* free to help out with Wave Fest.' Fliss wasn't giving up.

'Fliss, Lawrie isn't interested in the festival; she has a job to find. Plus, if she's still being paid by her firm then she won't be able to work for us—will you?'

'I'm not sure,' she said. 'It's not law, so it's not a conflict of interest, but I don't think I can take paid work whilst on gardening leave. I'll have to check the contract, but it would be unusual if it was allowed.'

'Volunteer! We could pay your expenses and it would look great on your CV, using your time to help out with a charity event. Come on, Lawrie. It's total serendipity, you being here just when we need you. You can't argue with fate!'

'Fliss!'

Jonas was sounding annoyed, but the word 'volunteer' had struck a chord with Lawrie. She tuned the pair out.

She liked to keep busy, and the thought of spending the forseeable future with nothing to do but job-hunt terrified her. Besides, her CV was already with the best recruiters in the business, so there was little she could do until they got in touch. Most importantly she had been racking her brains, searching for a likely explanation for her sudden departure from Forrest, Gable & Garner that prospective employers would find acceptable—laudable, even. If she could tell them that she'd taken the opportunity of severance to help out with a charity festival surely that would stand her in good stead? Every company liked a bit of free CSR in these straitened times.

Okay, it wasn't part of the ten-point plan, but which part of the last few weeks *had* been? Not finding Hugo labouring over his naked secretary, not watching the senior partners close ranks as they took his side and forced her out with a nice settlement and a good reference for keeping her mouth shut.

She had returned to Trengarth to lick her wounds, to regroup. Why not wring something positive out of her situation?

'Please?' Fliss looked pleading. 'Come on, Lawrie, you'll be perfect.'

'I'll do it.' The words left her mouth before she knew exactly what she was going to say.

Fliss squealed and flung her arms around Lawrie, but Jonas took a step back, his mouth tight, his eyes unreadable.

What have I done?

'If that's okay with you, of course, Jonas,' she added, not entirely sure what she wanted his answer to be—whether he would give her a get-out clause she didn't even know she needed. But he didn't answer—just continued to look at her with the same cool, steady regard.

Fliss jumped in before the silence stretched too far, got too awkward. 'It's fine, isn't it, Jonas? This is *fantastic*! I was going to get all the stuff from Suzy today, but why don't you come with me and meet her? Is tomorrow okay? Oh, Lawrie, it'll be just like old times, us working together.'

Fliss beamed at Lawrie, who couldn't help but smile back. Her old friend's joy was infectious.

'It looks like that's settled, then.' Jonas's face was still blank, his voice cool and professional. 'Lawrie, I'll chat to you tomorrow and go over the work involved, discuss how this will work as a volunteering role. Be sure this is something you can take on, though. Wave Fest raises tens of thousands for local charities. If you can't manage it it's imperative you let us know sooner rather than later.'

He sounded dismissive—as if he was expecting her to fail, to walk away.

How dared he? She'd negotiated million-pound contracts, painstakingly going over every single word, scrutinising each clause, routinely working sixty-hour weeks, often on short notice. One month sorting out a small local event would hardly tax her.

She lifted her head and looked straight at him, matching him cool glance for cool glance, every bit the professional, well-trained lawyer. 'I'm sure I'll manage. I like to see things through.'

He kept her gaze, scorn filling the blue eyes, turning them ice-cold. 'I'm sure you've grown up,' he said. 'But if there's a chance you'll get a job and leave before the contract ends I need to know. Promises aren't enough.'

She swallowed down her rage. If she had learnt anything from long hours of negotiating complex contracts it was how to keep her temper, no matter what the provocation. If he wanted to judge her on events that had happened nine years ago, so be it.

But she *had* promised to love him till death did them part. And that promise she had broken.

Did she actually need this hassle? The sensible thing would be to walk away, right now, lock up the cottage and go back to London. But then what? She had nowhere to live, nothing to do. At least in Cornwall she had a house, and now a way to occupy her time whilst finding the perfect job, getting her life back to the calm, ordered way it was supposed to be. And if that meant showing Jonas Jones that he was wrong—that the past wasn't as clear-cut as he obviously thought—well, that was just a bonus.

She smiled sweetly into the freezing eyes.

'I'll need to take time to sort out my move, of course,' she said, proud that her voice was steady. 'And there is a chance that I may need to travel abroad for interviews. But there will be plenty of notice. There shouldn't—there *won't* be a problem.'

'Then I'll see you tomorrow.'

The interview was clearly over.

'Enjoy the rest of your birthday.'

Fliss looked up in shock. 'It's your *birthday*? Here I am, thinking about spreadsheets and emails and offices, and what I should be doing is ordering you a cocktail to go with that cake. What are you doing later? I'm sure you have plans, but we could meet here for cocktails first?'

Lawrie's first instinct was to lie—to claim company, plans, unavailability. But Jonas had stopped, turned, was listening, and she couldn't let him know she was ashamed of her lone state. 'Actually, Fliss, I was planning a quiet one this year. I have a nice bottle of red and a good book saved up.'

It was the truth, and she had been looking forward to indulging in both. So why did it feel like a confession?

'A good book? I know you've been gone a long time, but nobody changes *that* much. Of *course* we're going to celebrate. I'll see you here for cocktails at seven, and then there's Open Mic Night later. Perfect! Jonas, you can pick her up. We don't want the birthday girl to be late.'

'Honestly—' Lawrie began, not sure what panicked her more: Jonas picking her up like old times, the chance that she might let her guard down after a cocktail, or spending her thirtieth birthday with the same people who had celebrated her eighteenth. 'I'll be fine.'

'Don't be silly.' Jonas's expression was indecipherable, his voice emotionless. 'Fliss is right. You can't spend your birthday alone. Besides, you used to enjoy singing. It'll be just like old times.'

And that, thought Lawrie, was exactly what she was afraid of.

CHAPTER TWO

'SO THIS IS where you're hiding.'

Jonas looked far too at home as he rounded the corner of Gran's cottage. And far too attractive in a pair of worn jeans that hugged his legs in all the right places, and a plain grey T-shirt emphasising his lean strength. 'I thought you had run away.'

'I thought about it,' Lawrie admitted, tugging at the hem of her skirt self-consciously.

It shouldn't take a grown woman two hours to get ready for a few drinks and some badly played guitar, and yet Lawrie had found herself paralysed by indecision. Her clothes were too conservative, too expensive, more suited to a discreet yet expensive restaurant or a professional conference than a small Cornish village.

In the end she had decided on a dress that was several years old—and several inches shorter than she usually wore.

Taking a deep breath, she pulled her hands away from the skirt and tried to remember the speech she had painstakingly prepared earlier, rehearsed at length in the shower.

'Thanks for coming to collect me—it's very nice of you. I know Fliss kind of forced your hand—' Lawrie stopped, her cheeks warm, the speech gone. 'Actually, she forced your hand in several ways earlier, and I should have thought... If you don't want me around—if it's awkward, I mean—then I'll tell her I can't do it.' She stumbled to a stop.

Great—in her former life fluency had been one of her trademarks. It looked as if she had lost that along with everything else.

'Fliss thinks she gets her own way, but if I didn't want you working for us you wouldn't be.' The blue eyes held hers for a moment. 'She's right. You'll do a good job—and, let's face it, we are a bit desperate. Beggars can't be choosers.'

Charming. It wasn't the most ringing endorsement she'd ever heard.

'I just don't want our past relationship to be an issue.' Lawrie was aware of how pompous she sounded. She'd been trying for offhand. A smirk at the corner of his mouth confirmed she had failed.

'We're both mature adults,' Jonas pointed out. 'At least I am. And it's your significant birthday we're celebrating, so hopefully you are too. I'm sure we can work together without too much bloodshed. In fact...' He moved away from the cottage and sauntered gracefully over the lawn towards her, a flat tissue-wrapped square in his hand. 'Happy Birthday.'

Lawrie stared at the proffered parcel in shock.

'Take it. It won't bite,' he teased. 'I promise. Think of it as a peace offering and a birthday present in one.'

He moved closer until he was standing next to her, leaning against the balcony, looking down on the curve of beach and sea below.

After a moment's hesitation Lawrie took the present, taking a moment to enjoy the thrill of the unknown. It was her only present, after all.

'Your gran always had the best view in the village,'

Jonas said. 'It's so peaceful up here.' He shot her a glance. 'I meant to write after she died, send a card… But I didn't really know what to say. I'm sorry.'

She turned the parcel round in her hands. 'That's okay. I think people were upset we had the funeral so far away, but she wanted to be buried next to Grandpa…' Her voice trailed away and there was a sudden lump in her throat. It had been six months since the funeral but the pain of loss still cut deep. 'I wish I had telephoned more, visited more.'

'She was very proud of you.'

Lawrie nodded, not trusting herself to speak. Swallowing back the tears, she turned her attention to the present, wanting to change the subject.

She slid her finger along the fold in the tissue, pulling the tape off slowly as she went, carefully opening the paper out to reveal a silk scarf the colour of the sea below. 'It's beautiful!'

His voice was offhand. 'It always used to be your favourite colour.'

'It still is.' She looked over at him, ridiculously overcome despite his casualness. *He'd remembered.* 'You really didn't need to, but thank you, Jonas.'

'No problem.' The blue eyes swept over her assessingly. 'It matches your dress.'

'I'll go and put it on. I won't be long.'

Walking through the back door, Lawrie felt yet again as if she had gone back in time—as if she was once again her sixteen-year-old self, skipping in to say goodbye to Gran before heading out on a date, full of possibilities, full of life and desperately, achingly in love.

Only there was no Gran.

And the world no longer felt full of possibilities. She was all too aware of her limits.

Oh, to be sixteen again, walking on the beach at night after her shift ended, unable to believe that her handsome boss had asked her if she fancied a stroll. She still remembered the electric shock that had run through her when his hand had first bumped against hers. The tightness in her stomach when his long, cool caressing fingers had encased hers. The almost unbearable anticipation drying out her throat, weakening her knees, setting every single nerveend ablaze as she waited for him to kiss her. And, *oh...!* The almost unbearable sweetness when he finally, oh so slowly, lowered his mouth to hers as the waves crashed against the shore.

It had been Lawrie's first kiss and for five years she hadn't thought she would ever kiss anyone else.

I haven't thought about that in years. She pushed the memory of vivid, haunting dreams filled with waves, passion and familiar blue eyes firmly to one side.

She glanced up at the wall, where a framed photo hung. A much younger Lawrie looked out from it, her hair whipped by the wind and framing her face in a dark, tangled cloud, laughing, her eyes squinting against the sun. Jonas had taken it twelve years ago, on her eighteenth birthday—their wedding day.

It was all such a long time ago. Who would have thought then that they would end up like this? Apart, near-strangers, exchanging polite remarks and stiff smiles. If she'd known what lay ahead would she have made the same choices...the same mistakes?

Lawrie shook her head wildly, trying to clear the questions from her mind. She couldn't allow this temporary setback to derail her, to make her question her choices, her past. It was time to face her future—and if the plan had gone awry...well, she would tweak it.

But first her birthday. She needed—she *deserved* some

fun. Maybe she could relax—just a little, just for a short while. Maybe Lawrie Bennett was allowed to let go for just one evening.

It was one of Jonas's favourite things, watching the Boat House being transformed from a family-friendly, light and airy café to an intimate bar. It was more than the deepening dusk outside the dramatic picture windows, more than the tea lights on the tables, more than the bottles of beer and wine replacing the skinny lattes, the tapas in place of cream teas.

It was the way the atmosphere changed. Grew heavier, darker. Full of infinite possibilities.

Tonight was the monthly Open Mic Night—a tradition carried through from the earliest days. Before he'd held a bar licence he used to invite friends over to the café after-hours to jam; he'd always fancied himself as a pretty mean guitarist. Once he'd licensed the premises it had become more of an organised event, yet still with a laid-back, spontaneous feel.

Folk violinists rattling out notes at an impossible speed, grungy rock wannabes, slow and sweet soul singers— there were no exclusions. If you had an instrument and you wanted to play, you could sign up. There was a magic about Open Mic Night, even after all these years. The room might be full of regulars but there were usually one or two surprises.

And yet tonight he was wound tight, the tension straining across his shoulders and neck. Even the familiar feel of the sharp strings under his fingertips, the crowded tables, the appreciative applause, the melding and blending of notes and beats and voices couldn't relax him.

His eyes, his focus, were pulled to the small table in the corner where Lawrie perched, toying with a glass of champagne, her head resting on her hand, her eyes dreamy as she listened. The dim lighting softened her; she looked like his teen bride again, her dark hair loose, curling against her shoulders, her huge grey eyes fixed unseeingly on the stage.

On *him*.

A reluctant tug of desire pulled deep down. It was definitely the memories, the nostalgia, he told himself grimly. Why was she back? Why had Lawrie Bennett, the girl who put her work, her career, her plans before everything and everyone, given up her job and moved back?

And why did she look so scared and vulnerable?

It was none of his business—*she* was none of his business. She had made that clear a long time ago. Whatever trouble Lawrie was in she could handle it herself. She always had.

Resolutely he tore his gaze away, focussed on the room as a whole, plastering on a smile as the song ended and the room erupted into applause. Jonas exchanged an amused look with his fellow musicians as they took an ironic bow before vacating the stage for the next musicians—a local sixth form experimental rock band whose main influences seemed to be a jarring mixture of eighties New Romanticism and Death Metal.

Maybe he was getting old, Jonas thought as he made his way back to the bar. It just sounded like noise to him.

'I should be getting home.' Lawrie got to her feet and began automatically to gather the glasses and bottles. Just like old times. She stilled her hands, looking around to see if anybody had noticed.

'Don't be silly—the night is just beginning,' Fliss said in surprise.

Lawrie looked pointedly at the people heading for the

door, at the musicians packing away their instruments, at vaguely familiar faces patting Jonas on the back with murmurs about babysitters, getting up for work and school runs. Since when had most of his friends had babysitters and office hours to contend with? The surf-mad mates of his youth had matured into fathers, husbands and workers. The night might feel like a step back in time, but everything had changed.

'This is the fun bit,' Fliss said, grabbing a tray filled with lurid-coloured drinks from the bar and handing a neon blue one to Lawrie. 'We get to hog the stage. What do you want to start with?'

Several pairs of eyes turned expectantly to Lawrie and she swallowed, her mouth dry. She took a sip of the cocktail, grimacing at the sweet yet almost medicinal taste. 'You go ahead without me. I don't really sing.'

'Of *course* you sing! You always used to.'

'That was a long time ago. Honestly, Fliss, I'd rather not.'

'But…'

'I thought all lawyers sang,' Jonas interceded.

Lawrie shot him a grateful glance. Fliss was evidently not going to let the point go.

'Didn't you have a karaoke bar under your office?'

'Sadly I didn't work with Ally McBeal.' Lawrie shook her head, but she was smiling now. 'The only singing I have done for years is in the shower. I'd really rather listen.'

'You heard her. And she *is* the birthday girl.'

'Which is why she shouldn't be sitting there alone,' Fliss argued. She turned to Lawrie pleadingly. 'Just do some backing vocals, then. Hum along. This is the fun part of the night—no more enduring schoolboy experiments or prog rock guitar solos. Thank goodness we limit each act to fifteen minutes or I reckon *he* would still be living out his Pink Floyd fantasies right now. There's only us here.'

Lawrie hesitated. It had been such a long time—part of the life she had done her best to pack away and forget about. Small intimate venues, guitars and set lists had no place in the ordered world she had chosen. Could she even hold a tune any more? Pick up the rhythm?

Once they had been a well-oiled machine—Fliss's voice, rich, emotive and powerful, trained for the West End career she had dreamed of, filling the room, and Lawrie's softer vocals, which shouldn't really have registered at all. And then there had been Jonas. Always there, keeping time. There'd been times when she had got lost in the music, blindly following where he led.

The thought of returning there was terrifying. Lawrie shivered, goosebumps rippling up her bare arms, and yet she acknowledged that it was exciting too. On this night of memory and nostalgia, this moment out of time.

And how lost could she get if she stuck closely to backing vocals? Stayed near Fliss, away from Jonas and that unreadable expression on his face? Did he wish she would just leave? Stay? Or did he simply not care?

Not that there was any reason for him to care. She had made sure of that.

She took another sip of her cocktail, noticing with some astonishment that the glass was nearly empty. She should be thinking about Hugo, Lawrie told herself. Mourning him, remembering their relationship so very recently and brutally ended—not mooning over her teenage mistakes. If she was going to work here, survive here, she couldn't allow her past to intimidate her.

'Okay,' she said, putting the now empty glass down on the table and reaching for another of Fliss's concoctions— this time a sickly green. 'Backing vocals only. Let's do it.'

* * *

She was seated on the other side of the stage, angled towards the tables, so that all he could see was the fall of her hair, the curve of her cheek. Not that he was attracted to her—he knew her too well. Even after all this time. It was just that she seemed a little lost, a little vulnerable…

And there had been a time when Jonas Jones had been a sucker for dark-haired, big-eyed, vulnerable types.

He'd learned his lesson the hard way, but a man didn't want to take too many chances—not on a night filled with ghosts. He looked around, half expecting to see the creamy painted wooden slats of the old boathouse, the rough floorboards, the mismatched tables. But a twinge in his fingers brought him back to the present, reminding him that he was no longer nineteen and that, although thirty-two was certainly not old, he was too old to be playing all night on a work night.

His mouth twitched wryly. Once a work night had meant nothing. His hobbies and his job had blended into one perfect hedonistic existence: the bar, the music, the surf. He didn't know what had infuriated his parents more. How successful his beach shack had quickly become or how effortless he had made it look.

But in those days it *had* been effortless.

It wasn't that easy any more. Would his parents be proud or smug if they knew how many of the things he loved he had given up for success? Or would they still think it was not enough.

Maudlin thoughts. A definite sign that it was late, or that he'd allowed Fliss to make the cocktails again.

Time to wrap things up.

Only Fliss had started another song, carefully picking out the tune on her guitar. The breath caught in his throat. His heart was a painful lump blocking its passage.

Not this song. Not this night. Not on what could have been, *should* have been, their twelfth wedding anniversary.

There was only so much nostalgia a man could take.

And then Lawrie picked up the tune and he was plunged into a whole other level of memory. Her voice wasn't the strongest—nothing in comparison to Fliss's—yet it had a true, wistful quality that tore at him, hooked him in, wringing truth out of the plaintive words.

Despite it all Jonas found himself playing the harmony, his hands surely and smoothly finding the right notes. They hadn't forgotten. He still knew—still felt every note, every beat, every word. How long was it since he had played this song? Not since Lawrie had left. Not even in the last desperate year of their marriage as he had watched her retreat further and further away, her eyes, her focus, firmly fixed on the gleaming spires of Oxford.

Suddenly simple folk tunes hadn't been her thing at all.

Yet she still knew all the words.

It was as if her whole body thrummed with the music. Her blood, her heartbeat, the pulses at her neck and her wrists. Long after the guitars had been packed away, the last few glasses cleared, the final lurid cocktail poured away—no one had felt able to risk the neon orange, not at past one in the morning—the beat still possessed her.

How had she managed to spend the last nine years without music? Had they even had music in the house? Music to listen to simply for the thrill it evoked deep down inside? There had been a stylish digital radio permanently tuned in to Radio Four, occasionally switched to Classic FM when they entertained. And Lawrie had attended concerts for corporate purposes—just as she had been to countless sporting events, black tie galas, charity auctions.

After a while they all blended together.

There was so much she had expunged from her life. Colour, impulsiveness, walking along a beach at dusk with the wind blowing salt-tinged tendrils of hair into her face. Enjoying the here and now.

She might have chosen a controlled, sleek, beige, stone and black existence. It didn't mean that she hadn't occasionally hungered after something a little more *vibrant*. But vibrancy had a price she hadn't been prepared to pay.

In the end control was worth it. It allowed you to plan, to achieve.

But, *damn*, the music had felt good. The right here, right now felt good. Even those ridiculously bright cocktails had been—well, not *good*, exactly but surprisingly palatable. Maybe coming back wasn't such a terrible thing after all.

'How are you getting back?'

Lawrie jumped, every sense suddenly on high alert. She didn't want to look Jonas in the eyes in case he read the conflicting emotions there. There had been a time when he'd been able to read her all too easily.

'I was planning to walk,' she said.

'Alone?'

'Unless there are suddenly bloodthirsty smugglers patrolling the dark streets of Trengarth I think I'll manage the mile home okay.'

'There's no lighting on your gran's road. I'd better walk you back.'

Lawrie opened her mouth to refuse—then shut it again, unsure what to say. Whether to make a joke out of it, point out that after negotiating London streets for the past few years she thought she could manage a few twisty Cornish lanes. Whether to just say thank you.

Jonas took her silence for acquiescence and strode off towards the door. Lawrie stood indecisively, torn between a childish need to stand her ground, insist she was fine, and a sudden hankering for company—any company—on the walk back up the steep hill.

She had been all too alone these last weeks.

Without thought, almost impulsively, she followed him.

The night was warm, despite the breeze that blew in from the sea and the lack of cloud, and lit up by stars shining so brightly Lawrie could only stand and stare, her neck tilted back almost to the point of pain as she tried to take in the vast expanse of constellation-strewn night sky.

'Have you discovered a new planet?'

Lawrie ignored the sarcastic tone. 'I'm not sure I'd realise if I had,' she said. 'It's just you never see the sky like this in London. I had almost forgotten what it was like.'

Another reclaimed memory to add to the list. Just how much had she shut out over the last nine years?

And how much could she bear to remember? To feel?

The shocking ache of memory—the whispers of 'what might have been'. If she hadn't walked in on Hugo she would still be in London, with Trengarth a million miles away from her thoughts, her ambitions, her dreams.

It was all so familiar. The dimly lit windy street, the harbour wall on one side and the shops on the other—a trendy mixture of surf-hire, arty boutiques and posh grub for the upmarket tourists who sailed or stayed in the village throughout the summer.

As they turned up the steep, hilly road that led to Lawrie's gran's house the shops became more prosaic: post office, grocer's, buckets and spades and souvenirs.

She stole a glance at the man strolling along by her side, walking up the hill with ease. He too was still the same in so many ways, and yet there was something harder, edgier. His very silence was spiky, and she had an urge to break it. To soften the mood.

'So...' Was that her voice? So tentative? She coughed

nervously and tried again—this time loud, abrasive. More suited to a confrontation than casual conversation. 'Are you married? Any children?'

He didn't break stride or look at her. Just gave a quick shake of the head. 'Nope.'

'Anyone special?'

'Not at the moment.'

So there had been. *What did you expect?* she asked herself fiercely. *That he's been living like a monk for the last nine years? Would you even want that?*

She wasn't entirely sure of her answer.

'A couple of times I thought maybe that there was potential. But it was never quite enough. I'm an old-fashioned guy.' He slanted a glance at her, cold, unreadable. 'Marriage should be for ever. Failing once was bad enough…'

'We didn't fail.' But her words had no conviction. Lawrie tried again. 'We just wanted different things.'

'If that's the way you want to remember it.'

Now this *was* familiar. The flush of anger, the ache of frustration as they stood on either side of a very deep chasm. *No,* Lawrie told herself. *Don't say anything.* What was the point in dredging up old arguments, conflict that should be dead and buried?

Only she had never been able to resist the opportunity to fight her corner.

'It's the way it was.' Cool, calm. As if it didn't matter. And of course it didn't. It was history.

Only it was *her* history. Theirs.

It was her job, knowing when to argue a point, knowing when to let it lie. There was nothing to gain from rehashing the same old themes and yet she felt compelled to go on.

'There's no shame in admitting something isn't working, in moving on,' she persisted as they reached the top of the hill and turned down the hedge-lined lane that led to the cottage. The bumpy road ahead was hard to make out, lit just by the brilliant stars and the occasional light marking out driveways and gates. 'I couldn't stay here, you wouldn't move—what else could we do? It all seems to have worked out for you, though. You seem to have done well for yourself.'

'Surprised?' The mocking tone was back. 'You always did underestimate me, Lawrie.'

'I didn't! I never underestimated you!' Her whole body flushed, first with embarrassment, then with indignation. 'We grew apart, that's all. I didn't think…'

'Didn't think what?'

How could those smooth, cream-rich tones turn so icy?

'That I was too naïve, too small-town for your new Ox-bridge friends?'

'Wow—way to rewrite history! You hated Oxford, hated London, disliked my friends, and refused to even consider moving away from Cornwall. It wasn't all me, Jonas. You wouldn't compromise on anything.'

He laughed softly. 'Compromise suggests some kind of give and take, Lawrie. Remind me again what *you* were willing to give up for *me*?'

'That's unfair.' She felt tired, defeated. She had just pre-sided over the death of one relationship—did she really have to do the post mortem on this one too?

'Is it?'

The worst part was how uninterested he sounded. As if they were talking about complete strangers and not their hopeful younger selves.

'Actually, I should thank you.'

She peered at him through the star-lit darkness. 'Thank me?'

'For forcing me to grow up. To prove you, my parents,

everyone who thought I was a worthless, surfing bum wrong.'

'I never thought that,' she whispered.

An image flashed through her head. A younger, softer Jonas, his wetsuit half peeled off, moulded to muscular thighs. Naked broad shoulders tapering down to a taut, perfectly defined stomach. Water glistening on golden tanned skin. Slicked-back wet hair. Board under one arm, a wicked smile on his mouth, an invitation in his eyes. A sudden yearning for the carefree boy he had been ran through her, making her shiver with longing. How had he turned into this cold, cynical man? Had she done this to him?

He laughed again, the humourless sound jarring her over-wrought nerves.

'Oh, Lawrie, does any of it matter? It was a long time ago—we were practically children. Getting married in our teens…we must have been crazy—it was always going to end in tears.'

'I suppose it was.' Her voice was tentative.

Was it? Once she'd thought they would be together for ever, that they were two halves of one whole. Hearing him reduce their passion to the actions of two irresponsible teenagers nearly undid her. She fought against the lump in her throat, fought for composure, desperate to change the subject, lighten the mood which had turned as dark as night.

'Here you are.'

He stopped at the gate that led into the small driveway and Lawrie skidded to an abrupt stop—close, but not touching him. She was achingly aware of his proximity, and the knowledge that if she reached out just an infinitesimal amount she would be able to touch him made her shiver with longing, with desire, with fear. She wanted to look away but found herself caught in his moonlit gaze, the blue eyes silvered by the starlight.

'It wasn't all bad, though. Being a crazy teen.'

The cream had returned to his voice. His tone was low, almost whispered, and she felt herself swaying towards him.

'No, of course not. That was the happiest time of my life.'

Damn, she hadn't meant to admit that—not to him, not to herself. It must be the cocktails talking. But as the words left her mouth she realised their truth.

'The happiest time,' she whispered, so low she hoped he hadn't heard her.

Just one little step—that was all it took. One little step and she was touching him, looking up at him. Her breasts brushed against his chest and just that one small touch set her achingly aware nerves on fire. She felt the jolt of desire shock through her, buzzing through to her fingers, to her toes, pooling deep within her.

Jonas's head was tilted down. The full focus of his disconcertingly intense eyes on her. Lawrie swallowed and licked suddenly dry lips, her nails cutting into her palms as she curled them into tight fists. The urge to grab him and pull him close was suddenly almost overwhelming.

'Jonas?'

An entreaty? A question? Lawrie didn't know what she was asking him, what she was begging him for. All she knew was that it was her birthday. And that she hadn't felt this alive for a long, long time.

'Jonas…'

He stayed still for a long second, his eyes still fixed on hers, their expression unreadable.

And then he took a step back. The sudden space between them was a yawning chasm. 'Goodnight, Lawrie.

I'll see you in the morning. Don't be late—there's a lot to go through.'

Lawrie suppressed a shudder. It was suddenly so cold. 'I'm never late.'

'Good.'

She stood by the gate, watching as he turned and began to stride down the path, ruthlessly suppressing the part of her that wanted to call after him, run after him. Yet she couldn't ignore the odd skip her heart gave as he stopped and looked back.

'Oh, and, Lawrie... Happy Birthday.'

And then he was gone. Swallowed up by the velvety blackness like the ghost of birthdays past.

Lawrie sagged against the gatepost, an unwelcome mixture of frustrated desire and loneliness pulsing through her. If this was how one night with Jonas could make her feel, how on earth was she going to manage a whole summer?

She forced herself upright. She was vulnerable right now, that was all. She would just have to toughen up even more—harden herself.

And stay as far away from Jonas Jones as she possibly could, boss or not.

CHAPTER THREE

LAWRIE WAS DETERMINED to be early.

'Don't be late' indeed.

Even if she *had* gone to bed long after one a.m., and even if she *had* spent half the night lying awake in a frustrated tangle of hot sheets and even hotter regrets, there was no way she was giving him the satisfaction.

Besides, she might be in Trengarth, not Hampstead, and in her old, narrow single bed and not the lumbar-adjusted super-king-size one she had shared with Hugo, but it was nice to retrieve a little of her old routine from the wreckage of the last week.

She'd been up at six sharp, showered and ready to go by seven.

So why was she still standing irresolutely in the kitchen at ten past seven, fingering the scarf Jonas had bought her? It looked good teamed with her crisp white shirt and grey pencil skirt, softening the severe corporate lines of her London work wardrobe, and yet she didn't want to give Jonas the wrong idea—come into work brandishing his colours.

She began to unknot it for the third time, then caught sight of herself in the mirror. Face drawn, anxious.

It's just a scarf, she thought impatiently, pulling the door shut and locking it behind her. *Not an engagement ring.*

She looked down at her left hand, the third finger bare—bare of Hugo's exquisite princess cut diamond solitaire, of Jonas's antique amethyst twist.

Two engagement rings before turning thirty. Not bad for someone who had vowed to remain independent. Her mother had been married three times before thirty; maybe Lawrie wasn't doing so badly after all.

It was another beautiful day, with the sun already shining down from a deep blue sky completely undisturbed by any hint of cloud, and the light breeze a refreshing contrast to the deepening heat. This was Cornwall at its best—this was what she had missed on those dusty, summer days in London: the sun glancing off the sea, the vibrancy of the colours, the smell of grass, salt and beach. The smell of home.

Don't get too used to it, Lawrie told herself as she walked along the lane—a brighter, far less intimate and yet lonelier walk in the early-morning light. *This is just an interlude.* It was time to start focussing on her next step, giving those recruitment agencies a quick nudge. After all, they'd had her CV for nearly a week now. She should have plenty of free time. How much work could organising a few bands be?

Five hours later, after an incredibly long and detailed handover by the sofa-bound Suzy, Lawrie was severely revising her estimate of the work involved. Just when had Wave Fest turned from a few guitars and a barbecue on a beach to a three-night extravaganza?

Walking back into Jonas's office, files piled high in her arms, her head was so busy buzzing with the endless stream of information Suzy had supplied that Lawrie had almost forgotten the ending to the night before—forgotten the unexpected desire that had flared up so hotly, despite thinking about nothing else as Fliss drove her through the narrow country lanes to Suzy's village home.

But walking back into the Boat House brought the memory flooding back. She had wanted him to kiss her.

It wasn't real. This was Jonas Jones. She had been there, done that, moved on. Besides, Lawrie told herself firmly, she couldn't afford any emotional ties. She was already mentally spinning this volunteer role into a positive on her CV. This could be the way to set her aside from all the other ambitious thirty-somethings hungry for the next, more prestigious role.

Volunteering to manage a high-profile project raising money for charity—an environmental charity, at that—would add to her Oxford degree and her eight successful years at an old City firm and she would be a very promising candidate indeed. She might even have her pick of jobs.

Only, Lawrie thought as she clasped the large, heavy files more firmly, negotiating contracts was a very different skill from organising a festival. She was used to representing multiple companies who thought they had first dibs on her time *all* the time, but at least there was uniformity to the work, making it simpler to switch between clients. This was more like running an entire law firm single-handed, handling everything from divorces to company takeovers.

There didn't seem to be an aspect of Wave Fest that Suzy hadn't been in charge of—that Lawrie was now in charge of—from budgets to booking bands, from health and safety forms and risk assessment to portaloo hire.

And there was a file for each task.

Jonas was hard at work as she staggered into the office, but he swung his chair round as she dumped the heavy pile on the round conference table with a bang. His face was guarded, although she could have sworn she saw a fleeting smirk as he took in the large amount of paperwork she had lugged in.

'Changed your mind now you know what's in store?'

It was said lightly, but a muscle beating at the side of his jaw betrayed some tension. Maybe he wasn't as indifferent to her as he seemed. Or maybe it was another dig at her lack of commitment.

Stop trying to second-guess him, Lawrie. It was probably just a throwaway comment.

'No, but it's more daunting than I imagined,' she admitted honestly. 'This lot—' she gestured at the files behind her '—is just invoices, purchase orders, health and safety certificates, insurance documents. The actual work is being emailed as we speak.'

'Can you do it?'

'It's different to my usual line, and my secretary would have taken care of most of the admin-related work—but, yes, I can do it. I'll need to spend a couple of days reading this lot, though.'

'Here?'

'Sorry?'

'Are you intending to work *here*?'

Lawrie looked up, confused. Where else would she work?

Her eyes caught his. Held them. And for several long seconds she was aware of nothing but the intense blue, the flicker of heat at the heart of his gaze. She caught her breath, an ache suddenly hollowing in her chest, need mingling with the excitement clenching at her stomach. She dragged her eyes reluctantly away, loss unexpectedly consuming her as she stepped back, self-consciously pulling at a folder, looking anywhere but at him, doing her best to ignore the sudden flare of desire, her total awareness of every inch of him.

His shirt matched his eyes, was open at his throat, exposing a small triangle of tanned chest; his long legs were encased in perfectly cut charcoal trousers.

She smiled at him, making it light, trying to keep her sudden nerves hidden, her voice steady. *For goodness' sake, Lawrie, you're a professional.* 'I was planning on it. I could work at home, but it will be easier to get answers to my questions if I'm on site.'

He nodded shortly. 'I agree. That's why I thought you might be better off based at the hotel.'

'The hotel?' For goodness' sake, she sounded like an echo.

'Coombe End. I appreciate it's not as convenient as here—you won't be able to walk to work—but as it's the venue for Wave Fest it makes a lot of sense for you to spend most of your time there.'

His smile was pure politeness. He might have been talking to a complete stranger.

Lawrie shook her head, trying to clear some of the confusion. 'You hold the festival at Coombe End? Your parents *let* you?'

She knew things had changed, but if Richard and Caroline Jones were allowing rock music and campers through the gates of Coombe End then she hadn't come back to the Trengarth she remembered. She had entered a parallel universe.

'No.' His eyes caught hers again, proud and challenging. 'They don't. *I* allow it. Coombe End belongs to me. I own it now.'

She stared at him, a surge of delight running through her, shocking her with its strength. So his parents had finally shown some belief in him.

'They gave you Coombe End? Oh, Jonas that's wonderful.'

He shook his head, his face dark, forbidding. 'They gave me nothing. I bought it. And I paid handsomely for every brick and every blade of grass.'

He had *bought* Coombe End? Lawrie looked around at the immaculately styled office, at the glass separating them from the café below, at the smooth polished wooden floor, the gleaming tiles, the low, comfortable sofas and designer chairs and tables. The whole building shouted out taste, sophistication. It shouted investment and money. She knew things had grown, changed, but how much? Whatever Jonas was doing now it was certainly more than serving up coffee and cakes to friends.

A lot more.

'That's great,' she said lamely, wanting to ask a million questions but not knowing where to start.

Besides, it wasn't any of her business. It hadn't been for a long time.

'I was planning to head over there this afternoon, so I could show you around, introduce you to the rest of the office staff. It'll probably be a couple of hours before I'm ready to leave, though, is that okay?'

Lawrie shook her head, her mind still turning over the 'rest of the office staff' comment. How many people did he employ?

'No problem. I want to go through this lot and make some notes, anyway.'

'If you're hungry just pop downstairs. Carl will make you anything you want.'

And he turned back to his computer screen, instantly absorbed in the document he was reading.

She had been dismissed. It shouldn't rankle—this was hard enough without his constant attention. But it did.

Lawrie sat down at the table and pulled the first file towards her, groaning inwardly at the thick stack of in-

surance documents inside. Deciphering the indecipherable, crafting the impenetrable—those were the tools of
her trade and she was excellent at it—but today her eyes
were skidding over each dense sentence, unable to make
sense of them. She was trying to focus all her attention
on the words dancing on the page in front of her but she
was all too aware of Jonas's every move—the rustle as
he shifted posture, the tap of his long, capable fingers on
the keyboard.

Despite herself she let her eyes wander over to him,
watching him work. She tried to pull her gaze away from
his hands but she was paralysed, intent, as his fingers caressed the keyboard, pressing decisively on each key.

He had always been so very good with his hands.

'Did you say something?'

'No,' she lied, hoping he hadn't turned round, hadn't
seen her blush.

Please, she prayed silently, she hadn't just moaned
out loud, had she? For goodness' sake she was a grown
woman—not a teenager at the mercy of her hormones. At
least she'd thought she was.

It was coming home. She had been away too long and
this sudden return at a time of stress had released some
sort of sensory memory, turning her back into the weak-
kneed teenager crushing so deeply on her boss that every
nerve had been finely tuned to his every word and movement. It was science, that was all.

Science, but still rather uncomfortable.

'I'm thirsty,' she announced. 'I'll just go and get some
water.'

His satirical gaze uncomfortably upon her, she slid out
of the door, heading for the kitchens beneath, relieved to
be released from his proximity. If she didn't get a handle

on her hormones soon then she was in for a very uncomfortable few weeks.

Walking down the stairs, she pulled her phone out of her pocket, automatically checking it for messages. Just the simple act of holding it created a much-needed sense of purpose, of control.

Nothing. Not from her old colleagues, not from her friends in London, not from Hugo. It was as if they had closed the gap her absence had created so seamlessly that nobody knew she had gone. Or if they did they simply didn't care. Yesterday had been her thirtieth birthday. She was supposed to have been having dinner with twenty of their closest friends. Other professional couples. How had Hugo explained her absence?

Or had he taken his secretary instead? His lover. After all, they had been *his* friends first.

This was the year she had been going to get around to finally organising their wedding.

This was the year they'd been going to discuss children. Not *have* them yet, obviously, but start timetabling them in.

They were supposed to have been spending the rest of their lives together, and yet Hugo had let her go without a word, without a gesture. Just as Jonas had all those years ago. Just as her mother had.

She just wasn't worth holding on to.

Lawrie leant against the wall, grateful for the chill of the tiles on her suddenly hot face. *Don't cry*, she told herself, willing away the pressure behind her eyelids. *Never cry. You don't need them—you don't need anybody.*

A large glass of iced water and some fresh air helped Lawrie recover some of her equilibrium and she returned to the office feeling a great deal better. Turning her back determinedly on Jonas, she called on all her professional resources and buried herself in the insurance folder, finding a strange calm in returning to the legalese so recently denied her. Pulling a notebook close, she began to scribble notes, looking at expiry dates, costs, and jotting down anything that needed immediate attention, losing herself in the work.

'Lawrie…? *Lawrie?*' Jonas was standing behind her, an amused glint in the blue eyes. 'Fascinating, are they?' He gestured at the folders.

'A little,' she agreed, pulling herself out of the work reluctantly. 'I'm sorry—do you need me?'

'I'm heading off to Coombe End. Do you still want me to show you around?'

Did she? What she really wanted was more time alone—more time to get lost in the work and let the real world carry on without her.

But it would be a lot easier tomorrow if she knew what to expect.

'Oh, yes, thanks.' She pushed her chair back and began to pile the folders and her closely covered sheets of paper together. 'I'll just…' She gestured at the files spread all over the table and began to pull them together, bracing herself ready to scoop them up.

'Here—let me.'

Jonas leant over and picked up the large pile, his arm brushing hers and sending a tingle from her wrist shooting through her body straight down to her toes. She leapt back.

'If you're ready?'

'Absolutely, I'll just get my bag—give me two minutes.'

'I'll meet you at the car; it's just out front.'

'Okay.'

The door closed behind him and Lawrie sank back into her seat with a sigh. She had to pull herself together. Stop acting like the gauche schoolgirl she'd outgrown years ago.

* * *

Jonas pulled his car round to the front of the restaurant, idling the engine as he waited for Lawrie. Their first day working together was going well. He'd had a productive two hours' work just then, not thinking about and not even noticing the exposed nape of her neck, her long, bare legs, not at all aware of every rustle, every slight movement.

Well, maybe just a little aware. But they were just physical things. And Cornwall in summer was full of attractive women—beautiful women, even.

And yet during the last two hours the room he had designed, the room that had evoked light and space, had felt small, claustrophobic, airless. How could someone as slight as Lawrie take up so much space?

Jonas looked over at the Boat House impatiently, just as Lawrie emerged through the front door, a carefully blank, slightly snooty look on her face—the expression that had used to mean she was unsure of the situation. Did it still mean that? He used to be able to read her every shifting emotion, no matter how she tried to hide them.

Then one day he simply couldn't read her at all.

She stopped at the gate, peering down the road, puzzled.

What was she looking for? He half raised one hand to wave at her, then quickly lowered it, leaning on the horn instead, with a little more emphasis than needed. He allowed himself a fleeting moment of amusement as she jumped at the noise and then, obviously flustered, crossed the harbour road, walking slowly towards the car.

He leant across to open the passenger door, sitting back as she slid in, looking straight ahead, trying not to watch her legs slide down over the seat, her round, firm bottom wriggling down over the padded leather, the sudden definition as the seatbelt tightened against her chest.

'Nice,' she said appreciatively, putting a hand out to

stroke the walnut dashboard as Jonas pulled the low, sleek car away from the kerb. 'I have to say I hadn't pegged you as a sports car man. I was looking for the camper van.'

'Oh, this is just a runabout. I still have the camper. There's no way I could get a board in here.'

He laughed as she grimaced.

'You and your boards,' she said. 'If they're that important you should have gone for a sensible people carrier rather than this midlife crisis on wheels.'

'Midlife crisis?' he mock-huffed. There was no way he was going to admit the secret pride he took in the car.

Jonas didn't care too much what people said, what people thought of him, but he allowed himself a little smirk of satisfaction every time he passed one of his parents' cronies and saw them clock the car and the driver and, for one grudging moment, admit to themselves that that no-good boy had done well.

'At least this has a real engine in it. I've seen that dainty little convertible you call a car. Do you actually put flowers in that holder?'

She shook her head, smiling. 'You have to admit it's convenient for parking. But I can see why you like this— she goes like a dream,' she said as he turned the corner onto the main road and the car began purring up the steep climb. 'And at least she isn't red, so not a total cliché! I'm glad that you kept the camper, though. I was always fond of the old girl. What?' she asked as he slid her a sly smile.

'I'm glad you've finally acknowledged that she's a she— you'll call her by her name next,' he teased.

'I will *never* call a twenty-year-old rusty van by such a ridiculous name—by *any* name. A car is not a person,' she said with a haughty flick of her ponytail.

But Jonas could hear the laughter in her voice as he

deftly swung the car round the corner and along the narrow lanes that led to the hotel, just two coves away.

'Go on—say it,' he coaxed her.

It had been a long time since he had seen Lawrie laugh. Judging by the wounded, defensive look in her eyes it was a long time since she *had* laughed.

'I'll help. Bar… Barb…'

'No!' But she was definitely trying not to laugh, and there was a dimple at the corner of her lush, full mouth. 'What about this one? What have you named her?'

'Nice escape, Ms Bennett. But I will get you to say her name before you leave.'

'We'll see.'

The words were dismissive but she still sounded amused. Jonas sneaked a glance at his passenger and saw her face was more relaxed, her posture less rigid.

'So go on—surprise me. What's she called?'

'Ah,' he said lightly. 'This baby doesn't have a name. It'd be disloyal to the camper.'

This time she did laugh—slightly croaky, as if she were unused to making the sound, but as deep and rich, as infectious as Jonas remembered.

'We wouldn't want to hurt the feelings of a rusting old van, would we?'

'I assure her every day that I only bought this to spare her tired old axles, but I'm not sure she believes me.'

'Nobody likes being replaced by a younger model.'

There was a dark undercurrent to her tone and he glanced at her sharply, but her face was as impassive as ever, the laughter gone as if it had never been, replaced by that cool mask she always put on.

It had been her coolness that had first attracted him— the innocent look on her face as she said the most outrageous things a stark contrast to the noisy beach bums he'd been surrounded by. It had been the unexpected moments when she'd opened up that had made him fall head over heels in love with her—the moments when her mask had dropped and she'd lit up with laughter, with indignation, with passion.

Dangerous memories. His hands tightened on the wheel as he navigated the narrow bends, the hedgerows high beside them as if they were driving through a dark, tree-lined tunnel.

'I'm glad you're driving. I'm not sure I'd find my way by road,' Lawrie said conversationally, as if she were discussing the weather.

As beautifully mannered as ever, Jonas thought.

'It's been a long time since I've been to Coombe End. I can't imagine it without your parents there—how are they?'

There were a million and one responses he could give to that. Jonas settled for the most polite. 'Retired.'

Lawrie made an incredulous noise. '*Retired?* Seriously? I didn't think the word was even in their vocabulary.'

'It wasn't. It took a heart attack to make them even talk about it, and a second one to make them do it.'

'I'm sorry to hear that. What are they doing now?'

Jonas's mouth twisted wryly. Making sure he knew just how much they regretted it. Just how much it hurt to see their profligate son undo all their hard work. Not that any of that was Lawrie's business. Not any more.

'Living in a respectable villa, in a respectable village in Dorset, and taking an inordinate amount of cruises—which they mostly complain about, of course. Still, every retiree needs a hobby.'

Lawrie looked at him, concern in the deep grey eyes. Of course she knew more about his relationship with his parents than anyone else. He wasn't used to that—to people seeing behind his flippant tone. He made damn sure that nobody did.

'I can't imagine it—your parents, of all people, taking it easy on cruise liners. How long since you bought them out?'

'Coming up to four years.' Jonas kept his answer short, terse.

'Are they still involved?'

'Now *that*, Lawrie dear, would mean them communicating with me.' All this talk of his parents—his least favourite subject. It was time to turn the tables. 'Talking about difficult relations,' Jonas said, 'how is your mother? Still in Spain?'

Lawrie twisted in her seat and stared at him. 'How did you know she was in Spain?'

Jonas grinned to himself, allowing his fingers to beat out a tune on the leather of the steering wheel. *Nice deflection, Jones.* 'I met her when she was over from Spain, introducing her new husband...John, isn't it? He seemed like a nice bloke. Didn't she come to London? She said she wanted to see you.'

Lawrie's mouth had thinned; the relaxed posture was gone. Any straighter and he could use her back as a ruler.

'I was busy.'

Jonas shrugged. 'I think this one might be different. She seemed settled, happy.'

Lawrie was radiating disapproval. 'Maybe five is her lucky number.'

'People make mistakes. Your mother certainly did. But she's so proud of you.'

'She has no right to be proud of me—she doesn't know me. And if she was so keen to see me she should have come back for Gran's funeral.'

'Didn't she?'

He should have been at the funeral too. He'd said his own private goodbye to Gran on the day, alone at the cottage. But he should have gone.

'She was on a retreat.' It was Lawrie's turn to be terse.

Maybe it had been too successful a deflection. Jonas searched for a response but couldn't find one. Lawrie had every right to be angry, but at least her mother wanted to make amends.

His parents wouldn't have known what they were expected to make amends *for*—as far as they were concerned any problems in their relationship were all down to him.

He was their eternal disappointment.

There was an awkward silence for a few long minutes, with Jonas concentrating on the narrow road, pulling over several times as tractors lumbered past, and Lawrie staring out of the window.

'I'm sorry,' she said suddenly. 'I'm glad she's happy— that five husbands and goodness knows how many boyfriends later she's settled. But it's thirty years too late for me.'

'I know.'

And he did. He knew it all. He knew how bitter Lawrie was about her mother's desertion, how angry. He knew how vulnerable years of moving around, adapting to new homes, new schools, new stepfathers had made her.

He knew how difficult it was for her to trust, to rely on anyone. It was something he couldn't ever allow himself to forget.

When it all got too much Lawrie Bennett ran away. Like mother, like daughter. Not caring who or what she left behind.

This time he was not getting to get left in her destructive wake.

CHAPTER FOUR

'WHAT HAVE YOU done with the helipad? And didn't the ninth hole start over there? I'm not sure your father ever recovered from that lesson. Or your mother...although I *did* offer to pay for the window.'

Lawrie would have bet everything she owned that a country house hotel catering for the rich was not Jonas's style. But now she was here it was hard to pinpoint the changes she instinctively knew he must have made. Coombe End *looked* the same—a tranquil Queen Anne manor house set in stunning acres of managed woodland at the back, green meadows at the front, running into the vivid blue blur of sea on the horizon—and yet something was different. Something other than the change in owner and the apparent loss of a golf course and helipad.

Maybe it was the car park? There were a few high-end cars dotted here and there, but they were joined by plenty of others: people carriers, old bangers, small town cars and a whole fleet worth of camper vans, their bright paintwork shining brightly in the sun. Last time she had been here the car park had been filled with BMWs and Mercedes and other, less obviously identifiable makes—discreet and expensive, just like the hotel.

Lawrie hadn't seen many camper vans in London, and the sight of their cheery squat box shape, their rounded curves and white tops, filled her with a sudden inexplicable sense of happiness. Which was absurd. Camper vans were for man-boys who refused to grow up. Ridiculous, gas-guzzling, unreliable eyesores.

So why did they make her feel as if she was home?

As Jonas led Lawrie along the white gravelled path that clung to the side of the graceful old building her sense of discombobulation increased. The formal gardens were in full flower, displaying all their early summer gaudy glory—giant beds filled with gigantic hydrangea bushes, full flowered and opulent—but the gardens as a whole were a lot less manicured, the grass on the front lawns longer than she remembered, with wildflowers daring to peek out amongst the velvety green blades of grass.

And what was that? The rose garden was gone, replaced by a herb garden with small winding paths and six wooden beehives.

'You've replaced your mother's pride and joy?' she said, only half in mock horror.

'Doesn't it all look terribly untidy?' Jonas said, his voice prim and faintly scandalised, a perfect parody of his mother.

Lawrie shook her head, too busy looking around to answer him, as they walked up the sandstone steps that led to the large double doors.

The old heavy oak doors were still there, but stripped, varnished—somehow more inviting. The discreet brass plaque had gone. Instead a driftwood sign set onto the wall was engraved with 'Boat House Hotel'.

'Come on,' Jonas said, nudging her forward. 'I'll show you around.'

He stood aside and ushered her through the open door. With one last, lingering look at the sun-drenched lawn Lawrie went through into the hotel.

She hadn't spent much time here before. Jonas had left home the day he turned sixteen—by mutual agreement, he had claimed—and had slept above the bar or in the camper van before they were married. He'd converted the room over the bar into a cosy studio apartment once they were. It had always felt like a royal summons on the few occasions when they were invited over for dinner—the even fewer occasions she had persuaded Jonas to accept.

They had always been formal, faux-intimate family dinners, held on the public stage of the hotel dining room. Jonas's parents' priority had clearly been their guests, not their son and his wife. Long, torturous courses of beautifully put together rich food, hours full of polite small talk, filled with a multitude of poisoned, well targeted barbs.

Her memories made the reality even more of a shock as Lawrie walked into the bright, welcoming foyer. The changes outside had been definite, but subtle; the inside, however, was completely, obviously, defiantly different. Inside the large hallway the dark wood panelling, the brocade and velvet, had been stripped away, allowing the graceful lines of the old house to shine through in colours reflecting Jonas's love of the sea: deep blues and marine greens accentuating the cream décor.

'It's all reclaimed local materials—driftwood, recycled glass, re-covered sofas,' Jonas explained. 'And everything is Cornish-made—from the pictures on the walls to the glasses behind the bar.'

'It's amazing,' Lawrie said, looking about her at the room at once so familiar and yet so new, feeling a little like Alice falling into Wonderland. 'I love it. It's really elegant, isn't it? But not cold. It feels homely, somehow, despite its size.'

'That's the effect I wanted.' His voice was casual but his eyes blazed blue as he looked at her. 'You always did get it.'

Lawrie held his gaze for a long moment, the room fading away. That look in his eyes. That approval. Once she'd craved it, looked for it, yearned for it. Like the perfect cup of tea at the perfect temperature. A slab of chocolate exactly the right mixture of bitter and sweet. A chip, crisp and hot and salty on the outside, smooth and fluffy as you bit down.

Of course the only tea she drank nowadays was herbal, and she hadn't had a chip—not even a hand-cut one—in years.

And she didn't need anyone's approval.

'Some of my clients own hotels,' she said, injecting as much cool professionalism into her voice as she could. 'I've seen some great examples of décor, and some fairly alarming ones too. This is really lovely, though, Jonas.'

The approval faded, a quizzical gleam taking its place, but all he said was, 'I'm glad you approve. Let's hear your professional opinion on the rest of the place. This way.'

And Jonas turned and began to walk along the polished wooden floor towards the archway that led into the main ground floor corridor.

Lawrie heaved a sigh. Of relief, she told herself sternly. Job done—professional relationship back on track.

So why did she feel as if the sun had just disappeared behind a very black cloud?

Lawrie followed Jonas through the foyer and down the corridor, watching him greet both staff and guests with a smile, a quick word, a clap on the shoulder—evident master of his empire. It was odd… He used to be so unhappy here, a stranger in his own home, and now he appeared completely at ease.

Jonas led her into the old dining room. A large, imposing space, dominated by the series of floor-to-ceiling windows along the far wall matched by a parade of pillars reaching up to the high ceiling. This room too had been extensively remodelled, with a similar look and feel to the café on the seafront, all the lace and delicate china replaced with light woods and cheerful tablecloths.

A long table ran along one end, filled with large jugs, chunky earthenware mugs and plates of small cakes and biscuits.

'Wouldn't want the guests to get hungry,' Jonas explained as he grabbed a pair of large mugs and poured coffee from one of the jugs, automatically adding milk to them before handing one to Lawrie.

She opened her mouth to decline but closed it as she breathed in the rich, dark aroma.

Why had she given up coffee? she wondered as she took a cautious sip. It was delicious, and the creamy Cornish milk was a perfect companion to the bitter nectar. Two milky coffees in two days—she was slipping back into bad habits.

The coffee was the least of it.

Jonas carried his cup over to the nearest window, which stood slightly ajar, allowing the slight summer breeze to permeate the room with the sweet promise of fresh warmth. The breeze ruffled his dark blond hair, making him look younger, more approachable.

Like the boy she had married. Was he still there, somewhere inside this ambitious, coolly confident man, that impetuous, eager boy?

Lawrie had promised herself that she wouldn't probe. The last nine years, Jonas's life, his business… None of it was relevant. Knowing the details wouldn't help her with her job. Or with the distance she needed to maintain between them. And yet curiosity was itching through her.

She wandered over to the window and stood next to him, every fibre acutely aware of his proximity. Of the casual way he was leaning against the window frame. The golden hairs on the back of his tanned wrists. The undone button at his neck and the triangle of burnished skin it revealed.

Lawrie swallowed, the hot clench at her stomach reminding her of her vulnerability, of the attraction she didn't want to acknowledge.

She looked out, following his line of sight as he gazed into the distance. The sea was clearly visible in the distance, calm and unruffled, the smell of it clear on the breeze. And the urge to know more, to know him again, suddenly overwhelmed her.

'Why here?' There—it was said.

Jonas looked mildly surprised. 'Where else? This room works well as a dining room, has good access to the kitchens. It would have been silly to change it just for change's sake.'

Lawrie shook her head. 'I didn't mean the room. I meant the whole thing,' she said, aware she was probing deeper than she had any right to. 'I mean here. You hated this place. I couldn't get you to set foot inside the gates without a massive fight. I could understand it if your parents had gifted the place to you, but if you paid full value for and then remodelled it? It must have cost a *fortune*!'

Jonas quirked an eyebrow at her. 'Oh, I get it. You're wondering about how much I'm worth. Regretting the divorce after all?'

Heat flooded through her. She could feel her cheeks reddening. 'That's not what I meant,' she protested. 'You know I wouldn't have taken a penny.'

'That's my Lawrie—still so serious.'

Jonas let out a laugh and Lawrie swatted him indignantly, trying to repress the secret thrill that crept over her at the possessive word 'my'.

'Oh, ha-ha. Very funny.'

Jonas leant back against the window pane, still grinning, and took a sip from the chunky Cornishware mug. 'You always were so easy to wind up. Good to know some things don't change.'

'So?' she pressed him, taking advantage of his suddenly companionable mood. 'How come you ended up at Coombe End?'

Jonas didn't reply for a long moment, and the mischievous glint in his eyes faded to annoyance. When he spoke his tone was clipped. 'This was my home once, Lawrie. It wasn't a big conspiracy or takeover, no matter what the village gossips say.'

Lawrie winced. She hadn't considered the inevitable fall-out the change of ownership must have caused. The whole of Trengarth—the whole area—knew how things stood between Jonas and his parents. And there were few without definite opinions on the matter.

'Since when did you care about what the gossips say?' They had always been different in that regard. She so self-conscious, he proudly indifferent.

His eyes were cold. 'I don't. My decision to buy Coombe End was purely a business one. I always knew this place could be more. Yes, it was successful—very successful—if that kind of thing appealed: a little piece of the capital by the sea. You could drive straight here, fly your helicopter here, use the private beach, play the golf course and return home without ever experiencing what Cornwall is about,' he said, his lip curling as he remembered. 'The kind of place your fiancé probably took you.'

'Ex-fiancé,' Lawrie corrected him. She shook her head, refusing to take the bait, but there was an uncomfortable element of truth to his words. Hugo had liked the luxury hotel experience, it was true, but they'd been so busy that just snatching a night away had been enough. There had never been time to explore local culture as well.

'Of course,' Jonas said, putting his mug down decisively and stepping away from the window. 'Ex. Come on. There's a lot to go through.'

No wonder she felt like Alice, being constantly hustled from place to place. She half expected Jonas to pull out a pocket watch. If there were croquet lawns she was in serious trouble.

Lawrie took a last reluctant gulp of the creamy coffee and placed her mug onto the nearest table before following Jonas once again. He led her back down the corridor, through the foyer and outside, along the winding path that led to the woods that made up most of the outside property.

One of Coombe End's winter money-makers had been shooting parties. Lawrie had hated hearing the bangs from the woods and seeing the braces of poor, foolish pheasants being carried back to the house, heads lolling pathetically.

Jonas was walking fast, with intent, and she had to lengthen her stride to keep up with him. It took her by surprise when he came to a sudden halt at the end of the gravelled path, where a long grassy track snaked away ahead of them up the small wooded hill that bordered the hotel gardens.

Lawrie skittered to an undignified stop, clamping down on the urge to grab onto him for support. 'A bit of warning would be nice,' she muttered as she righted herself cautiously.

Jonas ignored her. 'I never hated this place, Law,' he said after a while, gesturing out towards the woodland, its trees a multitude of green against the blue sky.

A secret thrill shuddered through her at the sound of the old pet name.

'I love it here. I always did. But I wanted a different way.'

He resumed walking, Lawrie kept pace with him, wishing she was wearing flatter, sturdier shoes. He had a fast, firm tread; she had always liked that. Hugo was more of a dawdler, and it had driven her mad—as had his admonishments to 'Slow down…it's not a race'.

Jonas didn't look at her as she reached his side but continued as if there hadn't been any break in the conversation. It was as if he was glad he had the chance to explain. And why shouldn't he be? The boy had done well. *Very* well. He hadn't needed her at all. It must be *satisfying* to be in his position. Successful, in control, magnanimously helping out your ex.

Lawrie clenched her fist, digging her nails deep into the palm of her hand. This wasn't how her life, her return to Trengath, was supposed to have been.

'By the time my father had his second heart attack I'd managed to expand the Boat House into twenty-seven seaside locations in the South-West and people were buying into the whole experience—branded T-shirts, mugs, beach towels. So, from a business point of view, expanding the dining experience into a holiday experience made sense.'

Lawrie pulled her mind away from her introspection. Self-pity had never been her style anyway. It didn't get you anywhere.

'I guess,' she said slightly doubtfully. 'But I don't go to my favourite coffee shop and think what this place needs is somewhere for me to sleep.'

'But your favourite coffee shop is near where you live or work,' he pointed out. 'Sure, we're popular with the local population, but in summer especially seventy per cent of our customers are tourists—even if just a small percentage of those people want to take the experience further and holiday with us then that's already a good deal of our marketing done.'

She looked at him in fascination. He sounded like one of her clients.

'I was writing the dissertation for my MBA on brand expansion at the time. Fascinating to put the theory into practice.'

An MBA? Not bad for a boy who'd left school at sixteen. Not that she hadn't known he was capable of so much more. But, truly, had she ever thought him capable of all this? Shame crept over her, hot and uncomfortable. Maybe he was right. She *had* underestimated him.

He flashed her a smile, warm and confiding—a smile that evoked memories of long late-night conversations, of dreams shared, plans discussed. Had she and Hugo ever talked like that? If they had, she couldn't remember.

'Luckily I had been planning what I would do with this place if I were in charge since I was a kid. I've left the hotel itself as pretty high-end, with the rooms still aimed at the luxury end of the market, but I've utilised the woods and the golf course more effectively and I began to reap the rewards almost straight away.'

They were near the top of the small hill. He reached it first and paused, waiting for her to catch up, an expectant look on his face.

She looked down and gasped. 'What on earth...?'

Set beneath them were the woods, which opened almost immediately into a large glade, easily seen from the top of the bank on which they were standing. Inside the glade were eight round white cotton objects that looked a little like mini circus tents.

'Glamping' he said, his voice serious. His eyes, however, had warmed up and were sparkling with amusement at her expression. 'Oh, come on—you're a city girl. Isn't this how the London middle classes enjoy the great outdoors?'

She found her voice. 'You've put *tents* into the woods?

Do your parents know? Your dad will have a third heart attack if he sees this.'

'Ah, but these are luxurious, fully catered tents,' he assured her. 'Perfectly respectable. People can enjoy all the hotel facilities, including their own bathrooms and food in the hotel—although there are barbecues if they want to be pioneer types. They arrive to fully made-up camp beds, there's space to hang clothes, armchairs, rugs, heating. Not what I call camping, but it's hugely popular. The traditional bring-your-own-tent-type campers are on what used to be the golf course, and there are lots of shower and toilet blocks for their use there. According to one review site they are the best camping loos in Cornwall.'

'Well, *there's* an accolade.'

'I'm hoping for a certificate.'

'Anything else?' she asked. 'Tree houses? Yurts? A cave with hot and cold water laid on?'

He chuckled softly, and the sound went straight to the pit of her stomach.

'Just a few stationary camper vans dotted around here and there.'

'Of course there are.' She nodded.

He looked at her, his blue eyes darkening, suddenly intense. 'They're very popular with honeymooners—complete privacy.'

She felt her breath catch as she looked at him, and a shiver goosed its way down her spine. 'A bit cramped,' she said, hearing the husky tone in her voice and hating herself for it.

'They're customised cosy getaways for two—big beds, good sheets and baskets of food delivered.'

'You've thought of everything.'

So different from the two of them, with a sleeping bag and a couple of blankets, a bottle of champagne, the moon, the stars, the sound of the surf. And each other—always each other. Bodies coiled together, lips, hands, caresses… She swallowed. How did these memories, buried so deep, resurface every time this man spoke?

'I had long enough to plan it, watching my parents cater for rich idiots who didn't give a damn where they were,' he said, his mood changing instantly from dangerously reminiscent to businesslike again. 'This place is so beautiful, and yet only a handful of people ever had the opportunity to enjoy it—and once they were here they had no idea what was outside the estate walls. Opening it up to campers and glampers means anyone can come here, whatever their budget. We make sure they have all the information they need to go out and explore, hire them bikes, provide transport. All our food is sourced locally, and we recruit and promote locally whenever possible.'

Lawrie laughed, shaking her head in disbelief. 'It's inspired,' she said honestly. 'Utterly inspired, Jonas.'

Without thinking, without even realising what she was doing, she put a hand on his arm, squeezed softly.

'Amazing.'

The feel of his arm was warm and firm under her hand, and the fine cotton of his shirt bunched up under her fingers. How many times had she slid her hand up this arm, admired the strength inherent in the toned muscles as he emerged, sleek and shiny, from the sea? Felt their gentleness as he pulled her in close, encircling her in the safety of his embrace?

'I'm glad you like it.'

Jonas stepped back. Stepped away from her hand, her touch.

'The hotel isn't just the base for the festival—it sets the tone. It's important you understand that. Shall we?'

He gestured back towards the hotel. She shivered, suddenly cold despite the balmy warmth of the day and the wool of her suit jacket. If only she was still with Hugo. If only she were secure in her job. Then seeing Jonas, speaking to him, would have meant nothing apart from a certain nostalgic curiosity. She was feeling vulnerable, that was all.

'You're right—this is the perfect setting for the festival. I see how it works now.' She could do businesslike as well. She'd practically invented it.

He registered the change, a querying eyebrow shooting up as she adjusted her jacket again, smoothing her hair back away from her face, plastering a determinedly polite smile onto her face.

'So, what other changes have you made?' Lawrie kept up a flow of light conversation as Jonas led the way back to the hotel, barely knowing what she was saying, what his answers were.

Thoughts tumbled around her brain. Coming back wasn't easy, starting again was hard, but she had expected that. What she *hadn't* expected, she admitted honestly to herself, was that anything would have changed.

Walking back into Gran's cottage had been like entering a time warp, and for the first couple of days as she'd holed herself up and licked her wounds it had looked as if Trengarth had stayed the same as well.

She had walked down to the harbour on her birthday looking for the safety and comfort of her past. She had truly expected to see the Boat House in its original incarnation—Jonas behind the bar, a little older, a little more thick-set, his mind firmly fixed on waves, on guitar chords, on fun.

She had wanted to validate her choices. To know that even if her present was looking a little shaky at least her past choices had been right. She had been so convinced, once, that Jonas was holding her back, but what if she had been the one holding *him* back?

He was obviously better off without her. Which was *good*, she told herself defiantly, because despite everything she was definitely better off without him.

Or she would be once she had decided exactly what she was going to do.

The familiar niggle of worry gnawed away at her. She had just a few weeks left of her gardening leave—just a few weeks to get a job so much better than her old one that to the outsider it would look like a planned move. Just a few weeks to show Hugo and the senior partners that she was better than their firm. Just a few weeks to get her plan back on track.

They had reached the front of the hotel again and she turned to face Jonas, her features deliberately smooth, matching his. 'This has been fascinating, Jonas, and I can't wait to get started. If you show me where I am to work I'll get set up.'

And then Jonas smiled. A slow, intimate, knowing smile. A smile that said he knew exactly what she was doing. A smile that saw right through her mask. It crinkled the corners of his eyes, drew her gaze to firm lips, to the faint shadow on the sculpted jawline.

It was the kind of smile that offered comfort, acceptance. The kind of smile that invited a girl to lean in, to allow those broad shoulders to take the strain.

It was almost irresistible.

But Lawrie Bennett was made of sterner stuff. Just.

She straightened her shoulders, met his eyes with a challenge. 'After all, you must have a lot to be getting on with.'

The smile deepened. 'Good to see work is still your priority, Lawrie.'

It was. And it evidently was a priority for him as well. So why did he sound so amused?

'The staff entrance is round the back, but you can use the front doors. Just this once.'

Once again Lawrie was following Jonas, moving behind the stylish reception desk and through a door that led to the offices, kitchens and staff bedrooms.

'I have an office here, of course,' he said. 'But I do prefer to work at the Boat House—whether it's because I designed the office there, or because it's where this all began I don't know.' He shrugged. 'A business psychologist would probably have a field-day, trying to work it all out, but I'm not sure I need to know as long as it works and the business keeps growing.'

'You don't live in your parents' apartment?'

He looked surprised at the question. 'Oh, heavens, no. This place needs a whole team of managers and some of them live in. The general manager and his family have the apartment. I bought a place on the seafront a few years ago. One of the old fishermen's cottages by the harbour. You'd like it.'

She nodded, maintaining her cool, interested air even as a stab of pain shot through her. It had always been her ambition to own one of the stone-built cottages clustered around the harbour. On moonlit nights she and Jonas had strolled along, hands entwined, as she'd pointed out her favourites, and they had laughingly argued over decorating plans, colour schemes, furniture.

Now he lived in one of those cottages, without her.

It was ridiculous to feel wounded. To feel *anything*. After all she had spent the last five years living in a beautiful flat with another man; very soon she fully intended to be in an apartment of her own somewhere completely new. Yet the thought of Jonas living in the dream house of their youth filled her with a wistfulness so intense she could barely catch her breath.

He had opened a door to an empty office and held it open, motioning her to move inside. Swallowing back the unexpected emotion as she went through, she saw the office was a large room, distinguished by two big sash windows, each with a cushioned window seat, and furnished with a large desk, a small meeting table and a sofa.

'This is supposed to be my office,' he explained. 'I never use it, though, so you may as well have it while you're here. As I said, it'll be useful for you to be based on site. I'm sure it's all in your notes, but the hotel itself usually hosts the bands, VIPs and essential staff, and most festival-goers camp in the grounds—although quite a lot book out the local B&Bs and caravan parks too.'

She nodded. Of course she had read all this yesterday, but it was still hard for her to comprehend.

Jonas had started this festival during her first year at Oxford, getting local rock and folk bands to play on the beach for free, raising money for a surfing charity that campaigned against marine and beach pollution. The first ever festival had been a one-night affair and the festival-goers had slept on the beach…if they'd slept at all. Food had, of course, been provided by the Boat House. Lawrie was supposed to have returned to Cornwall for it, but at the last minute had decided to stay in London, where she'd been interning for the summer.

Her refusal to promise that she would attend the third festival had led to the final argument in their increasingly volatile relationship. She had packed her bags on the eve of her twenty-first birthday and gone to London for another summer of interning. At the end of that summer she had returned to Oxford for her fourth and final year. She had never returned to Cornwall.

Not until a week ago.

And now that little beach festival had grown—just like the Boat House, just like Jonas's business. Everything was so much bigger, so different from the small, comforting life she remembered. Three nights, thirty-six bands, family activities, thousands of festival-goers, raising substantial funds for charity—yet still local, still focussed on the best of Cornish music, food, literature. It was daunting.

Not that she was going to confess that to the imposing man standing before her.

Lawrie had never admitted that she needed help before. She wasn't going to start now.

'This is great, Jonas,' she said. 'I can take it from here.'

His mouth quirked. 'I have complete faith in you,' he assured her. 'You know where I am if you need me.'

She nodded, but her mind was completely made up. She did not, *would* not need Jonas Jones. She was going to do this alone. Just as she always did.

CHAPTER FIVE

JONAS LOVED THIS drive. The winding lanes, the glimpses of sea through the dense green hedgerows. If he put the top down he could smell the intoxicating scent of sweet grass and gorse, feel the sea breeze ruffling his hair.

And he loved the destination. The hotel *he* owned. The hotel *he* had bought. The hotel where his ex-wife was right this moment sitting at his desk, taking care of his festival.

It had been an unexpected couple of days. Of course the village gossips were having a field-day. Again. What would they do without him? He should start charging a licence fee for the resurrection of their favourite soap opera. He would always be that no-good boy who'd broken his parents' hearts, and she would always be the no-better-than-she-should-be teen bride, flighty daughter of a flighty mother. Their roles had been set in stone long before no matter how they tried to redefine them.

Well, the viewers were doomed to disappointment. Reunion episodes were always a let-down. He had no intention of allowing this one to be any different.

Pulling into the gates of the hotel, he felt the usual spark of pride, of ownership, zing through him. Who would have thought the prodigal son would return in such style?

It would be nice, though—just once—to drive through the gates and not be assailed by memories. By the disapproving voices of his parents and their disappointed expectations.

When he'd failed his exams at sixteen his parents had wanted to send him away to boarding school—ostensibly to do retakes, in reality to get him away from his friends. It showed a lack of character, they'd thought, that rather than befriend the other boys from the private school they'd sent him to he preferred to hang around with the village kids.

His hands tightened on the steering wheel. Yes, he probably should have studied rather than sneaking out to swim and surf. Taken some interest in his exams. But his achievements—his interest in food, his surfing skill, his hard-won A* in Design and Technology—had meant nothing. His father couldn't, or wouldn't, boast about his son's perfect dovetailed joints on the golf course.

His parents hadn't ever lost their tempers with him. Cold silence had been their weapon of choice. There had been weeks, growing up, when he could swear they hadn't addressed one word to him. But they'd come close to exploding when Jonas had refused to go to the carefully selected crammer they had found.

Some parents would have been proud, Jonas thought with the same, tired old stab of pain, proud that their child wanted to follow in their footsteps. He had thought his plan was a winner—that he would finally see some approval in their uninterested faces.

He'd been so keyed up when he'd told them his idea to run a café-bar on the hotel's small beach. One that was aimed at locals as well as tourists.

He had even offered to do a few retakes at the local college before studying Hospitality and Tourism.

It hadn't been enough. Nothing he did ever was.

In the end they had reached a grudging compromise. They'd given him the old boat house they hadn't used, preferring to keep their guests—and their guests' wallets—on the hotel grounds, and they'd cut him loose. Set him free.

They'd expected him to fail. To come back, cap in hand, begging for their forgiveness.

Instead, twelve years later, he'd bought them out.

And it had been every bit as satisfying as he had thought it would be. It still was.

And, truth be told, Jonas thought as he swung his car into the staff car park, it was quite satisfying having Lawrie here as well. Working for him once again. Seeing just how much he had accomplished. Just how little he needed her.

Whereas she definitely needed him. She was doing her best to hide it, but he could tell. Her very appearance in Trengarth. Her acceptance of the job. None of it was planned.

And Lawrie Bennett didn't *do* spontaneous.

There were just too many ghosts, and Jonas felt uncharacteristically grim as he walked through the foyer—although he did his best to hide it, playing the jovial host, the approachable boss. If growing up in a hotel, then running a café at sixteen, had taught him anything it was how to put on a mask. Nobody cared about the guy pouring the coffee—about his day or his feelings. They just wanted a drink, a smile and some easy chat. Funny how he had always accused Lawrie of hiding her feelings. In some ways they were exactly the same.

Walking along the carpeted corridor that led to his office—now Lawrie's—he felt a sense of *déjà vu* overwhelm him. Once this had been his father's domain. He had never been welcome here—summoned only to be scolded. Even stripping out the heavy mahogany furniture and redecorating it hadn't changed the oppressive feeling. No wonder he preferred to base himself at the harbour.

He paused at the shut door. He didn't usually knock

at his employees' doors, but then again they weren't usually shut. And this was *his* office, after all. Jonas felt his jaw clench tight. Nothing was simple when Lawrie was involved—not even going through his own damn door in his own damn hotel.

He twisted the heavy brass door and swung it open with more force than necessary, striding into the room.

Then he stopped. Blinked in surprise.

'You've certainly made yourself at home.'

There was a small overnight bag open on the floor. Clothes were strewn on the table, chairs and across the sofa—far more clothes than could ever possibly fit into such a small case. Jeans, tops, dresses, skirts—all a far cry from the exquisitely tailored suits and accessories that in just two days Lawrie was already famous for wearing to work.

If Jonas had to hear one more awed conversation discussing whether she wore couture, high-end High Street or had a personal tailor, then he would make all his staff—no matter what their job—adopt the waiting staff's uniform of bright blue Boat House logo tee and black trousers.

Lawrie was on the floor, pulling clothes out of the bag with a harassed expression on her face.

'Have you moved in?' he asked as politely as he could manage, whilst making no attempt to keep the smirk from his face.

Lawrie looked up, her face harassed, her hair falling out of what had once, knowing Lawrie, been a neat bun. She pushed a tendril of the dark silky stuff back behind an ear and glared at him. 'Don't you knock?'

'Not usually. Are you going somewhere?'

'Road trip,' she said tersely. 'And I have nothing to wear.'

Jonas raised an eyebrow and looked pointedly at the sofa. And at the table. Finally, slowly, he allowed his gaze to linger on the floor. A pair of silky lilac knickers caught his eye and held it for one overlong second before he pulled his gaze reluctantly away.

'Half this stuff is mine. Only it's about fifteen years old—whatever I still had at Gran's. The rest is Fliss's, and as we aren't the same height or size it's not really much use. The truth is I don't really know how to dress down. Where I live it's all skinny jeans and caramel knee-length boots, with cashmere for shopping and lunch or yoga pants at home. None of that is very suitable at all,' she finished, with a kind of wail.

'Suitable for what?' Jonas decided not to ask why she was packing here and not at home. He wasn't sure she even knew.

'The road trip,' she said.

He cocked an enquiring eyebrow and she rocked back on her heels and sighed. Irritably.

'*You* know! Suzy always gets a couple of local bands to come and play Wave Fest. They send in their CDs, or links to their downloads or whatever, and she whittles them down to a shortlist and then goes to see them play live. At a *gig*,' she said, pronouncing the word 'gig' with an odd mixture of disdain and excitement. 'I haven't been to a gig in years,' she added.

'Not much call for yoga pants at Cornish gigs.'

'Or cashmere,' Lawrie agreed, missing his sarcasm completely, or just ignoring it. 'Three of the shortlisted bands are playing over the next three nights so I'm going to see them all. Two of them are in the county, but tomorrow's gig is in Devon, so it made sense to plan a whole trip and do some mystery shopping at some of the caterers and cafés we've got tendering as well. We're behind in letting them know. Only that means a three-day trip and I don't have anything to wear. Why do you have to be so inclusive and get other people to provide the food?' she ended bitterly.

'Because we couldn't possibly feed thousands of people, and it's good publicity to make the festival a celebration of local food as well,' Jonas said, his mouth twitching at Lawrie's woebegone expression.

She looked like somebody being dragged to a three-day conference on dental drills—not like someone heading out for a long weekend of music and food, all on expenses.

He took pity on her.

'Right, unfortunately packing light may not be an option,' Jonas said, gesturing to the small bag. 'Three gigs in three nights? You'll need to be prepared for beer-spills,' he clarified at her enquiring expression.

Lawrie pulled a face. 'I'm not planning to *mosh*.'

'You did once.'

Lightly said but the words evoked a torrent of memories. Lawrie, so small and slight. Vulnerable. Hurling herself into the mass of bodies right at the front of the stage. It had taken him a long time to make his way through the tightly packed, sweaty mass to find her, jumping ecstatically to the beat of the music, eyes half closed. He'd liked staying near her, to protect her from the crush as the crowd moved to the music.

Lawrie's eyebrow furrowed. 'What did I wear?'

He looked at her incredulously. 'How am I supposed to remember? Probably jeans...' A memory hit him, of thin straps falling off tanned shoulders, a glimpse of skin at the small of her back. 'And a top?' he added. 'Was there a green one?'

Her eyes lit up. 'Hang on!' She jumped up and ran over to the table, where she sifted through a pile of brightly coloured tops. 'Do you remember this?' She held up a light green floaty top.

Jonas wouldn't have said he was a particularly observant man, especially when it came to clothes. His last girlfriend had claimed that he said, 'You look nice...' on autopilot. And it was true that he generally didn't notice haircuts or new outfits. He knew better than to admit it, but he preferred his women laid-back and practical. Jeans, trainers, a top. Even a fleece if they were out walking. There was nothing less sexy than a woman stumbling along the cliff-tops in unsuitable shoes and shivering because her most flattering jacket proved useless against a chill sea breeze.

But the sight of that green top took his breath away, evoking the beat of a drum, the smell of mingled beer, sweat and cigarettes in the air. Not the most pleasant of smells, yet in the back room of a pub, a club or a town hall, as guitars wailed and people danced, it fitted. Dark, dirty, hot. The feel of Lawrie pressed against him in the fast-moving, mesmerised crowd.

He swallowed. 'I think so,' he managed to say, as normally as he could.

Lawrie regarded it doubtfully. 'I guess it will fit. I'm the same size, and luckily Gran had them all laundered.' Now it was her turn to swallow, with a glint in her eye.

Had she grieved properly for her gran? For the woman who'd brought her up? The woman who had provided him with a sanctuary, a sympathetic shoulder and a lot of sound advice?

Had helped him become the man he was today.

'There you go, then,' he said. 'Three tops like that, some jeans for the gigs, something similar for the day, and pyjamas. Easy.' He tried not to look at the lilac silk knickers. 'Plus essentials. Where are you staying?'

'I'm not sure. Fliss was supposed to have sorted out accommodation. Wherever I can get in last-minute, I guess.'

She didn't look particularly enthusiastic and he didn't blame her. Three nights alone in anonymous, bland rooms didn't sound like much fun.

'I'm looking into buying a small chain that covers the whole of the South-West,' he said. 'We could see if any of those are near where you need to be and you can do some evaluation while you're there. Let me know what you think of them.'

She nodded. 'I'm near Liskeard tonight, then over to Totnes tomorrow, and back towards Newquay on Saturday. I could drive straight back from there, but there are several food producers I want to sample around that area so it makes sense to stay over.' Her eyes darkened. 'I wish Fliss hadn't bailed, though. It would be nice to have a second opinion.'

'Isn't she going with you?'

'She was supposed to be—we were going to road-trip. Like Thelma and Louise—only without guns or Brad Pitt. But Dave has tickets for some play she really wanted to see and I think he wants to make a weekend of it. It's fine. I'm quite capable. Only she was going to sort out the accommodation and didn't get round to it.'

Her face said exactly what she thought of such woeful disorganisation.

Jonas suppressed a chuckle. He'd have liked to see them set off—Fliss laid-back and happy to wing it, Lawrie clutching a schedule and a stopwatch. 'I'll have a word with Alex and get him to find you some appropriate rooms. What time are you off?'

'After lunch, I think. If I can get packed by then.' She cast a despairing look at the clothes-strewn room.

'I'll let you know what Alex says. Let him arrange your bookings—he knows all the good places. That's why I employ him.'

'Thanks.' She was trying to hide it, but there was still uncertainty, worry in the dark eyes.

'No need to thank me; it's his job. I'll see you later.'

Jonas needed some air. The room suddenly felt hot, claustrophobic. He'd been working too hard, that was the problem. Head down, losing himself in spreadsheets and figures and meetings. He hadn't been near a board for days, hadn't touched a guitar.

He needed a break. Lucky Lawrie. A road trip sounded perfect.

Good food, music, and some time on the road.

It really *did* sound perfect.

If only he had known earlier he could have offered to go instead. A trip was just what the doctor had ordered.

Lawrie checked her watch. Again. This was ridiculous. She had planned to be on the road fifteen minutes ago. Nothing was more irritating than being behind schedule.

Even worse, she was hungry. It must be the Cornish air, because far from acting like a normal jilted bride, and existing on tears alone, for the first time in years Lawrie had a real appetite. Every day she went to the staff dining room promising herself she would just have the soup. A *small* bowl of soup. Because she strongly suspected it was made with double cream.

Yet every day she would find herself drifting over to the bread. Carbs, wheat, gluten. Things that Lawrie had been depriving herself of for so long she had completely forgotten why. Bread covered with real butter, with rich, creamy cheese…sharp, tangy cheese. Even worse, she sometimes had crisps on the side, and the handful of lettuce and tomatoes she added to her heaped plate went no way to assuaging her guilt.

Only—as the pang in her stomach reminded her all too well—she was skipping lunch today. The first stop on her schedule was a baker's, and she had an Indian restaurant and an ice cream maker to fit in today. She might be the same size as her teen self right now but, she thought, the chances of her remaining that slender were looking very, very slim.

She checked her watch again and shook her head. She couldn't wait. Her schedule was packed. Alex would just have to leave her a message and let her know where she would be staying that night. She swallowed. That was okay. He would hardly leave her to sleep in the car. So what if she hadn't checked out the hotel website and printed out directions in case the sat nav didn't work? This was a road trip, not a military manoeuvre.

Lawrie grabbed her handbag and moved towards the door, picking up the stuffed overnight bag and the shopper she had quickly bought in the hotel shop to carry the overspill as she did so. She averted her eyes from the mass of clothes on the sofa. She had tried to tidy up but it still looked as if a whole class of fifteen-year-olds had done a clothes-swap in the normally tidy office.

'Okay, then,' she said out loud, but the words sounded flat in the empty room and her stomach lurched with the all too familiar panic she'd been trying to hide since Fliss had pulled out last night.

Lawrie was no stranger to travelling alone, to making decisions alone, but usually she was clothed with the confidence of her profession. Sharp suits, intimidating jargon, business class flights. This time it would just be Lawrie Bennett, unemployed and jilted. Alone.

She dropped her bags, pressing a fist to her stomach, trying to quell the churning inside. For goodness' sake, she dealt with CEOs all the time. How could standing in a dark room listening to music be scarier than walking into a hostile boardroom?

But it was.

It had been so long. Gigging belonged to a younger, more

naive Lawrie. A Lawrie she had said goodbye to many years before. Still, she thought grimly, it would all make an amusing anecdote one day—possibly even at a job interview. An example of how she was prepared to go the extra mile.

The trill of her desk phone made her jump. Good—Alex at last. Walking over to it, she prayed for a reprieve. There were no hotel rooms left in the whole of Cornwall…. She was needed elsewhere…

'Sorted out your sartorial crisis?'

Not Alex. Warm, comforting tones, as caressing as a hot bath on a cold night. A voice she wanted to confide her fears in—a voice that promised safety. Sanctuary.

'I'm running late,' she said, more sharply than she had intended. The last thing she needed was for Jonas to guess how relieved she was to hear his voice, to know how scared she was. 'Did your guy manage to sort out a place for tonight? I really can't hold on any longer.'

'Everything's organised. Come and meet me in the car park.'

Was that laughter tinting the deep tones? 'Fine. I'm on my way.'

Laden down, it took Lawrie a few minutes to make her way along the corridors and through the staff door that led to the car park.

The weather had cooled suddenly, and the sky was a mixture of grey and white with occasional glimpses of hopeful blue. It meant nothing. Cornwall was full of micro climates, and she had packed for every eventuality bar blizzards.

Her convertible Beetle was tucked away in the far corner of the car park. Hugo had laughed at it—told her that she was obviously still a hippy surf girl at heart—although she had eschewed all the pretty pastel colours for a sensible metallic grey. She had thought of it as the perfect choice for a city car: small and compact. But its rounded lines and cheerful shape fitted in here. Maybe Hugo had been right about that part of her at least.

She pushed Hugo from her mind. He didn't belong here, in this world dominated by the sea and the open country. In the new life she was trying to make for herself. She looked around for Jonas but he wasn't by her car or by the hotel entrance.

'Lawrie?'

There he was, predictably enough standing by one of the camper vans that were always dotted around the car park, several of them staff vehicles. She was pretty sure ownership of one guaranteed you a job here.

This van was freshly painted a minty green, its contrasting white trim bright. Jonas leant against it, arms folded, one long leg casually crossed over the other, a look of enjoyment on his face. The same feeling of safety she had experienced on the phone rushed over her as she walked towards him.

'I'm behind schedule, so this had better not take long,' she said as she stopped in front of him, dropping her bags at her feet.

She wasn't going to give in to temptation, to allow her eyes to flicker up and down the long, muscled legs, the firm torso that broadened out in exactly the right place. She wasn't going to pause at the neck—what *was* it with this man and his unbuttoned shirts? One button lower and it would look sleazy, but as it was he managed to show just enough chest to tantalise. And she wasn't going to linger on the perfectly defined jawline, on the cheekbones wasted on a mere man—even on this one. She certainly wasn't going to step closer and allow her hand to brush that lock of dirty blond hair back from his forehead, no matter how much her hand ached to.

'You have a schedule?' He shook his head. 'Of course you do. A timetable, printed maps, telephone numbers all printed out. I bet there's a clipboard.'

Hot colour crept over her cheeks. 'There's nothing wrong with being organised.'

He raised an eyebrow in pretend surprise. 'I didn't say there was. It's an excellent quality in a festival-planner and an equally excellent one in a navigator. Come on—hop in.'

Confusion warred with panic and a tiny, unwanted tendril of hope. 'What do you mean?'

Jonas gestured to the van. 'She doesn't know whether to be pleased or offended that you don't recognise her, even though she spent a good six months being restored.'

'They all look the same,' Lawrie replied automatically, but her eyes were searching the camper van, looking for the tell-tale signs, looking for the rust, the dents. 'That's not Bar...? Not your old van?'

'You nearly said her name.' A smirk played around the firm mouth. 'Not looking so old now, is she? A facelift— well, an everything lift, really—new custom interior, new engine. She's never been in better shape.'

'Boys and their toys,' Lawrie scoffed, but secretly she was impressed.

The old van did look amazing—a total change from the ancient rust bucket whose tattered interior might have been original but had definitely seen better days. The same magic wand that had been waved over the Boat House, over the hotel, even over Jonas himself had been hard at work here.

'She looks good, but I still don't get what that has to do with me.'

The blue eyes gleamed. 'You said yourself you needed a second opinion.'

The tiny tendril of hope grew larger, bloomed. Lawrie

stamped down on it. Hard. 'I said Fliss was going to *give* me a second opinion—not that I needed one.'

'And I realised that I need to recharge my batteries.'

He carried on as if she hadn't spoken, pushing himself away from the van and sauntering slowly towards her. Lawrie fought an instinctive urge to take a step back. With his unhurried grace he reminded her of a predator, blue eyes fixed on her, hypnotic.

Lawrie swallowed, her mouth suddenly dry, her heart pounding so loudly she was sure he could hear it. 'I'm not sure it's a good idea. Working together is one thing, but spending time alone after everything...' Her voice trailed off. Lost for words again. It was becoming a habit around him.

Jonas paused in his tracks. 'But we *will* be working. Second opinions, remember?'

'Alone—we'll be working together alone,' she snapped.

He quirked an eyebrow. 'Oh, I'm sorry. I totally misread the situation. I thought you were totally over me, what with the divorce and the fiancé and the nine years apart, but if this is awkward for you maybe I had better keep my distance.'

He stood grinning at her. He obviously thought he had the upper hand.

Lawrie could feel her teeth grinding together. With a huge effort she unclenched her jaw, forcing a smile onto her face. 'I hate to burst your highly inflated opinion of yourself,' she said, as sweetly as she could, 'but I was only thinking of you. If this isn't awkward for you, then great— by all means join me.'

He moved a step closer, so close they were nearly touching. She could see the smattering of freckles that dusted the bridge of his nose, the tops of his cheeks. They gave him a boyish air, emphasised by the hair falling over his forehead, the impish grin.

But he was no boy. Jonas Jones was all grown up.

'Ready?' he asked, eyes locked on hers.

She stared straight back at him, channelling every ounce of cool professionalism she had right back at him. 'Of course.'

'Then let's go.'

'Did Alex book the hotels? I can plot out the best routes for the entire weekend once I know where we're staying.'

Jonas had to hand it to her. Lawrie was never knocked down for long. He could have sworn that his decision to crash her trip had completely thrown her but she was hiding it well. The road atlas open on her lap, clipboard and pen in hand, she was seemingly back in control.

For now.

Of course she had a point. A very good point. Spending three days on the road with any colleague would be testing. Make that colleague the person you'd once thought was the love of your life and things got a little more difficult.

But this was purely business. Lawrie had been thrown in at the deep end, after all. She might be a whizz with a spreadsheet and able to decipher the finer points of contracts in the blink of an eye, but Jonas was prepared to bet good money that she hadn't been anywhere near a tent or a crowded gig in years. This was his festival—his reputation at stake. He might agree that in the circumstances Lawrie was the right person to help them out, but she still needed hand-holding. Metaphorically, of course.

Of course he *might* be playing with fire. But what was life without a little danger? He'd been playing it safe for far too long.

Time to light the fireworks.

Jonas nodded towards a folder on the dashboard. 'Our accommodation is in there.'

Concealing a smile, Jonas watched out of the corner of his eye as she slid the folder onto her knee and pulled out the sheaf of paper from inside.

Her brow crinkled. 'These aren't hotels.'

'Excellent opportunity to check out some of the competition,' he said.

'You own a hotel.'

'And a campsite,' he reminded her.

'But I'm not set for camping. I don't camp—not any more.' Her voice was rising. 'I don't even own a sleeping bag.'

'Relax,' Jonas said easily. 'I'm not subjecting you to a tent. Barb has everything we need. You won't even need a bag. I have sheets and quilts. Even pillowcases.'

'We're sleeping in *here*? Both of us?'

'She's a four-berther, remember?' He flashed a grin over at her, looking forward to her reaction. 'Do you want to go on top or shall I?'

'I'm not nineteen any more, Jonas.'

Lawrie's face was flushed, her eyes dark with emotion. Anger? Fear? Maybe a combination of both.

'This really isn't acceptable.'

Jonas raised an eyebrow appraisingly. What was she so scared of? 'I'm sorry, Lawrie, I didn't think this would be a big deal. I really do want to see how the facilities at the sites compare with mine. Look, if you feel that strongly about it I can drop you at a motel or a B&B after tonight's gig. But I promise you you'll get a better night's sleep here than in some anonymous hotel chain bedroom.'

'Call me old-fashioned, but I like en-suite facilities.'

But his conciliatory tone seemed to have worked as she

sounded more petulant than angry. He decided to push it a little.

'I promise you we won't be roughing it. Barb's newly sprung and very comfortable. All these sites have electric hook-up and plenty of shower blocks. The place I have picked out for tonight has a very well-regarded organic restaurant too. I thought it would be good to compare it with the Boat House. And Saturday's site prides itself on its sea views, which is one thing we're lacking. I really would value your opinion.'

'But I thought you had the best toilets in Cornwall? I won't settle for less.'

Was that a small smile playing around the full mouth?

'If I didn't think every single one of these toilets weren't a serious contender I promise you I wouldn't have dreamt of bringing you along. Come on, Lawrie, it'll be fun. Food, music and the stars. I know I need the break. And...' he slid his eyes over to her again, noting the dark shadows under her eyes, the air of bewildered fragility she wore whenever her professional mask slipped '...I'll bet everything I own that you do too.'

'This isn't a break—this is work,' she reminded him primly.

'True,' he conceded. 'But who's to say we can't have fun while we're working?'

She wound a tendril of hair around her finger, staring out of the window, lost in thought. 'Okay, then,' she said finally. 'I'll give it one night. But if it's cold or uncomfortable or you snore—' she gave him a dark look '—then tomorrow we're in a hotel. Deal?'

'Deal,' he said. 'Okay, then, woman-with-clipboard, which road do you want me to take?'

CHAPTER SIX

'This is so good.'

'Better than your Pinot Noirs and Sauvignon Blancs?'

Lawrie took a long sip of the cool, tart cider and shook her head. 'Not better—different. I'm not sure I'd want to drink it in a restaurant. Too filling, for a start,' she finished, turning the pint glass full of amber-coloured liquid round in her hands, admiring the way it caught the light.

'They have a micro-brewery on site.' Jonas was reading the tasting cards. 'Rhubarb cider—that sounds intriguing. I wonder if they would want a stall at the festival? Talking of which, have you made a decision on the bands yet?'

Lawrie pulled a face. 'It's so hard,' she said. 'They were all good, and so different. Seriously, how do you compare punk folk with rock with acoustic?' She shook her head. 'Who would have thought punk folk even worked, and yet they were fab. Can I ask them all?'

'You're the organiser; it's up to you,' Jonas said. He gave her a mock stern look. 'Not last night's support, though. We want people to *enjoy* their festival-going experience.'

'Oh, I don't know.' Lawrie smiled at him sweetly. 'I thought the part where she read out poetry to a triangle beat was inspiring. Especially the poem about her menstrual cycle.'

'Stop!' Jonas was covering his ears. 'Those words are

seared onto my brain. As is that triangle. I swear I could hear it in my sleep. *Ting, ting ting.*' He shuddered.

Lawrie laughed and took another sip. 'I think the triangle represented her feminine aura.'

It was amazing, how comfortable she was. How comfortable *they* were. Having him around, driving, tasting, listening, bouncing ideas—it had made the whole trip easy, fun. And it hadn't been awkward. Well, hardly at all. Lying in the upper berth listening to his deep breathing had been a little *odd*. A little lonely, maybe. But nothing she couldn't shake off.

And he'd been a perfect gentleman. Which was good, obviously.

'It was a good idea of yours to stay an extra night,' she said with a small, happy sigh.

Jonas had been right about the views. The final campsite was perfectly placed in the dip of a valley, with the beach and sea clearly visible from their sheltered pitch. Lawrie wriggled back in her chair and closed her eyes, savouring the feel of the late-afternoon sun on her face.

'It seemed a shame to get a pitch with these views and then not be around to enjoy them,' Jonas said. 'Besides, we deserve some relaxation. And we discovered this cider.' He held up his pint with a satisfied smile. 'And that crêperie this morning. I think you should consider that patisserie too—their croissant was a work of art.'

'Hmm…' Lawrie opened her eyes and reached down to the folder at her feet. Picking it up, she flicked through it thoughtfully. 'They were good, weren't they? And the bakers near Liskeard were superb. I think that's enough pastries and bread though, don't you? We need some diversity. Two ice cream suppliers, four breweries, one Indian, one Thai and an Indonesian takeaway. Paella, the baked potato stall…'

'Stop right there.'

Jonas held his hand up and, startled, Lawrie let the folder slip shut.

'Lawrie Bennett, it is Sunday afternoon. You have been working day and night all weekend. Relax, enjoy the view, and drink your cider.'

A warm glow spread through her at his words. Nobody else had ever cared about how hard she worked, told her to slow down. She needed it. Somehow, when brakes were being handed out Lawrie had been last in line.

They lay side by side, sprawled out in the deckchairs, united in a companionable silence. That was another thing, she thought drowsily. He was easy to talk to but she didn't *have* to talk to him, to entertain. She was free to be lost in her own head if she wanted.

It was nice to be sitting here with no plans, nothing to tick off on her physical or mental to-do list. It was just... Lawrie shifted in her seat. What were they going to do tonight? At least her schedule had meant there were no awkward gaps to be filled. Their conversation had revolved around the food they were tasting, the music they were listening to. But tonight stretched ahead—empty. Maybe there was another band playing locally. Or another restaurant to check out. A seafood stall might be an interesting addition to the mix.

'Stop it.'

Lawrie turned her head in surprise. 'Stop what?'

'Timetabling the evening.'

How did he know? 'I'm not,' she said. Then, a little more truthfully, 'I was just thinking about later. Wondering what we were going to do.'

'We haven't stopped for three days,' Jonas pointed out. 'Do we have to do anything?'

'No...' she said doubtfully. 'Only what about food? Or

when it gets dark? Not that I'm not enjoying the sun and the view, but it will start to cool off in an hour or so.'

'Good thing we packed jumpers, then.'

The teasing tone was back in his voice and Lawrie squirmed, hot with embarrassment. It was unfair of him to make her feel uptight. Just because she liked to know what was coming next. Hugo had liked her organisational skills. Maybe that was what had attracted him to his secretary? Not the leopard print thong but the way she organised his diary.

'Okay.'

Jonas was sitting up in his chair and she could feel his eyes fixed on her, despite the sunglasses shielding them.

'I haven't made notes *or* a list, and I don't own a clipboard, but I had vaguely thought of a walk, finishing up at the farm shop for cheese and bread and more of this excellent cider. Then back to the van, where I can finally take cold-blooded, nine-year-old revenge for *quilling* on a triple word score. If you're up to the challenge, that is?'

That sounded really pleasant. In fact it sounded perfect. Almost dangerously so.

'Misplaced confidence was always your problem,' Lawrie said, adjusting her own sunglasses, hoping he couldn't see just how much the evening he had outlined appealed to her. 'There have been many high-scoring words since then, Mr Jones. But if you are willing to risk your pride again, I am more than willing to take you down.'

Jonas leant forward, so close his face was almost touching hers, his breath sweet on her cheek. 'I look forward to it.'

'That is *not* a word!'

'It is.' Lawrie couldn't hide the beam on her face. Ah, the sweet smell of victory. 'Check the dictionary.'

'I don't care what the dictionary says,' Jonas argued. 'Use it in a coherent sentence.'

Foolish, foolish boy. He should know better than to challenge Lawrie Bennett at Scrabble. Or at any game.

'How many *exahertz* are these gamma rays?' she said, sitting back and enjoying his reaction.

'You have never, ever used that sentence in your whole life!'

'No,' she conceded. 'But I could. If I went to work at CERN, for instance, or had a physics laboratory as a client. Besides, the rules don't specify that you have to have used the word in everyday conversation.'

'They should do,' Jonas grumbled, staring at the board in some dismay.

As he should, she thought, looking at the scores neatly written down on the pad in front of her. There was no way he could win now. And if she could just prevent him from narrowing the gap too much…a two-hundred-point lead was so satisfying.

Leaning back against the bench, she began to add up her points. They were both sitting on the floor of the camper van, the amost full board between them. The van doors were slid fully open, giving the scene a dramatic backdrop as the sun sank into the sea, leaving a fiery path on the top of the calm waves.

'That is thirty-one tripled, plus fifty for getting all my letters out. It's a shame it's the H on the double letter score, but all in all not a bad round. Okay, your turn.'

'I don't think I want to play any more,' Jonas said, disgust on his face as he surveyed his letter tiles. 'Not even *you* could manage to make a word out of three Is, a U, two Os and an R.'

Lawrie bit back a smile as she surveyed the board. 'Oh, dear,' she said, keeping her face completely serious.

'I think the official Scrabble term for your situation is screwed. *Ow!* What was that for?'

'Excessive smugness.' Jonas held up a second cushion. 'Don't think I won't,' he threatened.

Retrieving the cushion he'd already lobbed in her direction, Lawrie held it up in front of her, half shield, half offensive weapon. 'You just try it, Jones.'

He eyed her. 'A challenge? Really, Lawrie? You may, on this occasion, have won on brains, but I am always going to win on brawn.'

'Brawn,' she scoffed, uneasily aware of a tightening in her abdomen—a kind of delicious apprehension uncoiling—as she brandished her pillow. 'At your age?'

'In the prime of my life,' he said. 'Never been in better shape. What?' He laughed indignantly as Lawrie collapsed into giggles. 'It's true.'

'Says the man sat on a caravan floor, unshaven and holding a cushion!' It was hard to get the words out.

'It's not a caravan, you blasphemer. This is a classic and you know it. Besides, *you* can't talk. If only all your fashion admirers could see you now they would be totally disappointed. Nothing chic about leggings and a sweat-shirt—even I know that.'

Swallowing back the laughter, Lawrie hugged her knees to her chest. 'Yoga pants and cashmere, actually.'

It felt good to laugh. Free.

Trying hard not to think about how long it had been since she had laughed like that, Lawrie fastened onto Jonas's last words. 'Hang on—what do you mean, fashion admirers?'

Jonas shook his head and pushed the Scrabble board away, sliding down so only his head and shoulders were propped up against the bench seat, the rest of his long, lean body sprawled comfortably along the floor.

He took up a lot of room. A lot of air. Lawrie swallowed and adjusted her gaze so that she was looking straight ahead, at the glorious sunset, at fresh air. Not at the denim-clad legs lying close to her. Close enough to touch.

'I dress really conservatively for work,' she said, probing for an answer as Jonas seemed disinclined to speak. 'And my only night out was on my birthday.'

'Apparently West London's "conservative" is Trengarth's cutting edge,' Jonas said, swirling the Scrabble tiles around on the board and mixing up the words. 'It's all about the cut, or so I've heard. Definitely not High Street, they say.'

'I *do* get my suits made for me by a tailor who specialises in women's clothes.' Why did it feel like an admission of guilt? 'They fit better, though I wouldn't call them fashionable. But I don't know why I am explaining this to you.' She rounded on Jonas. 'If your suits aren't handmade I'll eat a Scrabble tile.'

He grinned, picking up an *I* and holding it out to her. 'Here you go—there are too many of these anyway.' Lawrie raised an eyebrow at him and he palmed the tile. 'Okay, you win. I *do* frequent an establishment in Plymouth run by a gentleman who trained on Savile Row.'

'I knew it!' The moment of triumph was shortlived as the impact of his words hit. Lawrie's chest tightened painfully and she breathed deeply, slowly. 'Why do people care about what I wear?'

Jonas looked surprised. 'They don't—not really. Only you're new, have history with me, and you look smarter than anyone else. It was bound to make a bit of a stir. It's not a big deal.'

But it was. 'I don't like being talked about. No one even noticed my suits in the City. Maybe I should get some new clothes for the rest of the summer.'

'What on earth for?' He sounded incredulous.

A wave of irritation swept over her. 'To blend in. The last thing I want is to be noticed for anything but my work.'

'People aren't exactly staring at you as you walk down the street,' Jonas pointed out. 'Wait...' He pulled his legs in and sat up, facing her. Blue eyes studied her face intently. 'Is this why you were so stressed about what to bring on this trip? You wanted to blend in?'

'There's no reason to sound so judgmental.' Lawrie could feel her face heating up, a prickly and uncomfortable warmth spreading down her neck and chest. 'I'm not comfortable standing out from the crowd. No big deal.'

He was still looking at her. Looking into her, as if he could see her soul. As if he was unsure about what he was seeing there. It took every bit of self-control that she had not to squirm or pull away.

'Is it, Law?' he said softly 'Is it just about blending in?'

'I don't know what you're talking about.' She wanted to pull away, look away, but it was as if his eyes had a hypnotic effect on her. She was paralysed, stuck to the spot, as he stared at her searchingly.

'You didn't sing in London. Not once in nine years.'

'For goodness' sake, Jonas, I was busy!'

'What *did* you do? Apart from work.'

She tried to remember but it was all fog. It seemed like a lifetime ago. 'We had dinner with friends. Went to the theatre, to museums and exhibitions. The usual things.'

'Usual for who? West London professionals like you?' His gaze sharpened. 'You're a tribal animal, aren't you, Lawrie? You like to dress the part, act the part—whatever that part might be. What is it you really want? You like? Do you even know?'

'What do you care?' The words were torn from her. 'As soon as my life diverged from yours you gave up on me.

So don't you dare be so damn superior—don't act like I'm letting you down by trying to fit in.'

'But you're not.' He looked surprised. 'Why would you be letting me down? But are you letting yourself down, Lawrie? If you spend your whole life hiding your own needs and wants away can you ever be really happy?'

'Happiness is not about *things*.' The words snapped out of her, surprising her with their fierceness, their certainty. 'Clothes, hobbies, food—they're just trappings, Jonas. I don't care about any of them. All I want—all I have ever wanted—is to be successful, to be independent. To stick to the plan.'

'Is this the plan? To be here with me?'

It was like a punch straight to the stomach, winding her with its strength. 'No,' she said after a long pause. 'No, this wasn't in the plan. But I'm adaptable, Jonas. I'm strong. Don't ever mistake a desire to fit in with weakness. Lions blend in with the Sahara, you know.'

He threw his head back and laughed. The sound jarred with her jangled nerves.

'Weak is the last word I'd use to describe you. Lioness, on the other hand…'

It was his turn to duck as she threw a cushion at him.

'I was just agreeing with you,' he protested.

'If you had lived with my mother you'd have learned to fit in as well,' Lawrie said. She didn't know why she was telling him this—why she needed him to understand. But she did. She needed him to know that she wasn't shallow or weak. 'One moment I'm living in Stockbrokerville in Surrey, learning French and pony-riding, the next we're in a commune near Glastonbury and my mother is trying to make me answer to the name of Star. She changed completely, depending on who she was with, and she never went for the same type twice.'

'I know,' Jonas said, pity softening the keen eyes. 'It was hard for you.'

Lawrie shook her head. 'I don't need you to feel sorry for me. I'm just explaining. What I wore, ate, did, the friends I had—they were interchangeable, dependent on her whims. If I had cared, had tried to hang on to *things*, it would have been unbearable. So I kept my head down, I worked hard, and I vowed that I would be so successful that I would never have to be dependent on anyone. And I'm not.'

'Is that why you and the fiancé split? Because you didn't need him?'

'No.' Of course it wasn't. Hugo had *liked* her independence. Hadn't he? 'It was…complicated.' That was one word for it. 'Is that why you wanted out? Because I didn't need *you*?'

'Oh, Lawrie.' There was no lightness in his voice, in his face, at all. 'I was used to that. Not being needed. And, if you remember, in the end you were the one that walked away.'

'Maybe…' Her voice was low. 'Maybe I was afraid that I did need you.'

'Would that have been so bad?' He examined her face, searching for answers behind the mask.

She shook her head and another lock of hair fell out of the loose ponytail, framing her face. 'Bad? It would have been terrible. I was barely started on my path. Oxford, an internship at one of the best City firms… And I seriously, *seriously* considered giving it all up. For you. For a man. Just like my mother would have. Just like she did again and again. I *had* to leave, Jonas.' She turned to him, eyes wide, pleading for understanding. 'I had to hold on to me.'

And in doing so she had let go of him. Jonas closed his eyes for a second, seeing a flash of his heartbroken younger self frozen in time. He hadn't wasted a single emotion on his parents' rejection, pouring all that need, all his love, into the slight girl now sitting beside him. It had been far too much for someone so young to carry.

He reached out and cupped her cheek. Her skin was soft beneath his hand. 'I guess I needed you to choose me. I needed *somebody* to choose me. I still needed validation back then. It was a lot to put on you. Too much.'

'Maybe you were right. We were too young.' Her eyes were filled with sadness and regret. 'I didn't want to agree with you, to prove all the *I told you so* right, but we had a lot of growing up to do. We weren't ready for such a big step.'

He nodded. Suddenly he didn't feel any anger or contempt towards her or towards their shared past. Just an underlying sadness for the idealistic kids they had once been. For their belief that love really was all they needed.

He was still touching her cheek. She leant into him trustingly and he turned his hand to run the back of it down the side of her face, learning once again the angle of her cheekbone, the contours of her chin, the smoothness of her skin.

Jonas had made some rules for himself before he came on this trip. No talking about the past, no flirting, and definitely, absolutely no touching.

But sometimes rules were meant to be broken.

Slowly, deliberately, he let his fingers trail further down her face, brushing her full mouth before dipping down to her chin. He let them linger there for one long, agonising moment, tilting her face towards him, giving her ample time to pull away, to stop him, before he leant in slowly—oh, so slowly.

It was a butterfly kiss. So light, so brief, their lips barely touching. Jonas pulled back, searching her face for consent. Her eyes were closed, her face angled towards his, lips slightly parted. Expectant. It was all the agreement he needed.

He shifted closer to her, closing the space between them as he slid one arm around her slender shoulders. The other hand moved from her chin to the sweet spot at the nape of her neck. She moved in too—an infinitesimal shift, yet one that brought her body into full contact with his. Her face lifted, waiting, expecting. Jonas looked down at her for one moment—at the face at once so familiar and yet so strange to him, at the dark eyelashes, impossibly long, improbably thick, the creamy skin, the lush, full mouth waiting for him.

And a gentleman should never keep a lady waiting.

Another fleeting kiss, and another, and another. Until, impatient, she moaned and pressed closer in, her mouth opening under his, seeking, wanting. She tasted of cider, of sunshine. She tasted like summer, like coming home, and he deepened the kiss, pulling her even closer until they were pressed together, her arms wound around his neck. His own arms were holding her tightly to him, one bunching the silky strands of her hair, the other caressing the planes of her back through the lightness of her top.

It was like being a teenager again, entwined on the floor of the camper van, mouths fused, hands roaming, pulling each other closer and closer until it seemed impossible that they were two separate bodies. There was no urgency to move, no need to start removing clothes, for hands to move lower. Not yet.

Seconds, minutes, hours, infinities passed by. All Jonas knew was the drumming of his blood in his ears, the fierce heat engulfing him. All he knew was her. Her touch, her taste, her mouth, the feel of her under his hands. When she pulled back it was as if she had been physically torn away from him, a painful wrench that left him cold. Empty.

She looked at him, eyes wide, dark with passion, her pupils dilated, mouth swollen. 'I think…' she began, her voice husky, barely audible.

Jonas readied himself. If she wanted to be the voice of common sense, so be it. He looked back at her silently. He might not argue, but he wasn't going to help her either.

'I think we should close the doors.'

Her words were so unexpected all he could do for a moment was gape. The van doors were still open to the night sky. The sea breeze floated in, bringing the taste of salt and the faint coconut-tinged smell of gorse.

Then the meaning of her words hit home. Anticipation filled the air, hot and heavy, making it hard to breathe as excitement coiled inside him.

'There's no one out there.'

They were in a secluded spot, parked at the very edge of the field. As private as you could be in a campsite full of tents and caravans. Not as private as they could have been if he'd planned for this.

'Even so…'

She smiled at him, slow and full of promise, and slowly, as if he were wading through treacle, he got to his feet and swung the sliding door firmly closed. The outside world was shut out. It was just the two of them in this small enclosed space. The air was heavy with expectation, with heat, with longing.

'Satisfied?' He raised an eyebrow and watched her flush.

'Not yet.' She was turning the tables on him. 'But I'm hoping to be.'

Passion jolted through him, intense and all-encompass-ing. In swift, sure steps he closed the space between them, pulling her in tight. 'Oh, you will be,' he promised as he lowered his mouth to hers once again. 'I can guarantee it.'

CHAPTER SEVEN

'Ooof!' WHEN HAD breathing got so *hard*? Bending over to catch her breath, the tightness of a stitch pulling painfully at her side, Lawrie conceded that a ten-mile run might have been a mite ambitious.

Of course, she reassured herself, running outside was harder, what with all those hills and the wind against her, to say nothing of no nice speedometer to regulate her stride. Straightening up, one hand at her waist, Lawrie squinted out at the late-afternoon sun. On the other hand, she conceded, although her late, lamented treadmill came with TV screens and MP3 plug-ins it was missing the spectacular views of deep blue sea and rolling green and yellow gorse of her current circuit. It was definitely an improvement on the view of sweaty, Lycra-clad gym-goers that her old location had provided her with.

Taking a much needed long, cool gulp of water, Lawrie continued at a trot, looping off the road and onto the clifftop path that led towards the village. If she continued along to the harbour she could reward herself with a re-fuelling stop at the Boat House before walking back up the hill home. No way was she going to try and run up that hill—not unless her fitness levels dramatically improved in the next half an hour.

Just keep going, she thought fiercely. *Concentrate on that latte...visualise it.* It was certainly one incentive.

And if Jonas just happened to be working at the Boat House today then that, just possibly, could be another incentive. The pain in her side was forgotten as the night before flashed through her mind, her lips curving in a smile as she remembered. Another night of heat, of long, slow caresses, hot, hard kisses, hands, tongues, lips. Bodies entwining.

Lawrie's pulse started to speed up as her heartbeat began racing in a way that had nothing to do with the exercise.

She upped the trot to a run, her legs pumping, her arms moving as she increased her pace. She wasn't going to think about it. She wasn't going to dwell on the delicious moment when day turned into evening. She wasn't going to remember the tingle of anticipation that ran through her as she sat on the terrace in the evening sun, an untouched book and an iced drink before her, pretending not to listen for the purr of his car. Pretending not to hope.

She was most certainly not going to recall the thrill that filled her entire body, the sweet jolt that shot through her from head to toe, when he finally appeared.

Time was moving so fast. She had less than a month left in Trengarth. So she wasn't going to question what was going on here. She was going to enjoy the moment. And what moments they were. She couldn't remember the last time she and Hugo had made love twice in a week, let alone in a night, whereas she and Jonas... Well...

Sure, she hadn't planned for this, and for once she was being the exact opposite of measured and sensible. But wasn't that the point? She had to make the most of this enforced time out. It would all get back to normal soon enough.

Starting with today. Her first interview.

It was all happening so fast. Just a few days since the initial approach, the phone call, and now a face to face interview. In New York.

It was perfect. This would show Hugo and the partners. She could just imagine the gossip. *Lawrie Bennett? Out in New York, I believe. A most prestigious firm.* Anticipation shot through her. It was as if a load had been lifted. To be approached for such a role meant that her reputation was intact. It should be, but sudden departures were responsible for more scurrilous gossip in the legal world than any tabloid could imagine.

Lawrie slowed her pace as the cliff path began to wind down towards the harbour and the pretty stone cottages clustered beneath her. Which was Jonas's? He hadn't asked her over and she was certainly not going to invite herself, to admit she was curious.

Even if she was.

Was it the one overlooking the harbour, with the pretty roof garden situated in exactly the right place for the afternoon sun? The three-storeyed captain's house, imposing its grandeur on the smaller houses around? The long, low whitewashed cottage, its yard covered in tumbling roses?

What did it matter anyway?

Despite herself she slowed as she jogged along the harbour-front, looking into the windows, hoping for some clue. She didn't care, she told herself, but she still found herself craning her neck, peeking in, searching for a sign of him.

Beep!

A car horn made her jump. The follow-up wolf whistle which pierced the air brought her to a skidding halt.

Lawrie turned around, hands on hips, ready for battle, only to find her mouth drying out at the sight of Jonas

Jones in that ridiculous low-slung sports car, top down. She coloured, looking around to make sure nobody had heard, before crossing the narrow road and leaning over the car. 'Shush. People will hear you,' she hissed.

He raised an eyebrow mockingly and Lawrie clenched her hands, controlling an irresistible urge to slap him. Or kiss him. Either would be inappropriate.

'Let them,' he replied nonchalantly, that annoying eyebrow still quirked.

She wanted to reach out and smooth it down, caress the stubble on the strong jaw, run her fingers across the sensual lips. She clenched her hands harder. She wouldn't give him or the curious onlookers openly watching them the satisfaction.

Jonas leant closer, his breath warm and sweet on her cheek. 'They all think they know anyway.'

'Let them think. There's no need to confirm it.' She was painfully aware of people watching them—many openly. How many times had she seen neighbours, parents at the school gates, people in the local shop watch her mother in the same way as her latest relationship began to disintegrate? 'I hate gossip, and I really hate being the focus of it.'

'Just a boss having a chat with his festival-organiser—nothing to see…move it along,' he said, an unrepentant grin curving the kissable mouth.

She bit her lip. She was *not* going to kiss him in public, no matter how tempted she was. But how she wanted to.

Her eyes held his, hypnotised by the heat she saw in the blue depths. The street, the curious onlookers faded away for one long moment. She didn't know whether to be relieved or disappointed when he leant back, the grin replaced with a purposeful businesslike expression.

'I was on my way up to collect you—thought you might appreciate a lift to the airport. Yet here you are.' He ran his eyes appreciatively over her and she fought the urge to tug her running top down over her shorts. 'You're not really dressed for flying, though. And I don't mean to be offensive, but...'

Lawrie snorted. 'That will be a first,' she muttered.

'But I'm not sure eighties aerobics is really the right look for business class *or* an interview. You might want to get changed,' he continued, ignoring her interruption. 'I could give you a lift up—or, if you really want to finish your run, I can pick you up in ten minutes.'

'If you're in such a hurry I'd better take the lift,' Lawrie said, opening the door and sliding in, her pride refusing to admit to him that she'd had no intention of running up the hill. 'I was planning to drive myself, though. I do appreciate the offer, but can you spare the time?'

She sounded cool enough—shame about her hair, pulled high into a sweaty bun, the Lycra shorts, the sheen of sweat on her arms and chest.

'Actually, it's on my way—that's why I'm offering. I'm heading over to Dorset to look at some potential sites. I'll be passing Plymouth so I might as well drop you off.'

'Oh.' He wasn't making the journey especially. Of course he wouldn't—why would he? Her sudden sharp jolt of disappointment was ridiculous. 'Well, it's very kind of you.'

There was a long silence. She sneaked a look over to see him pushing his hair out of his eyes, his face expressionless.

'It's nothing,' he said. 'As I said, I was passing the airport anyway.'

Neither of them spoke for the two minutes it took to drive back to the cottage, and as soon as the car pulled up in the driveway Lawrie was ready to leap out. The atmosphere was suddenly tense, expectant.

'I'll be five minutes,' she called as she hurried over the lawn and round to the back door. 'Make yourself at home.'

She fumbled with the key, breathing a sigh of relief as she finally pushed the door open, almost collapsing into the sanctuary of the kitchen, then heading straight to the bathroom to peel off her sweaty clothes and get into the welcome coolness of the shower.

The same peculiar feeling of disappointment gripped Lawrie as she lathered shampoo into her hair and over her body. What did it matter if he was dropping her off in passing or making the journey especially? Either way she ended up where she needed to be. Her trip to New York would be short—just a few days—but it meant time away from Cornwall, from the festival, from Jonas. Which was good, because their lives were already re-entangling, boundaries were being crossed. This interview was a much needed reminder that there was an end date looming and neither of them could or should forget that.

It had been a sweet kind of torture, watching her Lycra-clad bottom disappear around the corner. Jonas had to hold onto every ounce of his self-control to stay in the car and not follow her right into the shower, where he would be more than happy to help her take off those very tight and very distracting shorts.

He grabbed his coffee and took a long gulp.

This was temporary. They had always had an undeniable chemistry, even when nothing else between them had worked. And now they were both single, available, it was silly to deny themselves just because of a little bit of history.

Besides, they both knew what this was. No messy emotions, no need to prove anything. No need for words. It was the perfect summer fling.

It was all under control.

She'd said five minutes so he settled in for a half-hour wait, roof down, coffee in hand, paper folded to the business pages. But in less than fifteen minutes she reappeared, wheeling a small suitcase, laptop bag and handbag slung over her shoulder. She looked clean, fresh, so smooth he wanted nothing more than to drag her back inside and rumple her up a little—or a lot.

His hands clenched on the steering wheel as his pulse began to hammer, his blood heating up.

Damn that chemistry.

He dragged his eyes down from freshly washed, still-wet hair, combed back, to creamy skin—lots of it. Bare arms and shoulders, with just a hint of cleavage exposed by the halter-necked sundress, skirting her waist to fall mid-thigh.

He stifled a groan. He had a couple of hours' driving ahead of him and it was going to be hard to concentrate with so much skin nestled next to him.

'Is that suitable for flying? You'll need a cardigan,' he bit out, wrenching his gaze from the satisfied smile she gave him as she pulled a wispy wrap from the bag hung over her shoulder. 'Hurry up and get in. There's bound to be a lot of traffic.'

The powerful sports car purred along the narrow, winding lanes connecting Trengarth to the rest of the county. Lawrie leant back in the low leather seat, feeling the breeze ruffle her hair and watching the hedges and fields flash by. The blue glint of the sea was still visible in the distance, but soon the road would take them through the outskirts of Bodmin Moor, its rolling heathland and dramatic granite tors a startling contrast to her coastal home.

Home? She felt that pang again. Home was a dangerous concept.

'Lawrie?'

She jumped as Jonas repeated her name.

'Sorry, I was just daydreaming.'

'I know. I recognised that faraway look in your eyes,' he said wryly. 'Where were you? Round some boardroom table in New York?'

'Actually, I was thinking how beautiful it is round here.' That felt uncomfortably like a confession. 'No moors in New York.'

'No.'

Now it was his turn to stay silent, a brooding look on his face, as he navigated through open countryside and small villages until they met the main road. Suddenly the silence didn't feel quite so companionable, and after one uncomfortable minute that seemed to stretch out for at least five Lawrie began to search desperately for a topic of conversation.

It felt like a step backwards. Things had been so easy between them for the last few days—since the road trip, since that last night in the van. They had fallen into a pattern of colleagues by day, lovers by night—professional and focused at work, equally focused in the long, hot evenings.

Now she suddenly had no idea what to say.

'Will you be visiting your parents when you're in Dorset?'

Whatever had made her say that? Of all the topics in the world.

His face darkened. 'I doubt I'll have time.'

'You'll pass by their village, though, won't you? You should just pop in for a cup of tea.'

He didn't say anything, but she could see the tanned

hands whiten as he gripped the steering wheel. She tried again, despite the inner voice telling her to back off, that it was none of her business. 'They must know the areas you're looking into. It might be interesting to hear their thoughts. Seems silly not to canvas local opinion, even if you don't take them into account.'

He was silent again. Lawrie sneaked a quick glance over, expecting to see anger, irritation in his expression. But he wasn't showing any emotion at all. She hated it—the way he could close himself off at will.

'I just think it's worth one more chance,' she said hesitantly. Why did she feel compelled to keep going with this? Because maybe this was one relationship she could fix for him? 'If they understood why you work the way you do—understood that you love Coombe End, that your changes are an evolution of their work, not a betrayal—maybe things would be better.'

He finally answered, his face forbidding. 'What makes you think I want things to be better?'

Lawrie opened her mouth, then shut it again. How could she tell him that where his parents were concerned she understood him better than he understood himself? That she knew how much he was shaped by his parents' indifference, how much he craved their respect?

'You're going to be in the area,' she said at last. 'Is popping in to see your parents such a big deal?'

He didn't answer and they continued the drive in silence. Lawrie stared unseeingly out at the trees and valleys as they flashed past, relieved when Jonas finally turned into the airport car park and pulled up at the dropping-off point.

'That's great—thank you.'

He didn't answer. Instead he got out of the car and walked round to the boot, retrieved her bag and laptop case as she smoothed her dress over her thighs and pushed herself out of the low seat.

It was hard to be dignified, getting out of a sports car.

'What time is your connection?'

She stared at him, wrenching her mind away from her thoughts to her surroundings. Back to her plans, her flight, her interview, her future. 'Oh, two hours after I get to Heathrow—which is plenty of time for Security, I hope.'

'Should be. Let me know if there are any changes with your flight back, otherwise I'll see you here.'

He was going to pick her up? Her heart lurched stupidly. 'You don't have to.'

'I know.'

'Okay, then.' She picked up her bags and smiled at him. 'Thanks, Jonas.'

'Good luck. They'd be mad not to offer you the job.'

'That's the hope.' She stepped forward and gave him a brief, light kiss, inhaling the fresh, seaside aroma of him as she did so, feeling an inexplicable tightening in her chest. 'Bye.'

He stood statue-still, not reacting to the kiss. 'Bye.'

She paused for a split second but she had no idea what she was waiting for—why she had a sudden leaden feeling in the pit of her stomach. Taking a deep breath, she picked up the bags and, with a last smile in Jonas's direction, turned and walked away towards the sliding glass doors.

'Lawrie?'

She stopped, turned, unexpected and unwanted hope flaring up inside her.

'I'll make a deal with you. I'll go and visit my parents if you email your mother.'

The familiar panic welled up. 'I don't have her email address.'

'I can forward it to you.'

'Oh.' She searched for another excuse.

'Scared?' His voice was low, understanding, comforting.

'A little.' Not that she wanted to admit to fear—not to him. 'I don't know, Jonas. I feel safer with her not in my life.'

'I know.' His mouth twisted. 'It's just one step. It doesn't have to be more.'

Just one email. It sounded like such a small gesture and yet it felt so huge.

'One step,' she echoed. 'Okay.'

'Good. I'll see you here in four days.'

And he was gone.

Five hours later Lawrie was ensconced in a comfortable reclining seat, her laptop already plugged in on the table in front of her, her privacy screen blocking out the rest of the world.

Wriggling down into her seat, Lawrie squared her shoulders against the plump supporting cushions. She loved business class! The firm's willingness to pay for it boded well.

Ostensibly her ultra-comfortable journey should ensure she arrived in New York both well rested and prepared, but although her research on the firm was open on the laptop she had barely glanced at it.

Instead she had spent an hour composing an email to her mother. Lawrie reread the few short lines again and sighed. For goodness' sake, how hard could it be? She was aiming for polite, possibly even slightly conciliatory, but she had to admit the tone was off. The words sounded snooty, accusatory, *hurt*.

Exasperated, she deleted the lot and typed a few stiff sentences as if she were addressing a stranger.

She supposed she was. Would she even recognise her mother if she sat next to her? Her early teens were so long ago. Had it hurt her mother, leaving her only daughter in Trengarth? Never seeing her again?

Did she ever wonder if she had done the right thing? Regret her past?

She wondered how Jonas was doing with his parents—if his efforts were any more successful than her own.

She shook herself irritably. For goodness' sake! She was supposed to be preparing for her interview. This was it—her big chance.

So why did she feel so empty?

Lawrie slid a little further into the plush seat and looked out of the small window at the wispy white clouds drifting lazily past. What was wrong with her? Surely she hadn't let a blue eyed surfer derail her the way he had done twelve years ago?

Hot shame flushed through her body. She couldn't—wouldn't repeat the mistakes of her past. *Because let's face it*, she thought, *ambitious little Lawrie Bennett wanted many things.* She had planned her whole life through, and getting married the year she left school, before she'd received her A-level results, going to university as an eighteen-year-old bride had not been part of that plan.

Yet she had still said yes.

Lawrie pulled a piece of hair down and twizzled it around her finger. That moment—the utter joy that had suffused her whole being the second he'd asked her. Had she felt like that since? Not when she'd graduated with a first, not when she'd got hired at a top City firm.

And certainly not when Hugo had proposed.

She shook herself irritably, tucking the strand of hair back into her ponytail. Joy? 'For goodness' sake, grow up,' she muttered aloud. She was in business class, flying to be interviewed for the job of her dreams, and—what? It wasn't enough?

It was everything.

She had to remember that. *Everything.*

Jonas pulled over and typed the address into his phone, but he knew long before the icon loaded that he was in the right place. Looking around the tree-lined lane, he saw a row of identikit 1930s detached houses, all painted a uniform white, every garden perfectly manicured, every drive guarded by large iron gates, every car a sleek saloon. There wasn't a plastic slide or football goal to be seen.

The quiet, still road was crying out for bikes to be pedalled along it, the wide pavements for chalk and hopscotch. But there was no one to be seen.

Jonas sighed. What was he doing here? How many times could a guy set himself up for disappointment? He wouldn't be welcome. Even if his parents liked surprises his unheralded appearance wasn't going to bring them any joy.

But he had made a deal. And he might not know much about Lawrie Bennett any more, but he did know that there was something lost at the heart of her.

That desperate need to fit in, to be in control. To follow the plan...

He'd tried to fill that void once. Maybe someone in New York could, if she could just let go of her fears. And if he could do that much for his ex-wife—well, maybe their marriage wouldn't have been such a disaster after all.

A sharp pain twisted inside him at the thought of her with someone else but he ignored it. One of them deserved to be happy; one of them should be. And himself? Well... He smiled wryly. There were moments. Moments when a deal went well, when a chord was played right, when he looked around at a café full of content customers, when a wave was perfect.

Those moments were gold. He didn't ask for more. He wasn't sure he was capable of more.

Sighing, Jonas looked down at the icon on his phone, busily flashing away, signalling a road just to the left. He was pretty sure the next few moments were going to be anything but gold. But he'd promised.

And he always kept his word.

Why did his parents favour cups that were so damn small? And chairs that were so damn uncomfortable? And wallpaper that was so very, very busy? And, really, would it hurt them to smile?

The silence stretched on, neither side willing to break it. Side? That, thought Jonas, was a very apt word. Somehow—so long ago he had no idea when or why—they had become entrenched on opposite sides of a chasm so huge Jonas didn't think there was any way across it at all.

'So...' he said slowly. Speaking first felt like giving in, but after all he *had* intruded on them. 'I was just passing...'

'Where from?'

Did he just imagine that his mother sounded suspicious? Although, to be fair, he hadn't been 'just passing' in four years—not since the day he had told them that he had bought their beloved hotel.

'I was dropping Lawrie off at the airport.'

'Lawrie? You're back together?'

Now *that* emotion he could identify. It was hope. Even his father had looked up from his teacup, sudden interest in his face. Lawrie was the only thing he'd ever done that they'd approved of—and they hadn't been at all surprised when she'd left him.

'She's working for me this summer. Just a temporary

thing before she moves to New York. And, no, we're not back together.' It wasn't a lie. Whatever was going on, they weren't back together.

'Oh.'

The disappointment in his mother's voice was as clear as it was expected. Jonas looked around, desperate for something to catch his eye—another conversation-starter. A spectacularly hideous vase, some anaemic watercolours… But something was lacking—had always been lacking. And it wasn't a simple matter of wildly differing tastes.

'Why don't you have any photos?' he asked abruptly.

The room was completely devoid of anything personal. Other people's parents displayed their family pictures as proudly as trophies: bald, red-faced babies, gap-toothed schoolchildren, self-conscious teens in unflattering uniforms.

The silence that filled the room was suddenly different, charged with an emotion that Jonas couldn't identify.

His mother flushed, opened her mouth and shut it again.

'Dad?'

Jonas stared at his father, who was desperately trying to avoid his eye, looking into the depths of the ridiculously tiny teacup as if it held the answer to the secret of life itself.

'Dad,' he repeated.

The anger he had repressed for so long—the anger he'd told himself he didn't feel, the anger that was now boiling inside him—was threatening to erupt. He swallowed it back, tried to sound calm, not to let them know that he felt anything.

'I know I'm not the son you wanted, but—really? Not even one photo?'

'Leave it, Jonas,' his father said loudly, putting his cup down so decidedly it was a miracle the thin china didn't break in two.

'Why?' he persisted.

He would not leave it. For so many years he had endured their disapproval and their silence, their refusal to engage with him. He'd listened to their instructions, to their plans for his life—and then he'd gone ahead and done what he wanted anyway. But suddenly he couldn't leave it—didn't want to walk away.

He wanted answers.

'I appreciate that I don't live my life the way you want me to, that I didn't make the most of the opportunities you gave me, and I admit that failing my exams at sixteen wasn't the smartest move.'

He tried a smile but got nothing back. His father was still trembling with some repressed emotion; his mother was pale, still as stone.

'But,' he carried on, determined that *this* time they would hear him, *this* time he would have his say, 'I have an MBA, I have a successful business, I own a house, I'm a good boss, I give to charity.' Despite himself, despite his best intentions, his voice cracked. 'I just don't know why I have never been good enough for you.'

There. It was said.

The silence rippled round the room.

His mother got to her feet, so pale her carefully applied make-up stood out stark against her skin. 'I can't do this, Jonas,' she said.

He stared at her in astonishment. Were those tears in her eyes?

'I'm sorry, I just can't.' She laid one, shaky hand on his shoulder for an infinitesimal second and then was gone, rushing out of the room.

What the hell…? He'd expected indifference, or anger, or some lecture about what a waste of space he had always been, but this tension strung as tight as a quivering bow was unexpected. It was terrifying. Whatever was going on here was bigger than the fall-out of some adolescent rebellion.

Jonas glared at his father, torn between utter confusion and sudden fear. 'Dad? What *is* going on? I think I deserve the truth, don't you?'

CHAPTER EIGHT

IT WAS HORRENDOUSLY hot, and the airport was overcrowded as families, couples, grandparents waited anxiously, pressing close to the gate, necks craning for the first glimpse of a loved one.

Some had even brought signs—handwritten, decorated. Jonas looked over at the young man barely out of his teens, standing at the very end, as close as he could get to the gate without crossing the yellow line. He had love hearts all over his sign. The poor sap.

He even had flowers, Jonas noted. A bouquet so big it almost obscured the sign.

Whereas it was all Jonas had been able to do to turn up at all. He was still processing the afternoon he had spent with his parents. He wasn't sure he could share it with anyone, and Lawrie was bound to ask.

After all they had a deal.

'Hey.'

He hadn't even seen her come through the gate. 'Hey, yourself. Good trip?'

She beamed. 'The best. They're a really exciting firm, with some great projects, so fingers crossed they liked me.'

'I bet they loved you.' He took her bag from her and led the way out of the airport to the short-stay car park. Suddenly, despite everything, the day seemed brighter, the clouds drifting away. It was too nice to be shut away in an office—even his office.

'Are you exhausted?' he asked.

Lawrie shook her head. 'I might have had a red-eye flight, but I was spoiled enough to spend it tucked up in business class. I feel fresh as a daisy! I swear those seats are comfier than my bed.'

'I was thinking a picnic,' he said. 'There's a nice farm-shop about twenty minutes away where we could grab some supplies. Unless you want to get back?'

Lawrie looked down at herself and pulled a face, although Jonas thought she looked immaculate, in dark skinny jeans that clung to her legs in a way he definitely approved of.

'I need a shower at some point in the next few hours,' she said. 'No matter how air-conditioned the airport and plane are, I still land feeling completely grubby. But fresh air sounds good, and I guess I could eat. My business class freshly cooked breakfast seems a long time ago now.'

'Nice subtle reminder of your exalted status.' Jonas nodded approvingly. 'You'll need to up the stakes when you get to New York, though, I believe lawyers on the Upper East Side only travel by private jet.'

'Ha-ha.' Lawrie stuck her tongue out at him as they reached the car and he opened the door for her before stowing her cases in the boot.

'Your post is on your seat,' he called over. 'I knew you would want to look through it before you relaxed properly.'

'Thanks,' she called back.

Closing the door, he saw she was already engrossed, flipping through the pile and sorting the mail into order. She was up to date with her emails too, he knew. Lawrie wouldn't allow a little thing like the Atlantic Ocean to stand between her and her work.

A good reason to make sure she had the afternoon off. And it would probably do him good too. He'd barely left his desk these last two days. Sometimes hard work was the only way to cope.

He slid into his seat and looked over at her. She was staring at an envelope, her cheeks pale. He recognised it: a thick, expensive cream envelope with the name of her old firm stamped on the back. It was probably her P45 or something.

It didn't explain the pallor in her cheeks, though.

'Everything okay?' He turned the key and felt the engine purr into life.

She didn't answer.

'Law?'

She looked across, a dazed expression on her face. 'Hmm? Yes, I'm fine.'

But she didn't sound convincing.

'Are you going to open that?' He nodded towards the envelope. She was turning it over and over, as if she could read the contents through touch alone.

'Yes, of course. It's probably some HR stuff.'

But she looked anxious as she tore the envelope open, pulling out a handwritten letter with another slip of paper clipped to the outside. It looked like a cheque.

'What on earth…?'

'Redundancy?' he suggested.

She shook her head. 'That will get paid with my last month's salary, and not until my notice is completely served,' she said, unfolding the letter and slipping the cheque out. Her eyes widened. 'My goodness—how many noughts?' Then, her voice seemed strangled with what sounded suspiciously like tears. 'It's from Hugo.'

The ex.

Jealousy, ugly and hot, seared through him. What was he doing writing to her? Sending her cheques?

Grimly he set his eyes on the road ahead, concentrating on the exit from the airport, trying to give Lawrie the space she needed as she fought for control.

'It's for my share of the house,' she said after a while, her voice a little croaky. 'He didn't have to. I mean, yes, I contributed to the bills, of course—paid for decorating and stuff. But it was his house. Legally I'm not entitled to anything. My name wasn't on the mortgage.'

Was she regretting leaving him? A man who made such generous gestures? Thoughtful? 'Will you accept?'

There was a pause.

'Yes,' she said finally. 'My pride tells me to shred it and return it to him, but he's right. If I hadn't moved in with him I'd have bought my own place, made money on that. This cheque is enough for a reasonable deposit so I can buy in New York, or wherever I end up. I'd be a fool to turn it down. And I guess morally I do deserve it.'

She was silent again as she read the rest of the letter, all her attention on the closely written lines until an exclamation burst out, her voice high with shock 'He's getting married! In September. His fiancée is pregnant so they're rushing it through.'

Indignation replaced the jealousy.

'He has a *fiancée*? A *pregnant* fiancée? How on earth did he manage that? You've only been apart a couple of weeks! Unless he was cheating on you?'

The colour in her cheeks gave him the answer.

Jonas whistled softly. 'What a bastard!'

Lawrie didn't answer for a bit, turning the letter over to read it again. 'No. He isn't—not really.'

It was odd, listening to her defend another man. A man she had lived with.

'Okay, that's not entirely true. He behaved horribly, but I think it was my fault—at least partly.' She whispered the last part, tears choking her voice again.

Jonas's first instinct was to pull over, to pull her into his arms and comfort her. But one look at her rigid face as she fought for control dissuaded him. She was so private, so secretive, he instinctively knew she'd clam up if he offered sympathy.

He kept his voice impersonal. 'Your fault how? Because you left?'

'Because I didn't love him. Not in the way he deserved to be loved. I see that now.' She looked away, out of the window, and when she spoke again her voice was level. Composed. 'I wasn't entirely honest with you. It was just too humiliating. I didn't leave Hugo. I didn't change the plan. It was changed for me the day I found him with someone else. If it had been up to me I'd still be there, working towards making partner, putting off planning my wedding, engaged to someone I couldn't admit I didn't love.'

'He didn't deserve you.' Jonas knew that absolutely. If he had he would have been faithful.

She shook her head. 'He really did love me once. And I wanted to love him, I thought I did, but…' She faltered. 'Ouch—honesty hurts, doesn't it? Truth is, I think it was the lifestyle I wanted—the package. He should have someone who doesn't care about the package, who wants him because he is kind and decent.' She sniffed. A slight sound that almost broke his heart. 'I hope he's found that.'

'That's big of you. Really.'

When Lawrie had left him the last thing he'd wished for was her happiness. It shamed him to remember how bitter he had been.

'There was a point when I could happily have castrated

him with a spoon,' she admitted. 'And strangled *her* with her own leopard print thong.'

Jonas's eyebrows rose at the extraordinary visual and he tried his best to control a smirk. A watery giggle next to him confirmed his failure.

'But I was more unhappy about having to leave the firm than about the infidelity. I think, if he'd offered I would have allowed him to grovel and pretend I hadn't seen anything. Wow, I'm pitiful.'

'That *is* a little sad,' he agreed. 'But why did you have to be the one to go?'

'Because his grandfather founded the firm. Oh, my payoff will be good, my reference glowing—as it should be!—but it was made clear that they would prefer me to pack up, get out and keep my mouth shut. And I was too embarrassed to fight.' She sighed. 'So there you are—the big, ugly truth. The real reason I turned up at the Boat House alone on my thirtieth. Do you hate me?'

'I think you're amazing,' Jonas said.

He honestly did. This woman was strong—a survivor.

'And I'm glad you found your way home to Trengarth. Even if it's just for the summer.' He reached over and put his hand on her knee. 'I'm glad I've had this opportunity to know you again. And,' he added with a teasing smile, 'you're a great project manager!'

'So...' Lawrie lay back on the picnic blanket, looking up at the sky. 'I did it. Are you proud?'

'Did what?'

Jonas knew exactly what she was talking about. He still didn't know what he was going to say—if he could be honest.

He opted for diversionary tactics. 'Ate your own body

weight? Because I have to say that was a pretty impressive amount of food.'

'I blame the sea air,' Lawrie said thoughtfully. 'I never ate like this in London. It's a good thing I'm off soon—there isn't enough exercise in the world… But, no, that's not what I meant. I emailed my mother. Proud?'

'Mmm,' he said noncommittally. Aware of her sudden keen scrutiny, Jonas tried for more enthusiasm. 'That's great. Did she reply?'

It was Lawrie's turn to sound less than enthusiastic. 'Oh, yes—a great long stream of consciousness that was all about her.' She pulled a face. 'Not one question about me or what I'm doing.'

Jonas propped himself up on an elbow and looked down at her. 'I'm sorry.'

'Don't be.' Lawrie sat up, wrapping her arms around her knees and staring out to sea. 'Of course she *is* monumentally self-centred—I knew that. What kind of woman ditches her teenage daughter to go trekking? Doesn't come to her own mother's funeral? Truth is, I've spent my whole life hating her and at the same time wanting her to put me first, you know? But reading that email I just felt sorry for her. Which is an improvement, I guess. And I know she isn't capable of more. I just have to accept that.'

She turned to him, her face alight with interest.

'So…?'

'So?'

Here it was. And he still didn't know what to say.

'Did you go?'

The sand suddenly felt lumpy, hard beneath his elbow, and Jonas lay down. It was his turn to look up at the clear blue sky, the wisps of cloud lazily bobbing overhead. The weight of his newly acquired burden pressed down on him. Maybe sharing would help.

If anything could.

And Lawrie would be going soon. She wouldn't be there to constantly remind him, asking him how he felt, looking at him with sympathy or pity. And if she recoiled from him in disgust—well, maybe he deserved it.

'Yes,' he said slowly. 'I went.'

'And...?'

She seemed to sense the turmoil in him, was looking down at him in concern.

'Jonas, what is it? What did they say?'

He took a deep breath. 'I asked them why they had no photos of me—not one anywhere.' The words were almost dragged out of him, yet the very act of saying them relieved some of the almost unbearable load his father had bequeathed to him.

Lawrie was utterly still, her concentration all fixed on him. 'And...?'

'At first? Nothing. Then finally my father admitted they couldn't bear to—couldn't bear to have pictures of their only son. It was too painful a reminder.' He exhaled noisily. 'My presence, my *existence*, is too painful a reminder.'

He turned his head to look at her, to see her reaction as he finally said the words.

'There were two of us, Law. I had a twin—a sister. But we were early...too early. I was a lot bigger than her, so when we were born I had a better chance. She was too small.' He paused, remembering the utter look of desolation, of loss, on his father's face as he'd stumbled through the family secret.

'The doctors said if I hadn't taken up so much of the blood supply things could have been different—they might have saved us both. But as it was I killed her, Law. I killed my twin sister.'

For an agonisingly long time Lawrie didn't say anything. Was she horrified at him? By him? By what he had done? Because *he* was. This explained everything, and suddenly he couldn't blame his parents at all.

She was bolt upright, one hand covering her mouth, tears swimming in her eyes. One was falling and rolling unheeded down her cheek. With a muffled sob she turned to him, her arms reaching out, enfolding him, pulling him close, pulling him in.

'You poor boy,' she whispered, her tears soaking into his hair. 'It wasn't your fault—you hear me? Don't let *anyone* put this horrible thing onto you. It wasn't your fault.'

Jonas knew he should pull away, that the temptation to sink into her and never let go was too strong right now— that letting her go might be the hardest thing he had ever had to do. But the relief of another person's touch, another person's warmth, was too much, too intoxicating for a long, blissful moment, and he bathed in her warmth, in her understanding, before pulling back, reaching for her hand, lacing her fingers into his.

'If I had been a different kind of boy it might all have been easier,' he said after a while, caressing the soft smoothness of her hand. 'If I had been more like them… quieter…maybe they could have accepted me. But I was so boisterous, so energetic—always wanting to be different. I was always showing them how strong I was, how healthy. A constant reminder that if I had been a little *less* strong then she might have made it too.'

'No.'

The strength in her voice surprised him, her conviction ringing true.

'No. You mustn't ever think that. What happened was horrible—*horrible*. Your poor parents…I can't even imagine…' She shuddered. 'But it was no one's fault. Especially not yours.' She shook her head. 'And although I feel desperately sorry for your parents I could also shake them. Pushing you away, rather than thanking God every moment that they were blessed with one healthy, amazing boy? That's their tragedy. And they have to live with it. But you...' Her fingers tightened on his. 'You let this go.'

They sat, hands entwined, staring out to sea, neither of them speaking, and gradually, slowly, Jonas felt some of the darkness lift. He would always have to carry this knowledge, this loss, with him, but Lawrie was right. He didn't have to let it define him—even if his parents had allowed it to define their lives, their relationship with him.

There was nothing he could do about that. His card had been marked from the moment of his birth. He just had to live with that and move on—properly this time.

'At least...' he said slowly. 'At least I know it wasn't me—some terrible defect in me. I used to wonder, you know...wonder why they couldn't love me...why I was so damn unlovable.'

'Lots of people love you.' Lawrie leant in close, her hair soft on his cheek. 'Gran loved you—she adored you. When I left—when we split up—she told me I was a fool, that there was no finer man out there. Who knows? Maybe she was right.'

'She was definitely right,' he said, and was rewarded with a low laugh. 'Thank you,' he said. 'For listening.'

She turned to him, eyes serious. 'You know, I thought coming back here was going to be the most humiliating experience—facing you again, no job, no Hugo.' She shook her head. 'And it was pretty awful at first, but in a way I'm glad. That we got the chance to reconnect. To be friends again.'

'Is that what the kids call it nowadays?'

She smiled, moving her hand up to push the hair from

his eyes in an old, intimate gesture. 'I believe the phrase says "with benefits".'

He stared deep into her eyes, watched her pupils darken, grow, heard her breath quicken. His hand caressed hers, moving down to circle the delicate skin at her wrist. Right now all he wanted, needed, was to lose himself in this person who believed in him, who had once needed him.

'I, for one,' he said, 'am a great fan of benefits. I think they should be explored in much greater detail.'

Her pulse leapt at his touch. 'How great?'

'Let's go home,' he said. 'And I'll show you.'

CHAPTER NINE

DAMN, SHE WAS daydreaming again.

It was this office. Too much space, too many large windows with far too beautiful views. It just wasn't conducive to concentration. She'd choose her old windowless, airless, tiny internal office over this spacious luxury any day. At least she'd never been distracted there.

And it *was* the view, the sun, the come-hitherness of the summer's day that was the problem. It was not—most certainly *not*—the last few days.

Lawrie gazed unseeingly at the complicated document in front of her, detailing band schedules, riders, accommodation, entourage lists, her mind churning.

After the initial awful shock, the sudden grief and guilt, Jonas had seemed freed, unburdened. And hellbent on getting as much benefit out of their newfound friendship as he possibly could.

And she was matching him every step of the way.

She told herself it was because she was worried about him, because he seemed to be coping too well, because she could still see the hurt behind the playboy smile, but the selfish truth was that the benefits were working both ways.

Working really well.

It was no good. For once work was letting her down. Maybe she needed to take a break.

Sitting up, she grabbed her phone and flicked to her personal emails—belated birthday greetings from friends who didn't even know she'd left London, the usual deluge of sales emails offering her shoes, spa days, holidays, clothes. None of it mattered. Not any more.

'That's rather a scary grimace. Planning some street theatre?'

She looked up with a start. 'Some warning would be nice. You shouldn't sneak in like that.' It was the shock that had made her heart leap—not the sight of Jonas, immaculate in tennis whites, legs bronzed and muscular, hair damp with exertion pushed back off his forehead.

After all, *any* passable man looked good in tennis clothes.

Still, despite herself, she let her gaze travel from the dark blond tip of his head down over broad shoulders to his chest, clearly outlined through the fine white material, down past the shorts that clung to his narrow hips far too comfortably for her peace of mind and down those rather magnificent legs.

Lawrie swallowed, desperate to moisten her suddenly dry mouth as a jolt of desire pulsed through her, as a sweet, persistent ache settled in the pit of her stomach.

'You look like you've been busy.'

'Got to make sure all the facilities are in perfect working order.' He grinned at her boyishly. 'It's a hard job, but someone has to do it.'

Sauntering across the room, Jonas perched next to her on the edge of her desk.

Lawrie swallowed, the spreadsheet, her emails all forgotten. There was so *much* of him, and it was all so close. So much toned, tanned flesh, perfectly set off by the white fabric. Too much of the overwhelmingly male scent evoking grass, sun and sea. She licked her lips nervously, unsure whether she wanted to push the self-assured interloper off the desk or push him back and straddle him.

'And are they? In working order?'

Goodness, why did everything sound like a *double entendre*?

'Of course.' He smiled at her, slow and sweet. 'Want to find out?'

'No, I haven't played in years.' And she looked away from his knowing grin, feeling the heat spreading downwards, pooling in the pit of her belly. She tried again. 'I don't really have time to play. I watch a little, though. The firm had a corporate box at Wimbledon.'

He pulled a face. 'Wining and dining clients, hospitality boxes—it's all right for some, I suppose. It's not the real deal, though, is it?'

'It's different,' she said, ruthlessly pushing aside memories of being trapped in conversation with CEOs who knew nothing and cared less about the top-quality tennis being played out before them, who were there solely because it showed that they were *somebody*.

'But not better?' He was still sitting by her, disconcertingly close, one trainer-clad foot swinging. 'Although I hear the queuing facilities are much better now, and people have proper tents and loos and everything.' He put on a quavery voice. 'People today don't know they're born. In my day a couple of fold-up chairs and a sleeping bag did us.'

'Men's quarter-finals day,' she remembered. The sound of the racket hitting the ball, the smell of grass mingling with traffic fumes and sun cream, the taste of sweet, succulent strawberries, rich cream, and Pimm's fizzing on her tongue. 'Seems so long ago. We saw Agassi!'

He laughed. 'You can keep your Seychelles and your Maldives. A dusty pavement and top-quality tennis is the perfect honeymoon destination in my book. You wanted me to buy you an Agassi T-shirt!'

She laughed with him, couldn't help it. 'Well, I *was* eighteen,' she defended herself. 'Have you been since?'

He shook his head. 'June and July are such busy times for me. Pete, our pro, usually goes—takes some of the local kids he coaches—but I haven't joined them yet. One day.'

She nodded her agreement and tried to think of something else to say. Hard to think with him so close, so casual, so overpowering, so very male. Her mouth was dry, her mind suddenly empty. *Say something, damn it,* she thought. She opened her mouth but no sound came out.

'I was going to go for a swim,' Jonas said, seemingly unaware of her awkwardness.

Didn't he feel the uncomfortable silence? The weight of their past happiness?

'Fancy it?'

'Oh, I…well…' She fumbled desperately for the right words. If she was finding Jonas hard to cope with when he was semi-respectably clad in tennis whites then how would she manage with him wearing nothing but swim shorts? 'I haven't brought anything suitable to swim in,' she finished.

'Good thing we have a shop,' he said, and his eyes took on a disconcerting gleam. 'Or you could just wear nothing at all…'

For a long second Lawrie couldn't breathe. All she could do was stare at him, hypnotised by the heat in his eyes, the way the blue deepened until she was drowning in their azure depths. The ache in her stomach intensified, moved even lower, and for one hot, blazing moment all she was aware of was him.

Zzzzzzzz.

Lawrie jumped. The buzz of her phone as it signalled

the arrival of a text message broke the spell. Blinking her way slowly into reality, she realised in one mortifying moment that she was leaning forward, moving closer to him. With an effort she wrenched her gaze away, leaning back and looking intently at her computer as if all the answers were to be found there.

She summoned up a light, amused tone. 'I thought this was a respectable family hotel?'

Jonas still looked ridiculously at ease, seemingly unaware of her struggle to stay focused. 'It is—and I have something a bit more refreshing in mind than a pool full of overtired toddlers and harassed parents. Ready?'

Sensible Lawrie, clipboard-touting, plan-making Lawrie, knew it was a bad idea. She glanced at the spreadsheets still open on her desk. The safe, easy option. The right option.

But not the only option.

Just a couple of weeks left. A short while to be someone else. Someone less measured, less careful, less controlled. Someone free.

And then she would go to New York, Sydney, Toronto—wherever—and this summer would be a dream, a memory.

Someone else.

A smile curved her lips. She took a deep breath, kicked the chair back, away from the desk, and swivelled it towards Jonas, still sitting there on the desk, one bare leg idly swinging, watching her with an impenetrable gaze.

'Let's go,' she said.

Lawrie felt like a schoolgirl playing hooky as Jonas led her across a field at the back of the hotel garden towards the path that led down to the cove bordering the hotel property. It wasn't a private beach, but as there was no public right of way to it, it was used solely by hotel guests and anyone with access to a boat.

'Feels good doesn't it?'

'What does?'

'Being outside when you should be at work.'

'But you're my boss,' she pointed out as they slowed to a jog. 'And as I'm not being paid I'm not sure this technically counts as skiving.'

He shook his head, a mischievous smile playing around the sensual lips. 'Admit it—you still feel half guilty, though, I bet this is the first time you've ever bunked off work.'

She didn't answer, increasing her pace so that she sprinted past him, enjoying the sun on her face, the slight breeze ruffling her hair, the unusually giddy feeling of being free. Jonas gave a startled shout as she raced ahead, before also breaking into a fast run, catching her up with long-legged strides, elbowing his way past her to reach the stile first.

'Aren't you glad I made you get changed?' he asked, glancing down at her shorts and vest top appreciably. 'Those power heels of yours wouldn't have lasted five minutes.'

She pulled a face before darting round him and jumping over the stile onto the path that wound round the cliff, sniffing appreciatively. Gorse—how she loved it.

Jonas leant against the stile post, watching her. 'You look like a Labrador off after a scent.'

'It just smells so good,' she explained, knowing how idiotic she sounded.

It was funny... She'd read that smell was the best sense to evoke memories but she had never really noticed it personally before. Yet ever since she had returned to Cornwall she'd found herself reliving, remembering, her memories triggered by the very air about her. A primal creature after all, despite her veneer of city sophistication.

Jonas stepped up beside her and his hand brushed against hers. Such a small touch to provoke such intense memories. Long, lean, capable fingers entwined round hers. She felt the coolness of his palm, the slight roughness of his skin. She was preternaturally aware of every tiny square millimetre where their flesh touched, of little trickles of desire rippling up her arm. Her breasts suddenly felt full, heavy, aching, and an almost painful pressure behind her ribs echoed the intensified beating of her heart. Did he know? Was he aware of the effect his slightest touch had on her?

She didn't speak. Didn't look down at their hands. Didn't acknowledge him in any way. But she didn't pull away either.

Lost in a haze of feeling, Lawrie was unaware of where they were walking, knowing only the heady joy of touch, smell, sensation until they reached the top of the cliff.

'Where are we?' she asked looking about her in some confusion. 'This isn't the hotel beach.'

'Nope, this is the next cove along,' he explained. 'The hotel beach will be full of guests and their families, and mini-tot surf schools, sandcastle-building. All perfectly lovely, but a little more crowded than I had in mind.'

He looked back and flashed her a grin of such pure, seductive wickedness that her knees weakened and she nearly stumbled, steadying herself against the sparsely covered cliff-face with one trembling hand.

He means swimming, she told herself. *Get a grip.*

'Careful,' he called back as she picked her way down the dirt track. 'There're lots of little stones—it's easy to slip.'

'I do know how to walk down a cliff path,' she told him, but she slowed down a little, dragging her mind away from his earlier comments and her own overheated imaginings until she reached the bottom and looked about her.

It was a tiny little cove—a perfect little semi-circle of fine sand leading down to lapping waves, hidden from the rest of existence by the tall cliffs whose arms reached out into the sea on either side. A few rocks clustered at the foot of the cliff.

Jonas was standing by a large flat one and had laid the small rucksack he was carrying on top, was already shaking out the tartan blanket and laying out a couple of towels.

'It's beautiful,' Lawrie said, looking around in delight. 'I can't believe I've never been here before.'

'You can't access it from Trengarth,' Jonas said. 'With the hotel so close nobody ever comes here. Which is why I like it.'

Having taken care of the contents of the rucksack he was kicking off his trainers, pulling his T-shirt over his head. She stared, fascinated, at the still slim but perfectly toned chest, at the smattering of golden hair over his well-formed pecs turning into a fascinating line running down his taut stomach and disappearing into the top of his swim shorts.

Lawrie swallowed, an insistent pulse of desire throbbing through her entire body.

'Come on,' he teased her, moving from foot to foot.

Reluctantly she tore her eyes from his torso and looked out at the sea. Yes, it was calm, blue, inviting, and it was August, but even so…

He followed her gaze and sighed. 'Wimp,' he said. 'Honestly, when we were kids we swam in just our costumes Easter to October—now it's wetsuits all year round. Does no one like the feel of water on their skin any more?'

'You always liked your wetsuit well enough,' she retorted. But, stung by his words, she reluctantly pulled off her vest top, glad that she had bought a modest one-piece from the hotel shop and not the skimpy bikini he had picked out for her.

'I like my wetsuit for surfing, when I'm in the water for hours at a time, not for a good swim. The cold's half the fun.' He eyed her as she slipped the shorts off, an appreciative glint in his eye. 'That's not the itsy-bitsy polka-dot bikini I picked out, but it's rather nice.'

She looked down at herself. The fifties-style swimsuit suited her, she thought. The nipped in waist added curves to her leanness; the halter-style neckline lifted her breasts. He was still looking at her, his eyes lingering on the hint of cleavage, the exposed tops of her breasts. Feeling suddenly, unaccountably shy she took a step back, towards the sea.

'Last one in is a rotten egg,' Lawrie said, and took off, running towards the sea.

Jonas stood still for one disbelieving second before he took off after her, running up behind her, swinging her into his arms and running them both headlong into the sea until he was waist-high when, despite her laughing entreaties, he dropped her straight into the cold, clear water.

It was freezing. Like little shards of ice on her overheated skin. She sank beneath the surface, spluttering with outrage, with laughter, with cold. Her feet found the sandy bottom and she steadied herself and stood up, revenge on her mind.

Jonas had already anticipated her mood and was swimming away from her, widthways across the bay, reaching out with sure, sharp strokes. She stood for a minute, pushing her wet hair away from her face, blinking the water out of her eyes and watching him—sleek, strong, completely at home in the marine environment he loved. He turned, floating onto his back, and gave her a little ironic wave.

Right. She set out across the water. Goodness, it was

hard work swimming against the waves; a flat gym pool was no substitute for the sea. Forgetting Jonas for a second, she stopped swimming, treading water and allowing the waves to bob her up and down, closing her eyes and enjoying the sensation of the hot sun contrasting with the cold sea, the sound of the waves, the seagulls overhead— until a splash of sea water on her face brought her back to the present with a startled cry.

'You...' she threatened scooping up some water and flinging it at him.

Laughing, he dodged out of the way. Lawrie pursued him, pushing more and more water at him, until with a triumphant yell she doused him, moving in, holding him back whilst she thoroughly dunked him, enjoying the feeling of power, the play of muscles in his shoulders as she held him down, enjoying the way their bodies entwined as they play-fought. The hardness of him, the strength... She shivered.

He stopped fighting her, suddenly still, waist-deep in the sea. Her hands stilled on his shoulders as he straightened, and her wet body was close to his as one of his arms came to rest loosely round her waist. The other was at the nape of her neck until he drew a slow, tantalising line down her bare spine, his hand coming to rest on the small of her back, his long, oh, so capable fingers drawing a slow circle. Every sense she had seemed to be centred in that small area of sensitised skin.

'Jonas?'

It was such a small sound—a question, an entreaty? She couldn't have said. She just knew that she needed something—something more, something only this man could give her. She moved in closer, leg against leg, her aching breasts pressed against the tautness of his chest, her face raised pleadingly to his. This was why they had come here, wasn't it? For this…for the sheer sweetness of the moment as he finally lowered his mouth to hers.

Light kisses, delicate kisses, lips against lips, murmured endearments and still such restraint. One of his hands was still caressing the small of her back, the other was lightly on her waist as she held onto his shoulders, pressing herself closer against him, trying to get more of him, to deepen the kiss, to lose control.

Just for a while. Just for now, for this moment.

He picked her up again, swinging her up as if she weighed no more than a child, his arms tight around her. Without saying a word he strode towards the shore.

Lawrie felt a dreamlike calm mixed with an almost unbearable anticipation as she wound her arms around his neck and snuggled in, pressing small butterfly kisses onto the side of his neck. Her tongue flicked out, tasting the salt, and he gave a groan. Emboldened, she carried on exploring the wet, golden flesh, following drops of water with her lips, enjoying the effect she was clearly having on him.

He reached the picnic blanket and knelt down, placing her carefully onto it. She lay there waiting, welcoming, wanting, rolling towards him as he lay beside.

She needed this…she *deserved* this.

'Lawrie?'

His eyes were dark with desire, and the fire she saw in them elicited a primal response in her. The ache pulsating between her thighs was insistent, strong, powerful. She didn't answer. Words were beyond her. She was all instinct, all desire. She rose to her knees and leant over, pressing her mouth to his, her arms on either side of him supporting her weight.

With a groan he grabbed onto her, rolling her on top of him, deepening the kiss as his hands finally moved away from her waist, roaming over her body, touching, caressing, lighting sparks everywhere they travelled. She was aware of nothing but him, the planes of his body, the sensations his oh, so skilled fingers were inducing in her, his kiss, the taste of him, the feel of his lips, his tongue.

Sun, sea, salt, sensation overwhelmed her, whisking Lawrie away to some faraway place where all that existed was this. All that existed was them, just as it had used to be. She closed her eyes, allowing his touch, his mouth, his body to take her away, to soar over the cliffs and spiral up into the sky.

Jonas lay stretched out on the blanket, Lawrie curved into his side, one arm flung lightly across his chest. She was dozing, almost asleep but not quite, her eyes closed, her breathing even. Despite the lateness of the hour the air was still warm, sticky. He felt…*content*. That was the nearest word for the relaxed laziness of his body and mind.

For once Jonas didn't want to jump up, make his excuses and leave, break the intimate silence with meaningless small talk designed to keep a clear distance between his companion and himself. He wanted to stay here, holding Lawrie Bennett, and just *be*.

Although he really ought to think about getting dressed. He had been to this cove many times, and had yet to see another living soul beyond the gulls, but there was always a first time, and he'd rather not be naked when that time came. He ran a hand along the length of Lawrie's body, shoulder to hip, feeling the slight curves, marvelling at the silkiness of her skin. Even now, unclothed, half-asleep, there was a quiet dignity to her—a dignity that had been noticeable by its absence during the last hour.

He smiled to himself as he ran his hand back up her body, feeling her quiver under his touch. Passionate, unguarded, fiery, tender—she had been many things but not dignified.

'Lawrie?'

'Hmm?'

'Wake up, honey, it's getting late.'

She muttered something indistinguishable, rolling over away from him. He flicked his eyes down her graceful back, lingering at her curved behind, before trying again.

'Come on, Lawrie, time to get dressed. You wouldn't want some ramblers copping an eyeful, would you? Though it'd probably make their day—do wonders for the local tourist economy.'

She muttered again but rolled back, pushing herself up until she was sitting, legs drawn close to her chest as she flicked her hair out of her still sleepy eyes. 'What time is it?'

He held up his bare arm. 'No watch…no phone,' he teased. 'Can you cope with being so far from communication and order?'

She smiled, but warily. 'Good thing I brought my bag,' she said. 'I think I should probably get dressed, though. Erm…could you possibly…?' She gestured at her clothes, neatly folded on top of the rock.

'Of course,' he said, getting to his feet and noticing how her eyes were drawn towards his body before she lowered them, a faint blush staining her cheeks. Taking pity, he threw her shorts and T-shirt to her before retrieving his, unable to keep from watching her as she wriggled into her clothes in as discreet a style as possible.

'Don't mind me,' he said, and grinned as her head came up and she glared at him.

'A gentleman would turn his back.'

'Poor gentleman—he'd miss out.'

She stood up slowly, stretching out her arms and legs

with a lithe grace. 'Do you want a hand?' She gestured at the blanket and towels.

'Do you want to rush off? I brought food and wine.'

She eyed him nervously. 'You said it was getting late, that we should get back.'

'It is, and we should,' he agreed. 'But we can stay a little longer if you want—or do you have plans tonight?'

'No, but if I drink that I won't be able to drive home,' she pointed out as he reached into the rucksack and drew out a bottle of wine encased in a cooling holder.

'I own a hotel. Finding a bed for the night is never a problem.' He unscrewed the top and handed it to her. 'You're not too posh to drink from the bottle, are you?'

'Seriously?'

Her face spoke volumes but at his amused nod she screwed up her nose and raised the bottle to her lips. Only Lawrie Bennett could make drinking from a bottle look refined. And sexy.

'I, however, don't own a hotel.'

'We may have a spare tent somewhere—*ow!*' This as she flicked his shoulder smartly. 'What was that for?'

'Seriously, Jonas. What are you suggesting? That I stay at the hotel tonight with you? People are already talking...' Her voice trailed off.

'So what?' People always talked. They'd been talking since the second she'd sashayed back into town. Let them. 'Come and eat something. I brought all of this for you. I'm not lugging it back up the cliff.'

Lawrie flopped down onto the blanket next to him and took the paper plate he was holding out to her, loading it daintily with a selection of breads, cheeses and salads. She began to build a towering sandwich of cheese, salad, grapes and coleslaw.

Jonas watched, fascinated. 'That's quite some sandwich,' he said.

'Hmm, I'm not quite sure how I'm going to manage to bite into it,' she admitted. 'Maybe sandwiches could be my thing?'

'What thing?'

'Well, you said it yourself—I'm a blender. I don't have an interest that's really mine,' she said, reassembling the sandwich into several smaller parts. 'Maybe it's time I did. In New York they asked me what I liked to do in my spare time and I told them about going to museums and exhibitions. But of course that was Hugo's interest, not mine. I enjoyed them, but would I go by myself? And then I said singing, but I only do that when I'm with you. I don't know *what* I like to do apart from work.'

'And sandwich-making is your new hobby?'

'Being a foodie might be. I've had a lot of practice. Or I might take up art? What?' she asked as he shook his head.

'I've played Pictionary with you. Believe me when I say that art is *not* your thing.'

'Good point. Well, maybe quilting, or distressing furniture.'

'You could… But you don't have to decide right now, do you?'

'But if I decide before I go then I can research,' she said, taking a bite of the newly assembled sandwich. She chewed, then swallowed. 'I'll tell you what I'm not going to do, though. I am not going to date anyone I work with. Especially not my boss. Twice bitten, three times shy. Or something.'

Jonas grinned. 'Interesting statement, considering I am kind of your boss now.' His smile grew wider, more wicked, as he saw the blush colour her pale cheeks, the answering smile in her eyes. 'And, considering how you've been spending your nights lately, I have to conclude that you haven't started to enforce that rule too strictly.'

She laughed and her colour was high, her lips reddening, full, inviting. 'Ah, but we're not dating.'

'No?'

'No.'

'Then…' He leant in, close. Took her hand in his, turning it over to slowly trace a circle on her palm. 'What *are* we doing late at night, Miss Bennett?'

She swayed towards him, her hand closing onto his. Jonas slid his thumb over the plump flesh of her palm, every sense suddenly heightened. The brightness of the sun illuminated the scene in honey-coloured light: her glorious hair, the creaminess of her skin, the crash of the waves onto the shoreline, the call of the birds swooping high above, the distant coconut smell of gorse mingling with her light, fresh perfume, the silky smoothness of her hands in his. The anticipation of taste. The so very sweet anticipation…

He pulled her closer, sliding his hands out of hers and up her bare arms, then down her back, where they rested on the soft skin of her shoulderblades. His thumbs moved in small circles. She shivered under his touch, her breath speeding up, coming in small gasps, as one finger slid leisurely down her spine and then up to the nape of her neck. She swayed towards him, her face tilted up, eyelids half closed, desire and need in her expression, her eyes, her mouth. He leant in, brushed her mouth with his oh, so slowly, before trailing kisses along her jaw, down the side of her neck, to the soft pulse beating insistently in her throat.

She sighed, leaning against him as his tongue flicked out, tasted her warm skin. His hands were still playing up and down her spine, enjoying her uninhibited response to his touch, his kiss, the feel of her quivering beneath him.

'Jonas...' she began, one hand coming up to clutch his T-shirt, the other to encircle his neck.

But whatever she'd been going to say was interrupted by the shrillness of a ringtone from her bag, flung carelessly at his feet. Lawrie pulled back slowly, her expression clearing, releasing him. Reluctantly he let her go, his hand lingering against her back as he did so.

She gave him an apologetic smile. 'I should get this.'

Jonas nodded, standing up and taking a step away to recover himself as she rooted in her bag and pulled out the insistently shrieking phone.

He closed his eyes, inhaling the sea air deeply. He felt so alive. At some point in the last few days his eagerness for life, his zest, had returned—and yet he hadn't even noticed that it was gone

'Yes...yes. Absolutely. That sounds great—thank you. Yes, okay. I will. Bye.' Lawrie switched the phone off and stood still, a dazed expression on her face.

He looked over at her enquiringly. 'Bad news?'

'Huh? Oh, no.' She looked a little dazed. 'No, it was the agency.' A wide smile broke out on her face. 'The New York firm want me! They were really impressed with my interview and want me to start the day my gardening leave finishes. Isn't it wonderful?'

'Yes, wonderful.' Jonas forced a smile onto his face, made himself move over to her, pull her close into a hug. 'Of course they want you. They'd be mad not to.'

She returned the embrace, then stepped back, excitement filling her vivid dark eyes. 'New York...' Her face glowed. 'It's all coming together, Jonas.'

'Of course it is. You've made it come together.'

She had. She'd worked hard for it, picked herself up when it all had been snatched away from her. She deserved this.

So why did it feel as if the bottom had dropped out of his world?

'So?' She was tugging at his hand, playfully. 'You were saying before we were interrupted…?'

'I think we should head back,' he said, still with that forced smile on his face. 'News like this calls for champagne.'

She looked slightly surprised, a little disappointed, but didn't demur, helping him pack up, chattering about New York, the firm, the work she hoped to be doing. He listened, agreed, asked questions, and the topic lasted them all the way home.

Her eyes were firmly fixed on the bright lights of a big city once again.

CHAPTER TEN

THE FIELDS WERE full of life. Families, couples, groups of friends, were laughing, chattering, wandering into one of the myriad teepees, tents and yurts to enjoy theatre, story-telling, music or poetry readings. Food stalls offered local beers and ciders, and every type of food, from traditional Cornish cream teas to Indian street food. Meanwhile over on the main stage one of Cornwall's best-known folk bands was entertaining a large crowd. It was exhausting. It was exhilarating. Lawrie was loving every minute of it.

When she had a chance to stop and think about it, that was.

She reached up a hand to check the earpiece that kept her connected to the main radio network bleating out se-curity breaches, lost children, petty theft, missing artists. She was aware of every single incident taking place on the festival site. Even last night, when she'd stayed in Jonas's camper van, parked backstage so she was in the midst of the activity at all times, she'd kept it switched on. Her bulg-ing file and her phone had been close by the bed, ready to be snatched up at a moment's notice.

She hadn't slept a wink.

But here they were: Day Two. The sun was still mirac-ulously shining, no musician so lost he couldn't be found and shoved out on stage on time, every sobbing child reunited with grateful parents. No food poisoning—yet, she thought anxiously—no serious crimes or marauding youths. Just a happy, laid-back vibe. Like a swan, with the festival-goers the body, floating serenely along, whilst she and the other members of staff paddled furiously to keep the whole thing afloat.

Goodness, what an overblown simile. She must be tired.

'When did you last eat?'

She jumped as a pair of hands landed on her shoulders, squeezing lightly.

'Have you even sat down once in the last two days?' Jonas continued mock severely. 'Taken time to listen to one of the bands you booked?'

'They were mostly booked before I started,' she protested, resisting the urge to lean back against him, to surrender the worries, the responsibilities into his oh, so capable hands for just a few seconds.

'It's on; we're live; it's all good,' he said, turning her round to face him. 'You should relax and start enjoying it.'

Lawrie hugged the black file that had been her constant companion over the last month closer to her chest. 'I'll enjoy it in twenty-four hours' time,' she told him. 'Once I know the last bands have turned up and that tonight has run smoothly.'

'Or once you've picked the last piece of litter up from the campsite in a week's time?'

She smiled. 'Maybe.'

Like her, Jonas was dressed casually. There was no sign of the successful businessman in the cut-off denims and orange T-shirt, a baseball cap covering the blond hair subtracting years from him.

'Well, at least let me buy you some lunch.'

'I'm not really hungry,' she demurred.

But, too tired to make a fuss, she allowed him to lead

her to a falafel stand and order her a humus salad wrap. The smell of fried onions and spicy chickpeas hit her as she stood there; they smelt like summer. A hollow feeling in her stomach reminded her that actually she had barely touched her breakfast that morning, nor supper the night before.

'Part of the fun of Wave Fest is the food,' he scolded her as she nibbled at the edges of the wrap, trying to avoid spilling what was inside down her top. 'You should be getting out there, experimenting.'

She licked humus off the top of the wrap. 'I'm not really the experimenting type.'

He leant in close. 'I don't agree.'

His breath tickled her ear, soft, tantalising, like a soft summer breeze. The faint brush of air on her sensitive earlobe spread through her body, warming her right down to her toes. She was almost paralysed with a sudden stab of desire—hotter, needier, more intense than ever. She swallowed, willing her knees to stay up, her stomach to settle, trying to control her traitorous body. It was the hunger, the lack of sleep, the craziness of the day. She couldn't still want him—not this much.

Her time here was almost over.

The thought was a short, sharp shock. The sweet, languorous need that had enveloped her fled as quickly as it had come. Their time together was nearly at an end—as it should be...as she wanted.

Autumn was coming. By the time the leaves had turned she would be across the ocean, beginning her new life. Jonas would be here.

They both knew long-distance didn't work. They had failed so spectacularly before.

Lawrie plastered a bright smile on her face, turning

to look at him, hoping that no trace of her thoughts remained visible.

'Have you seen many of the bands?' she asked, before taking a bite of the wrap. She nearly moaned out loud. Maybe it *was* lack of food that had caused her earlier weakness, because the combination of crisp wrap, rocket, humus and freshly made falafal was sensual overload.

'Is that good?'

Amusement was written all over his face as she nodded mutely, cramming another mouthful in.

'Maybe I was hungry,' she mumbled as she swallowed it down.

'Maybe.' His eyes were bright with laughter. 'You'll be admitting you need a nap next.'

She shook her head. 'Try coffee—caffeine might help,' she allowed.

He took her elbow, steering her effortlessly through the partying crowds. 'At least come into the hotel and sit down while you drink it,' he said, and the thought of a comfy armchair was too tempting.

She allowed him to lead her away, finishing off the wrap hungrily as they walked back to the hotel.

'Are your parents still here?' she asked as they mounted the steps and made their way through the crowded foyer to the desk. The hotel itself was strictly VIP for the duration of the festival, but it was no less hectic than outside, with staff, guests and the bands not camping backstage all based there.

'No, they left after a seafood lunch.'

His voice was non-committal. She sneaked a peep at his face but it was expressionless. Her heart sank. Getting his parents to agree to visit the hotel during the festival had seemed like a major coup; she hoped it hadn't backfired.

'That's a shame,' she said carefully. 'I would have liked to see them again.'

'Maybe it's for the best.' He flashed her a warm smile. 'My mother, despite thinking that you are far, far too good for me, has not-so-secret hopes that we may get back together and she can have her dream daughter-in-law again. Don't worry—I warned her that you're off again soon.'

He could at least sound a little regretful about it.

If only she wasn't so tired, could think more clearly. Where was that coffee?

She followed Jonas into her office and curled up thankfully on the large squishy sofa.

He cast her a concerned look. 'You are done in.'

'Not at all,' she protested. 'A coffee will sort me out.'

He looked unconvinced, but made her promise not to try and get up, no matter what, and then disappeared off to fetch her a drink. Lawrie leant back against the cool, plumped-up cushions and sighed. She *had* hoped that seeing the festival in full swing would help his parents appreciate all that Jonas had achieved, but maybe she'd been wrong.

Maybe she needed to accept that some things were best left alone. If she had kept to her original plan and stayed clear of Jonas then she would be in such a different frame of mind as she contemplated her life changing move.

She sighed. She should be much more excited, optimistic. This was what she wanted.

And yet it was as if her life had been beige and grey for the past nine years and colour had suddenly returned to it. It was bright, and it hurt sometimes, but oh, the difference it made. She just had to figure out how to keep the Technicolor when she left. When she started again.

'I managed to get you carrot cake as well.' Jonas returned to the room, carefully carrying a tray holding a cafetière of deliciously pungent coffee and a large slab of spicily fragrant sponge cake. 'Sugar and caffeine should sort you out.'

He placed the tray onto the small coffee table and poured out a cup of coffee, adding cream and handing it over to Lawrie, who sniffed ecstatically.

'I can't believe you've got me addicted to coffee again,' she said accusingly as she took a sip of the bitter brew.

'You are moving to New York,' he pointed out as he poured a cup for himself and sat next to her on the sofa. 'You don't want to be seen as a strange tea-drinking Brit who spends the whole time complaining that she can't get a proper brew, do you?'

'Well, no,' she conceded, leaning forward to hook the plate of cake off the tray. She forked a small portion of frosting and sponge and sat looking at it for a second.

'Are you going to eat that or just study it?'

'Eat it,' she retorted, and suited her action to her words.

She sucked the fork appreciatively, her mind still whirling.

'Did you serve them the shellfish special or the fried fish platter?' She attempted to keep her tone light, nonchalant, and licked the last bit of frosting off the cake fork.

'Huh?'

Jonas's eyes were glued to the fork, to her tongue flicking out and licking it. She coloured, forking up some more cake casually, as if she hadn't noticed his intense gaze, the disconcerting gleam in the blue eyes.

'Your parents? I think they're more shellfish people myself, but the whitebait on the fried platter is so delicious.' She was on the verge of babbling, but her words had the desired effect. Jonas pulled his eyes away from her mouth distractedly.

'My parents? Oh, the shellfish. They like big, extravagant gestures so it had to be lobster, really.'

'And did they see any bands?'

'Oh, yes. They had the full guided tour.'

'And...?' she prompted him.

He gave her a rueful grin. 'They didn't throw themselves on my neck with tears of apology for neglecting me all these years and promises of a brighter tomorrow,' he said.

His words were light, almost jocular, without the slight undercurrent of disappointment or the hint of bitterness talk of his parents usually brought out in him.

'On the other hand they didn't criticise, cry with disappointment or walk out in disgust. They stayed for lunch and even said it was "rather nice" so overall a success, I think.'

'A complete success,' she agreed.

He reached out his hand, tucking back a lock of her hair. She sat frozen, aware of nothing but his touch, the unexpectedly tender look in his eyes, the sound of her own heartbeat hammering.

Their eyes continued to hold. Her mouth was dry, she flicked her tongue out nervously to moisten her lips. They had been alone, been intimate, so many times—every night for the last few weeks—but this...this felt different. It felt *more*. But even as part of her welcomed it, thirsted for it, another, larger part of her shrank from it. It was too much.

Because they had been here before.

'I should go.' Was that really her voice? So hesitant, so unsure? She pushed herself up, legs wobbly. 'Wave Fest won't run itself, you know.'

He was still seated, still looking at her with that disconcertingly knowing gaze, as if he could see right inside her. He was so close. He just needed to reach out, pull, and she would be in his lap.

But if she allowed herself to settle there she would never want to leave.

He didn't. Didn't move, didn't pull, didn't try and dissuade her. He just watched her as she drank down the rest of her coffee, grabbed her file and walked out of the office. He didn't say a word.

Work. It was always the answer. And this was a workaholic's dream. The second she left the office Lawrie was pounced upon to sort out some problem with the evening's line-up, and by the time she'd pacified the disgruntled artist who expected a higher billing she'd managed to push all thoughts of Jonas to the back of her mind—where, she told herself sternly, he had better stay until she felt more like herself again.

Whatever and whoever herself might be. She certainly wasn't the brittle London girl who had arrived here just over a month ago, but she wasn't the Cornish girl in vest top and shorts she appeared to be either. She was only playing at her role here.

But, playing or not, there was a lot to do.

Eight hours later her lunch was just a distant dream. She had barely had the opportunity to grab any water, despite the heat of the sun, and must have walked miles. Next year she would recommend golf carts, she thought.

'There you are.'

Lawrie turned around, blinked blearily. Everything was suddenly amplified. The light was almost blinding; people and objects were a mingled blur. The sounds were an amalgamated cacophony of discordant notes and loud voices.

She swayed, pressing a trembling hand to her head.

'Lawrie! Are you okay?'

Jonas. How broad he looked…how comforting. She took

a small step towards him, then stopped, trying to summon up the energy to reply. 'Yes, just tired still. I'll be fine.'

It had been such a warm day. And yet now she was shaking with cold, wrapping her arms around herself, trying to press some warmth into her bones.

A touch on her chin tilted it upwards. She tried to meet his probing gaze but had to close her eyes.

'I told you to take a proper rest. There are another twenty-four hours of this festival, and you are not going to last,' Jonas said grimly and, disregarding her protests, whirled around, taking her elbow and pulling her along.

'What are you doing?' she said, trying unsuccessfully to pull her arm out of his grasp.

'Taking you home for the night. If you are on site you won't switch off,' he said pulling out his handset. 'Fliss, you are in charge for the next twelve hours. Lawrie is taking a few hours off.'

Lawrie could hear Fliss's voice floating up from the handset, worrying, agreeing, admonishing Lawrie to get some rest.

She wanted to argue, to tell them she was fine but the words wouldn't come. 'Are you all ganging up on me?'

'If that's what it takes.'

She felt as if she should fight harder but she didn't have the strength. 'Just a short nap,' she conceded.

'You are having the whole night off. You can come back tomorrow morning, but not a second before.' There was no trace of humour in his voice, just worry. 'And I'll see how you are then.'

'Yes, boss.'

But it was an effort to form the words, and she didn't demur as Jonas led her through the crowds and round to the staff car park, where he gently helped her into his car.

Lawrie sank into the seat and closed her eyes. Half

asleep, she didn't notice the route Jonas took until he stopped the car with an undignified squeal of brakes. She prised her eyelids open and looked about her. They were in the tiny old town, amongst the fishermen's cottages that clustered around the harbour.

'This isn't home,' she murmured sleepily.

'This is my house,' Jonas told her, and he unbuckled her seat belt before getting out and coming round to open her door and help her out. 'I don't trust you not to be logging on and fussing if I let you go back to yours.'

'Too tired to log on,' she protested, but obediently followed him along the street.

They were at the very top of the old town, with the cliffs towering above them and views over the rooftops down to the harbour below. Jonas came to a stop by a long crooked house that lurched drunkenly along the street and opened the door. Lawrie stopped on the doorstep and stared at him, suddenly more awake.

'The crooked house? You bought it?'

'Yep. Come in.'

She looked at him. Didn't he remember? That this was *the house*—the one that every time they played the 'one day when we are rich' game they had decided they would buy. Some were bigger, others more imposing, cuter, older, quainter, but something about this last house in the old town had appealed to her the most. The funny little corners, the different levels, the roof garden… It had always drawn her in, and now it belonged to Jonas.

'Lawrie, are you all right?'

'Yes, I'm coming.'

Slowly she stepped into her dream house. Inside it was just as she'd imagined. The hall that bisected the mismatched halves of the house was covered in grey flagstones, a wooden bannister curved around the crooked staircase.

She didn't have time to see more as Jonas ushered her straight upstairs. He turned down the winding passage to his left and stopped at the first door, pausing with his hand on the handle, a look of slight embarrassment on his face. 'I haven't made the other beds up but my sheets are clean on…' He trailed off.

She stared at him incredulously, then laughed. 'Jonas, we have been sleeping together most nights for the last month—plus, I am so tired I wouldn't care if your sheets hadn't been changed in weeks.'

He grinned. 'Good point,' he said and, turning the handle, ushered her inside.

It was a large, rectangular room, with two small windows cut into the deep walls, the stone window seats covered in plush cushions. An oak bedstead dominated the room and was made up in a rich, dark chocolate linen. It was the most inviting thing Lawrie had ever seen.

'Right…' He still stood at the door. 'I will leave you to…ah…make yourself comfortable. There's a bathroom just there.' He gestured at a door set in the far wall. 'I'll be back in the morning with some clean clothes and a meal, so just sleep, okay?'

''kay…' She nodded, but her eyes were already fixated on the plump, cool-looking pillows, the king-size comfortable bed.

Jonas had scarcely pulled the door shut behind him before she'd started to undress, kicking off her shoes, slipping off her shorts and unhooking her bra, manoeuvring it off under her vest top. Clad just in her top and knickers, she climbed into the bed and closed her eyes.

As she drifted off to sleep the events of the day replayed themselves. Why had Jonas been so funny about her sleeping in his bed? Of *course*, she thought drowsily as sleep began to overtake her. They had only shared a bed to have sex—sometimes sleeping together afterwards, sometimes he would leave her and go home. But this—this letting her into his bed, into his home—this was intimacy.

It scared her…it comforted her.

Lawrie drifted off to sleep.

It wasn't worth going back to the hotel, Jonas decided. After all, Fliss could cope for a few hours, and if she couldn't he was just fifteen minutes' drive away; it could take longer than that to walk from one side of the site to the other.

Dropping by Lawrie's to pick her up a change of clothes had taken him far longer than he'd anticipated. Choosing an outfit had felt almost uncomfortably intimate— which, considering some of the truly intimate actions he had been performing with and to her on a nightly basis, was just too weird.

He hadn't wanted to dwell on why that might be, choosing a dress and cardigan almost at random and plucking underwear out of her drawer with his face averted.

Well, maybe he'd had a little peek. But not a long one— he wasn't one of *those* guys.

Back at his house, he wandered into his sitting room, falling onto the leather corner sofa with a sigh, his mind fixated on the room above, where Lawrie slept. He had avoided bringing her here, to his home, to the house she had once loved so much.

He dragged his eyes away from the ceiling he was staring at as if he had X-ray vision—as if he could see through to the room, to the bed, to the sleeping girl above—fixing his gaze instead on the large watercolour portrait that hung above the open fireplace. It was a sea scene, of course—

every work of art he owned reflected the coast in some way—in which a girl sat on a rock, staring out to a wild sea, her hair whipped and blowing. She was turned away from the artist, so only a small part of her face could be seen.

Lawrie. A portrait painted by a summer visitor years ago. Jonas had tracked it down and bought it several years ago.

He didn't really like to examine his reasons why. Just as he didn't like to examine his reasons for buying this house in particular. The house he and Lawrie had play-furnished in their dreams time and time again. He could easily afford something bigger, fancier, more luxurious, but he felt grounded here—at home.

In the house she'd loved, with her portrait on the wall.

He sat bolt upright, adrenaline running through him. What was he *doing*? What had he been doing these last nine years?

He was pathetic. All these years he had prided himself on how independent he was, how he needed no one but himself, and look at him.

No wonder he was still single. How could any real woman compete with the ghost at the feast? They had never had a chance, had they? No matter how fun or accomplished or sexy they were, they had always been missing something very important.

They weren't Lawrie.

Maybe part of him had held on, hoping for her return. And here she was. Back in his life and back in his bed.

About to leave again.

He could try and change her mind. He could ask her to stay, beg her to stay. Rush up there now and tell her how he felt.

And then what?

Jonas got to his feet and walked over to the painting. There she was, her eyes fixed on the horizon, on the future. She had always dreamt big.

Right now she was vulnerable, more scarred by the loss of her job and her fiancé than she would ever admit. He could play on that fear and she might stay.

And then what?

He knew too well how *that* scenario played out. He would watch her feel more and more confined and constricted. Watch her start to blame and resent him. Again. Watch her walk away, walk out of his life, and this time never come back.

Or he could let her go and then move on himself. Finally, *properly* move on.

He looked at the clock sitting on the mantelpiece. Eight hours before he needed to wake her. It wouldn't hurt if he just stretched out for a while himself. The sofa was long enough, wide enough, comfortable enough… And yet he couldn't relax.

This was ridiculous. He had a perfectly good bed upstairs. Lawrie wouldn't mind.

She was fast asleep, the covers kicked off, exposing long, lean legs. The curve of her bottom encased in sheer black silk was a stark contrast to the cream of her skin. The strap of her vest had fallen down, showing a rare vulnerability in the usually self-possessed, contained, organised Lawrie. Looking down at her, he felt a tenderness creep over him for his beautiful, intelligent wife.

Ex-wife. Just two letters made such a difference.

Jonas kicked off his shoes and quietly slipped his shorts off, hanging them on the chair before crossing the room to get into bed beside her. He fitted his length against her, pulling her in close, one arm holding her tight.

'I love you,' he whispered. 'I'll always love you.'

Eyes open, thoughts racing, Jonas lay there, holding Lawrie close, willing time to slow, wishing that the night would last for ever.

CHAPTER ELEVEN

IT WAS THE campfire's fault. If Lawrie hadn't attended the end-of-festival campfire—hadn't met up with old friends, hadn't found herself singing songs she had forgotten she had ever known, hadn't cooed over babies and admired stroppy, tired toddlers, hadn't met new couples and heard one hundred stories about how they'd met…

If she hadn't spent the evening watching Jonas, golden in the flickering firelight, laughing, relaxing, looking over at her with laughter, with tenderness in his eyes.

If after the campfire they hadn't sneaked back to the camper van. If they hadn't made love with an intensity she couldn't remember having ever experienced before.

She should have left the minute the festival finished—packed her bags and disappeared without a word.

Then she wouldn't need to find the words to say goodbye. Find the will to turn and walk away.

'You're very quiet.'

Jonas was once more driving her to the airport.

Only this time there would be no return trip.

She forced a smile. 'I'm a little apprehensive,' she admitted.

He raised an eyebrow. 'Lawrie Bennett, lawyer, festival-organiser, campfire chanteuse…apprehensive? I don't believe it.'

He was so calm, so *cheerful*. As if her leaving didn't matter at all.

And, although she couldn't handle a scene, a little regret might be nice—a sign that their time together had meant something to him.

What if he asked you to stay?

Where had that thought come from?

She pushed it to one side, searching for something to say. 'Do you think I'm like my mother?'

As soon as she asked the question she regretted it, not sure she could bear to hear the answer.

Jonas looked surprised. That was good, right?

'I can't imagine you abandoning your teenage daughter while you go and party in Goa, no,' he said finally. 'Why?'

Immediately Lawrie wanted to backtrack. What could she tell him? That she wasn't sure about leaving? Didn't know if she could do this alone?

She fell back on an old conversation. 'I don't even know what I like, for goodness' sake. Is festival-going, shorts-wearing, beach-loving Lawrie more real than the suited and booted City lawyer? I worry that I'm a chameleon, Jonas, just like she is.'

Excuse it might be, but there was truth there. She had always defended her need to blend in. Maybe it was time to learn to stand out.

He was silent for a moment. 'Your mother spent her life searching—you've spent yours *doing*. You have spent your life trying to achieve something, Law. You have been working for it since I knew you. You're dedicated, single-minded. That's nothing like her. You never wasted your time on dreams and fairytales.'

That was true, but not enough. 'But I don't even know whether I like the stuff I like because of me, or because of you or Hugo. See? Chameleon!'

He laughed, and the warm humour caressed her taut nerves.

'We're back to this, are we?'

She nodded, slightly shame-faced.

'You're not a chameleon, I promise. Maybe you've just found it easier to adapt to other people's interests as that gives you more time to concentrate on what really matters to you.'

He was silent for a moment, concentrating on overtaking, and Lawrie took his words in, a warmth stealing over as she did so.

He understood her. In some ways better than she understood herself.

He spoke again, quiet and serious. 'For what it's worth, I think you're both of those people. Even city slickers are allowed to be beach bums occasionally. You don't have to choose. Okay—we're here.'

Looking up with a start, Lawrie realised Jonas was taking a left hand turn—the one that led to the airport short-stay car park. He was planning to come in.

Panic clawed at her chest. She couldn't handle a long, protracted goodbye. Memories flashed through her of tearful train station farewells, clutching desperately on to Jonas as the train drew in, suitcase at her feet.

She'd never been good at goodbyes.

'You don't need to stay, honestly. Just drop me off.'

He flashed her a quick glance. 'You sure?'

She put on her brightest smile. 'Goodness, yes. You don't want to waste an hour hanging out at the airport, and I don't have much luggage—most of my stuff was shipped out last week. I'll head straight to the departure lounge and read there. You go.'

There was a slightly desperate tinge to her voice as she

finished speaking but Jonas didn't seem to notice—he just turned the car around to drive into the drop-off area.

He pulled up to the kerb and they sat there. Silent. Lawrie stared at her hands, twisting them nervously together.

'Okay, then, this is it.'

'Yep.'

'I'll get your bag.'

Once again he was walking round the car to fetch her bag. Once again she was sliding out of the low-slung seats, stepping onto the grey paving slabs, ready to walk through the sliding glass doors.

Once again she was leaving.

'Right—you have your suitcase, laptop, handbag, jacket, tickets, passport?'

She nodded. 'I'm all good.'

'Okay, then.' He was moving away, the few steps back towards the car. It was just Lawrie and her bags, alone on the pavement. Just as she wanted. *Fight me on this,* she thought desperately. *Come in with me. See me off. Ask me not to go.*

The need was getting louder, harder to ignore.

Lawrie picked up her bag, testing its weight. This was it. She shot a look over at him, leaning against the bonnet, oblivious or uncaring of the cars lined up behind, waiting for a drop-off spot. His face was calm, set. Inscrutable.

'Law...?'

She paused, a fizz of hope bubbling up inside her, shocking her with its intensity.

'Just remember: tea is drunk hot, not iced, and jelly wobbles and is always eaten with ice cream.'

And just like that she was flat.

She attempted a smile. 'I thought you wanted me to fit in?'

'Fit in? Yes. Go native? No.'

The world had fallen away. All she was aware of was him. The foot between them seemed an ocean already—that solid, comforting presence a continent away. It was up to her. Only her.

And it terrified her.

Lawrie took a deep breath. 'I could stay if you wanted me to. If you asked me I would consider it, definitely.' *Ask me,* she begged silently. *Tell me you need me...you can't live without me. Tell me it will be better this time. Tell me we can make it.*

His expression didn't change. 'Why?'

Lawrie didn't know what she had expected him to do. To regretfully but politely turn her down and send her on her way? To run over to her, swoop her up, twirl her, like a montage of every rom-com she had seen? To be embarrassed?

But she hadn't expected that one-word question. She hadn't expected the warm blue eyes to turn to steel.

'Last-minute nerves,' she said as brightly as she could, pulling the tattered shreds of her pride around her, trying to match his cool expression. 'You know I hate saying goodbye. It's been a good few weeks. I got carried away, sorry. Forget I said anything.'

'What if I did ask?'

How could she have thought him calm? His voice reverberated with suppressed emotion. But not the emotion she'd hoped for. It wasn't warm, comforting, loving.

'Would you make it till the end of the year? Till next summer? How long before you blame me because you're stuck here and not in New York?'

Wow. Lawrie had never really believed that words could hurt before, but that hit deep—painfully deep. 'I can't believe you said that...' she almost whispered, torn between hot tears and plain old-fashioned anger. 'I only asked you...'

'You asked me to make a decision for you. *Again*. You want to stay, Lawrie?' The words whipped through the air, taut and clear. 'You stay. *You* make the decision and *you* live with the consequences. Don't ask somebody else to shoulder the responsibility for you so you can blame them the second it goes wrong.'

'I'm not!' All her verbal skills had deserted her. She was defenceless against the unexpected onslaught.

'No?' His laugh had no humour in it. 'You didn't blame me for keeping you here before? For getting married so young?'

The warmth of the summer's day had disappeared and a chill wind goosepimpled her bare arms, making her shiver. 'We were young!'

'You said yourself you would still be with your ex, making wedding plans, if he hadn't forced your hand. Now you want me to force it again?' Jonas shook his head. 'I don't think so, Lawrie. Take some responsibility for yourself, decide what the hell you want—what you *really* want—and then maybe we can talk.'

'I don't need to talk.' Lawrie's uncertainty and shock had disappeared, been replaced with a burning anger. How dared he speak to her like that? 'I made a mistake. Clearly. Thanks for pointing that out. Message received.'

And, picking up her bag, she turned and strode away as confidently as she could, his steel-blue gaze burning into her back as she did so.

No one had warned her how cold New York could be. It was barely autumn—fall, she corrected herself—and already the temperatures were dropping, the wind was howling through the island city, and the rain lashed down in great dramatic storms.

Not that Lawrie had much time to concentrate on the weather. New York prided itself on being the city that never slept and its standards were high. She was no shirker, but it was taking everything just to keep up.

And keeping up wasn't enough. She needed to excel. Others might skate in Central Park, go for coffee wrapped up in giant jumpers and cashmere scarves and hats; Lawrie worked. She had found a small studio flat close to the office, but spent so much time at her desk it really was just a base to sleep, shower and eat. Ostensibly she was apartment-hunting, looking for a place of her own to buy. In reality her attempts mirrored her wedding-planning with Hugo. Non-existent.

Hugo was now married to his secretary, Helen—happily, she assumed. His social media pages certainly painted that picture, showing a beaming Hugo—he had put on weight, she thought critically—with one arm possessively around his blooming bride. Every detail of Helen's pregnancy was detailed, along with scans, possible baby names and more information about her physical symptoms than Lawrie was entirely comfortable with.

On the surface she was cynically amused, but buried deep down inside—*very* deep down—she was touched and a little jealous. Not of Helen and Hugo, exactly, but of the absolute patent happiness that glowed out of every sentimental update. No amount of completed contracts, of senior partner compliments could compete with that.

And Jonas didn't get in touch. Not one word. No apology.

And she didn't contact him.

His last words reverberated around her mind, echoing at unexpected times. Not just when she was alone, and not just in the dead of night as she lay sleepless in an unfamiliar bed in a strange city, but in meetings, at the gym, as she walked down the street.

Take some responsibility.

And then the anger flared up again, but it was getting weaker as the days slowly passed.

And at the same time that unwanted voice was whispering insistently, *What if you could do it again? Would you ask him or would you tell him? Would you tell him you were staying and want to be with him?*

Would you tell him that you love him?

'Are you having a party this year?'

Jonas looked up irritably. 'What?'

'I asked,' Fliss repeated equably, 'if you want to have a birthday party again this year?'

As Jonas's birthday coincided with the final weekend of the season—the start of autumn proper—he usually had a big party at the Boat House. A chance for the locals and the villagers to let their hair down and reclaim their home after months of incomers.

He couldn't imagine anything worse, but the speculation if he missed a year would be unbearable.

'I haven't really thought about it. I suppose so.'

'Oh, great!' Fliss was obviously annoyed. 'Masses of preparation for "I suppose so". What you mean is, *Thank you, Fliss, I would love to—and, yes, I will of course be leaving the grumpy expression and the grunting at home and try to enjoy myself for once in my miserable life.*'

That was a little too close for comfort. 'That's enough,' he snapped.

Fliss looked anxious. 'Honestly, Jonas, you've been the proverbial sore-headed bear for weeks. Even *I* am finding you pretty difficult, and I have a much higher Jonas tolerance than most.'

Jonas swung his chair round and stared at her. 'Oh, come on. I know I've been a bit short—'

'A *bit*?' she interjected.

'Busy—'

'A reclusive workaholic.'

'And I don't suffer fools gladly.' He shot her a look as she opened her mouth and she snapped it shut. 'There has been a lot happening, as I am sure you have noticed: new cafés, two new hotels, getting the clothes line launch ready for next year.'

'I know,' she said. 'I work here too, remember?'

'Well, then, life isn't all surfing. Sometimes it is pure, hard, exhausting work.'

'But a balance is always good. When did you last take a board out? Not since the day after Lawrie left.'

'Don't say her name!'

It was involuntary, and he cursed himself for revealing so much—for revealing everything. But Fliss didn't look shocked or horrified. She looked knowing. She looked… heck…she looked *sorry* for him. Jonas gritted his teeth.

'Just because L… Because her departure coincided with a busy period does not mean that my present mood has anything to do with her.'

Fliss looked apologetic. 'But we've been here before,' she reminded him. 'That summer she left, before the third Wave Fest, you changed. You went curt and mean and nearly drove all your staff away. You worked twenty-four-seven and a year later—*voilà*—five more cafés and a mini-chain.'

'And a career for you.'

'And a career for me,' she agreed. 'But I bloody earned it, Jonas. And I am earning it now, acting as a buffer between you and the staff, trying to keep up with your break-neck speed, going along with the vision whilst making sure that we don't over-expand—and that we don't lose all our staff while we do so.'

His voice was icy. 'I know what I'm doing.'

'Well, yes, we all know what you're doing. You're throwing yourself into work to forget about Lawrie. After all, it worked once before. Is it working now?'

Not really. His mouth twisted. 'She wanted me to ask her to stay.' The words were out before he could stop them.

Fliss didn't look surprised 'Did you?'

Jonas stared at Fliss. 'No,' he said bleakly. 'No, I told her to go.'

'Why?'

The same question he'd asked Lawrie. The question that had swept the hope out of her eyes and left her looking broken.

He shook his head, trying to clear her stricken face from his mind. 'Because it's not my decision to make. If she wanted to be with me she would. I shouldn't need to ask.'

'Jonas, I love you, and I love her too, but you—you're my best mate as well as my boss and I'm worried about you. So I am begging you, for everybody's sake, win her back or get over her once and for all.'

Win her back. The words reverberated around Jonas's head as he walked along the harbour wall back home—back to the house that no longer seemed so cosy, no longer a sanctuary. She had spent less than twelve hours there, yet memories of her permeated every corner, every shadow. Lying there at night he could remember how her body fitted against his, the sound of her breathing, the silky texture of her hair as he stroked it.

How could he win her back when she'd never been his

to start with? He had tried marrying her, binding her close to him with legal ties, but she had left anyway.

He stopped and looked into the inky black water broken up by the reflected light from the street lamps.

If you love someone set them free. What kind of crazy thinking was that? If you loved someone you should never let them go.

Or, just possibly, you could go with them.

He had never done that. Never supported her, taken the journey with her.

He circled slowly, looked at the village that was his only home, his whole life.

It felt like a prison.

Slowly he began walking again, his brain whirring, re-living the past once again. And it wasn't comfortable viewing. He had only visited Oxford a handful of times. The beach-bred boy had been uncomfortable with the city of dreaming spires, and he had flat out refused to go to London at all the first summer she had interned there.

Shame flooded through him. He had been her husband and he had let her down. Badly. What must it have been like for her alone, renting a room in a far-flung suburb, travelling for an hour every morning in her one good suit to work twelve hour days in a city where she knew no one? She must have been so lonely. And yet he had never visited, never surprised her by showing up unexpectedly at her door. What kind of husband did that make him?

It was cold, with a chill wind whistling in off the sea, but he barely felt it wrapped in his ski jacket—a jacket that had never seen snow because he rarely took time off work. He'd blamed her workaholic nature for their inability to stay together; he was just as bad. If he couldn't survive outside of Cornwall, away from the comfort of his home seas, then was he any kind of success at all?

And if he was destined always to live alone then probably not much of a success at all.

If he had taken a chance, moved to be with Lawrie all those years ago, would they still be together now? He'd always thought that would have spelled disaster, that she would have been embarrassed by her non-professional husband and he would have struggled to find work. Jonas shook his head. He had underestimated her. Even worse, he had underestimated himself.

He looked out into the darkness, listening to the eerie voice of the wind, the crash of his beloved surf against the harbour wall. The wind blew spray up and over and he flinched as the icy drops flicked his skin, tasted salt. His beloved home. He'd always thought his heart was right here. But, if so, why did he feel so empty?

He turned his back to the sea and with a heavy heart made his way back to the cottage, alone.

'Lawrie, we're heading up to the Hamptons this weekend. My wife would love you to come. We can introduce you around.'

The older man's expression was sincere and Lawrie felt a rush of gratitude as she shook her head.

'Honestly, Cooper, I am fine,' she assured him. 'I've worked through every weekend since I arrived, and I think it's time I got to know the city a little. Some other time, maybe, if you'll ask me again?'

'Any time,' he assured her. 'Have a lovely weekend.'

'I will,' she promised.

And she meant to—or to try at least. She had been here nearly a month; it was time to put down some roots. Buy an apartment of her own, get a cat—she'd never had a pet. Pets were a sign of belonging.

Then she'd get out more, make some friends, date. Okay,

dating was a slightly terrifying prospect for an English girl who might have been married once and engaged twice but had never dated—especially New York style, whereby men seemed to think nothing of chatting to you in bookstores, in coffee shops, in lifts—*elevators*: she was a New Yorker now—and asking you out. She might have been with Hugo through most of her London life, but she was fairly sure men didn't behave like that there. It was most disconcerting.

But if dating was what it took to make her a native of New York then date she would.

But not yet.

Pulling her long cream coat on and wrapping her cashmere scarf securely round her neck, Lawrie left the office. It seemed that the whole city was heading out this weekend, and at almost seven on a Friday night the building was eerily empty. The Friday before she had worked until after ten. The Friday before that the same. The evening stretching ahead of her seemed very long and very empty.

This is the city that never sleeps, she reminded herself. *I am going to have some fun.* She could shop, she thought. Go to Barneys or Saks, buy an outfit. Go for a cocktail. A small stirring of interest reared its head in her breast. Yes, shopping. How long since she had done that?

An hour later Lawrie was feeling a little bit better. A beautiful wool wrap dress and a pair of designer leather boots had helped. *Maybe clothes will be my thing,* she thought, admiring her reflection one more time. *I'm well paid, single, and living in New York. Dressing well is a duty.*

Walking through the ground floor of the store, watching the sales assistants as they got ready to close, she found her eye caught by the displays of men's accessories. Butter-soft wallets, discreet briefcases, exquisitely cut gloves.

It wasn't just the women who knew how to look stylish in this city.

And then she saw it. A beautiful cashmere scarf. Dark greys, velvety blacks and inky purples combined in a pattern that reminded her irresistibly of a winter's night in Cornwall. Lawrie came to a sudden halt and, almost against her will, reached out to caress the soft wool. The feel of it filled her with a sudden yearning for wind, waves and the tang of salt. On autopilot she picked up the scarf and took it to the desk to be gift-wrapped, managing not to gasp when the assistant asked for a truly exorbitant amount of money.

It was Jonas's birthday in just a couple of days. It would be polite to send him a gift, surely.

Lawrie stood stock still, clutching the gift box, sudden homesickness hitting her like a punch to her stomach. She needed to snap out of it. Once New York felt like home it would all be easier. A cocktail was definitely next on the list. Possibly two.

Heading out of the store, she flung her arm out as a yellow cab cruised by. 'Taxi!'

Sometimes, no matter how good the intention, it was impossible to get in the right frame of mind. She was trying. But being perched on a high stool in the plush bar, reading the cocktail menu, watching the chattering, laughing clientele, was strangely distancing—as if she were in the audience of a play. She looked like them, these young, affluent, attractive people with designer clothes and salon-dried hair, but she was apart. Not just because she was on her own, but because she knew that all this was a charade....

Take away the dress and the heels, the artfully done make-up and the professionally glossy hair, and who was she? Lawrie Bennett, daughter of a teen mum, stepdaughter, granddaughter, young bride, divorcee. All those links and yet she was completely, utterly alone. She could disappear here and now and nobody would know until the office opened again on Monday morning.

Lawrie smiled to herself with bitter humour, imagining their shock if she wasn't at her desk by seven-thirty, skinny latte in hand, freshly showered after a half-hour session in the gym.

It didn't have to be like this. She could do anything, grab a flight, go anywhere. Be impulsive. Of course the last time she was impulsive she had ended up kissing Jonas Jones, and look where *that* had got her.

Well, it had got her some pretty amazing sex. It had got her fun and laughter and time spent with a man who understood and accepted her.

Maybe being impulsive wasn't such a bad thing after all.

Looking up, she caught the bartender's eye and beckoned her over. No, she wouldn't have one of the more obvious cocktails.

'A gin gimlet, please,' she ordered. She wasn't entirely sure what a gin gimlet was, but it made her think of intrepid bohemian flappers, drinking gin on safari, quite possibly in the middle of a thrilling adventure.

When was she going to have *her* thrilling adventure?

She took a sip and grimaced, but the second sip was strangely refreshing and led quite naturally to a third. She leant back and looked round. Opposite her was another lone drinker—a woman. Perfect hair, discreetly expensive clothes, sipping a cocktail while she typed busily on her laptop. It was hard to tell but she looked ten years older than Lawrie—although this *was* New York. She probably had an excellent surgeon.

As Lawrie watched her the woman looked up from her laptop and stared out at the laughing throng. An expression of such desolation, such loneliness, such sadness swept over her face that Lawrie quickly averted her eyes, embarrassed to be looking at such unvarnished pain. When she looked back the woman looked calm again, blank, coolly professional.

That could be me, Lawrie thought. *That could be me in ten years if the dates and the cat and the making an effort don't work. If I keep doing nothing but working I could make partner, be respected, be admired—and find myself drinking alone every Friday night, watching the happiness but being apart from it. Just like I am today.*

Panic caught her chest and for one horribly long second she couldn't breathe. The rush in her ears was drowning out the chatter and the laughter; her heart was swelling and aching. Was this what she wanted? Was this what she was working towards? Dinner for one and a taxi home?

Was this *living*?

She pulled out a crumpled note and put it on the table with shaking fingers, downed the rest of the cocktail—a drink that no longer seemed reckless and fun but tart and bitter—grabbed her bags and hurried out of the bar.

She managed to flag a taxi straight away and, after giving the driver her address, sat back, staring out of the window as the city changed. Shoppers and workers were making way for the partygoers, the theatregoers, the young and the beautiful, the wealthy and the stylish. The atmosphere had subtly changed to one of excitement, anticipation. It was Friday night and the city was truly waking up.

When was *she* going to wake up?

Almost panicking, Lawrie pulled her phone from her pocket and brought up her emails. Selecting an address, she began to type, jabbing at the keys in her anxiety to get it written and sent. She had to make a decision. She had to make a change. She had just seen her future, sitting across from her, and it hadn't been a pretty sight.

The clothes, the cocktails, the success. None of it mattered if she was this empty inside.

And she *was* empty. Without Jonas she had nothing.

It had only taken her nine years to work that out.

He was just relieved it was over. Spending the first Sunday lunch with his parents for twelve years had been challenging. The fact it was his birthday hadn't made it any easier.

But it had been the right thing to do. They had even smiled a couple of times.

It was odd, but it was the first time they'd ever had a celebratory dinner with just the three of them. Before, every holiday, Easter, Christmas, birthday had been spent in the hotel dining room, publicly celebrating with the hotel guests. Their whole family life played out in a public arena.

No wonder Jonas liked to be alone. He couldn't wait to get home, to relax.

But there was a party waiting for him at the Boat House, whether he wanted it or not.

It was a beautiful autumn night, although a definite chill in the air heralded the change of seasons. A perfect night for a stroll. If he parked the car back at his house he could walk along the harbour, clear his head, think about his plans one more time.

The streets leading from the harbour were narrow, twisting, but navigating them was second nature to him. On autopilot he reversed his car into a parking space and thankfully unfolded himself from the driver's seat, taking a deep breath of the cold sea air.

He stood still for a moment, gazing down the hill at the sea, lit only by the moon and stars. It was his favourite view. It made him feel alive, grounded.

He would miss it.

For one moment he stood indecisively. Home was so close. A glass of his favourite single malt, music, a good book... But he had promised Fliss.

He took a few steps down the hill, coming to a standstill as a car swung round the bend. Automatically Jonas pressed himself against the rough stone wall. Not every driver was as careful as he. The headlights were blindingly bright, sweeping up the hill as the car drew to a stop outside his house.

Who on earth could be visiting him at this hour?

A figure got out and shut the door, standing still as the car revved up and watching it drive away. A slim, graceful figure, a bag over one shoulder, another in her hand, shoulder-length hair silhouetted against the street lamp on the corner.

His heart sped up as the figure crossed to his door. And stood there.

'Lawrie?'

Rich as Cornish cream, deep as the Cornish sea.

She jumped. 'Happy Birthday.'

'You came all this way to wish me a Happy Birthday?'

'No, actually I came to bring you a present. I left it too late to post it, so here...'

She held out the box she had kept on her knee for the six-hour flight. 'Open it.'

'Out here?'

She shrugged, her eyes drinking him in as he stood lit up by the street light.

Jonas Jones. His face grey with tiredness, his hair ruffled, but so handsome, so alive, so close that her heart nearly flooded. And he was grinning as he opened the box, the corners of his eyes creased—grinning that same wicked grin she had been banishing from her thoughts, from her dreams, over and over again.

'It's a scarf,' Lawrie said shyly.

'I can see that. You really bought it for me?'

'It reminded me of you. Do you like it?'

His heart was in his eyes, so blue, so warm, so full she couldn't meet them, looking down at the dark, uneven flagstones instead.

'I love it. Is this what we do now?'

'What do you mean?'

'Buy each other scarves?'

She looked up, startled, laughed. 'Looks like it.'

'I like traditions. I think we should have one.'

'We should?'

He nodded, his eyes fixed on hers. 'A long-standing tradition. The kind grandkids find amusing and cute.'

'Grandkids?'

'I'm in favour, are you?'

Her palms were clammy, her stomach tense. Surely he didn't mean what it sounded as if he meant?

'I've never really thought about it,' she lied. Because the alternative life she could have had with him was something she liked to torture herself with on long, sleepless nights.

'Of course to have grandkids you need to have kids,' he continued, still in that calm, conversational voice whilst his eyes burned with passion. 'Shall we have kids, Lawrie?'

'We?'

Damn it, why was she croaking?

He stepped forward, took her trembling hands in his, looked down at her, and his face was filled with so much tenderness, so much hope, so much love, that she was bathed in it, suddenly calmer, suddenly braver, suddenly ready to hear whatever it was he had to say.

'I love you, Lawrie. I have loved you since you were

sixteen and I have never stopped—not for a day, for a second. I was a fool to let you go once, but to let it happen twice…? If you will just let me I promise to spend every second of our future making it up to you.'

The lump in her throat had doubled in size and her chest tightened even more. She could hardly see his face through the tears in her eyes.

'I…'

His grip tightened. 'I'm too hands-on. I know that. I don't need to interview every damn gardener, every cook, source every piece of fabric, every spoon. I pay people to do that. Obviously I would need to travel back and forth, but I could be based anywhere, really. I could be based in New York. Or Sydney, Kuala Lumpur. I can be based wherever you are—if you want me to be, that is.'

The tears were spilling, falling down her face as her hands returned his grip. 'You'd move for me?'

'Anywhere. I should have it done nine years ago, but if it's not too late I will now. Please tell me I'm not too late.'

The crack in his voice nearly undid her. She was crying openly now, but laughter mingled with the tears, breaking out into a smile as she stepped into him, pressed herself against his glorious, solid strength.

'Okay.'

He put his hands on her shoulders, pushing her back to look into her eyes. 'Okay?'

'Okay, kids, grandkids, traditional scarves. I'm in,' she said. 'I'm in for the whole crazy ride. I love you, Jonas. I missed you too. There I was in this amazing place, doing my dream job, and I was so *empty* I couldn't bear it. When you didn't email, didn't call, I thought I'd missed my chance with you again. And I didn't know where to go. I thought I'd go crazy. I missed you so much. I had to come home.'

His smile, his kiss, his arms were tender as he pulled her in. 'You came home.' He grinned at her, boyish and unafraid. 'Seems only fair—after all, I see a lot of flying in my future.'

Lawrie raised her head, pressing close, lips trailing sweet, teasing kisses across his jaw, towards the corner of his mouth. 'It might not be necessary,' she whispered in between kisses.

His hand tightened possessively around her waist, drawing her closer, loosening her belt, undoing her coat buttons with his capable hands.

'Hmmm?' he breathed as he slid his hands inside her coat and under her cardigan, one hand sliding underneath her top to draw circles on her bare tummy.

She shivered.

She arched back to allow his mouth access to her throat, to the pulse beating so insistently, desperate for his attention. 'I spoke to my firm.'

The hands stopped, the mouth moved away, and she gave a little moan of loss. 'And...?'

Damn, he wanted to talk. Talking was very overrated. 'We talked about setting up a European office. I'd still need to travel: London a couple of times a month at least, Paris, Berlin pretty regularly. But I could be based anywhere. I could be based here.'

His face lit up, love and happiness shining out. 'You'd be based here? You're coming home?'

Home. The word sounded so good.

She looked away, suddenly shy. 'If you want me to.'

'If I want? Lawrie, without you nothing works, nothing fits. If I *want*? I don't want anything else. Are you sure?'

'All this time I thought my job defined me, was all I needed. All this time I was wrong.' She stood on her tiptoes, nestled in close, seeking his warmth, his strength.

'All I need is you. You were right. I needed to be strong enough to admit it.'

Jonas shook his head, his expression rueful. 'That day at the airport I was harsh. I'm sorry.'

'You were a little harsh,' she conceded, allowing her mouth to find the strong lines of his jaw, to travel slowly towards his throat. 'But you were right too. It was unfair of me to ask.'

He looked over to the harbour at the lights shining brightly in the Boat House. 'There's a party going on at the café,' Jonas said, dropping a kiss onto the top of her head as his arms circled her. 'Or—and I would just like to point out that this is my preferred option—we could go into the cottage, barricade the doors and not come out for a week.'

'I like the idea of barricading ourselves away,' Lawrie said, smiling up at him suggestively. 'But I was hoping we could celebrate your birthday the old way: you, me, a sleeping bag and Barb, parked up on a headland somewhere? What do you say?'

His eyes were blazing with laughter, love and a promise so intense she could barely breathe.

'You said her name! I guess that means you really are back.'

'And this time it's for good,' she promised him. 'I've come home to you.'

* * * * *

CONVENIENTLY
ENGAGED TO THE BOSS

ELLIE DARKINS

For Mike

CHAPTER ONE

'COULD YOU HELP me with this zip, or are you just going to watch?'

Instinctively Joss shut the door behind him, wondering if anyone else had seen, and glanced through the window of the office to make sure his father wasn't nearby.

'Sorry, Eva. I was looking for my dad. What are you doing in his office? And why does it involve being undressed?'

Eva shrugged—he watched her shoulder blades move under pale, exposed skin where the dress's zip was gaping at the back.

'Edward's already gone to the boardroom. Shouldn't you be there too? Never mind. Could you help? I should have been there five minutes ago, but I spilt a cup of coffee over myself and now I've got the zip stuck.'

'Okay, okay—sure,' Joss said, with a glance back at the closed door. 'My dad wanted to see me in here before the meeting, but I couldn't get away from my last call.'

He reached Eva and gently batted her hands away

from the zip, pulling the slider to the top as quickly and impersonally as he could manage.

Eva turned her head to look over her shoulder, and as his eyes met hers he felt the tug of attraction that was ever-present around his father's executive assistant.

'Um… Joss, I meant *un*zip.'

Oh, no, that was *not* what he'd signed up for. No way was he that stupid. He'd been keeping his eyes, hands and mind off this woman for years. He knew the limits of his self-control, and just this proximity to her was pushing it—never mind anything else.

'I'm not sure that's…'

'Joss, would you just do it? Shut your eyes, if you want, but get me out of this thing! It's not like I'm naked under here, in case you're worried about your delicate sensibilities.'

He took a deep breath and unzipped, but the teeth snagged halfway down her back.

'It's stuck.'

'Still? Brilliant. I was hoping it was just the angle I was pulling it. Can you unstick it?'

He wasn't sure he wanted to—not when unsticking it meant exposing more creamy skin and finding out exactly what she'd meant when she said that she wasn't naked under there.

Joss fiddled with the zip, passing the teeth slowly through the slider and unpicking the threads that had got caught. Finally it gave way and slid smoothly down Eva's back, revealing a silk slip in a soft pink colour, edged with delicate cream lace. Worse than naked, perhaps, to be so close to seeing the body that he'd dreamed of, only to find it tantalisingly out of reach.

'At last! Thank goodness for that,' Eva said, stepping quickly out of the dress and reaching for another, which Joss had just noticed draped over his father's chair. As the fabric was sliding over her head he turned for the door, but Eva stopped him. 'Wait—can you zip up this time? I don't want to be any later than I already am.'

Joss let out a sigh, but crossed the office again and reached for the slider of the zip, his fingertips very close to the rose silk at the base of her spine. He lingered for a moment as he swept her hair away with his other hand, revealing the wispy baby hairs at the nape of her neck and the invitingly soft skin behind her ear.

But before he could cover her safely, the door behind him opened.

'Eva, are you in—?'

Damn his father and his terrible timing.

'I'm sorry, Edward. I'll be right there,' Eva said, reaching for the zip herself and pulling it further down in the process of twisting round.

'No, no—I can see I'm interrupting,' Edward said. 'I trust you're both on your way.'

Joss couldn't bring himself to look, but he could almost *hear* the huge grin on his father's face, verging on a full-on laugh.

'We're waiting for you.'

His father left the room before Joss could explain that nothing had been going on between him and Eva. He shot a look at her, and saw she looked as taken aback as he did as she struggled with her dress. He pulled the zip up for her—no lingering this time—and strode for the door.

'What are we going—?' Eva started.

'I'll handle it,' Joss said.

He walked into the boardroom, still fighting images of Eva's lingerie-clad body and the look of intrigue and delight on his father's face when he'd so clearly misinterpreted what had been going on in his office.

He was more used to seeing disappointment from his father, especially when it involved him and women. Since Joss's first marriage had failed, his father had tried to hide his disappointment that he'd not been able to settle down with anyone else. He knew that when he'd first told his parents he was getting a divorce, they'd blamed the break-up on him.

And then, when he'd walked into the office as a single man, emerging from the dark clouds of clinical depression and divorce, he had realised the strength of his attraction to his father's executive assistant.

He'd told himself that he would not be going near her—under any circumstances. His father doted on her, and would not take kindly to her feelings being hurt. And after what Joss had done to his marriage—the destruction he'd been powerless to prevent—he knew that he couldn't expect to make any woman happy.

At least his father respected him professionally. He'd been working for the family's chain of luxury department stores since he was in primary school, and had earned his position as Vice President of UK Stores. But professional respect and personal pride were two very different things, and Joss knew that an abundance of one would never compensate for the lack of the other.

All eyes turned to him as he entered the full board-room, with Eva right behind him. They found a couple of spare chairs in the corner. Sunlight flooded in through the old lead-paned windows, brightening the panelled room, which could feel oppressive on a gloomier day.

Joss tried to catch his father's eye, but he was either deliberately avoiding his gaze or so entranced by the view out of the window that he couldn't bring himself to look away. The well-heeled streets of Kensington were bustling below, and Joss could tell just from the hum of the traffic that the pavement outside the store was filled with shoppers and tourists, stopping to take in the magnificent window displays for which the store was renowned.

Eventually, though, the old man cleared his throat and looked around the room, glancing at each of the board members in turn.

'I'd like to thank you all for being here,' Edward began, with a smile that Joss couldn't interpret. 'Especially at such short notice and on a Friday afternoon, when I'm sure you'd all rather be at a long working lunch. I'm afraid that, as some of you may have guessed, an emergency board meeting is rarely called to share good news, and today is no different. So, it is with regret that I have to announce that due to ill health I will be resigning from the company in all capacities with immediate effect.'

Joss felt fear and dread swell in an all too familiar

fashion in the base of his stomach as the deeper meaning of his father's words sank in. His father *must* be ill—seriously ill—to even consider leaving the business.

But Edward carried on speaking, leaving him no time to dwell.

'You all know that over the years we have taken steps to ensure a smooth transition when the time came for me to hand over the reins, and so—if you are all still in agreement—I will be leaving you in the capable hands of my son, Joss, who will become Managing Director and Chairman of the Board in my place. Eva, of course, will be assisting Joss in his new role, as I suspect she knows more about my job than I do. I know you will continue to support them, just as you have supported me. Now, I imagine there will be questions, so I'll answer them as best I can. Who's first?'

The room sank into silence as Edward finished speaking. Joss looked closely at his father. Ill-health? His father hadn't taken a day off sick in his life, and yet now he was resigning completely? Yes, they'd talked about succession plans. Any sensible businessman had contingencies for all eventualities, and Edward would not have wanted to leave the company in chaos if anything had happened to him. But had there actually been more to it than that? Had his father known that he would soon be stepping down?

The dread in Joss's stomach twisted into stark fear as the implications of the announcement sank in and he realised what this must mean. His father wouldn't resign because of a dodgy hip or 'a touch of angina', as he'd once described a health scare. He'd always sworn he'd be carried out of a Dawson's department store in his coffin. For him to resign must mean he had had some terrible news.

Panic and grief gripped his throat as he noticed for the first time the slight grey tinge to his father's skin, and the lines around his eyes that suggested a habitual wince of fatigue. Why hadn't he noticed before? Why hadn't he been looking? His father wasn't exactly a spring chicken, and he was still working sixteen-hour days long past the age when most people would expect to retire.

He should have made his father take things easier—should have taken more off his plate.

He met his father's eye and saw sympathy and understanding in his father's gaze. He wanted to rush to embrace him, but something froze him to his chair, chilling his blood.

And then warmth crept from the tips of his fingers as a hand slid into his and he heard Eva's voice.

'Edward, are you in pain? What can we do to help?'

Joss's eyes swam and he clenched his jaw, determined not to allow a single tear to fall, to keep control over his emotions. Besides, swiping a falling tear before anyone saw would mean taking his hand from Eva's, and at that moment he couldn't see how he was meant to do that.

'Perhaps we should speak in my office?' Edward said to Joss, his voice gentle. 'And you lot—' he addressed the remaining members of the board 'you have a good gossip while I'm gone and think of what you need to ask me. Head back to the pub and finish your lunch, if you want to. But get your questions to me sharpish, because I'm planning on being on a sun lounger by the end of next week.'

Edward rose and Joss noticed, as he hadn't before, that his father leaned heavily on the table for support.

Joss snapped out of his trance and back into business mode as they walked down the corridor and back to Edward's office, firing questions all the way.

'Dad? What's happening? Are you okay? Was this what you wanted to talk to me about?'

Edward collapsed into the chair behind his desk and rested back against the padded seat. 'Yes. I'm sorry, son. Of course I wanted to tell you first, but you didn't arrive for our meeting—'

'Dad, if I'd known—'

'I know.' He softened the words with a smile. 'I know. But it was difficult for Eva to get everyone here at such short notice. I couldn't delay it any longer.'

'Couldn't delay? What's wrong with you, Dad?'

'Sit down, son.' His father indicated the chair opposite. 'And you, Eva. You both need to hear this. It's cancer, I'm afraid, and there's nothing they can do about it. I ignored it for a bit too long, it seems. So I thought it was about time I took that holiday I've been promising myself for the last thirty years and let you get on with running the business while I'm still around to answer your questions—there's no deadline for you two, of course.'

Joss stared at his father, unable to take in his words. His hand found Eva's again and he gripped it hard, taking strength from the solid presence of her, the warmth that always radiated from her.

'How long, Dad?'

'Oh, you know doctors. Never give you a straight answer. A few months, it seems. Long enough to have a little fun before I go. I love this business—you know that I do—but news like this makes you rethink, and I don't want these four walls to be the last thing I see before I go.'

'I'm so sorry, Edward.'

Joss could hear the tears in Eva's voice, and he squeezed her hand. He knew how fond she was of his father, and that her grief must mirror his own. 'Are you sure you're comfortable? Is there anything we can do?'

'Quite comfortable for now, my dear. Thank you for your concern. Now it's my turn to ask the questions.' He glanced at their clasped hands. 'Is there anything you two would like to tell me?'

Eva sat in shock, silenced by Edward's words. She couldn't believe that the old man was dying. Sure, he'd looked a little creaky around the joints lately, but he'd never complained of so much as a runny nose. It just didn't make sense that he could be terminally ill.

Joss had taken hold of her hand and she could feel the contact burning her skin. She hadn't thought about it when she'd slid her fingers between his back in the boardroom. Hadn't thought about all the times she'd imagined the slide of his skin against hers over the years. All she'd been able to feel was the grief and fear radiating from him, and she had acted on instinct, trying to ease it in any way she could.

And now Edward was calling them on it. Under normal circumstances she'd have cleared up the understanding with Edward the minute it had happened. But this was Joss's father, and they had both just been hit with shocking news. It was Joss's place, not hers, to explain.

'I'm sorry you saw that, Dad—' he started.

'Oh, don't be sorry—I'm delighted. I *do* remember what it was like to be young, believe it or not. I'm just pleased that you two have finally found each other. I can't deny that I've been waiting for this for some time. I take it that if you're bringing your personal life with you to work then it's serious?'

Eva felt her mouth fall open and waited for Joss to correct his father, to sum up what had happened with the dress and the coffee and the zip. But expressions chased across Joss's face faster than she could read them.

She was just about to jump in and explain for herself what had happened when Joss finally spoke.

'Yes, it's serious,' Joss said. 'In fact, we're engaged.'

She was about to call him on being completely ridiculous when she clocked the look on Edward's face. A smile had brought a glow to his face, and he was beaming at them both. Just a moment she was so shocked she couldn't speak. And then real life kicked in, and she remembered the news that Edward had just delivered, that Joss had just received. She found that she couldn't contradict him.

Still, she gently withdrew her hand. She had to maintain some semblance of control if she was going to keep
her head.

She'd been trying to pretend to herself for years that
she didn't have an enormous crush on this man. That he
didn't enter her mind when she was out on a date with
any other guy. And now he had to go and pretend to be
in love with her. And the only result of calling him on it
would be to hurt the man she'd come to care for almost
as a parent. She couldn't do it to him. She'd have to talk
to Joss in private. He could break it to his father gently.

Funny how being angry with him made him that little bit less fanciable—she'd been looking for something
to knock the shine off him for years.

It wasn't as if she *wanted* to be attracted to him—
she told herself that often enough. She couldn't think
of anyone less suitable for falling in love with than the
son of her boss, who spent half his time on the road
visiting the UK stores, and the other half in his office,
buried in spreadsheets and dodging calls from disappointed would-be dates.

Secretaries talked—hardly breaking news.

As soon as she'd recognised where her feelings were
going—the irritating pitter-patter of her heart, the annoying dampness of her palms, not to mention the completely inappropriate but delicious dreams that had her
waking flushed and impressed by the breadth of her
own imagination—she'd acted.

She'd put space between them at the office, avoided
him in the break room and at the pub. She'd thrown
herself into dating in a way that was the opposite of

Joss's clinical style: enthusiastically, prolifically, discriminately. She'd found handsome, eligible bachelors who weren't intimidated by her salary or her seven fluent languages—or the handful of conversational ones. She'd dated in Russian, Greek and German, and once— haltingly, but memorably—in Mandarin. She'd gone dancing, cocktail-making, picnicking. Tried blue blood and blue collar.

And not a single one of the men she'd kissed so demurely on the cheek at the end of the night had helped her even start forgetting about Joss. He was beginning to appear annoyingly unforgettable, and now he was pulling her into a deceit that she knew, unhesitatingly, was a BAD IDEA. All caps.

'Well, like I said, I can't say that I'm surprised. I've suspected for a while that you two have a soft spot for each other,' Edward said at last, still smiling.

Eva groaned inwardly. Oh, no, how much of her stupid crush had he seen? How much was he going to figure out? How much was *Joss* going to figure out for himself?

'And it makes me a very happy man to see you settled and in love before I go.'

The three of them sank into silence as the meaning of his words hit home and the reality of his illness intruded once again on the completely insane situation Joss had just created.

'But now I've got work to do—so get out of here, the pair of you.'

Eva kissed Edward on the cheek and mumbled something indiscernible, then let Joss follow her from the room, past the open-plan desks and into Joss's office.

'What the *hell* was that?' she demanded as soon as they were alone, staring at Joss as he sank into his chair and rested his face in his hands.

'Not now, Eva.'

'Not *now*? You just told your father we're engaged— I think I'm entitled to an explanation.'

'He's just told me he's dying. I can't talk about this now.'

She dropped into a chair opposite him, feeling sick to her stomach. Joss was right—he'd just had terrible news. Much as she had every right to give him hell, perhaps now wasn't the time.

'You didn't know anything about it?' she asked gently.

'He didn't say *anything*. Just that he needed to speak to me before the meeting. But I was tied up on a call and I… I missed the meeting. He wanted to tell me.'

'You couldn't have known he was going to tell you that.' She crossed to stand beside him and rested a hand on his shoulder. 'It wouldn't have changed anything. The news would have been the same.'

'It would have felt different if he'd been able to talk to me before having to tell everyone else.'

'You're right. I'm sorry.'

He leaned his head against her arm and she let her hand brush against his hair.

'And I'm sorry for what I told him about us.'

Eva moved her hand away, aware of a sudden change

of the chemistry in the room. She hitched herself onto the corner of the desk, letting her stilettoed feet dangle.

'What was that about? The truth would have been a much simpler explanation. It's going to be a hundred times harder to explain things now. Engaged or not, who knows what he thinks we were up to in his office?'

'I was thinking on my feet. I didn't want him to think that you were involved in something sordid, and my brain went to "engaged" rather than "wardrobe malfunction". You saw his face when I told him that we were getting married. I knew that it would make him happy.'

'Marrying me?'

'Being happy…settled. It's all he wants for me. And since my divorce… You don't want to hear all that. Just trust me on this one. I know my father. I knew it would make him happy.'

'So what's it going to do to him when you tell him there's no engagement?'

And suddenly, from the defiant clench of his jaw and the killer look in his eyes, Eva knew that he wasn't planning on telling his father the truth at all.

'Don't be ridiculous,' she said, keeping her voice low and commanding. 'We have to tell him the truth. I'll tell him about the coffee and the dress. I'll sort this out.'

Joss shrugged, never breaking eye contact, never backing down from the challenge she'd made so clear in her voice.

'We'll explain about the dress. But I see no reason to drop the pretence of our engagement.'

She stood slowly from the desk and took a step towards him, letting him know that she found neither his position in the company nor the six inches in height he had over her intimidating in the slightest. Least of all when he was seated and she could tower over him.

'No reason, Joss? You just panicked and told a bare-faced lie that has implications for us both. I have no intention of lying to your father, so unless you want him to hear from me that you just fabricated a fiancée, I think you would do better to just tell him now.'

'Or we could make him believe that it's true.'

She took half a step back to stare at Joss. 'Have you completely lost your mind? Why would we want to do that?'

'Maybe I have lost my mind. It wouldn't be the first time. I don't know... What I *do* know is that my father has just told me that he's dying, and I—we—can do something to make him happy in the time he has left.'

'By lying to him? Do you think he'd really want that?'

'You saw his face. You tell me if you think the lie hurt him.'

She shrugged, unable to contradict him. 'I know he seemed happy, Joss. But it can't be right. I mean, how long would we have to keep this up?'

She sat down again, losing a little of her anger as she realised what she was asking.

'I'm sorry. I didn't mean...'

'I know. I know you didn't mean anything by it. But, yeah, we would have to keep it up until he dies. Which, apparently, won't be all that long. Don't worry—I don't expect you to actually say *I do*.'

She sat and thought on it for a moment. Remembered the look on Edward's face when Joss had told his lie. She couldn't deny that he'd looked happy. As happy as she'd seen him for a long time.

She loved Edward. He had been the one constant in her life for so long now, and she wasn't sure how she was going to manage without him. A sob threatened, and her hand lifted slowly to her throat as she forced it down. She slumped into the back of the chair, suddenly deflated. Surely if it made Edward happy she could do this. She *should* do this.

'I need some time to think about it,' she said eventually, not wanting Joss to know the direction her thoughts had been heading.

Goodness knew she'd been trying to keep the details of her mind secret from him for long enough. If they were to go through with this completely ridiculous idea, how was she meant to keep that up? To hide the fact that her mouth wanted to part every time she saw him? That she had to stop her tongue moistening her lips and her body swaying towards him?

'Take some time, then. No work's going to get done this afternoon anyway, by the looks of it.'

Eva shook her head. 'Your father will need me.'

'I'm going to my father's office now, and we're going to have a long talk. I'll make sure there's not a problem. If you want, I can say you went home with a headache.'

'While he's still at work with a terminal illness? Thanks but no thanks. Lock yourself in with your father if you want, but I'll be at my desk if either of you need me.'

Joss leaned back in his chair, raising his hands to admit defeat. 'We need to talk, though. And we can't do that in the office. Dinner tonight?'

Dinner tonight.

How many times had she imagined Joss issuing an invitation like that? Though she'd always known that she wouldn't accept. It wasn't even the time that he spent travelling around the country that made her think he was a million miles from boyfriend material. No, it was the fact that even when he was here he wasn't quite...*here.* There was an isolation about him. A distance. Even when he was close enough to touch.

She'd done long-distance before, with people in her life that she'd loved, and she'd hated every second of it. The last thing she needed was a man—a fiancé—who was distant even when he was in the room.

But she couldn't ignore him while he was going around telling people that they had got engaged. She had to convince him to tell his father the truth. And then figure out how they were meant to work together.

'Yes,' she agreed eventually. 'I guess we do need to talk about this. My place? I don't feel like going out after news like this. I don't suppose you do either.'

'No. That sounds good. Eight?'

She nodded, and scribbled down her address.

Walking back to her desk, she grabbed the coffee-stained dress and put it in the garment bag that she'd flung over her chair as she'd raced for the boardroom.

The blinds in Edward's office were drawn—a sure sign that he didn't want to be disturbed—so she sat at her computer, knowing that her work—the one constant she had in her life—was going to change irrevocably, and there was nothing she could do about it.

CHAPTER TWO

Eva checked on the food and resisted glancing at her reflection in the window. She didn't want Joss to think that she'd made an effort, so she'd not touched her hair or her make-up since she'd got home, and had just thrown on jeans and a comfy jumper. She always wore her skinnies and a cashmere sweater for a Friday night in—that was perfectly plausible.

She didn't even want to think about how the conversation over dinner was going to go, but she had to. Had to be prepared—set out in her own mind, at least, what was and wasn't going to be on the cards.

Joss was crazy, thinking that they could get away with a fake engagement. They'd be under scrutiny every minute they were together at the office. She knew how little fuel the gossip furnace needed to keep it alight. But every time she convinced herself of how terrible an idea it was, she remembered the happiness on Edward's face and the eagerness to please his father on Joss's.

She had to admit to being intrigued.

Joss was a powerful man. A director—now the MD—of a vast luxury group of department stores, with a presence on every continent, property in every major European shopping capital. He was notorious for the coldness of his personal life—the wife and the marriage that he'd neglected, and the transactional nature of the dates he took to industry functions. The women he dated were always clients and colleagues, there to further a business deal or a conversation, and they always went home alone.

She'd always seen something else in him. Something more. Something in the way that he joked with his father in a way he didn't with anyone else. Being so close to Edward, she'd seen their father-son relationship up close. Seen that Joss might not be the cold-hearted divorcee that everyone had him pegged as.

And now he'd invented an engagement just to please his dying father, and her curiosity was piqued again.

The two men didn't have much time left together—and they both seemed happier with this alternative reality than with real life. Who was she to judge? Who was she to tell them they were wrong? If she hadn't been personally involved she'd be telling them to do whatever they had to do in order to enjoy the time they had left together. But to say that she was 'involved' was putting things mildly—and this was *way* personal. She'd be as responsible as Joss if the truth came out and Edward's heart was broken in his last few weeks or months.

And maybe all of this was academic. Because it assumed that they stood a chance of getting away with this charade. Making everyone believe that they were in love. Well, it wouldn't be too hard to convince on her side, she supposed, given the attraction that she'd been hiding for years.

Through the break-up of his marriage—that time of dark black circles under his eyes and an almost permanent blank expression on his face—she was the only one who had seen him lean back against his father's office door after he'd left a meeting, composing his features and erasing all emotion before he went and faced the rest of the office. And in the time since, he'd been working non-stop—not competing with his colleagues but seemingly competing with himself.

It was hard to pinpoint when she had realised she had a heck of a crush growing. Perhaps after the dip in her stomach when she'd won a hard-earned smile, or when they'd argued in the boardroom and he'd held up his hands in concession to her point, never mind that he was a director and she an assistant.

Or when he'd walked in on her today, half-dressed in his father's office, and her whole skin had hummed in awareness of him. She'd had to hide the blush that had crept over her cheeks when his fingertips had clasped the zip and pulled it down—something she'd fantasised about more times than she wanted to admit, even to herself.

But nothing that she had done so far had worked in trying to get herself to forget him.

Perhaps it was time to do something different. She had proved that ignoring this thing wasn't going to make it go away. Maybe getting closer to him was the key. It was easy to maintain a crush, a fantasy, from afar. When you didn't have to deal with wet towels on your bed or dirty dishes left on the table. Maybe what she needed was some old-fashioned exposure therapy.

Because what did she really know about Joss, beyond what she saw when he was occasionally in the office? If there was one sure way to test a romance it was for a couple to move in together.

Was she completely losing her mind thinking that this was even a feasible idea—never mind a good one?

The doorbell rang, shocking her out of her internal debate. Good, she was getting sick of the sound of her own thoughts. At least with Joss here she would have a sparring partner.

She jogged down the stairs to the street-level door, trying to ignore the familiar flip of her heart at the sight of him. Not that he was looking his best—he had clearly come straight from the office. His shirt was creased, his collar unfastened and his tie loosened.

And then she remembered again how his day had been a thousand times worse than hers and had to resist the urge to pull him close and comfort him.

'Hey—you found it okay?'

'Yeah.' He waved his phone vaguely at her. 'Just a little help from this. I've not been here since I was a kid.'

'Of course—your dad used to stay here back then. I'd forgotten you must have been here too.'

She stepped back so that he could get through the door. From her little cobbled mews she could barely hear the traffic from the main road nearby, muffled by the square of white stucco pillared houses around the private, locked garden. She showed Joss upstairs to her apartment—a legacy of the time when the building would have had stables downstairs and living quarters for servants of the wealthy above, all tucked away behind the grand mansions on the square.

Eva loved the understated elegance of her home, with clipped bay trees at the door, original cobbles paving the passage and soft heritage colours on the doors and windows.

'It's beautiful,' Joss said as he reached the top of the stairs and crossed to the living room, where great tall windows flooded light in one side of the room. 'Have you been living here long?'

'Since I started at Dawson's.'

Joss looked intrigued. 'I thought my dad had got rid of this place.'

'He had—sort of,' Eva said, reaching for a bottle of wine and raising a glass in question at Joss.

He nodded and reached to take it from her when it was full.

'He realised it was mostly sitting empty while it was a company flat, so he decided to rent it out. When I started working for the company I was stuck for somewhere to stay. Your dad didn't have a tenant at the time, and needed someone to house-sit, so he offered me this place.'

Joss raised his eyebrows. 'Lucky you.'

'Yeah, I don't like to move a lot, and he offered me a long-term lease. I like it here.'

'So I'm going to have a hard time convincing you to move in with me?'

Eva snorted, and winced at the sting of wine in her nose.

'That part's non-negotiable,' she confirmed. 'This is my home and I'm not leaving it.'

'So you're coming round to the rest of it? Good.'

She should have given him an outright no—told him there and then that there was absolutely no way she was going along with his ridiculous scheme. But somehow, with him here in her home, in her space, she wasn't sure she wanted to. All of a sudden she wasn't sure about anything.

That was what happened when the only stable part of your life upped and threatened to leave. It had sunk in on her short walk home from the office that she could be about to lose her job—the first point of stability she'd ever had in her life. The safe place that she'd built for herself in the twelve years that she'd been with the company.

She would have thought she'd have been used to it by now. She'd had her whole childhood to practise, after all. Every time her mother or her father had shipped out, or they'd all packed up and moved to another army base, she'd told herself it was the last time she'd care. The last time she'd cry.

She'd not managed to stick to her word until the final time. The time her mother hadn't come home at all.

Her father had packed her off to boarding school then, not long after she'd begged him to leave the army, to stop moving her around and give her some stability. She'd taken herself straight off to university after school, and from there straight into business, landing in Edward's team and working her way up to be his executive assistant.

Her parents had never managed to give her the stability she'd craved, so she'd found her own—with Dawson's. It was a family business, its history stretching into the last century and the one before that. The company had been around long before Edward, and she had no doubt that it would continue without him.

But how was it ever going to feel the same after he was gone? And what else was going to change?

The succession plans that had been approved by the board had appointed her as Joss's new EA—she was tied to the job role, not to the holder—but once his father was gone Joss had no reason to stick with that decision. She could be out through the door as soon as Edward was dead.

An engagement to the heir apparent—even a fake one—was another tie to the company. To the family. Another bond to the life that she'd built for herself. An obstacle between her and everything falling away. Was that completely crazy? Maybe. But that didn't mean she didn't feel it.

'Here.' She passed Joss a bowl of potatoes and a salad. 'Can you stick these on the table? The chicken will be just another minute.'

He took the bowls from her and glanced at the pan on the hob.

'That looks amazing. You shouldn't have gone to so much trouble, though. We could have ordered something.'

She shrugged. 'It was no trouble. I'd have been cooking for myself anyway.'

'You cook like this every night?'

She narrowed her eyes as she tried to work out his angle. 'Are you asking if that's part of the deal?'

'I'm making conversation. At least, I'm trying to.'

'I'm sorry.' She shook her head as she grabbed a couple of plates and started serving up. 'Everything just feels so…weird. I can't get my head around it.'

'It doesn't need to be weird.'

'Joss, this afternoon you asked me to pretend to be your fiancée. Now you're asking me to move in with you. How can it be anything *but* weird?'

'Because it's not real, Eva.'

She brandished a set of tongs at him. 'That makes it worse! How can faking something like that not feel weird to you? Lying to your father won't feel weird?'

He held his hands up and shrugged, though his expression belied his casual attitude. 'Do you tell your parents everything that's going on with you?'

'There's just my dad. We're not close. But I've never invented a fiancé.'

Before now, she added in her head. Because this conversation seemed to be gathering momentum, and she wasn't sure she was going to put a stop to it. She hadn't come out and told Edward that it wasn't true yet, so at the very least she was complicit in the lie getting this far.

It was only when Joss had mentioned it that she'd even thought about the fact that she might have to tell her dad. How was it that she'd put more emotional energy into worrying that she was lying to Edward than into the fact that she would also have to lie to her own father? She'd not even considered that going through with this would affect him too.

Maybe it didn't have to. Maybe she could keep the whole thing from him—it wasn't as if they spoke often. Or at all, really.

'You're quiet,' Joss commented as they sat down to eat at the dining table tucked into the corner of the living room.

'Thinking,' she replied, helping herself to salad and potatoes.

'Enlighten me,' Joss instructed, equally economical with his words.

Eva sighed, but he was here to talk and they weren't going to get anywhere if neither of them opened up. And, if what she'd seen of Joss over the years was anything to go by, she would be waiting a long time for an emotional outpouring from his end.

'I'm not sure that this is a good idea.' A good start, she thought. Get her cards on the table. 'We're lying to your father. It's likely we'll be found out. It's a distraction when we should be concentrating on what he needs.'

Joss raised an eyebrow.

'What?' Eva asked.

'We're doing it *for* my father. You saw how happy it's making him.'

Joss had said that they needed to talk, but it was only now she realised that he thought he was here to sort out details—not to convince her. He was assuming that she would just go along with it. He'd taken her decision not to tell Edward the truth from the start as approval, and he was here to iron out the fine print.

'You really think I'm going to go along with this?'

Joss looked up and held her gaze for a beat longer than was comfortable.

'I think you already are.'

A shiver ran through her at the tone of his voice. So commanding. So sure of himself. So arrogant. She'd had no idea before this moment that that did something for her, but the heat between her legs and the tightness in her belly told her it definitely did.

'If you were going to back out,' he continued, 'you would have done it back at the office. Or just told my father the truth on the spot. Why are we bothering to dance around this when we both know you've made up your mind?'

She fixed him with a stare and muttered an Arabic curse under her breath, trying not to show him how right she knew he was. Because she *could* have called a halt to this hours ago. The fact that she hadn't told them both all they needed to know.

'I'm doing it to make your father happy,' she clarified, still holding that gaze, making sure Joss could see that she wasn't backing down or giving in to him. She was making her own decisions for her own very good reasons.

'I know.' He nodded, taking a sip of his wine, breaking their eye contact and cutting into his chicken.

'I mean it,' he said, after he'd polished off half the plate. 'I could get used to this.'

'Good,' she said, standing up and picking up her

plate, suddenly losing her appetite. 'You can get used to doing the washing up as well.'

Joss finished his food and followed her through to the little kitchen. 'You think you're going to scare me away with threats of stacking the dishwasher?'

She gestured around the bijou kitchen. 'You see a dishwasher in here?'

He glanced around. 'Fine. So we'll get someone in. I'll pay,' he added when she started to shake her head.

'It's not about the money.'

'What? It's about me being willing to get my hands wet? Fine. But I'm not a martyr, Eva. If you're hoping to scare me then I might as well tell you now that it's not going to work.'

'You don't want to move in here. There's no space.'

He leaned back against the kitchen counter, a hand either side of his hips. His man-spreading made his intentions clear. It would have been more subtle if he'd marked the doorframe with his scent.

'I decide for myself what I do and don't want, Eva. This is where you live, so it's where I'll live too. You've stated your ground rules; now I'm stating mine.'

She folded her arms and leant back against the kitchen counter. 'There's not even any space in the wardrobe.'

'You can't expect us to live apart.'

'We're going to see each other all the time at work. Isn't moving in together a bit much?'

He took a step towards her, and Eva had to admit that his height *was* a little intimidating in the tiny kitchen.

'And how many people are going to believe our story if we're not living together?'

'We could tell people we're waiting until after the wedding.'

He shook his head and, much as she hated it, Eva knew he was right.

'They'd ask us which century we're living in. Perhaps if this was a real relationship we'd say to hell with what they think. But we need to make them believe us. I don't want to give them any reason not to. I'll start moving some stuff in on Monday.'

He moved to leave, and somehow, although it was what her rational brain wanted, it seemed her body wasn't expecting it. Disappointment washed through her. It wasn't as if she wasn't used to living alone. She loved having her own space. But they'd been through a lot today, and she wasn't particularly keen on being left alone with her thoughts.

'Do you want a coffee before you go?' she asked, flicking on the kettle behind her.

'Sure,' Joss said, watching her carefully. 'Something wrong?'

'No,' she replied, rubbing her forehead and realising she wasn't being very convincing. 'Just a lot to take in. Weird day.'

'Tell me about it,' Joss said, leaning back on the counter.

Eva looked up and realised that it wasn't a figure of speech.

'No, no—it's fine,' she said.

'I can listen. Even help.'

'I can't, Joss. He's your dad. You don't want to... It should be me asking if you're okay.'

'I don't get an exclusive on it, Eva. I know you care for him too.'

'I just can't believe I didn't know...you know.'

She made two coffees and carried them back through to the living room. Plonking them on the coffee table, she just had time to wish she had space for a bigger sofa before Joss appeared behind her.

'Do you sit and spy on your neighbours?' Joss asked, pointing out the way the sofa was angled towards the big picture window out onto the mews.

'More like bask in the sun. I get enough gossip at work.'

He looked surprised.

'What? Don't tell me you hadn't noticed.'

He shook his head. 'What do people gossip about?'

'Oh, you know—the usual. Who's sleeping with who. Who's angling for a promotion. Who's getting fired.'

'So why don't I hear any of this?'

Eva rolled her eyes. With all his expensive business education, did he seriously not understand how an office worked? She was clearly going to have to spell this out to him.

'Of course you don't hear the gossip,' she said. 'One, you're practically the boss. No one gossips in front of the boss. Two, you're hardly ever in the office. And three, you're not exactly Mr Friendly over the coffee machine when you *are* there.'

'People don't think I'm friendly?'

'*I* don't think you're friendly. I can't speak for anyone else.'

He folded his arms and fixed her with a stern look. She was tempted to laugh.

'What's so unfriendly about me?'

Should she go for it? Unload all his faults? All the reasons she'd been telling herself for years why he was a million miles from boyfriend material.

Why not? Perhaps it would be the final straw in this idiotic deception.

'Fine—if you want to hear it. You're not exactly an open book, are you, Joss? You don't talk to people unless it's directly about the business.'

'I don't do small talk. There's a difference.'

'Right: the difference between being friendly and not friendly. It's not a criticism. Just an observation.'

'You think I should be friendlier?'

She sighed and shook her head. Seriously, this man's emotional intelligence didn't even register on the scale. 'I didn't say that. I don't think you need to change. But just don't be surprised if people don't open up around you.'

'Well, *you* don't seem to be having a problem with that.'

She shrugged and gave a resigned laugh. 'Proposing to a girl will have that effect. If you didn't want to know, you shouldn't have asked.'

'Might as well know what people think of me. So— office gossip. Is there going to be a lot of it. About us?'

'Are you kidding?' She laughed properly, genuinely

amused for the first time all day. 'I'm going to be grilled like a fish about this on Monday morning.'

'You could just not go in,' Joss offered. 'Take a few days off. Benefits of dating the boss.'

The smile dropped from her face as the insult hit. As if she could just not show up for work, with no notice, and it wouldn't make a difference to anyone.

'I think we need to get a couple of things straight, Joss. One—I work very hard with your father. My job is important, and I can't just swan off because you say so. Unless you fancy handling his correspondence in Arabic, Italian and French on Monday morning, I'll be at my desk as usual. Two—we are not now, nor will we ever be "dating". If I'd wanted to date you, I'd have asked you out for dinner. I'm going along with your little charade because I care about your father. Don't confuse the two.'

'Would you?' He leaned into the arm of the sofa with a smile that was verging dangerously on smug.

'Would I what?'

'Have asked me out for dinner?'

She sighed. Bloody man. 'The key part of that sentence, Joss, was *if*. I've never asked you because I don't want to date you.'

'You know, you sound like you've given that quite a lot of thought. Should I be flattered?'

'Honestly. Only a man with your ego could find a way to take that as a compliment. Listen to me carefully, Joss. I don't want to date you. I don't want to be engaged to you. I'm going along with it for now. But when the time comes we'll both extract ourselves from this situation with as much dignity as we can muster and forget it ever happened.'

CHAPTER THREE

Eva SPENT THE weekend in a daze. The further she got from having seen Joss the more ridiculous the whole thing seemed. So when she pitched up at her desk at eight o'clock on Monday morning she was almost surprised to see him there waiting for her.

'You're in early,' she commented, unwinding her scarf from around her neck and draping it over the coat-stand. 'Trying to impress somebody?'

'I told you—my father wants to start handing things over today. I thought we'd need an early start.'

'Well, we've both beaten the boss in.' She glanced through the blinds to Edward's darkened office beyond. 'Did you see him at the weekend? How is he?'

'*He* is marvellous, Eva, dear,' Edward said, bowling up behind her. 'Thank you for asking. And I was out of the city this weekend, so I've not seen anyone since I left the office on Friday. How about you two? I hope you did something nice with your weekend and didn't spend it worrying about me.'

'Dinner on Friday night,' Joss supplied truthfully.

'And Borough Market on Saturday,' Eva added.

No need to mention that she'd gone alone. She disliked the taste of the half-lie in her mouth, but the smile on Edward's face softened the blow.

'And arriving together on Monday morning. Were you this indiscreet before or am I really getting old?'

'Actually,' Joss said, 'we thought that now everyone will be finding out our news there's no reason we can't arrive together. In fact, I'll be moving my things over to Eva's place tonight.'

'Well, that's marvellous. Wish it had all worked like that when your mother and I were that age. Now, I'm glad I've found you two alone—I've been thinking, and there's something I want to say to you. I don't know what your plans are, but I don't want you to rush them for me. I know my news has been upsetting, but I don't want you hurrying anything up for my sake. Please?'

It was perfect, in a way, Eva realised. They wouldn't have to find an excuse not to marry before he died.

'But enough about that. I need the two of you in Milan as soon as you can get there. The store manager's feeling jumpy, and we have a couple of major suppliers over there as well who would probably appreciate a visit. I need you to smooth things over. Let people see that you're more than ready for the big job.'

Joss's eyebrows drew together, and she knew he wasn't happy at the implication that his employees didn't trust him.

'Dad, I met Matteo at the conference earlier in the year and it was all fine. The managers all know me. Surely you want me here? I'm not sure now's the time for me to be travelling.'

'Now's the perfect time, son. We need to steady things. You're going to have to visit all the flagship stores. The big suppliers too. They're worried—it's been a long time since this company faced big changes. This is part of your job now.'

'But what if something happens here?'

Eva winced. She knew exactly what Joss meant.

'What if I pop my clogs, you're asking? It's not going to happen overnight, son. We have some time. And I'd like to see the old girl looking straight before I go. I promise if anything changes you'll be the first to know. If it helps you make your mind up, I'm not planning on hanging around London waiting to die. Some places I want to see before I go. But you two need to be on a plane before lunchtime, and I've got an inbox the size of Milan Cathedral to work through with Eva before you go.

Joss walked away, leaving Eva and his father huddled around his computer monitor. Eva was making notes on a pad and occasionally reaching across to touch the screen. It was clear to him how fond she was of his father, and how distressed at the news of his illness.

And now he'd told them that he didn't want a hasty wedding. Yes, it got them out of having to take this charade too far, but Joss saw something else in it.

How much did his father know about his last marriage? About how he had felt rushed, unable to stop the oncoming commitment even after he'd realised it was a bad idea? More than he had let on at the time, it seemed.

He'd been rash and stupid announcing their non-existent engagement to Edward, and he supposed that he should be grateful that Eva had agreed to go along with it.

She'd told him that it was because she cared for the old man, and Joss didn't doubt that. But that didn't mean he believed she'd given him the whole story. There were things that she was hiding. Layers of secrets, he suspected, from the frequently veiled expressions that crossed her face. Well, he was going to find out what they were—they had hours of travelling ahead of them, and she couldn't dodge his questions the whole way to Italy.

Or maybe he'd sleep instead of quizzing her, because that definitely hadn't been happening enough since his father had dropped his bombshell. He'd have liked to say it was grief over his father's illness that was causing his insomnia, but he knew that it was something else.

It was sleek chestnut hair and hazel eyes. The memory of a rose-pink slip under a serious navy dress. It was the thought of his holdall of clothes stashed in his office, destined for her flat just as soon as they got back from their trip. The thought of living in such close quarters with a woman he'd determinedly avoided since he'd noticed his attraction to her.

Back in his office, he dug out his toothbrush and a change of clothes from the holdall. If they weren't on a plane until lunchtime, he knew that they'd need to stay over. With his dad sending him off in such a hurry, he guessed it wasn't going to be a short meeting at the other end.

A noise caught his attention and he looked up to see

Eva, stalled at the entrance of his office. He felt that familiar pull, the heat in his body he knew was inevitable when he was near her. Again he silently cursed whatever impulse it was that had made him lie to his father.

He felt a twist of pain in his belly. He knew how dangerous secrets could be—keeping his feelings bottled up had turned toxic before, and lying to his father felt unnatural now.

Intellectually, he understood the reasons he'd done it. Because he'd let his father down so many times over the years. He'd married his university girlfriend, a friend of the family, because she was 'the right sort of girl' from 'the right sort of family', and everyone had expected it to happen. He'd done what he'd thought was the right thing—stood up in front of their friends and their family and made the commitment that was expected from him, no matter how wrong it had felt inside.

As his depression had grown and his marriage had darkened, he'd ignored the problems. Blinkered himself against his wife's pain and buried himself in his work rather than go back on his word and end a marriage that was never going to make either of them happy. Until she'd upped and left, and he'd seen the disappointment in his parents' eyes that he had failed. Failed his wife. Failed both their families.

It had only been after the breakdown of his marriage that he'd realised he needed help. He'd gone weeks with barely a couple of hours' sleep a night. Seen his weight drop and his appetite disappear. It had only been when he'd looked up his symptoms on the internet that he'd realised they were classic signs of depression.

As soon as he'd read that, everything had fallen into place—that was the dark tunnel that he'd found himself in as his personal life had hurtled towards marriage while he'd buried his head in the sand, concentrating on the business.

So he'd gone to his doctor, worked hard at therapy. Eaten and exercised well. Taken the meds he'd been prescribed. And he'd recovered from his illness with a clarity and a focus that he'd not felt in years.

He shouldn't have been in that relationship to start with. He should have called it off as soon as he'd had doubts—before his illness had blinkered his vision and left him feeling that he didn't have a way out.

His parents had hinted over the years since his divorce that he should start seeing someone else, get back out there. But he knew he didn't want to be a bad husband, a bad partner, again. He couldn't risk doing that to someone else.

But he also knew that his father wanted to see him settled and happy—that was what had made it so easy for those words to slip out of his lips in the heat of the moment. And it was what made him burn with guilt now, knowing that he was misleading him. He suspected his father felt partially responsible for Joss feeling he had to go along with family expectations. If this lie made Joss feel uncomfortable, it would be worth it if it meant that his father could let his guilt rest before he died.

The recent spate of sleepless nights was a worry, though. It was years since he'd felt this drag of fatigue, and it reminded him of a time in his life he had absolutely no wish to revisit. This time it carried with it an extra shade of dread. He didn't want to be ill again. Didn't want his world to shrink and pale as he fought with his own brain chemistry to feel even the smallest amount of hope.

And right there was another good reason not to listen to the pull of his body when Eva was near. No. They had to keep real life, real feelings, and their charade separate. Regardless of how attracted they were to each other.

He considered his own thoughts. Was he right? Was she attracted to him as he was to her?

'Hey, come in,' he said, remembering that she was still standing, watching him from the doorway.

She shut the door behind her and Joss shifted in his chair at the sudden charge in the room that their isolation created.

'How's Dad getting on?' Talking about his father seemed like the safest option.

'He's great. Same as always. If he hadn't told us, I still wouldn't know there was anything wrong. Says he's looking forward to some more time out of the city. You?'

'I'm good. Could do without this trip, if I'm being honest.'

'Yeah.' She glanced at her watch. 'That's what I wanted to talk to you about. Your dad's asked me to book us a room. Said he thought the meetings might go on a bit. I need to go home and pack a bag, so I'll just meet you at the airport.'

'It's easier if I come with,' Joss said, leaning back

in his chair. 'You're only around the corner. We'll get a cab from there. It means I can drop my stuff off too.'

'You brought it to the office?' Eva looked horrified.

'What? Are you still worried about the gossip?'

'It's easy for you to joke about it. You've not been grilled about our grand romance every time you've so much as looked at the coffee machine.'

'I'm sorry you're getting the brunt of it. Do you want me to say something?'

She sighed and shook her head. 'What? A formal announcement about our fake relationship? A little weird, Joss.'

'Fine. Well, we'll be out of here in an hour. Think the news has reached the Milan store already?'

'Oh, I can guarantee it'll travel faster than we do.'

As the plane lifted from the runway Joss itched to reach into his bag for his laptop, hoping to relax in the familiarity of a working journey. He'd travelled between stores more times than he could count, and he knew he could get plenty of work done before their meeting. Plus staring at the screen of his computer was safer than glancing across at the woman sitting beside him.

He remembered the first time he'd seen her. Well, the first time that he'd really noticed her. For so long during his marriage and his illness, he'd not been able to see any beauty in the world, never mind in a woman. And then one morning, newly divorced and with a fresh hold on his psychological wellbeing, he'd walked into his father's office and heard Eva speaking in quick-fire Italian—to the Milan store, perhaps. Or one of the luxury fashion suppliers. She'd burst into laughter, and as she'd thrown her head back in amusement she'd caught his eye.

Something had caught inside him, too. A spark of intense attraction he couldn't remember feeling since... Forget that. He'd *never* felt anything like that before—the intense pull not only to a beautiful woman, but to one he knew could joke and laugh in half a dozen languages when he was struggling to do it in one.

There had been a time in his past when an attraction like that would have felt like a red rag to a bull. But he knew better now. He knew where a relationship with him would leave a woman, and he had no desire to inflict that on Eva.

The 'Fasten Seatbelt' light was switched off, and Joss kept his eyes down as they both pulled out their laptops. Eva started muttering under her breath as she read through a document, the sound almost lost in the rustle of her hair as she tucked it behind her ear.

Please, not Italian, he pleaded silently. He wasn't sure what it was, but the sound of that language on her lips was his weak spot. He breathed a sigh of relief when he caught an Arabic phrase—something to do with the Dubai store, perhaps. It wasn't Italian but, *God*, she made it sound sexy.

He remembered the last time he'd heard her speak Arabic—at the conference of all their international store managers—the way the sounds had rolled around her tongue, and the confidence and speed with which she'd spoken. It was too much, eventually, and he glanced up from his spreadsheet, promising himself just a quick look at her expression.

But when he looked at her, her eyes were already focussed on him, and once he realised that he couldn't look away.

'What?' she asked him, breaking off from reading, and he knew he'd been staring too long.

He raised his eyebrows and shook his head. 'Nothing. Just wondered if you knew you were talking to yourself.'

He returned his gaze to the columns of numbers that had been dancing in front of his eyes since he'd loaded up the file.

He kept his eyes decisively on his screen until he heard his name pass Eva's lips and couldn't help glancing up to see her expression—he wished he hadn't when he saw the exasperation there. She rubbed her forehead and he glanced at her screen, but couldn't make out any of the Arabic she was reading. From her frustration, it was pretty clear that there was a problem, and he suspected he knew what it was.

'Trouble in Dubai?' he asked.

'They're worried,' Eva replied. 'Your father was due to have a phone conference with the manager of the store tomorrow. Edward's cancelled and asked me not to reschedule yet and the manager is worried about business continuity. I'm going to have to call your dad. See if he'll rearrange.'

'I'll take the meeting,' Joss said. 'What?' he added when Eva grimaced slightly.

'I'm not sure that'll work. In fact, I already tried that. They say they want to speak to Edward.'

'Well, if Dad's taking time off it's not like he doesn't have a good reason.'

'I know that. We'll talk to him about it when we're back in the office. But this is two stores just this morning who are going into crisis mode. I think we have to assume that others will react in the same way.'

Joss stared her down, not appreciating her doubting his ability to do his new job. 'I'm perfectly capable of running this business. I've been preparing for it for long enough.'

'I know that, Joss.' Eva relaxed back into the seat as she spoke. 'Your father does too—and every Dawson's employee, really. But knowing it and feeling it aren't necessarily the same thing. As a rule, people don't like change, and—like it or not—you at the head of the company *is* change.'

He shrugged off her concerns. 'So I'll go to Dubai too. To every single store worldwide if I have to.'

'It might help,' Eva said. 'In Dubai at least.'

Joss nodded, trying to mentally rearrange the next couple of weeks to accommodate another overseas trip. Dubai was too far to hop on a plane for just the day.

'You should come,' he said, thinking how valuable having his father's right-hand woman by his side would be in showing the store that nothing was going to change with him in charge. Yes, that was the only reason he was inviting her along. 'As a show of continuity. They might not know me well, but they know you. It will be reassuring.'

'I don't know, Joss.'

Eva didn't look convinced by his reasoning.

She leant forward, her elbows resting on the table in front of her. 'I never went with your dad. I can make the time to be out of the office for this one meeting, but I can't be constantly on the road or in the air.'

He watched her closely for a minute. The way she shifted in her seat and wouldn't meet his eyes. She might be worried about the business, but that wasn't really why she was refusing to go.

'That's not why you don't want to go. What is it—afraid of flying?'

She snorted a laugh. 'Did I miss you dragging me on here kicking and screaming? As if! And I'm an army brat, remember.'

'You *were* an army brat,' he corrected her. 'You look all grown up to me.'

He could have cringed at his cheesy line, but when her gaze finally locked on to his he didn't care—it was the truth. He didn't want to talk about her childhood. He wanted to talk about them on an all-night flight to Dubai and then getting hot and sweaty together in the desert.

He shook his head, hoping to scatter those dangerous thoughts. Eva was strictly off-limits, and he'd do well to remember that. Even if she agreed to this trip, as she'd agreed to the engagement, it would be strictly business. There would be no hot and sweaty—in the desert or anywhere else.

'So it's not the flight,' he said. He was intrigued. Who would turn down an impromptu trip to Dubai, with a visit to the city's most luxurious shopping mall guaranteed? 'What is it, then? Fear of catching some tropical disease?'

'It's nothing remotely exciting, Joss.' Eva flicked her fingers at an invisible piece of fluff. 'I prefer not to travel much. I love living in London and I like to stay there.'

Joss laughed with incredulity. 'But you speak six languages. Don't you ever want to use them?'

'Seven, actually. And, hello? How long have we been working together? I use them every day.'

'But is that really the same? Just saying the words, I mean. Or reading emails? Don't you want to go and experience the different cultures? Hear the dialects and the slang on the streets?'

Eva shrugged. 'I've done different cultures, thanks. I've done trying to learn what slang the cool kids are using. I'm happy where I am.'

'So why learn the languages at all?' He knew that talking about something so personal was probably a bad idea. But he couldn't help being intrigued by her. Couldn't help wanting to know more. 'There are plenty of jobs you could do without them.'

'It was a case of necessity at first, I guess,' Eva said. 'When we moved to Germany I wanted to do more than speak to the other kids on the base and at the army school. If I was going to be dragged to another country, I was determined to learn how to express myself there. The same when we went to Cyprus. And, to be honest, it came naturally. I loved learning to speak other languages. Maybe my brain likes the patterns of different grammar. Or hearing sounds that we don't even have in English. Words that can't be translated, because speaking another language makes you think in another language.'

'Okay, so German and Greek I get. But what about Arabic? Did you live in the Middle East?'

There was something more to this, he realised. Something about her parents. Something they'd never talked about before.

She shook her head. 'No, we were based here while Mum and Dad did their tours in Iraq. I'm not sure why I decided to learn. I quite liked the challenge of another new alphabet. A completely different written form of language.'

'And maybe it made you feel closer to your parents?' Joss asked gently. 'To speak the language they would be hearing around them every day?'

Eva remained silent, her eyebrows pulling together in a frown. Had she never considered that? he wondered.

'So, anyway, these meetings this afternoon,' Eva said, shaking off any suggestion of a personal conversation. 'What do you need from me? I've already requested an update from the supply management team on any issues they've had in the last few months, and pulled together the minutes from relevant meetings. As for the manager of the store, Matteo Lazzari, I've put all the correspondence between him and Edward in a folder and given you access. Is there anything else you need me to prepare?'

Joss looked at her closely, noting the swift change of subject but not pushing back. If she didn't want to talk about her personal life, then that was up to her. If this had been a real relationship then maybe he'd have encouraged her to open up, but this was just for show. She wanted to draw a line and that was fine by him.

He drew his eyes back to the spreadsheet in front of him, determined that the rest of the flight would be spent working, rather than trying and failing to guess what was going on in Eva's head.

When the announcement came to pack away all electronic devices and return their tables to an upright position, Joss congratulated himself on his self-control. Just as he'd promised himself, he'd got his work done with barely a thought for Eva.

He glanced sideways, to see if she was still working too, and realised the reason he had been so free from interruptions was because at some point, with her fingers still resting gently on her laptop keys, she had fallen asleep. Perhaps he wasn't the only one to have struggled with insomnia last night.

The cabin crew were making their way down the centre aisle, checking that their instructions for landing had been complied with, so he gently shifted Eva's hands from the computer onto her lap, then closed the laptop and folded up the table. She stirred a little in her sleep, shifting to get comfortable, and then eventually rested her head on his shoulder, letting out a deep sigh and settling back into sleep.

Joss watched her for a moment, unsure whether he should move her. But he thought it was unlikely he could do that again without waking her. So he left her where she was: with the gentle weight of her head against his arm and the smell of her hair temptingly close. The armrest between them was up, and as she fell deeper and deeper into sleep her body pressed closer, relaxing into him as he grew more and more tense.

He couldn't allow himself to enjoy this.

He mustn't allow himself to think about how he had seen that body covered only by the fine silk of a slip. How he'd wanted to run his hands inside her dress to clasp her waist, to pull her back against him as he slid her zip all the way down.

He couldn't allow himself to think about all the places his mind had taken him after he'd left her flat that night. Alone at home, he'd imagined pushing her dress off her shoulders, it gliding down to the floor and landing at his feet...

Another announcement from the cabin crew broke into his thoughts and was loud enough to wake Eva, who sat up with a start.

'Did I—?' Eva began, smoothing down her hair with a shaking hand before she stopped herself. 'Sorry— must have fallen asleep,' she said, briskly this time, looking around her in confusion. 'Did you put my laptop away?'

'They put the lights on for landing,' Joss offered by way of explanation.

'You should have woken me.'

He shrugged. 'Looked like you needed the sleep. I know the feeling. We'll be landing any minute,' he added, keen to move the conversation away from the question of them sleeping even in the same vicinity as one another.

An hour later their car passed the extravagant frontage of the Milan store on its way to their hotel, and he looked up at it in wonder. It didn't matter how many times he saw it, it never lost its magic. He thought of his great-grandfather, who had built up this business in a different century, a different world. And not for the first time he thought how lucky he was to be part of this family, to have such an inheritance, such a legacy to care for. His determination to continue that success, to prove himself, rallied.

And, much as he might protest to Eva that he had spent his life preparing for the top job, and much as that might be true, the job was his far sooner than any of them had imagined. He had thought he had a few more years to work on his relationships with the managers of the overseas stores. To build the connections that would be so important when his father was no longer around.

He was certain he had the experience and the expertise to continue the family success—now he had to prove himself to the rest of the business.

CHAPTER FOUR

EVA STEPPED UP to the desk at the hotel and pulled out the paperwork with the details of their reservation. The receptionist took their reservation number and tapped the screen of the computer for a seemingly endless time, until eventually she looked up with a smile and called over a bellboy.

'Thanks so much,' Eva said, excited to be speaking Italian face to face, despite everything she had said to Joss on the plane. 'Could you send some lunch up to the room?' she asked as the bellboy took their bags.

Their meeting was in an hour, but with the prospect of Italian cuisine when they arrived she hadn't been able to face the thought of airline food.

'Something quick and simple, please.'

She hovered behind the bellboy as he jiggled the key card and opened the door into their room. As she followed him in, she realised that there must have been some sort of mistake, in spite of how long the receptionist had taken to check them in.

Her eye was first caught by the extravagant bouquet of flowers on the beautifully polished table in the centre of the suite's foyer. A bottle of champagne and a note sat beside it, with her and Joss's names picked out in a stylish copperplate hand. Through the open doors leading from the foyer she could see at least one bedroom, a marble-lined bathroom, and a terrace overlooking the city. It was luxury far beyond anything she'd ever experienced. Was this what she had to look forward to as part of the Dawson family?

Not that she was part of the family yet. *Or ever would be*, she reminded herself. This engagement was all for show, no matter how real this suite was making it feel.

She picked up the envelope and turned it over, feeling the heavy weight of the paper in her hand. She read the note inside, fighting against the tear that was threatening at the corner of her eye.

Dearest Joss and Eva,
Consider the suite a little engagement present
from me. Enjoy Milan and don't hurry back.
Love,
Dad

Those last two words made her feel something she had been looking for for as long as she could remember. Included. Accepted. Part of a family. Something her own family had never managed.

Some parts of her childhood had been so privileged she knew she shouldn't complain. She'd always had a roof over her head and food on the table. While her mother and father had taken turns to be away on tour, among families and homes torn apart by conflict, whoever had been left behind had tried their best to fill the space that was left.

But that didn't change the facts. Both her parents had been happy to leave her for months at a time. Hugging her goodbye and promising to be home soon, all the while aware that they had no way of knowing if they could keep their promises. And then—inevitably, it had seemed—her mother had kissed her goodbye, told her she would be home soon, and instead they'd had a visit from a sombre-looking man in uniform. Eva had been left with the knowledge that her mother had never loved her enough to want to spare her the pain that her death would bring, even though she'd tried to convince herself that she didn't care enough to hurt.

She'd thought that would be it for her father. That he would be repulsed by the thought of leaving her again. Of taking the chance of making her an orphan.

She'd been wrong.

Joss came up behind her and took the note gently from her hand.

'The old romantic,' he said, with the beginnings of a laugh. He stepped around her to examine the champagne, but when he caught sight of her face he replaced the bottle in the ice bucket and reached to touch her cheek. 'What is it?' he asked, alarm evident in his expression.

'It's nothing,' Eva said, painting on a fake smile. 'You're right—it is romantic. Shame it'll be wasted on us.'

A knock at the door signalled lunch arriving.

'You show them in, I'll be back in just a minute.'

In the bathroom, she patted cold water on her cheekbones and took a few deep breaths, trying not to think about romance, or the suite, or Joss. It was probably a good job that they were going to be in meetings all the time they were out here. It didn't matter what Edward said—she would be hurrying home. The less time they spent closeted in a luxury hotel suite the better. Or safer, at least. There were a lot of reasons why she might enjoy being locked away with Joss, but it was absolutely not a good idea to think about them. Definitely safer not to.

She left the bathroom and grabbed a couple of pieces of ciabatta from the tray the waiter had left on the table. Eating while she worked, she sifted through the files that she had brought with her, stocking her bag and ensuring that her tablet had enough charge to last the rest of the day. She had access to all the information that Joss might need for their meetings. This was his first test as Managing Director of the company, and it was a matter of professional pride for her that nothing went wrong for him.

She glanced at her watch as she pulled on a jacket. 'Are you ready?' she called to Joss, who had disappeared into one of the bedrooms.

'Be right out,' he called back.

She checked her phone as she waited by the door and was relieved to see a text from their driver, letting them know that he was waiting for them outside.

Joss emerged wearing a fresh shirt and she deliberately averted her eyes, not wanting to give herself any excuse to appreciate the way that man wore simple white cotton. It was a thought that she'd blocked out a lot over the years—when she'd caught sight of Joss in a meeting or walking through the office and tried to work out exactly what it was that made this man so attractive to her.

It wasn't as if he was even *nice*. Sure, he was courteous. He was professional. She couldn't think of a time when he had been outright rude. But definitely not nice. He wouldn't go out of his way to make someone feel comfortable. Wouldn't remember her birthday and drop something small and wrapped on her desk in the morning without a word.

He was nothing like his father, whom she adored. So how was it that for years she hadn't been able to get him out of her head? Why was he the man she measured every date against and found them lacking?

She reached behind her and grabbed the door handle, opening the door into the corridor and stepping out of the suite when Joss was a few feet away. A buffer zone: that was what was needed. Safe space between them that couldn't be breached.

But would people think that was odd? she wondered. She had no doubt that news of their engagement would have reached the Italian store before they did. Her standoffishness might cause more gossip—make people start to question whether the relationship was real. Make them ask what she hoped to get out of it.

She shook her head. It was far more likely that people would see that they were two professionals at work, acting professionally. No one would expect them to be all over each other. Respectful distance worked *for* their story, rather than against it.

'So, when was the last time you met with Matteo in person?' she asked Joss, determined to keep their conversation on a work footing after their earlier diversion into her personal life.

'In the spring,' Joss said. 'But it was at the conference for all the international store managers. You know what that thing is like—between meetings and presentations there's hardly time for a business conversation, never mind anything more personal.'

'Well, we should have lots of time today. You two have all afternoon pencilled in, and there's nothing in your diary for tonight either, so you can always take it to dinner if you feel you need to. Just remember you're trying to make a personal connection. He knows that you're capable. You've been with the company for ever. Just show him that you're someone he's going to enjoy working with.'

Joss caught up with her in the hallway. 'What? You want me to flirt with him? Seduce him?'

Here she was, trying to be professional, and he had to mention flirting and seduction pretty much the minute he opened his mouth. Was he determined to make this impossible for her?

'You know, I think he's been happily married for the last twenty years or so. I'm not sure flirting will get you anywhere.'

Joss tutted. 'You know what I mean. You think I should charm him. That's what he wants?'

'I don't think he wants to be charmed, Joss. I think he wants to get to know you. You could be friendly. That would be a start.'

Friendly. There was that word again. Was that what she wanted from him? For him to be friendly to her? Hardly. That would make things impossible. At least when he was terse and short and—well, *un*friendly— she could remind herself of all the reasons why she shouldn't indulge this crush of hers. If he were to actually start conversing, or—God forbid—laughing like a normal human being, then she was going to be in big trouble.

'I thought we'd already established that I can't do friendly.'

'No, we established that you *don't* do friendly. Only you know whether that's out of choice or not. Do you try to be unfriendly?'

'I just try and get the job done, Eva. It doesn't normally require chatting over a cup of tea.'

'Well, your new job does, Joss. People need to see you, to get to know you. Your dad's illness has been a big shock to everyone. They're going to miss him enormously. It's a big gap to fill.'

Joss stopped in the hallway and fixed her with a stare.

'I'm well aware of that, thank you, Eva.'

She let out a breath and reached out a hand to his arm. 'I'm sorry, Joss. I know you are. And I'm not trying to criticise. Just trying to fill you in on what your father's relationship with his store managers is like. I'm not saying that you need to do business in the same way—I'm just giving you the information that you need to manage this transition. We're all trying to manage this situation as best we can. Myself included.'

He turned back to the lift and pressed the button to take them to the lobby. 'Well, thank you for the information. I'll take it under advisement.'

So that was how today was going to be. Icy cool. Well, that was fine by her, but she wasn't sure what Matteo would make of it.

They walked into the grand entrance of the Milan store to see Matteo waiting to greet them. 'Eva, *bella*. It is always such a pleasure.' He greeted her with a kiss on each cheek and warm enquiries about her health. 'And Mr Dawson, of course.'

He held out a hand to Joss and received a brusque handshake in return.

'Please, call me Joss.'

Unfortunately Joss's tone didn't match the friendliness of his sentiment, but Eva resisted the urge to roll her eyes in front of Matteo.

'And I hear from a little voice back in the office that congratulations are in order! You are to be married?' He kissed Eva again on both cheeks and shook Joss's hand again. 'An office romance. How lovely.'

He picked up Eva's left hand and let out a murmur of dismay.

'Oh, but no ring?'

'Oh, no,' Eva said, trying to think on her feet. 'Everything happened rather quickly, and with Edward's news…'

She let the sentence sit in the air and hoped that her allusion to terminal illness would do away with the need for further explanations.

'Oh, but you have some time now,' Matteo exclaimed with pleasure. 'And you are in the most beautiful store in the world! If you will forgive the slight to your English stores, Mr Dawson. I absolutely insist you come and choose something before our meeting.'

Eva looked at Joss, expecting him to shut down any discussion of shopping and insist they all get to work. But he wore an inscrutable expression that was heading towards a smile, and somehow she knew that meant trouble.

'If you're sure you don't mind waiting a little longer for our meeting, Signor Lazzari. Eva and I would love to do that.'

As they walked through the lobby towards the fine jewellery department, Eva grabbed Joss's hand and hung back a little, allowing the distance between them and Matteo to stretch beyond his hearing a whisper.

'What are you doing?' she asked out of the side of her mouth, glancing round to make sure that no one else could be listening in.

'Being friendly,' Joss replied with that same almost-smile.

'If you're doing this to make a point to me, it's fine. I get it—you're Mr Friendly. Time to drop it.'

Joss shook his head. 'Matteo wants to spoil us in his store. Show it off at its best. I thought it was politic to go along with him. Anyway, we will need a ring. If we wait too long people will start to talk.'

'You know,' she said, a touch of sharpness in her voice, 'some people think of that before they pop the question.'

'Yes, well, I'm not "some people", am I? I have the feeling that you never would have agreed to this if I was.'

She stopped, a hand on his arm turning him towards her. 'And what's that meant to mean?'

'Oh, nothing, darling,' Joss replied as he realised they had reached the gleaming glass counters of the jewellery department and Matteo was looking at them expectantly. 'So—where do you want to start?' he asked.

Matteo pulled out a few rings from the nearest cabinet—diamond solitaires all of them, ranging from the shockingly big to the tastelessly huge.

'Something classic, perhaps?' Matteo said, handing her a platinum diamond ring that must be a good three carats.

Eva held it between her fingertips and then looked up to Joss. He must have sensed her discomfort, because he took the ring from her and placed it back in the tray.

'Something a little more unusual for Eva, I think,' he said, reaching for an equally huge stone, this time flanked with pretty yellow pear-shaped diamonds. 'What about this,' he asked, meeting her eyes as he slipped the ring onto her finger.

She stood staring at it for a moment, reality and make-believe clashing. She knew this wasn't real. She knew it was all for show. But with this rock on her finger the lines were less clear than ever before.

She couldn't deny that she'd fantasised about this moment. All she wanted in her life was constancy... stability. Perhaps, one day she'd meet a man who she wouldn't want to let go. He'd slide a ring onto the third finger of her left hand and she would know without doubt that it was staying there for life.

It wasn't meant to feel like...*this*. It was never meant to be temporary. All she could see when she looked at this ring was the day when she would have to take it off. When Edward was gone, and she and Joss gave up their pretence, she'd have to return it to its snug velvet box and hand it back to him.

Her eyes filled with tears, but she fought them back, knowing that she couldn't lose it in front of Joss, never mind in front of Matteo.

'Ah, look at you. This is a special moment,' Matteo said with a smile. 'And I see I am not quite needed here. If I say I will see you again in an hour, will that be enough time for you?'

He handed Joss the keys to the jewellery cabinets and clapped him on the shoulder. 'I leave you two young lovers alone. Choose something special, yes?'

They both watched in silence as Matteo crossed the jewellery hall, waiting until they were alone and could speak safely.

'You don't like it?' Joss asked eventually, picking up her hand again and examining the ring.

'It's spectacular,' Eva replied with honesty.

'Then why the tears?' he said, gently this time, brushing a finger across her cheekbones.

'I'm not crying.'

'You're not letting them fall. I can see that. But you're upset. Why?'

'It's nothing, Joss. It's just that this is all a bit unnecessary. It feels strange. Wrong.'

'Why?'

There was no impatience in his voice, nor in his expression, as she took her time choosing the right words.

'Because it's all a lie. And a ring like this—it deserves something better. It's meant to be a symbol of love and commitment. We both know that we're not promising either of those things.'

He looked down at the ring for a moment, and then gently pulled it over her knuckle. 'Nothing that looks like an engagement ring, then. That narrows our options. What about this?' he asked.

'That's an eternity ring, Joss. Same problem.'

'You know, I don't think the ring is going to mind.'

She shook her head, not sure if she could make him understand without revealing too much of herself. '*I* mind. I might want one of these things for real one day. When I buy my engagement ring—or an eternity ring for that matter—I don't want to be keeping the receipt for when I have to return it.'

'So that's the problem.' Joss nodded, looking as if he had cracked a particularly difficult problem in the budget spreadsheet. 'You don't want something you like because you won't want to give it back? You can keep the ring, Eva. With everything you're doing for my father, for the business, it's the least I can do.'

Eva let out a breath in frustration. 'It's not about the money, Joss. It's the symbol. It's what the ring's meant to mean. I can't accept an engagement ring when there is no engagement.'

He looked thoughtful, and remained silent for a few long minutes, before reaching for her hand and pulling her gently to another case. 'What about if the ring symbolises something else, then? What if it's a gesture—a friendly gesture—of thanks. Thanks for caring for my father enough to go through with this. Thanks for looking after him and the business for so long. It's a gift—from a friend. The meaning doesn't change, whatever happens between us. And I absolutely won't accept it back from you when this ends.'

She looked at the case of jewellery he had brought her to, and thought about what he had said.

A gift like that she could accept, she thought. A ring was part of making this engagement look realistic, but these didn't look like engagement rings. They looked more like garlands of flowers, or boughs of blossoms. Tiny diamonds, sparkling and weaving their way across bands of yellow gold.

Joss unlocked the case and brought out one of the rings, with pink and blue sapphires scattered amongst bigger diamonds. He slipped it on to her third finger and they both stared at it in silence for a moment, taking in the effect.

'What do you think?' Joss asked.

'Better,' Eva said. 'It feels…friendly.'

Joss breathed a laugh. 'You old romantic. You're right. It's better. But it's not perfect. It's too heavy for those slender fingers. Too busy.'

He slipped it off again, and swapped it for a more delicate one—just diamonds this time, set in a meandering line like a trailing spray of flowers. This time when Joss slipped it on her finger she had no doubts.

'It's the one,' she said, gazing down at her finger.

'Perfect,' Joss agreed.

And before she realised what he was doing he had lifted her hand to his mouth and the warm heat of his lips was pressing against her knuckles.

She stood and stared at him, not quite sure where to begin with her line of questioning on this one.

'Joss... I don't think...'

His lips left her hand and he looked up, meeting her eyes with his intense gaze. She forgot what she had been going to say. Something about how this wasn't a good idea, probably. Except with her hand still encased in his, with the ring warming on her finger, it suddenly felt like the best idea they'd had for a while.

Joss's other hand landed lightly on her waist and for a moment neither of them breathed. Then, as one, they took in a sharp breath, and nudged closer towards one another.

Joss's hand snaked around her back, taking hers with it, twisting her until her back was against the jewellery cabinet. And it would have been so, so easy to relax into him, to loosen her body and let his arms take her weight. Take her anywhere he wanted to go.

Another half-step closer and his body met hers, pressing lightly against her from knee to chest, setting off fireworks everywhere in between.

This was all for show, she reminded herself. Joss was playing a part. For him, all this was just a way of making his father happy. Nothing about this was real for Joss—not in the way that the feelings she could feel growing for him were real.

At that moment she heard Matteo's voice from somewhere behind Joss and pushed gently against his chest, putting some much needed distance between them.

'Ah, I see you two have chosen something. Come—let me see.'

Eva held her left hand out to Matteo, hoping that she would be able to control the slight shake she could feel deep inside.

'It is beautiful,' Matteo said. 'A wonderful choice. But then I would expect nothing else. So, perhaps now we are ready to get to work?'

'Of course,' Joss said, his voice brusque, nothing like the soft tones she had heard when they were discussing her engagement ring.

She hoped that Matteo would put it down to an excess of emotion over their engagement rather than unfriendliness, otherwise the whole 'choosing the ring' exercise would have been wasted.

'And I have just spoken to Signora Lazzari—Giulietta—and she insists that you join us for dinner tonight,' Matteo said.

'Oh, I'm not sure if we—' Eva started.

'We'd love to,' Joss said, interrupting Eva's plan for a polite refusal.

But Joss was probably right. He was here to show the manager that he was the sort of man they could work with. It made sense for them to have dinner together. Eva herself had suggested that they might spend some time together this evening. But eating together as a foursome—that was inviting a world of trouble.

When they were working, it would be simple to explain away the lack of intimacy between them. They *should* keep a professional distance when they were in the office or one of the stores. But at dinner, perhaps at Matteo's home, that would be personal. They would be expected to look like a couple—and they'd have to make it convincing.

But now that Joss had agreed she didn't have much choice. She could hardly *un*accept a generous invitation from the man they were here to charm.

'But I insist that you allow us to take you out,' Joss said, allaying one of her concerns.

At least if they were safely out in public then they would be expected not to indulge in too many displays of affection.

CHAPTER FIVE

EVA PULLED ON the black dress that she always packed in case of emergencies. There was no situation she'd discovered yet that a simple black shift couldn't handle. She caught sight of the diamonds on her left hand and decided to leave off the statement necklace she'd also packed—it would be a shame to overshadow the pretty, understated ring that she and Joss had chosen together.

They'd agreed on dinner in the hotel restaurant downstairs. Its reputation was unparalleled in the city, and Matteo and his wife had happily accepted Joss's suggestion.

She checked her reflection quickly in the mirror and rubbed away a smudge of eyeliner. She'd kept her make-up simple, professional: a subtle reminder to herself that she hadn't knocked off for the day. She still had a part to play.

She heard the shower being shut off in the other bathroom and wondered whether Joss had thought to pack something to wear out to dinner. If it had been Edward taking the meeting she would have provided him with an itinerary of their trip—including likely social possibilities as well as all the meetings that were confirmed in the calendar. She hadn't found that familiarity with Joss yet. That closeness. A way of anticipating his needs even before he did.

She shivered slightly at the thought of developing such a thing with Joss. Even without their fake engagement, the changes at work would have been enough to turn their relationship completely on its head. To break down those careful barriers she'd built to keep herself distant from him at work. To keep her mind from wandering in his direction.

With everything else that had happened, she hadn't stopped to consider the alternative reality that might have existed if Edward had never walked in on them in the office and got the wrong idea. It wasn't as if her life would have carried on unchanged. She and Joss would still be in Milan, for a start. In separate rooms, though, instead of this suite. And Joss would still be moving in to Edward's office, sitting every day in her direct eyeline, on the other end of an intercom, occupying a huge part of her work life.

Joss's presence in her life would have grown anyway. So maybe by agreeing to this engagement she'd actually gained more control than she would otherwise have had. More freedom to discuss the nature of their relationship. To make clear to him that, however it might seem, a romantic attachment was absolutely *not* on the cards between them and never would be.

She shook her head. Most people didn't feel the need to have that sort of conversation with their boss. With most people it was just assumed that there would be nothing extracurricular going on. Just the fact that she was thinking it proved that these changes were always going to have caused trouble.

'Are you ready?' Joss called from the other side of the bedroom door.

What a question. She was ready to jump in a car, get on the first plane home, and pretend that none of this was happening. But was she ready to go out and fake a relationship with the man she'd been burying her feelings for since his divorce? She wasn't sure she wanted to admit the answer to that one.

Instead she opened the door, shut out her feelings and faked a smile.

'Ready,' she said, doing a last-minute check on the contents of her bag as they headed to the front door of the suite.

'You look nice,' Joss said as they headed out into the corridor.

He'd barely looked at her, she noticed. But she couldn't fault his manners.

'You too,' she replied, trying just as hard not actually to look at him.

Spending so much time together was meant to be curing her of her crush—but so far all the evidence was that it was having the opposite effect. It really was in no way fair. Perhaps it was the vast suite that Edward had arranged for them. With their separate bedrooms the size of palaces they might as well be living in separate apartments, as they had been back in London.

But this was only temporary, she reminded herself. Tomorrow they would be flying back to London, where there was a holdall of his clothes waiting for them in her spare room. And an empty drawer and a few inches of wardrobe space she'd managed to clear out for him.

They rode the lift down to the lobby in silence, and Eva deliberately avoided meeting Joss's eye in the mirrors that surrounded them. Then she remembered what they were doing here, the lie they were meant to be living, and risked a glance at him. She found him already watching her, and gave him a small smile.

'Ready for this?' he asked.

'No. You?'

'No.'

At that she felt the smile spread from her lips and across her cheeks, and saw it was reflected in Joss's eyes. She even risked a small laugh.

'Well, as long as we're in agreement, I suppose.'

She grabbed his hand as the lift doors slid open, and they were greeted by the sight of Matteo and his wife waiting for them in the lobby. Good job they'd got their faces sorted out before the lift stopped, Eva thought.

She greeted Matteo and Giulietta with kisses to both cheeks, but Joss kept her hand locked in his. She held on, in case he needed the support. Anyway, with her body anchored to his like this it made it easier to remember what she was doing—the part she was supposed to be playing. She wasn't just his assistant, greasing the wheels of conversation, providing snippets of information when they were needed. She was half of a couple.

Even as they were chatting over an aperitif she could still feel the warmth of Joss's hand against her skin, and she wondered if that would ever go. This hyper-awareness of his body whenever it was in contact with hers. In twenty years, would she still be getting fireworks if their fingers brushed when she handed him a letter to sign, or a contract to approve?

Twenty years.

Working with Edward, she'd never had any trouble envisaging her future. She'd felt secure. She'd known— or thought she had known—that she would always have a place with Dawson's. But now... Now she couldn't be sure.

One of the reasons she'd agreed to this charade in the first place was because she'd thought it would bind her more closely to the company, and then Joss wouldn't be able to show her the door as soon as his dad was gone. But was that naïve? Did this fake relationship make it more likely, rather than less, that Joss would want to see the back of her once this was over? Surely it would be more realistic that they *wouldn't* want to work together any more if they 'broke up'.

And if people found out that the whole thing was a sham, of course Joss would want her out of the way.

The thoughts crashing through her brain made her realise how naïve they had been, thinking that they could just start this thing with no idea when or how it was going to end. And how had she thought that Joss would want to keep her around after it was over?

A shiver ran through her, and she felt rather than saw Joss turn towards her.

'Cold?' he asked, dropping her hand and placing an arm around her shoulder.

'Just from this,' Eva said, faking a laugh and gesturing to the Prosecco in her hand, condensation beading on the glass.

As they took their seats at the table Eva was still incredibly aware of her body language, and that of Joss, sitting beside her. Were they playing it too cool? This was a dinner with colleagues, and they were out in public, so no one would expect them to be all over each other. But since she'd shaken off Joss's arm, with protestations that she wasn't cold, she was more aware than ever of his presence beside her, of having him so close but not touching.

Should she do something? she wondered, as she stared at the menu in front of her, unable to take in a single word. She glanced at his hand, resting on the table, and wondered if she should reach for it. She could just slide her fingers between his, the way she remembered doing instinctively the day Edward had announced his illness. It would look like the most natural thing in the world to Matteo and his wife. Or maybe she could rest a hand on his thigh, feel under her fingertips those firm muscles which just a couple of hours ago had pressed her against a jewellery cabinet.

She resisted the urge to sigh and tried to concentrate on her menu instead, picking it up from the table and attempting to focus.

'Oh, what a pretty ring,' Giulietta said from across the table. 'Matteo told me you chose it together today.'

Eva smiled at Giulietta and glanced down at her hand. She remembered what Joss had said about it symbolising friendship, her place in the family, and looked up at him with a smile.

'Ah, but you two are so in love,' Giulietta said with a laugh, and Eva felt her cheeks colour. 'It is good that you can be happy after such sad news. I was so sorry to hear that Edward is not well.'

This time she didn't think about it. She reached for Joss's hand and squeezed it tightly in her own, knowing how raw his pain must be, if it was anything like her own.

'Thank you,' Joss said, carefully steady.

Eva glanced up at him and could see from the set line of his jaw how much of a struggle he was finding that composure.

'I know my father values your efforts here highly.'

'And I know that he is so sorry that he's not able to be here himself,' Eva added, hoping that she'd be able to make up for Joss's lack of warmth.

Edward and Matteo had been friends for years, and she knew that the Lazzaris would be feeling the sadness of his loss too. Joss had his own grief to deal with—but she had to make sure that this meeting achieved everything they needed it to. Matteo *had* to see that he would be happy working with Joss.

'I know that he would love to be at this dinner with us.'

'Ah, we understand,' Giulietta said with a kind smile. 'We are just happy to have *your* company this evening. And to be able to send our warmest wishes with you when you return.'

'Of course we will take them,' Eva said, and glanced up at Joss.

They were here to try and show Matteo a more

human, personal side of Joss, but so far he was too distracted. He seemed more buttoned up than ever, and she still had no idea how to get him to open up.

'If you'll excuse me?' Giulietta said, pushing her chair back. 'I'll be back in a few moments.'

Three at the table felt a whole lot more uncomfortable than four, Eva realised after a few seconds' awkward silence.

She attempted to start up a conversation a couple of times, but nothing was thawing between them. Matteo's phone rang, and he excused himself from the table with apologies, saying that it was his deputy at the store.

'What?' Joss asked, as she turned towards him with a concerned look.

She took a bracing breath, knowing that this conversation had to be quick, discreet and effective. 'We're here to show Matteo a warmer side to you, yes? Well, we're not doing a good job so far.'

He sat up a little straighter in his chair. 'We were talking about my terminally ill father. Would you like me to be cracking jokes?'

She shook her head—a small, efficient movement. 'Of course not. And I understand how difficult it will be. But we've come all this way. If we're not going to make it count, then why did we bother? Do you want to go back to the office having failed to achieve our objective?'

She knew that the business-speak would win him over—she'd worked with him for long enough to understand that the company director in him wouldn't be able to resist the threat of a missed objective or deadline.

Giulietta returned to the table and Eva greeted her with a smile, and an offer to top up her glass. Signora Lazzari took hold of her hand and looked again at her ring.

'Forgive me,' she said. 'I can't help looking. They're pretty stones—and such an unusual design. You really have an eye.'

It was the perfect opening she needed—cue Joss's human side.

'Actually, it was Joss's choice. He understood exactly what I would want.' She turned to him with what she hoped would look to their guests like an adoring smile.

'After a couple of false starts,' Joss added with a laugh.

Eva could hear that it was slightly forced, but from the look on Giulietta's face she hadn't noticed.

'Let's just say that Eva had to point out the virtues of "less is more".'

Joss leaned over and pressed a kiss to her temple, and for that second when his lips were on her skin everything else stopped. The noise of the restaurant… the conversation around the table. Her breathing and her heartbeat. Everything was *him*. His lips, his touch, his heat.

And then it was gone, and the world crashed in again—noisy and brash.

'Well, you must be an attentive pupil,' Giulietta said. 'It's truly beautiful. And have you set a date?' she asked as Matteo returned to the table, tucking his phone into the inside pocket of his jacket.

'It is to be soon?' Matteo asked as he took his seat. 'Your father must be so excited to see you married.'

'We don't want to wait longer than we have to,' Joss said, taking Eva's hand. 'But we're not ready to set a date yet. My father has asked us not to decide anything until we've had time to come to terms with his news and all the changes it will bring. He wants us to concentrate on business at the moment. We feel that's the least we can do for him, to ensure the continuation of his legacy.'

'Ah, well, a long engagement is very romantic,' Giulietta said with a sigh. 'Sometimes I wish we could go back and do it all again.' She looked wistfully at her husband. 'Be newlyweds again.'

'I can drink to that,' Joss said with a smile that looked a little more relaxed. He lifted his glass. 'To engagements.'

'And being a newlywed,' Giulietta added.

Matteo lifted his glass as they all toasted.

'And to Edward Dawson,' Matteo said before they all went to replace their drinks on the table. 'He can never be replaced, but I am looking forward very much to getting to know his son better.'

Eva breathed a sigh of relief, and for the first time since they had arrived in Milan thought that maybe this might turn out not to be the disaster she had feared.

The rest of the dinner passed quickly, with conversation flowing in tandem with the wine. They eventually kissed Matteo and Giulietta goodbye in the lobby, late in the evening, and walked towards the lift, still hand in hand, just in case the Lazzaris should look back and see them.

Except Eva didn't drop Joss's hand once they were in the lift. She felt warm and comfortable, relaxed in Joss's company in a way she hadn't been since the day Edward had shared the news of his illness and Joss had come up with his absurd plan.

Until the lift doors slid shut and they were completely alone.

Not so relaxed any more.

In fact every muscle in her body tensed as she glanced around her, seeing them reflected in the mirrors on every side of them. Still their hands were linked together. She looked up at Joss, to find that he was already staring down at her, his expression inscrutable.

She opened her mouth to speak, but the ding of the lift stopping and the doors opening halted her.

Hand in hand, they turned towards their suite, and Joss dipped his free hand in his pocket for the key card, smoothly opening the door so that they barely had to break stride.

Eva realised she was holding her breath. She wasn't sure when she'd started to do it, but as the door closed behind them, and they were truly private for the first time all evening, she let it out—long and slow. All she could think about was Joss's lips. Warm on her hand that afternoon as he sealed their friendship ring with a kiss. And then tender on her temple over dinner.

She stopped at the door, not trusting herself to go any further into the suite. After all, her hand was still locked in Joss's, and neither of them was showing any sign of letting go.

She leant back against the door and Joss stood in

front of her, filling her vision with the wide shoulders of his exquisitely cut suit.

'Everything okay?' he asked, his voice low and sensual.

Eva nodded, when what she really wanted to do was shout. To tell him that no, she wasn't okay. That things were far, far from okay. This was confusing and terrifying and oh, so much more complicated than she had ever wanted her life to be.

But she couldn't let go of his hand. Couldn't be the one to break that connection between them.

She'd felt it growing as they'd played their parts over dinner. A touch of the hand here. A brush of fingers over an arm there. A quick kiss to the temple and too many shared smiles.

The intimacy had grown and grown between them, in some strange simulacrum of the relationship they had invented. But she had expected them to walk away from it. Expected to leave it at the table as they had their dirty glasses and used tableware. She hadn't expected it to stalk them into the lift and back up to their suite.

Intimacy was safe in public, where neither of them could act on it. But with her back against this door and Joss in front of her—looking serious, smelling delicious—it was a more dangerous prospect. And Joss knew it too. That much was clear from his expression. And she wouldn't be the first person in her family to walk headfirst and knowingly into danger. Maybe she had more in common with her parents than she'd realised.

A shiver went through her as the moment to push

him away, to break their contact, came and went, and she knew that she had made a decision. She closed her eyes and pushed herself onto her tiptoes, then gently, as gently as he'd kissed her, she pressed her lips to his.

For a moment she thought she'd miscalculated, misjudged, and that this *hadn't* been where the evening had been heading since the moment she'd walked out of her bedroom and set eyes on Joss. But then his lips came alive beneath hers, tasting, touching, caressing. She let out a long sigh—her body's relief after so many years of imagining this moment.

But her body wasn't the one in charge here—her brain was, and it wasn't exactly cheering her on. She could feel his restraint, too. It was there in his jaw, when she touched it gently with her fingers. It was there when he lifted his hand and it came to rest on the door beside her head instead of on her cheek or in her hair. It was there in the way he held his body ever so slightly away from hers, instead of pressing her hard into the wood.

And it was there in the way she had her hand on his chest, making sure he couldn't get too close.

She broke the kiss and rested her head back against the door, a chagrined look on her face.

'Bad idea,' she said at last as their breathing returned to normal. 'Too complicated.'

'I wish it wasn't,' Joss replied, and she could tell that he meant it.

Except they'd known each other for years before it had got so complicated, and they had known then, too, that this wasn't a good idea. At least it was a kind lie.

'Goodnight,' Eva said at last, after a few long moments during which one or the other of them might have decided that the complications didn't matter that much after all. But this wasn't a fairy tale, and the realities of their lives weren't going to melt away because of one kiss.

She pushed herself away from the door, determinedly avoiding eye contact, and brushed her hand gently against his arm as she slipped past him and into her bedroom.

CHAPTER SIX

'*BAD IDEA,*' EVA had said. Joss couldn't argue with that. It would undoubtedly have been a very bad idea. But a bad idea had never looked so good in his life.

They could have just gone for it. One kiss—how much damage could that have caused? But instead they'd both held back, and the whole moment had turned into a glimpse of what it might have been. Stirring his imagination without satisfying anything.

The next morning that kiss was on his mind all through his meetings with the Milan-based suppliers, even as he was reassuring them that there was no reason to think that there would be any drop in demand for their luxury goods throughout the Dawson's network of stores. And there would be absolutely no problems with the transition from Edward's leadership to his.

And on the plane, with Eva so close and so untouchable, the impression of her lips on his remained distractingly present.

It wasn't until they walked into their office at three o'clock in the afternoon and saw his father packing the contents of his desk into cardboard boxes that he was able to push that kiss from the forefront of his mind.

'What are you doing?' Joss barked at his father as he reached his office, though the answer was startlingly obvious.

'Sorry, son,' Edward said. 'I thought I'd be finished before you were back from the airport. You're the boss now—it's only right that you have the office that goes with it.'

Joss folded his arms, looking around the messy office, unable to believe his father was really going to be gone. 'Dad, I don't need your office. I don't *want* your office.'

'Well, I don't have much use for it now, and it would be silly for it to sit here empty.' Edward held up his hands and shrugged. 'And, really, I'd quite like to see you sitting here. If it makes you feel any better, it means Eva won't have to move desks. You'll want her close, believe me. She knows this job as well as I do. Better.'

He'd want her close. Well, there was the problem, wasn't it? It seemed that neither of them knew exactly how close they wanted to be.

She'd kissed him yesterday, all the while keeping him at a safe distance, never really giving in to what she wanted, even when they were alone. And he'd held back too. Warring with himself, telling himself that he had to stop this. He'd not been able to drag his lips from hers. All he'd been able to do was keep some emotional distance and try as hard as he could not to be dragged by those sensations into doing something they would both regret.

He whipped his head around as he heard the familiar click of her heels behind him.

'Edward—no. You can't be packing up already.'

'Ah, my dear, you as well. It is good to see you and my son so in tune with one another but, really, you must both see that I'm not needed here any more. Joss is more than capable of running this company and, to be perfectly honest, I've got places I would rather be. You know how much this business means to me—both of you do. But a prognosis like mine helps you to see what's really important. I've given this business fifty good years. Now, if I only have a few months left, I'm going to spend them doing some of the things I've been putting off for too long.'

He taped up the box with what seemed to Joss to be an unnecessarily dramatic flourish.

'Now...' He glanced at his watch. 'I've got an appointment, so I guess the rest of this will have to wait until tomorrow.' He laid a hand on Joss's shoulder as he passed him. 'I know this is hard, son. I'm here if you need to talk.'

He left the office and Joss couldn't breathe. It was as if he'd taken all the oxygen with him. He sat stiffly against the edge of the desk, among the abandoned staplers and office supplies that Edward had left lying there.

'Do you?' Eva asked.

Joss stared at her, unable to work out what she meant.

'Do you need to talk? Because I'm here too.'

He absolutely, definitely did not want to talk. What he wanted was to go and lock himself in his own office and get on with his job as if none of this was happening. There was a budget spreadsheet in his inbox that he could happily lose himself in for hours.

But he'd been down that route before, and it hadn't led anywhere good. Anywhere healthy. He had no intention of going there again. Talking to Eva… He wasn't sure that was a good idea. But when he thought about it he wasn't sure there was any other good option. She was the only one who knew the secret they were keeping after all. But what about *his* secrets? What about all the things in his past that he'd carefully hidden from everyone around him.

'Maybe I *should* talk, Eva. But I'm not sure that talking to you is the best idea. After last night…'

'What about last night?'

Really? Was she just going to pretend that it had never happened? Maybe they both should. After all, forgetting about that kiss was just about the most sensible—albeit impossible—option at this point.

'That kiss. It was…nice.'

He had a feeling it might have been incredible—if they hadn't both been holding back. He didn't know what her reasons were, but he was going to have to share his if that was what it took to keep them both from the mistake of making this fake relationship real. She had to see what a bad idea it would be, getting involved in a relationship now, with his father's illness and the knowledge that they would lose him soon.

'But I think we were right to stop it when we did. Taking it any further… It just wouldn't be a good idea.'

'Oh!' Eva's left hand flew to her chest. 'You mean

this isn't for *real*?' She subtly waved her engagement ring at him, but the rolling eyes gave her away. 'I *do* know that, Joss. Really, you need to get over yourself.'

'I know I wasn't the only one holding back, Eva. And I don't need you to tell me your reasons. But I want you to hear mine. It's not like I didn't want—'

He stopped himself before he said something stupid.

He started again. 'I want you to understand why. You know that I've been married before?'

Eva nodded.

'Well, it didn't end well. For either of us. The thing is, before I got married I was ill. But I didn't realise.'

She looked curious at that, but didn't interrupt.

'It was clinical depression. I hid it from everyone. From my family. From my then girlfriend, now ex-wife. I didn't get the help I needed, and then the wedding gathered pace around me, and I found myself in the position of being a really terrible husband.'

Her eyes softened with sympathy. 'But you were ill, Joss. It wasn't your fault. Maybe you need to be kinder to yourself.'

He stood stiffly, determined that she would understand him. 'I know that depression is an illness, but that didn't make our marriage any easier for my wife. Or our divorce, for that matter. I realised after it was all over how wrong it had been to feel the way I had for a long time and I finally got help. Got better. But none of that changes what I put her through. Or the fact that I know that it could come back. I'll never be completely free from it. And I'm determined not to do to anyone else what I did to my ex.'

Eva took a step closer to him and he took half a step back. 'You don't know that you will get ill again,' she said.

'And I don't know that I won't. What I *do* know right now is that my dad is dying, and that seems as good a recipe for depression as any other I can think of.'

'And don't I get a say in this?'

He looked at her closely. Had he missed something? This had started as a way of getting things off his chest, just to make things clear to her. A way to avoid the bottling up of his thoughts that he knew could lead somewhere toxic. She had been holding back too last night, and he'd assumed that meant that she was as wary of this chemistry between them as he was. But was he wrong? Did she want more?

Her answer unsettled him—he'd never really thought that she'd want a say in it.

'Don't look at me like that,' she said. He hadn't realised he was looking at her like *anything*. 'I'm not saying that we were wrong to stop things.'

He walked away from the desk and she shifted herself up to perch on the edge of it. He couldn't tear his eyes away from her ankles, slender and vulnerable-looking atop her smart spike heels.

'Look,' she continued. 'I think we can both say that there is an attraction between us. After what happened last night it would be stupid to attempt to deny it. But I'm as scared of this thing as you are. No offence— and this has nothing to do with what you've just told me—but a relationship with you would scare the hell out of me. I want commitment and stability, and even before I knew what you just told me it was abundantly clear that those things are not of interest to you. I fancy you—okay. But that doesn't mean that wanting you is a good idea. We got carried away last night. It was the first time that we really had to act this thing out, and it was trickier than I expected to slip in and out of character. We'll get better at it. We have to.'

She fancied him? It shouldn't really be news to him—not after that kiss last night. But somehow, despite everything else she was saying, that was all he could hear. And not because it was a nice boost to his ego. But because it made him question so many things from the last few years. All those times he'd avoided her, knowing that she was too much temptation, had she felt the same?

'But just because I don't think this would be a good idea, Joss…' she slipped off the desk and came towards him, laying a gentle hand on his arm, '… I don't think having an illness in your past is a good enough reason to shut yourself off from the idea of having a relationship in the future. There's probably some woman out there who thinks you'll make the perfect boyfriend—and she should probably be allowed a say in what happens. Why don't you give it a chance?'

He thought for a long moment. Some mystery woman who might come and convince him that he had been wrong about the decisions he had made in his life? He just couldn't see that happening. If he couldn't find it in himself to bend his rules for Eva, he just couldn't imagine any other woman who would make him want to.

'Well, we don't need to worry about that, do we?'

he said briskly, wanting out of this conversation before he started questioning his own better judgement. 'For now, I'm an engaged man. And one relationship—even a fake one—is enough.'

'Fine.' Eva said, crossing her arms. But then her expression and her body language softened. 'But I meant what I said. If you want to talk, Joss, or if you think your depression might be coming back…you can come to me. I mean, a fake fiancée can still be a pretty good listener.'

Joss smiled. If things had been different—if he hadn't had this illness lingering in his past—he was pretty sure she'd made a damn good *real* fiancée.

'I appreciate that. So, what about you? No luck finding a stable, committed guy to do this for real?'

'Plenty of candidates,' Eva said, with a shrug that wasn't as nonchalant as he thought she was hoping for. 'None that quite match up to my criteria.'

'Lucky for me, I guess.'

'Damned lucky for you.'

CHAPTER SEVEN

Eva sat at her desk, watching the clock on her screen ticking ever closer to seven o'clock. It was already dark outside and the office had emptied a couple of hours ago—everyone except her and Joss were long gone.

She wondered whether Joss was working late for the same reason she was—putting off the moment when they would have to go back to her little apartment and start living together for real. Her stomach gave a growl, and she wished she had picked up something more substantial for lunch.

Well, one of them was going to have to be the first to make a move, and she was too hungry to wait and see if Joss would cave. She shut down her computer and straightened up her files for the morning.

Joss appeared in the doorway to his office, leaning against the frame.

'Heading home?' he asked.

'Yeah, I'm all done for the day. And starving,' she added truthfully. 'I'll see you back there.'

She opened the door to her flat and headed straight for the kitchen. She hadn't shared her living space since she had left university and started working at Dawson's, and she realised that she had no idea how adult flatmates really worked. Or any form of cohabiting other than student living, really. She'd not seen her parents living together often enough to have formed an idea of it at an early age. How *did* a relationship work with both parties present at least most of the time?

She hated feeling so uncertain in her own home. For as long as she had been working at Dawson's she'd felt settled, secure. She'd known how things worked in the office; she'd had her own place to come home to. No one had started changing things up just when she'd got settled. And now her security at the office had gone, and even her home wasn't the safe haven it was meant to be with Joss moving in.

She chucked the leftover sauce she'd found in the freezer into the microwave and tested the pasta. Still way too *al dente*. A glance out of the window showed no one coming up the mews, and she felt relieved. Perhaps she'd be able to eat and zone out in front of a box set for an hour before Joss came home. At which point she could invent some excuse and escape to her bedroom for the rest of the evening.

Really, Eva, she chastised herself. *Hiding? Not exactly your style.*

But then the glow of a mobile phone outside the window caught her eye and she knew that her plans for a solo dinner had just been thwarted.

When she heard the knock at the door she remembered that Joss didn't have a key—something they'd have to fix. As she walked down the stairs it really hit her. He was going to be here. Every day. Even if not in person, his stuff would be here. He was going to be a permanent presence in her life for the next few months at least.

She tried to think of the last time she'd had a relationship, even a friendship like that, and came up blank. The last man she'd lived with was her father. And that hadn't exactly been plain sailing.

She opened the door and stood aside to let Joss pass her on the stairs, but instead he stopped in the doorway and gave her a considering look.

'What's wrong?'

'Nothing,' she replied automatically, trying to shake off the mood that thinking about her parents always caused. 'Just thinking that we need to get you a key cut. Come up—I've put some pasta on.'

'I thought you told me not to get used to being cooked for?'

'You shouldn't. You're cooking next time.'

'Fine. It's a date. I told you—you're not going to scare me off with threats of domesticity.'

A date. She hadn't meant it to sound like that, but intentionally or not she'd just arranged one. Did Joss see it like that too? Or was it just a figure of speech?

She shook her head as she went back up to the kitchen and gave the sauce a stir. Of course he didn't see it like that. He couldn't have been clearer with her that he didn't want to date her. Good, because she'd already told him—more than once, and in no uncertain terms—that she didn't want to date him either.

And where did that leave her? she wondered, thinking back over the last few years of her love-life—or lack of one. If she didn't want to date the only man she had been remotely interested in in years, then was she resigning herself to a lifetime of being alone?

Maybe there wasn't anything wrong with that. Lots of people never married. Stayed single. Perhaps that was the life she was cut out for. When this engagement was over Joss would move out, she would move a couple of cats in, and settle for the next few decades.

But if she really thought that why had she bothered dating at all? Why download the apps and accept the blind dates and chat to the hopeful-looking men in bars if she wasn't looking for something more?

Window shopping—that was what she had been doing. After their visit to the Italian store's jewellery department yesterday, she recognised it for what it was. Looking at all the pretty things on offer, knowing they weren't right for her, and that she would never be interested in actually buying them. So why wasn't she interested in dating Joss either? If the only reason she hadn't wanted those other guys was because they weren't *him*, surely she should want him if he were offered on a plate.

But it wasn't just about him, she realised. Maybe it had never been about him. If she refused to accept anyone who wasn't Joss, but didn't want the real thing either, then that left her where? On the shelf? Off the market? It left her alone, as she had been for all of her life. Where she was comfortable.

Was that what this was?

'Hey, is it terrible to open a bottle of wine on a Tuesday night?' Joss asked, grabbing one from the rack beneath the kitchen counter.

'After we spent most of Monday night on the Prosecco? I don't think anyone will judge us too harshly.'

She was glad of the distraction as she opened the bottle and found glasses.

'So, what have you got planned for the rest of the week?' she asked, trying to keep their conversation on a safe work footing as they went through to the living room and settled with bowls of pasta on their knees and their wine on the coffee table.

'Ah, I actually need to talk to you about that.'

'Sounds ominous.'

She'd expected him to brush the comment off, but he nodded. *Not good.*

'It's Dad. He's invited us to spend the weekend with him. He wanted an engagement party, inviting the great and the good. I managed to talk him out of it, but he still wants us to spend some quality time together.'

'Just the three of us?'

It was a lovely idea, in theory. She couldn't think of a better way for Joss and his father to spend the time they had left. And she loved Edward—of course she wanted to spend time with him. But this charade of a relationship with Joss made everything more complicated. By spending time together, were they going to expose their secret and do more harm than good?

After what had happened in Milan she knew that spending more time in close quarters with Joss and an audience wasn't a sensible idea. Acting out their relationship with the Lazzaris had led to acting out her desires, and they had both agreed that that had been a bad idea. The last thing they needed was a whole weekend of blurring the boundaries.

But they had to put Edward first. And if it was a weekend of quality time that he wanted, then that was what he deserved.

'Yeah, just the three of us,' Joss replied. 'Unless you want half the county and your business contacts list invited too?'

She shuddered. She wasn't sure what was worse—the scrutiny of the single person who knew them both better than just about anyone, or of everyone either of them had ever met.

'The whole weekend?' she checked, thinking that maybe, if they went for just a few hours over lunch, they might be able to keep up the pretence without doing too much harm to her self-control. Being together a whole weekend, there was no way that they'd be able to get away with separate bedrooms—not when Edward thought they were living together.

'That's what he said. And, given the circumstances, I want to go. It's not like we have time to waste.'

'And he wants me there too? Are you sure?'

Joss nodded. 'Of course he does. He thinks you're my fiancée. He just assumed that you would be coming. And you have to admit it would look strange if you didn't.'

Of course it would.

'Okay. And it's just one night, isn't it? Two at most?'

Joss nodded. 'We'll drive down after work on Friday. Be back on Sunday.'

She drew her brows together in confusion. Edward's house was no more than a fifteen-minute walk from her mews, on one of the smart garden squares that filled this part of London.

'Drive there? Wait—where are we going?'

'The house in Berkshire. I thought you realised that's what I meant?'

She sat back in the sofa cushions, temporarily lost for words at the thought of being isolated down a country lane with Joss. Somehow the seclusion of a country house seemed more intimate than being in London all together. If they were in the city she could make excuses to give Joss and Edward time alone together—pop out and fetch them all coffee, suggest a trip to the gallery she knew was opening on Saturday. In the countryside she didn't even know if there would be a pub nearby to escape to if it all went wrong.

She shook her head, but knew that she couldn't refuse. 'Of course I'll come—it'd be my pleasure.'

Oh, she shouldn't have used that word. Because now all she could think of was all the different types of pleasure that Joss could show her in an isolated country house. Hot breath on cold cheeks after a walk to a secluded spot in the woods... Cold hands on warm skin in front of a roaring fire...

'And the rest of the week?' she asked, knowing that she needed to distract Joss from what she was sure was a tell-tale blush on her cheeks.

'Dubai,' he said, giving her a curious look. 'You were right. I need to show my face. Let them know everything's going smoothly. Make sure everyone's happy with how things are going to work from now on.'

She nodded. 'Sounds like a good idea.'

'I need you to let me know if there are any problems here,' he went on. 'Make sure the place is running okay with Dad not coming in to the office any more.'

'I'm your eyes and ears on the ground. I get it. Do you want me to book your tickets?'

'It's done,' Joss said.

Eva felt piqued that he had bypassed her.

'What?' he asked, when he saw the look on her face.

'I know all this fiancée stuff is pretend, but you *do* know that the job isn't? I'm your assistant. I should know about your travel plans.'

'You're angry that I got someone else to book my plane ticket?'

'I'm angry that you're not letting me do my job. The other thing doesn't trump that, you know. I know it's hard, with everything else that's going on, but we have to find a way to work together as well. Otherwise how will that look? Like you've taken over and I'm instantly getting an easy ride.'

'Well, at least one of us is…' Joss said.

Eva didn't want to begin to unpick all the potential meanings of that sentence. Way too dangerous.

'Fine,' he said. 'While I'm away you can take over everything that's needed. When I'm back you can brief me on anything you think I need to know about from my father's desk that he hasn't already covered. Does that meet with your approval?'

'Fine. Good.'

She knew she still sounded short with him as she took another sip of wine, but she prided herself on her professional skills. If Joss was going to work around her at every opportunity she couldn't see herself *wanting* to stay in her job for much longer—a thought that terrified her. If she didn't want to be at Dawson's any more she didn't know who she was, never mind what she wanted from life.

No, she was being silly. Her job at Dawson's went way beyond her relationship with Joss, and mattered way more. She wouldn't even consider leaving just because she and Joss hadn't worked out the finer details of their professional relationship yet.

'So, when do you leave for Dubai?' she asked, wondering when she would get back the safety and security of living alone.

'I thought I'd go Tuesday, then be back in time to drive us down on Friday. Does that work with my diary?'

'You'll have to tell me. Until we get to work tomorrow I'm officially off the clock,' she said, taking a glug of her wine to prove her point.

CHAPTER EIGHT

EVA GLANCED AT the time, hating herself for doing it even as her eyes were drawn once again to the hands on the old wooden grandfather clock in the far corner of Joss's new office.

Three forty-seven. Exactly four minutes after she had last looked.

And at least twenty minutes after she had expected to see Joss back in the office.

He had been on a half-nine flight, which the live arrivals board told her had arrived at Heathrow at thirteen thirty-three. If he'd jumped into the car that she had booked for him he should definitely be here by now.

It was professional concern, she told herself. He had a meeting at four o'clock. She'd told him he would be cutting it fine if they were to leave to pick up his father this evening and get to the house, but he'd insisted that he would be there in time.

Her eagerness to see him was nothing to do with the way she had lain in bed awake, remembering the hard press of his body and the gentle touch of his lips in that hotel suite in Milan. Thinking about the night they had spent together in her flat, knowing that he was just down the hall. Knowing she could bump into him on the way to the bathroom and get a glimpse of those firm, toned abs and muscular thighs.

She shook off the thought. No, it was absolutely nothing to do with that at all.

A noise behind her made her jump, and she turned to see Joss striding through the office, familiar holdall in hand, glancing at his watch.

'I know, I know—you told me it would be close.'

'And you told me you'd make it. I never doubted you,' she lied.

He came up to her desk and kissed her on the cheek, and it was only as the blush rose that she remembered he was only doing what would be expected from a man who'd just spent a few nights away from his fiancée. He was performing for their audience, who—a brief glance out of the corner of her eye told her—were appreciative of his efforts.

'I told him you'd meet him in his office,' she said after a pregnant pause, suddenly struck with stage fright, unsure of her lines.

'Great. I'll drop this bag and head over there now. We'll still be out of here by six. Promise.'

She smiled and waited for him to walk away, but his gaze hadn't broken from hers and the ghost of a smile passed over his lips.

'Did you miss me?' he asked.

She resisted the urge to draw in a shocked breath, keeping her breathing deliberately slow and even. Was he playing with her? Was this part of their act or was he really asking her—the *real* her, not the fake fiancée?

'Not even a tiny bit,' she said, with a proper smile of her own.

Any eager ears in the office could put that down to normal relationship banter, she decided. And it was worth it to see the expression on Joss's face. She liked taking him by surprise.

He reached out a hand to her cheek, just ghosting the tips of his fingers along the line of her jaw. 'Well, I guess that means I need to make more of an impression,' he said, his voice low. Too low to be for the benefit of their audience. 'Give you something to miss next time I'm gone.'

He brought his right hand up in a mirror of his left, bracketing her with his fingers. She should pull away. Turn her face to her computer monitor in an effort at professionalism. But then she might never know. She would be left wondering whether this was for play or for real. And suddenly, dangerous or not, she had to know.

For the fleeting half-second he held her gaze, she wondered if she would be able to tell. And then she remembered that kiss in Milan. The way that they'd read everything the other person was feeling through the touch of their skin. And she knew that his body wouldn't lie to her, whatever he might say out loud.

With the first fleeting, barely there caress of his lips, she knew that it was real. It held all the promise of their kiss in Milan. Set off all the same fireworks. She lifted her hand to his face, felt the same tension in his jaw—the strength of his desire battling with the strength of his self-control. She could feel herself teetering on the edge, just as she had in Italy, knowing that letting a crack in her resolve show for even a second would mean they were both lost.

Which was why—even as it pained her—she pulled away. Again. Put just a millimetre of space between them, waited for him to move further back. He didn't. Instead he leaned his forehead against hers, and she could sense rather than see his smile.

'Now I'm late,' he said, after what felt like an age but couldn't have been more than a second.

Eva bit her lip with a smile, unwilling to let the moment go just yet. 'Told you so,' she said, stifling a laugh.

Joss sneaked one last peck onto her cheek before he strolled out of the office with an irritating degree of calm and confidence.

When the door shut behind him Eva knew she couldn't avoid looking around her any longer. She glanced over the partition of her cubicle and saw that—as she might have guessed—all eyes had been on her and Joss. She waited for the inevitable jokey comments, but instead the women—and half the men—were looking at her wide-eyed.

Eventually her assistant blew out a slow breath in awe, and muttered something that sounded incredibly like, 'Lucky woman.'

If only she knew.

On the dot of six o'clock, Joss closed his laptop and reached for the jacket he'd chucked over the back of his chair. He'd promised Eva that he'd be done in good time for them to leave for his father's country house for the weekend, and he had no intention of breaking that promise. Especially after what had happened earlier.

What *had* happened?

He wasn't sure what had come over him. But as soon as he had walked into the office and seen her it had been as if something that had been missing for three days was suddenly back and in overload. As if he hadn't even known he needed something, and then was drunk on it.

It had been meant as a polite, friendly hello. The sort of public kiss that anyone would offer their fiancée when they'd been away for a few days. To do anything else would have looked suspicious. But as soon as their eyes had locked it had been so much more.

That night in Milan had come flooding back—everywhere that kiss might have led if they had decided to let it. And then it had been too late to back out, and he'd had no choice but to give in to what his body had been begging him to do. Let his fingers trace the soft skin on her jaw, let his lips brush against hers, setting off a chain reaction that was going to lead them somewhere dangerous.

Thank goodness they were in the office, with an in-built safety net of public scrutiny and didn't have to rely on their self-control. Or *his* self-control at least. Who knew? Perhaps hers was still rock-solid, and she'd only returned his kiss for show.

No, he knew her better than that, he realised. He had felt the passion in her, and the iron self-control that was holding her just as fast as it was him. She wanted him, but she wasn't going to let it get the better of her.

And now they were going to be spending a whole weekend together, holed up in an isolated country house. Most people would consider having their dying father there as having something of a chaperone effect—but, as he'd once said to her, they weren't 'most people'.

He had to stop overthinking this. It would only make them awkward. The only thing to do this weekend—if they wanted to keep the lie alive and his father happy—was to jump right in. Forget it was a lie. Live as if they were really an engaged couple, head over heels in love. And lust.

But where could that lead when sustained over a weekend? In Italy it had led to an aborted kiss, when they had both still had just enough self-awareness to keep it from going further. And—importantly—they'd had separate bedrooms to retreat to. When they found themselves alone behind a closed door with a four-poster in the corner how were they going to resist?

Well, they'd just have to find a way. Because the alternative was giving in to this attraction. Getting involved in something real. And he knew that if he let that happen Eva would get hurt—and he wasn't having that.

He opened the door to see that she was still sitting at her desk, concentrating on the screen of her computer, the pen in her hand tapping absent-mindedly at her lip. He couldn't look away, reminded of the feel of those lips less than a couple of hours ago. But she was obviously more aware of him than he realised, because she held up the pen in the universal sign for, *Give me a minute*.

She tapped a few more keys, and then looked up with

a beaming smile. 'Sorry—just had to get that done. Are we ready?'

He nodded, temporarily lost for words. He didn't know how she had that effect on him. But then, why would he? For years he'd been avoiding this. Avoiding finding out the effect that she might have on him. Well, there was going to be no getting away from it this weekend.

He wondered if she was as nervous as he was about them being in such close proximity. His father's house was far bigger than her flat, but there were fewer places to hide. Not when they couldn't drop their act as soon as they were inside the front door and start treating each other like indifferent colleagues again.

Eva wrapped a long scarf around her neck as she stood up, half an eye still on her computer before she finally shrugged her shoulders and shut it down.

'Problems?' Joss asked.

'No…nothing. I'd just hoped to be able to sort something out before we left. It's not a big deal.'

He held out her coat and she slipped her arms in while he resisted the urge to run his hands instead of the sleeves up her arms. To let them rest on her shoulders before brushing her hair aside and pressing a kiss at the nape of her neck.

Eva turned on the spot and was suddenly far, far closer than was comfortable. She barely had to look up to meet his gaze, and he resisted the sensible part of his brain that was urging him to take a step backwards.

'Ready, then?' she asked, glancing past him towards the door.

'As I'll ever be.'

Thankfully the drive out to the house was short and familiar—because, Joss thought, he really couldn't attest to his competency on the road with a car so filled with atmosphere.

His father had seemed chipper when they had picked him up, as Edward had slung his small bag into the boot of the car, but he had been asleep on the backseat within minutes.

'Everything okay?' Eva asked, after they had been driving in silence for another ten.

'Yeah, fine.'

He knew that he was killing any chance of conversation dead with his monosyllables, but for the moment he didn't care. The confined space of his car, with two people keeping secrets from each other, was more pressure than he could take.

It wasn't until he drew on to the driveway of his father's country house, between the old stone gateposts, that he finally felt himself start to relax. It wasn't so much that the pressure of having a fake fiancée was lessened. But out of the city, with space around them, it felt easier to breathe.

He parked close to the front door, and was relieved to see it open before they had stepped out of the car, and Thomas, their groundskeeper, pushing a wheelchair through.

Joss stepped out of the car and stared at the chair for a moment. He hadn't even realised that his father *owned* a wheelchair, never mind needed one. But Edward had slept the whole way here from London, and Joss suspected that he hadn't been entirely honest about how well he was feeling.

He waved at Thomas as he walked up to the steps at the front of the house. 'Thanks for this,' Joss said, gesturing at the chair. 'But he fell asleep while we were driving. We should probably just leave him a few minutes.'

'Probably for the best,' Thomas agreed with a nod. 'And this must be Eva.'

Joss looked behind him to see Eva stepping from the car, glancing briefly through the back window to check on his father. He felt a tug of tenderness at this obvious display of affection for the old man. He had no idea what the next few months had in store for them. How dark things were going to get while his father's body fought and then succumbed to this disease. But, however complicated things might be, he was glad that Eva was going to be by his side.

It was selfish, he knew, to look for her support. Especially when he knew that he wouldn't be able to return it. He was going to need all his strength to look after his father, to look after himself. And that was why he couldn't let this thing with Eva become real. Because she would get hurt.

He had to keep reminding himself of that. It didn't matter how good she looked, how incredible she smelled, how natural it felt to have her skin against his, her hand in his. Her life meshing with his. It didn't matter that it felt right, because it wasn't.

Except... That was not what Eva had said when he'd explained things to her. It wasn't what she believed. He had told her, plainly, the reasons he shouldn't be in a relationship, but they hadn't seemed to be good enough for her. He supposed he was lucky that she had her own reasons for wanting to stay single. Because she hadn't recoiled when he had told her of his depression. Hadn't blamed him when he'd told her about how his last marriage had ended. She had simply told him what he knew intellectually to be true: that he had been ill, and that what had happened had been out of his control.

Well, that might have been true then. But it wasn't now. He wasn't going to let this relationship get out of control. Because when that happened innocent bystanders like Eva got caught in the crossfire.

Eva walked towards him and threw a questioning glance towards Thomas. He loved the way she didn't even break her stride as she held out her hand to shake his. There was something in her posture, her confidence, her self-awareness, in the straightness of her back and shoulders, that he found completely captivating.

'Eva, this is Thomas. He looks after the house and the grounds. And perhaps he looks after my father, too, recently?' Joss said, glancing again at the wheelchair. 'Does he use this a lot, Thomas?'

'Ah…only now and then,' Thomas replied. 'More the last time he was here. He hasn't told you?'

'My father's been keeping secrets.'

'Well, he's not the only one, is he? It's lovely to meet you, Eva,' Thomas said. 'I hear that there are wedding bells in the offing. Congratulations to both of you.'

'Thanks,' Joss said, with a quick side-glance at Eva.

She was still smiling at Thomas, not showing any sign of discomfort at their lie. Once again he was blown away by her self-possession.

The sound of the car door opening behind them caused him to turn sharply on the spot, to see his father stepping out of the car.

'Sorry about that, folks. You know what it's like in the back of a car. Like being rocked to sleep in a cradle.'

Joss took the wheelchair from Thomas's hands and pushed it over to the car, but his father waved it away. 'No need for that, son. But if you don't mind I think I'll go and finish this nap inside. You show Eva around. Enjoy the last of the sunshine—it's been a beautiful day.'

Well, his father was right about that. The sun was low in the sky, casting long shadows over the garden through the leaves, which were just starting to turn shades of red and gold.

'Don't worry about the bags,' Thomas said. 'I'll get those. Your father's right. Go for a walk down to the village. The path's beautiful this time of year, and there's just enough light left.'

Joss turned to Eva with a questioning look, and she smiled. 'Good job I threw some boots in my bag. Sounds like a lovely idea.'

She pulled on her boots as she perched on the bumper of his car, and Joss watched his father walk slowly up the steps to the front door. It had only been a couple of days since he had last seen him, but his father seemed years older. And more sick.

When he reached Thomas he leaned on him for a few

moments before taking the last step up into the house. They would have to talk later. Have one of the difficult conversations they had all known must be coming about what his father wanted for the end of his life and how they could all keep him comfortable.

But for now the sun was just touching the tops of the trees, and he knew that the pub in the village would have good beer on tap. They could keep the real world at bay for an hour longer while his father rested.

He grabbed boots and a coat from the car and looked over at Eva, who was winding a scarf around her neck. Was she going to regret this in the weeks to come? Entangling herself with a man, a family, that was about to reach crisis point?

'Let's go,' he said, heading towards the path at the side of the house that would take them through the gardens and then down towards the village.

He walked quickly around the corner of the house, glancing up at the familiar red brick of the old building. This had never been his permanent home, but it had always been a happy place to escape at weekends and in school holidays. He knew every inch of the brickwork, every hollow and tree in the grounds. And soon it would be his, he realised. Along with the house in London and the dozens of Dawson's stores around the world. A whole portfolio of responsibilities was about to fall onto his shoulders.

'Is it far to the village?' Eva asked, catching up and walking alongside him.

'Not far—about fifteen minutes if we go down the

lane. If we want to stay for a pint we'd better walk the road way back. It'll be dark by then.'

'Sounds good to me,' Eva said, and they fell into silence as they walked.

Joss buried his hands deep into his pockets.

'Your father looked tired,' Eva said eventually. 'I'm glad he went for a lie-down. I was worried.'

Joss stopped for a second. 'Me too,' he said eventually. 'I should have expected it,' he added, walking on.

'Doesn't mean it wasn't a shock. Or that it won't be hard to watch.'

'I'm aware of that.'

As soon as the words were out of his mouth he regretted them. Or his tone, at least. He shouldn't be taking this out on Eva—it wasn't her fault. For a second he had a flashback to his marriage. Fights over nothing, and always with his dark mood at the start of them.

'I'm sorry, Eva. I didn't mean to snap.'

'It's okay. It's understandable,' she said, brushing a hand against his arm.

He shrugged it off. This was exactly what he was trying to avoid. Anyone being in the firing line if his depression came back. He was going to do everything in his power to stop that happening, but if he couldn't do that—if he couldn't beat it again—he was at least going to make sure that he wasn't taking anyone else down with him.

'It shouldn't be. You shouldn't let me get away with it.'

'You're under a lot of stress. I can't imagine—'

'Eva, don't make excuses for me. I don't need them. This shouldn't affect you.'

'If I didn't want it to affect me, Joss, I wouldn't have gone along with this whole charade in the first place.'

Joss turned to her, shaking his head and stopping his stride. 'That's different. Of course Dad being ill is going to affect you. But that doesn't mean that my moods should as well.'

Eva brushed her hand against his sleeve again, and this time he lost the battle to shrug it off.

'We're living together. I'm pretty sure that in a couple the other person's crappy moods are part of the deal. Trust me—give it a couple of weeks and I'll give you a run for your money.'

'We're not just talking about an occasional bad mood with me, though. This is something different.'

'Are you talking about your depression?' Eva asked. 'If you're telling me you think it's returning, Joss, then we can talk about that. We can think about getting you the help you need to get you through a bad patch. But snapping at people is something that we all do. It doesn't have to be a symptom of something bigger.'

'It's no excuse.'

'You're right.' She nodded. 'It's not. So apologise, think about what I've said, and we'll move on.'

'I'm sorry,' he said after a few long minutes of walking in silence. 'I don't want you to be brought down by this.'

'You know, maybe you could trust me to *tell* you when enough is enough. My happiness isn't your responsibility, Joss. I can look after myself. I always do.'

She was right—her happiness wasn't his responsibility. But he'd like it to be, he realised. He'd like his first task in the morning to be to put a smile on her face. He could think of a dozen ways right now that he'd like to try. And then he could spend his whole day keeping it there.

But another person's happiness was too big a responsibility on top of his own. Especially for someone like him, who had so spectacularly failed at the task in the past.

He also suspected there was more in what she said than first met the eye. She had always looked after her own happiness... Well, of course. Everyone had responsibility for their own happiness. But the way she'd said it—there was independence and then there was isolation. He suspected he knew which side of the coin she was on.

'So you always look after yourself?' Joss asked, brushing past some overgrown gorse, the thorns catching on his coat.

'No one else volunteered for the job,' Eva replied, with a flippant smile that didn't reach her eyes.

It was obvious that she didn't believe what she was saying. Which meant she was hiding something. After exposing so much of his own past, his own vulnerabilities, he suddenly realised how little he knew about her. And he hated how unequal that felt. Hated that she might be able to hold that over him. If he was exposed, then she should be too.

That was what was behind him needing to know more, he told himself. It wasn't that he had any other reason to want to know why she hadn't met someone and settled down already.

'Somehow I find that hard to believe,' he said. 'I have a suspicion that plenty of guys were interested and none quite measured up.'

'What makes you think that?'

'Oh, you know. You hear things.'

She gave him a sideways look that told him exactly how unbelievable she thought that was.

'Um… I think we've already established that you *don't* hear things. Try again.'

He shrugged. 'Fine—I'm guessing. Are you going to tell me I'm wrong?'

He watched her carefully, watched her eyes narrow and her forehead wrinkle as she thought hard. So he had hit on something, then.

'Why are you so keen to pair me off, Joss? You're not going to be one of those unbearable people who can't see a single woman in her thirties without assuming there's something wrong with her?'

He'd give her full points for deflection, but zero for accuracy. Well, if he'd hit a fault line it seemed to make sense to keep pushing.

'I don't know. *Is* there something wrong with you?'

Eva threw her hands up and picked up her pace, calling over her shoulder. 'So you *are* going to be one of those people? Great.'

He jogged a few paces to catch her up. 'I just wonder why you think you have to do everything by yourself.'

She slowed down again. 'I never said that I did,' she replied.

'No, but I've watched you. In the office. With me. You like to be in control.'

'So? Who doesn't?'

He gave her a meaningful look. 'But a relationship doesn't work like that, does it? Sometimes you have to give the other person a chance.'

She shook off his comment with a carefully neutral expression. 'Good job we're not *in* a relationship then, isn't it? We're just pretending—which means I don't need to change anything about who I am for you.'

'Right, because *that's* a healthy way to approach things.'

'So now I'm unhealthy? Is that what's wrong with me, or is there something else?'

He tried to reach for her wrist, slow her down, but she dodged away from him.

'I'm starting to think you're impossible—does that count?' he asked.

'Oh, sure—why not add impossible to the list as well? At least you don't have to wonder why I'm single any more. It should be self-evident by now.'

Oh, it was becoming that way. The way she deflected his questions. The way her arms had folded over her body, putting physical as well as emotional barriers between them. The way she was making every effort to appear as unavailable and unattractive to him as possible...

She wanted to be single—fair enough. Relationships weren't for everyone. He knew that. But he recognised something in the way she oh-so-casually brushed off the idea of being involved with someone. He recognised it because it was so familiar. It was the same brush-off he'd given his father for years when he asked if he'd considered dating again, giving married life a second chance. The same expression he'd doled out to concerned friends who asked if he wasn't lonely with his string of meaningless dates.

Something had happened to make Eva feel this way about relationships, and he wanted to know what it was.

'So have you always felt like this?' he asked, as the sun slipped behind the thick hedgerows, leaving them in a twilight that cast murky shadows across her face.

'Yeah, I suppose… Just never thought I'd be the settling-down type.'

'But you do date?' he clarified.

'Of course I date. I'm not a hermit.'

But why bother dating if you didn't want a relationship? He knew that one tended to lead to the other, which was why he had stayed clear of both.

'Why do you date?' he asked.

'I don't know—for fun? To meet new people? Do new stuff?'

'Why meet new people who you're not planning on seeing again?'

He could see from the tight expression on her face that he was annoying her. Well, good—if it meant that they got to the bottom of this issue and she stopped evading his probing.

'I see some of them again,' she said, a note of defiance—or was it simply irritation?—in her voice.

'What—two, three times, I'm guessing.'

'What is this, Joss? Are you stalking me now, or just planning to?' she asked as they reached the end of the lane.

He could see the lights from the pub across the road. They crossed to it in silence, and it wasn't until they were installed at the bar, each with a pint of real ale, that he picked up his line of questioning.

'I'm not stalking you,' he said, just in case she hadn't been kidding. 'I'm just guessing. But I'm pretty sure I'm right, or you wouldn't have reacted that way.'

She took a sip of her beer, and he could see the machinations behind her eyes as she tried to work out what his angle was. Why he was so interested.

'I just don't get why you want to know, Joss. Why it's any of your business, in fact.'

He managed a wry smile. 'You're right. It's not. I mean, if we were *friends* then it would be normal for us to talk about this sort of stuff—the guys you're dating, what you want for your future. But we're not friends.'

'We're not?'

'Of course we're not. How can we be when you're so intent on keeping me at arm's length?'

'Um… I thought we were keeping *each other* at arm's length? I thought we had decided that was the best thing to do? We both know that getting involved romantically is a complication this situation really doesn't need.'

'I'm not talking about romance, Eva. I'm talking about friendship. We've barely spoken since Milan. And I don't know about you but it feels weird to me. We're living together. We're working together. We're spending the bloody weekend together with my dad. If we can't even be friendly to each other it's going to be unbearable. And we don't know how long we're going to be keeping this up. Months in the same house but living as strangers—it just wouldn't feel right.'

'Now you're accusing me of not being friendly? You *do* remember we had this exact conversation the other day, except it wasn't me who was being standoffish.'

'You were talking about being friendly.' He laid a hand over hers, where it was fidgeting with a beer mat. He wanted her to focus on their conversation. He needed her to open up to him, and he didn't want to think too hard about why. 'I'm talking about being friends, Eva. Do you even know that there's a difference?'

'I have friends.' She shrugged his hand away with an annoyed flick of her fingers.

'Do you? Really? People you tell your darkest secrets to? Who know you as well as you do yourself?'

She looked up from the beer mat and met his eye— there was fire in her expression now, and he knew he was close to cracking her. Close to the truth.

'That's a pretty narrow definition of friendship.'

'I don't know… I think most people agree it involves opening yourself up. Being vulnerable.'

'Oh, and you're the expert on that, I suppose? Because you're so open to letting new people into your life. That's why you had to convince your assistant to pretend to be your fiancée rather than find yourself a real one.'

He choked on his beer and then looked at her for a few seconds without speaking. She was right. They had a lot in common—which meant he could tell her the truths he was pretty sure she needed to hear. It wasn't as if *she* was holding back. And she wasn't going to get out of talking about herself by turning the conversation to him. They'd already talked about his vulnerabilities—at length. He had no desire to go over that again.

'That's different. Other people got hurt. I'm protecting them, not myself.'

'You're *so* noble. The fact that you don't have to take a risk on anyone else—that's just a side benefit, I suppose?'

He reached for her hand again, hoping that the contact would bring her closer. Let her see that he was on her side.

'Don't turn this around. We were talking about *you*.'

'We were talking about vulnerability…about letting people get close. I think turning this around is pretty valid.'

'Fine, and we can talk about me later, if that's what you want. But right now we're talking about you. Why is it you don't want to let me in?'

CHAPTER NINE

'THIS ISN'T ABOUT YOU, Joss. It never has been.'

Her hand flew to her mouth as she took in a deep suck of air. She hadn't meant to say that.

Ever since he'd started digging, digging, digging—trying to get her to talk about why she didn't want to get involved—she'd told herself she shouldn't let him in. Letting people in never led anywhere good, and with Joss Dawson it would be downright dangerous.

It had been easier to dodge and deflect his questions when they'd been walking, with shadows to hide her face and the ability to walk off when he hit too close to the bone. But here in the cosy, intimate atmosphere of the pub, with the fire roaring behind them and Joss perching so close to her on a bar stool that she could see the golden flicker reflected in his eyes, she knew there was nowhere to escape.

The only way to shut this conversation down was to give him what he wanted—show him that a relationship wasn't an option for her, the same way it wasn't for him. Perhaps then he'd let the topic lie.

'Look, I know what it's like to have someone you

love leave you and hurt you, okay?' she said after a long pause. 'Is that what you want to hear? Because it's pretty much a description of my entire childhood. Both my parents in the army, taking it in turns to ship out while the other one was stuck at home with me. Me making friends and then being told we were leaving again. Until one day my mother didn't come home from her tour, and my dad—rather than be stuck with a grieving teenager—packed me off to boarding school so he could lose himself in his work. So for the love of God, Joss, don't talk to me about opening up. Some of us have perfectly good reasons for being happily closed books, thanks.'

She watched him as she waited for a response. Fine lines appeared at the corners of his eyes and a muscle in his jaw flickered. He was waiting, weighing, judging. Was he going to push further, or had she revealed just enough to make him back off?

'I'm sorry,' he said. 'I didn't know.'

Bingo. Well, her plan had worked, at least. But with the new information in the air between them, and old wounds exposed for the first time in years, she felt uncharacteristically vulnerable. Small and unprotected.

'It's fine. I just want to drop it now. We should change the subject.'

'Right.'

They sat in silence for a few minutes, while she tried to think of somewhere safe to take the conversation. Work? They had enough of that at…well, at work. His dad? That wasn't exactly going to lighten the mood. And there was no point waiting for Joss to pick up a small-talk baton. They'd already established he was all but incapable of that.

She glanced around them for inspiration and her eyes fell on a framed picture of the manor house, where they had left his father resting. Until she saw the picture, faded behind the bar, she hadn't really thought about the house as being part of the village, of Joss belonging to a community.

'So, has your family always owned the house?' she asked.

Joss's face relaxed immediately with relief at her opening small-talk gambit. Much as he had been pushing, it seemed he was as happy to see the personal topics dropped as she was. Perhaps because it meant that she wasn't turning the conversation back onto him, as she'd threatened.

'No, Dad bought it when I was small,' he said. 'After he and Mum divorced. He wanted somewhere in the country to bring us—get us out of the London fumes occasionally.'

Eva nodded slowly, raising her eyebrows. 'Well, when he wants to escape, he does it in style. How old were you when your parents split up?'

'Young enough not to remember it. It was all amicable. They're still good friends. No deep scars to probe there.'

'I'm glad to hear it.' She smiled, relieved the atmosphere really was lightening between them. 'So you used to come here at weekends?'

'And school holidays. You should see it in the summer—it's beautiful.'

'You're lucky.'

'I am.'

She could tell from the way he said it that he knew how incredibly privileged his life had been. But there was a tinge of sadness there, too. Because next time the house saw summer perhaps it would belong to Joss. And that could only mean one thing. She wondered whether Joss was making that same connection.

She finished her beer and glanced at her watch. 'Do you think your dad will have woken up?'

'Probably. We should head back anyway. I'm not sure whether Dad has asked Maria, Thomas's wife, to arrange dinner. But if he has you won't want to miss it.'

'Another woman who likes to cook for you—should I be jealous?'

Eva could feel a blush rise on her cheeks and turned her face to the fire so she could at least blame her colour on the heat from the flames. Thankfully Joss didn't capitalise on the potential of that sentence to get her confessing more secrets she didn't want to share.

'I'll drink up and you can find out for yourself.'

As they crunched up the gravel driveway towards the front door of the house Eva realised that there was one factor of spending the weekend with Edward they hadn't talked about yet—sleeping arrangements. Thomas had told them not to worry about their bags, which presumably meant that by the time they reached the house they would have been delivered to one of the dozens of bedrooms a house like this must contain—and, despite the copious number, they would have been delivered to the same one.

She could only hope that it contained an enormous bed, large enough for them to share without meeting in the middle at some point in the night. Or that there'd be an elegant chaise longue in the corner of the room that Joss could retire to in a show of gentlemanly manners.

If all else failed there were the flannel pyjamas—long legs and sleeves of course—that she'd packed just in case she found herself needing to protect her modesty.

They walked up the front steps and were met by Thomas at the door.

'How's my father?' Joss asked as soon as the door opened, and Eva couldn't help a small smile at his devotion to his father even in the sad circumstances.

'Still resting,' Thomas answered, with a concerned look. 'I've put you and Eva in your usual room, Joss, and Maria says dinner will be ready at eight. If you look in on your father, could you ask him if he'd like a tray instead and let me know? I think the journey must have taken it out of him.'

'Of course,' Joss said, his voice heavy with worry, and he gestured for Eva to go ahead of him up the stairs.

'Do you think he's okay?' Eva dropped her voice as they climbed, fearful of disturbing Edward, though with the treads carpeted in a lush, thick velvet, she supposed their voices wouldn't carry far.

'I'm shocked,' Joss replied. 'I didn't think that just driving to the country would tire him out so much. Either things are moving quicker than he expected, or he's not been telling the truth about what's going on.'

Eva had suspected as much herself. 'Are you going to ask him?'

'I already have. And I've offered to go to the hospital with him. He brushed me off with barely a word. He said he didn't want me dragged down by it.'

'Sounds like he wants to protect you.'

'Parents, huh?' A grimace crossed his face. 'Sorry, I didn't mean...'

'It's fine. You don't have to apologise for having a great dad. I just feel lucky that I got to know him too. You know, he's something of a father figure to me.'

'It will make him happy to know you think that.'

She shrugged, a little embarrassed. 'Well, let's not go telling him. We wouldn't want him to think we're getting all mushy.'

They reached the top of the staircase and Joss gestured her down the corridor in front of him. His steps slowed as they passed door after door, and eventually Eva had to laugh.

'My goodness—how many rooms *are* there in this house?'

'Last count? Fourteen bedrooms. And half as many bathrooms. Not sure about downstairs. I've never counted...'

'So, fourteen bedrooms and we end up—'

'Here,' Joss said, as they finally stopped and he opened the door.

Well, she'd been right about the chaise longue, at least. It was positioned under the elaborately draped Georgian paned windows, upholstered in a deep navy, with a pattern that caught the light from the chandelier overhead. A fire was set in the grate opposite the bed—a four-poster, naturally. It had a canopy up by the ceiling, and heavy curtains tied back in each corner. Crisp white pillows were piled up at the head of the bed, and instead of the sheets, blankets and eiderdown she'd been expecting there was a fluffy duvet, also covered in simple white cotton.

She turned to Joss and had to suppress a giggle.

'I know. It's a lot. But imagine a normal-sized bed in a room like this. You'd never find it.'

'No,' she said, shaking her head, her eyes wide. 'It's perfect. It's just…'

'Ridiculous? At least I drew the line at frilly sheets.'

'Yeah.' She let out a laugh. 'Yeah, a bit ridiculous.'

She crossed to the bed and had to do a little hop in order to hitch herself up onto the mattress. Joss came and sat beside her as she kicked her heels against the frame, and she turned to look at him, smiling.

'Here I was thinking it was going to be awkward, us sharing a bedroom, and I'm bursting out laughing as soon as we get in here.'

'Not what I'm usually aiming for when I show a woman to my bedroom,' Joss said. 'But I'll take it under the circumstances. You thought it would be awkward?'

'Well, of course. You didn't?'

'I hadn't really thought about it.'

'You're lucky to have me, d'you know that? To do your thinking for you. You really do need someone who knows how to do your job.'

'I never said I wasn't lucky.'

'Good. Let's keep it that way.'

She glanced around the room. Her comments on the decor and the house and the furniture had broken the ice when they'd entered the room but now, as they sat on the bed together she could feel tension mounting between them as they both looked around.

She presumed he was thinking the same thing she was—where were they going to sleep?

'I'll take the chaise longue,' Joss said eventually. 'I'll sneak some stuff from the linen closet.'

'And risk Thomas and Maria finding out that we're not what we say we are?'

'I'll blame it on you. Tell them you feel the cold,' he said, with a laugh that eased the tension again.

Eva pushed him gently on the arm. 'Throw me under a bus, why don't you? You know, the bed's the size of a continent,' she said. 'I trust you not to try anything if you want to share.'

'Wow. You have such a high opinion of me you feel you have to spell that out?'

'It was a generous offer and it comes with an expiry date. Just a warning.'

'Fine. Well I accept your offer.'

'Good.'

'Good.'

And all of a sudden awkwardness was back with a vengeance. She glanced across at Joss, then looked away as soon as she realised he had done the same. Being around this man was worse than being a teenager. At least then you could be pretty sure your crush was as messed up and confused as you were. But neither she nor Joss were hormonal kids. The decisions they made now would have real consequences over the coming days, weeks and months. There was no kissing now and then pretending it had never happened.

Except it was too late for that, Eva realised. Kissing without consequences was what they had tried in Milan, and if the tension between them right now was anything to go by there was no doubt that pretending it had never happened wasn't an option.

'I should check on my father,' Joss said at last, breaking the atmosphere between them.

It was a temporary reprieve; she knew that tension would be waiting for them when they climbed the stairs at the end of the night and found themselves locked in here until morning.

Joss disappeared for a few minutes, and then stuck his head round the door. 'Dad's going to join us downstairs, but I'm going to give him a hand getting ready. Do you need anything?'

She shrugged, and glanced pointedly around the room. 'Well, I didn't pack my tiara. Will I be needing one of those?'

'Oh, don't worry about it. Chuck on any old jewels. Kidding!' he added, when her expression must have shown her surprise. 'I'll see you downstairs.'

Eva descended the stairs, wondering how on earth she was meant to find the dining room without a map or a compass. When Joss had been trying to find her mews house he'd had the benefit of satellites and technology, but she suspected there wasn't an app for navigating your fake fiancé's country home.

She stuck her head around a couple of doors, reveal-

ing grand reception rooms with clusters of uncomfort-
able-looking furniture. In the end she followed her nose
down grand corridors to the back of the house, until the
sound of Radio 4 came into hearing and the smell of
roasting chicken grew stronger.

She checked another couple of doors until eventually she stumbled into a room with an enormous range
cooker and an elegant woman—seemingly in her fif-
ties, and certainly in charge—stirring something de-
licious-smelling.

The door hinges squeaked and the woman turned
around, her face lighting up with a smile. 'You must
be Eva,' she said. 'I'm Maria. I try and keep this house
in order and keep those men fed.'

Eva returned her smile, feeling instantly welcome.
'And you do a beautiful job of both, by the looks of
things. Roast chicken?' she asked, knowing that food
was always a safe conversation-starter.

'With lemon and garlic sauce,' Maria replied. 'Now,
don't tell me that the three of them have abandoned you
to find your own way here?' she said with a tut.

'Oh, Joss is—'

'Never mind what they think is more important.
You're our guest. If I'd known they'd left you to wan-
der the halls I'd have come and looked after you myself.
Now, take a seat and tell me what you'd like to drink.
Tea? Or something more appropriate to the hour? A
little aperitif?'

'Well, I suppose a gin and tonic would go down well,'
Eva said, after thinking about it for barely half a sec-

ond. 'But only if you join me. The dangers of drinking alone and all that.'

'Oh, well, I think I probably should—seeing as I appear to be in charge of you. Right, then, let me find us a lime. I know there were some in the delivery yesterday.'

Maria disappeared for a couple of minutes and returned with two glasses filled almost to the brim with ice, lime and clear sparkling liquid.

'I'm sorry—I should have asked if you want this in the drawing room,' Maria said, her brow suddenly creasing. 'Edward asked me to set the table in the dining room for dinner, but he normally has a drink in here with us first. You can go through, though, if you prefer.'

'No, not at all,' Eva said, raising her glass in a salute to Maria and taking a long sip. 'A drink in here sounds perfect to me. It's ridiculously warm, for one thing.'

'Decision made, then,' Maria said, opening the door of the Aga and peering inside. She pulled out a perfectly golden chicken and placed it on the warming plate on top of the range before sliding a meat thermometer into the flesh.

'Can't be too careful,' she said, glancing over at Eva. 'With Edward's health being what it is. I've tried to get the rest of the house warm for him, but a heater in his bedroom and the Aga in here seem to be the only things that work.'

Eva didn't have a chance to reply before the door of the kitchen opened and Joss, Edward and Thomas all appeared.

'Ah, about time. You gentlemen abandoned poor Eva,' Maria scolded them. 'We both had to take some medicinal gin for the shock,' she added, with a wink to Eva.

'Excellent idea,' Edward said. 'Think I'll have one of those myself. Anyone else?'

He made to walk away from where he was leaning on Joss's arm, but stumbled with his first step. Joss helped him over to a chair instead.

'You sit down, Dad,' Joss said, sharing a concerned glance with Eva over the top of Edward's head. 'I'll get the drinks.'

By the time they were all seated formally in the dining room Edward was looking tired again, ready for another lie-down. Eva and Joss shared another concerned glance, but this time Edward caught the look between them.

'Enough, you two. If you've got something to say, then just say it. I'm having a tiring day. Not sure why, but I suppose it's to be expected under the circumstances.'

'We're just worried, Dad. You seem more tired than you were last week.'

'I *am* more tired,' Edward said. 'But my doctor's not worried. I called him, you know. I'm not just pretending this isn't happening. He said it's completely normal. I just need to rest more. Which means we should get this conversation done with so we can all eat and get to bed.'

'What conversation?' Joss asked.

Eva felt a shiver of foreboding. She could guess what conversation.

Edward reached for a folder of papers that Eva realised he must have stashed on a chair earlier.

'We need to talk about my will,' he said.

'Dad—' Joss tried to interrupt.

But Edward wasn't having any of it.

'No, son. We need to have this conversation at some point and I'd like to do it now, while I'm still well and no one can accuse me of having gone doolally or anything like that. Not that it matters much *what* you say, actually, because it's all finished already. I just thought you might like to know what's in there.'

Joss pushed his chair away from the table and Eva could see him glancing at the door, wondering if he could bail out on this conversation. He'd better not dare leave it to her—she'd make him pay if he did.

'Dad, it doesn't matter to me what's in there.'

'Well, it matters to me. So you can sit there and listen, if you're quite finished talking.'

Eva shifted uncomfortably in her chair. It was hard enough being caught in a family argument. When it was about a will, and it wasn't even your family, she was all for bolting for the door herself.

'Maybe I should leave you two…?'

'Not at all, dear,' Edward said when Eva tried to excuse herself. 'You're part of this family now, and I'd like you to stay. I know Joss will tell you everything anyway, so this way we save him the trouble. Right, I'm not going to go over every detail, because you know all the business stuff already. But the personal stuff we've not talked about before. It's not complicated, though. I'm leaving your mother a large amount of cash, so neither of us have to worry about her being comfortable for the rest of her life. But most of the rest of it goes to you, of course, Joss. Including the London house and this draughty old place. But the mews house is yours, Eva. It's been your home for many years, and I would hate to think of you having to leave it. I hope that you'll accept?'

'Edward,' Eva protested straight away. It was too much. Too generous. 'I couldn't possibly—'

But Edward shook his head defiantly. 'I don't want to hear anything like that. A simple thank-you would be fine.'

She couldn't accept. Of course she couldn't under these circumstances.

If Edward knew the truth about their fake relationship he wouldn't be doing this. It wasn't fair to let him make decisions like this based on a lie.

'Edward, you don't understand. About me and Joss—'

'No, no.' Edward said decisively. 'I'm quite sure that your relationship is none of my business. Really, Eva dear. This is a gift for you. Quite apart from what you and Joss mean to one another.'

She shared a long look with Joss, and tried to communicate what she was thinking without speaking.

Was he angry with her? She would tell Edward the whole ugly truth if she had to. This had gone too far. It wasn't fair on the sick old man. She'd gone along with his misunderstanding when he'd assumed that she and Joss were a couple because it had seemed a small thing to do to make him so happy. But this—this was different. This was legal—a binding contract and the transfer of property—making their little white lie suddenly seem a whole lot more serious.

'The mews house *should* be yours,' Joss said at last.

She wanted to kick him under the table for continuing to lie to his father. They should just tell him the truth. Come clean. She turned and glared at him.

'I mean it,' he carried on. 'I'd give it to you anyway, if it came to me. I'm serious,' he continued, when she widened her eyes at him, trying to get him to stop talking. 'Don't fight this, Eva.'

His voice was softer now, gentler, and she found she couldn't argue with him when he was being reasonable.

And when she thought of her mews house as being really her own... It meant that she would have a little piece of the city that was always there—a safety net whenever she needed it. She fought back tears as she rose from her chair.

'Thank you, Edward,' she said, walking around the table to give him a kiss on the cheek. 'It means the world to me. It really does.'

'Well, let's hear no more about it,' Edward said, his cheeks flushed a little pink.

Maria appeared at the door with such promptness it seemed inevitable that she had been waiting outside, listening for an appropriate break in the conversation.

'This looks delicious, Maria. Thank you,' Eva said as the platters of food were set down in the centre of the table.

With the difficult topic of the will set aside, they all relaxed into friendly conversation, though she could see that Edward's eyes were fighting to stay open halfway through their main course. She glanced at Joss, and saw that he had noticed it too. As their eyes met she felt a flash of connection between them, and knew that in that moment she could read him completely. She wondered if she was as open to him as he was to her. What he could see if she was.

A warmth started in her chest and sank to her belly as she realised how close they had grown over the past week. How she had really started to know him, with their communication becoming subtler, more personal, more intuitive.

She didn't want to think too much about what that meant. About the risk that she was taking in letting him in. Because that *was* what she was doing. Whether she had intended him to or not, he was getting under her skin, into her thoughts, into her life. And now, when she looked at him, she saw something familiar—something that had been part of her life for so long she would recognise it anywhere. She saw the void that he would leave when he left. She saw her life without him. The spaces she would have to try to fill when he wasn't part of her world any more. The voids that would haunt her at night and occupy her thoughts during the day.

She'd seen those voids around both her parents when she was growing up, and had wondered how her life would look if they were gone—really gone—and she was left behind. And then her mother had been killed on duty and she'd found out. She'd lived longer with the space that her mother had left behind than she had with her mother there. It was like a shadow in the corner of the room, reminding her of what she'd lost. What she'd never had much of a claim on in the first place.

And she could see that void around Joss now. See the hole that would be left in her life when this was over.

She'd never meant to let it get this far. It was meant to be a lie. Their engagement *was* a lie. But these feelings that she was having for him—they were very, very real.

She didn't know what to do with them. Her instincts were telling her to run. To get away from him now, while she still had a chance of plugging that space, of rebuilding her life without him in it. But her heart wanted her to stay. She knew that from the way it ached when she thought about leaving. About what they were going to do when they had to get back to real life. When she thought about a life without him in it—or, worse, a life where they were polite to one another in the office and then tried to forget each other existed the moment they left.

Joss frowned slightly, and she realised she had shown too much in her expression. Even if he couldn't understand the minutiae of the struggle she was feeling at that moment, he knew something was wrong. And she had a suspicion that he was going to expect her to explain herself later.

A clatter disturbed her thoughts, finally forcing her gaze away from Joss's, and she realised that Edward had dropped his knife. He'd barely touched his meal, but now he lay down his fork too, and took a sip of wine.

'I think I'm going to retire and leave you young people to enjoy the rest of the meal,' Edward said. 'I'm sure that Maria will have a delicious dessert in store, so please don't let it go to waste.'

She called goodnight to Edward as Joss took his elbow and helped him out of the room and presumably up the stairs to bed. Left alone, Eva wondered whether she should make her escape. But what would Joss think if he came downstairs and found her not at the table? And even if she decided she wanted to, she had nowhere to go.

She could escape to the bedroom, but Joss would be there as well soon enough. She might remember how to get back to the pub in the village, but what would Edward, Thomas and Maria think of her taking off in the dark? They'd know that there was something wrong between her and Joss, and that was the last thing she wanted for Edward just now.

Joss appeared at the door a few minutes later, and made her glad that she had stayed. His eyes looked heavy, as if he was fighting off emotion, and she knew he needed company. That if he were alone his thoughts and fears would torture him.

'Is he okay?'

'Tired,' Joss replied. 'He says he's not in any pain, but I'm not sure I believe him. I'll check on him later, and if he's not sleeping soundly I'll call the doctor. I'm sorry, Eva. I should never have brought you here. You shouldn't have to go through this. It's not fair on you.'

'I'm glad I'm here,' she said automatically.

But as the words passed her lips she realised that she meant them. Even if it *did* mean facing the sadness of watching Edward fade by the day. Despite her earlier thoughts of escape, she knew that this was important. That if she left these men to fend for themselves at this crucial time she would be hurting both of them, and she didn't want that.

It was dawning on her just how far she had let both of them in already. She had told herself after her mother had died and her dad had sent her away that she wouldn't do that again. She would never let anyone leave a hole in her life that she didn't know how to fill. But somehow the two Dawson men had found a way in.

Her affection for Edward was nothing new, but since he had given her the news of his illness, since her closeness with Joss, it had changed. He was no longer the kindly old boss she'd always thought him. He'd become more than that. He'd become like family.

And Joss? She didn't know *what* to think about Joss and how she felt about him. She had never meant to feel *anything* about him. She'd had a crush, yes. But that was all it had been. An appreciation for a handsome face and an enigmatic attitude. So how, in a matter of a couple of weeks, had he come to be so much more than that to her? How was he suddenly so much a part of her life, a part of *her*, that all she could see was the dark outline of the shape he would leave in her life when he inevitably left her?

What she wanted to know was what she was meant to do about it. She knew it was too late to turn back without getting hurt. Hurting was inevitable now. But she needed a plan to get through it when the time came to end their engagement.

'How can you be glad?' Joss asked eventually, rubbing both his hands on his face and then reaching for his drink. 'I'd rather be anywhere than here.'

'I don't think that's true. I think you're glad to be spending time with your father. And I'm here for the same reason you are, I suppose. Because it's important to be with your dad right now. And because it's hard to do that alone.'

'You're right,' he said, looking up and meeting her eyes with a look that might burn her if she wasn't more careful. 'But it's not just that. It's not that I want *someone* here. I want *you* here.'

'Because your father thinks—'

'For reasons that have absolutely nothing to do with my father. Believe me, Eva. What I'm talking about has nothing to do with him.'

He wasn't kidding. She could read volumes in his expression, and filial duty was nowhere to be seen.

She dropped her eyes, breaking their connection. If she hadn't, there was only one place that the conversation would go, and she suspected neither of them was ready to go there. Yet. *Ever.*

The door opened and Maria appeared with a trolley to clear their plates. They sat in silence as she worked, only occasionally glancing across to one another. When they eventually had *tarte Tatin* and *crème anglaise* sitting in front of them, on elegant white and platinum plates, Eva let out a long breath, determined to start a conversation with something completely non-controversial.

But as she grappled around for a subject she found she was coming up with nothing. Everything felt so loaded with Joss. Their work, their home, their families… They all led to conversations more deep and meaningful than either of them wanted right now. And she hoped to 'goodness they were beyond the point where they would have to talk about the weather for lack of anything else to say to each other.

She pushed a piece of tart onto her spoon, and let out a sigh of anxious relief when Joss eventually spoke.

'I hear it's going to be a nice day tomorrow.'

So that was where they were. She didn't know whether that made her want to weep or laugh, but at least the ice was broken.

'We should take your dad out,' she said.

'He'd like that, I think. He's always liked to walk in the gardens.'

They fell into silence again, and Eva concentrated on finishing her dessert, counting down the pieces until this awkward dinner would be over. And then, with a mouthful left on her plate, she asked herself what on earth she was doing. The longer she could make this last, the better. At least with six feet of solid mahogany table between her and Joss she was safe from making any huge, irrevocable mistakes. Once dinner was over her safety net would be gone.

She lingered over the last mouthful, and responded enthusiastically and gratefully when Maria asked if they would like coffee. But as she drained the dregs of the drink she knew she couldn't delay any longer.

'Do you want to go straight up?' Joss asked.

And, although she had been expecting it Eva still felt wrong-footed. If she said yes, would that make it seem as if she was desperate to get to their room, into bed with him? If she said no, what would he read into that?

But she could feel her eyelids growing heavy, despite the coffee. It had been an emotionally draining evening, and although it wasn't late she wanted a bed—whatever the dangers of sharing it.

'I think I will,' she replied, stifling a yawn that just thinking about sleep had produced.

'Can you find your own way up?' Joss said. 'I think I'll use Dad's study and just finish up a few things.'

Eva let out a breath, trying not to show how her body had instantly relaxed, relieved at his words.

'I'll be fine. I guess I'll see you in the morning, then,' she said, standing up from her chair.

They both stalled by the table for a moment, and for a second she was unsure what they were waiting for. A formally polite kiss on the cheek? A handshake?

In the end, she darted past Joss, the lure of an empty bed too much to resist.

CHAPTER TEN

JOSS LISTENED TO her climb the stairs, her footsteps elegantly measured despite the way she had darted past him out of the dining room.

He sighed at the thought of having to crack open his laptop and put in another couple of hours' work. Since this thing had started with Eva his schedule had been punishing, with him trying to keep himself busy and out of her way as much as possible. Keeping himself from temptation. And now, knowing he would be returning to a shared bed, not just a shared house, the temptation was stronger than ever.

He wondered whether she had felt it too. That connection when their eyes had met across the dinner table... He shook his head. Of course she had felt it. Something like that couldn't be one-sided. It was the very fact that they were both feeling the same way that gave the moment its energy. Its power. He had to be more careful.

He turned on the computer and pulled up the latest reports from his store managers, scrolling through them without really reading. Despite his earlier concerns over how he was going to shoulder his father's business with so little notice, he needn't have worried. The transition plans they had put in place had worked just as they were supposed to. And, although there was still some anxiety in parts of the business, mostly things were going well.

He forced himself back to the start of the reports and made himself read them properly this time.

When he was done, he glanced at the clock and saw that an hour and a half had passed. Eva had looked pretty tired when she had left the dining room, so surely it would be safe by now for him to go up to bed? Everything would be simpler if she was asleep, he told himself. He could just climb into bed and pretend he was alone. Goodness knew, the mattress was big enough for the both of them.

He climbed the stairs slowly, and remembered the sound of Eva's feet on the treads. Had she been feeling as uneasy as him? Wanting to put off the inevitable?

How on earth was he meant to get any sleep in the same bed with her? Maybe he should stick to his chivalrous guns and sleep on the chaise longue as he'd suggested. If anyone caught him, it could be easy enough to explain away. An argument. Snoring. A dispute over the duvet. A sudden conversion to a conservative religious order. Or just a reminder that their sleeping arrangements weren't anyone's business but their own.

Who was he kidding? Sleep was in short supply these days, and if it was going to be difficult in bed with a woman he was attracted to, it wasn't going to be any easier a few feet away, freezing cold, wishing he were closer to her.

He turned the handle of the door to his room slowly, trying to remember where the hinges squeaked and where the loose floorboards were. If he could get into bed without waking her, maybe he could do an okay job of pretending that she wasn't there at all.

Fat chance of that.

He crept through the door, opening it as little as possible, and saw that Eva had left a bedside lamp on for him. He smiled involuntarily at the small gesture of consideration; it was probably more than he deserved.

Her dark hair was spread on the pillow, shiny with just a hint of red, like a conker, in the warm light from the lampshade. He silently gave thanks that the duvet was plump enough to hide any suggestion of what her body might look like beneath the covering.

And then cursed when his brain reminded him that he'd already seen enough to give him plenty of sleepless nights. That day in his father's office. Pale skin and delicate lace. Pink silk just skimming over the curve of her back.

He shook his head and turned his back to her as he slid open a drawer, careful to ensure that the wood didn't stick and make any unnecessary noise. He pulled out a T-shirt and started unbuttoning his shirt, trying not to think about the fact that he was undressing with Eva barely a couple of metres away from him.

If she were to wake up, open her eyes, what would—?

No. He stopped himself. There was no way he could let himself finish that thought. It wasn't fair on Eva, who had offered to share the bed on the understanding that he would be a gentleman.

It wasn't fair on himself either. He needed sleep, and it would never come if he was thinking about Eva watching him undress...maybe moving to kneel at the edge of the mattress as she watched, and then reaching out to help...

He struck a hand against his forehead. He really had to get this under control, he thought, taking a couple of deep breaths. Usually control was not something he struggled with. Since his diagnosis with depression he had taken back control over his life, bringing order to all those areas he had let his illness take over. Structured goals and routine had woken him from the fog that had clouded him for too long. Focussing on achievable objectives, sticking to his plan—even when he didn't feel like it—that was what had got him better. It would be foolish to slip now, to give the power back to his untrustworthy emotions rather than the techniques that he knew worked for him.

He flicked the lamp off, gently pulled back the duvet and slipped between the sheets, gasping at their icy touch on his feet and legs. For a moment he was jealous of the thick cotton pyjamas he had helped his father into earlier, though he hadn't owned anything like that in his life. Even the T-shirt was an out-of-character nod to decency for Eva's sake.

He glanced at the fire in the grate; it was burning low and doing as little as the central heating was to warm the room.

He shifted on the mattress, stretching his legs and wondering how far he could spread out without disturbing Eva. He needed to know where she was so that he could be sure he wouldn't touch her by accident. He reached out a leg experimentally, and breathed a sigh of relief when it encountered only more shiveringly cold sheet.

He turned on to his side, stretching out his arm as he did so, and his hand encountered warm softness. He froze, but the sharp intake of breath from beside him told him all he needed to know. Well, he'd worked out how much space he had—not enough. Eva must have rolled over at the exact moment he had turned, and landed on his hand. The weight of her was soft and heavy, and as he gently flexed his fingers he had to stifle a laugh. Turned out she had better protection against the cold and their attraction than he did.

'Flannel pyjamas?' he whispered.

He felt a shudder of laughter against his hand in return.

'Are you kidding?' she muttered, her voice heavy and slow with sleep. 'Of *course*, flannel pyjamas. It's freezing in here.'

Her voice was not much more than a breath, and the intimacy of whispering in bed with her made him ache.

She shifted and he acted on instinct, wanting to keep her near. As she turned over to face him he drew her closer, so when she eventually looked up they were practically nose to nose. He ran his free hand down her arm, feeling the cotton soft and warm beneath his fingers. The sensation made him achingly hard.

Who knew? he thought. *Flannel.*

Eva sucked in a breath and he realised she was feeling exactly what he was. That she was as keyed up as him, and had the same reservations.

'Still cold?' he asked, testing the waters.

'I've got goosebumps.'

It didn't necessarily answer his question, but it made him throb with the need to pull her even closer. His hand was still trapped beneath the curve of her waist, and finally it was too much to bear. He slipped it under her, until his arm encased her completely and his fingers could brush against the indentation of her waist.

'Better?' he asked.

She took so long to reply he was scared she'd changed her mind. That he was losing her.

'Hot.'

When she eventually spoke he closed his eyes with a groan. She had to know what she was doing, saying that. It was an invitation—or an acceptance. He wasn't sure who was leading this little dance. And he didn't care, because now his other arm was curving around her waist, drawing her against him until she could be in no doubt about how hot *he* was feeling right this second.

He nudged his nose against hers, asking a question he was already pretty sure of the answer to.

He wasn't wrong. Her hand came up to cup his face and she pressed her lips softly to his. Barely a whisper of a kiss at first. He held still, his arms squeezing her to him. It killed him, but he waited. Waited to see if she'd change her mind, as she had in Milan. If she was still holding back. Doing the sensible thing.

But the noise that came from deep in her throat told

him this was nothing like Milan. Her lips found his again—harder this time, demanding a response.

So he responded the only way he could, by possessing her mouth with his, exploring the textures and contours of her lips. Brushing soft kisses, tasting, touching with his tongue.

His hands bunched the soft fabric of her pyjama top at the base of her spine, pulling it tight across her breasts and revealing a couple of inches of bare skin above her waistband. She gasped softly as he did so, and then louder when his hands slipped beneath the cotton, desperate to know the feel of her skin.

'Okay?' he asked breathlessly, drawing away from her for a moment. It felt like ripping away a part of his own body.

'Freezing!' she said, with a gasp and a laugh.

She reached behind her back for one of his hands and drew it between them, rubbing his fingers and his palm between her own, blowing hot breath onto cold skin. He shivered and it had nothing to do with the temperature of the room. She kissed his palm and her lips branded him.

He barely had time to recover himself before she slipped his hand beneath the covers, cupping it around her breast.

'Better?' he asked, barely controlling the shake in his voice.

'Warm,' she replied, pressing another kiss to his lips, snaking her arms around him. 'Good. *Really* good.'

And then her hands were on his back, exploring, pulling at his T-shirt, and he didn't care whether they were fire or ice—he just knew that he wanted them. Everywhere.

He sat up so he could pull his shirt over his head and Eva rolled beneath him. When he looked down he could just make out her features in the warm glow from the fire. Her eyes were closed, her face relaxed, her body open and languid beneath him. He pinned her with his elbows either side, dipping his head to tease at her neck and her collarbone with his mouth and tongue as he unbuttoned her pyjamas, one tiny awkward button at a time.

With each inch of skin that was revealed he dipped his head lower, determined to learn every inch of her. And as the last button came open he kissed her navel, revelling in her gasp of appreciation.

He hooked his fingers into the waistband of her pyjama trousers, barely able to let himself believe that this was really happening. But her fingers were in his hair, encouraging, demanding. And as he skimmed the fabric down her thighs he kissed her lips again, hard. Knowing that every second of this night would be burned into his memory for ever.

CHAPTER ELEVEN

EVA WOKE WITH a delicious fatigue in her muscles, her head so heavy she could barely lift it to turn her other cheek to the pillow. She fought against the fluffy cotton duvet, which had formed a cocoon around her face, and stretched out a toe. The sheets on the other side of the bed were cold.

'Joss?' she called into the still room, lifting her head and propping herself onto her elbows. She strained her ears, listening for water running in the bathroom or footsteps on the landing. Nothing.

She reached for her pyjamas, where they had fallen by the side of the bed, and shrugged her arms into the soft flannel, which had long since turned cold, abandoned on the floor. Pulling on socks, she crossed the enormous bedroom into the en suite bathroom, where there were signs of a hasty exit from Joss. His toothbrush had been flung on the side of the cabinet, his T-shirt was still in a heap on the floor.

But there was no note. No explanation of his absence. No apology.

Nothing to explain the huge empty hole he had left in their bedroom or the ache in her chest as reality sunk in.

He had left her, just as she had always feared he would.

What on earth had she been thinking, going to bed with him?

She hadn't been thinking at all. Or at least not with her head. She'd woken up to find Joss behind her in the bed and herself practically rolling into his arms. He'd laughed about her flannel pyjamas, and then she'd gasped and sighed as they'd had precisely the opposite effect to the one she had intended.

In Milan she had held back, certain that giving in to her lust for Joss would lead to disaster. But things had been different last night. She had already accepted that he had a place in her life. That, however he left it, he was going to leave a space behind that was going to be hard to fill. But the way he made her feel when they were together—it would be worth it. She had never thought she would find a man worth that risk.

And now he had walked away from her without even a word.

Had he at least regretted it when he'd shut the door with her sleeping soundly on the other side?

She felt tears prick at her eyes and turned away from the mirror, not wanting to see them fall. A thick dressing robe hung on the back of the door and she pulled it on, aware how even her heavy-duty pyjamas weren't managing to keep out the chill.

She left the bathroom and glanced at the fireplace. She had no idea how to get any heat back into those dying embers, so she pulled the fabric of the robe tighter around her, holding her breath to avoid Joss's lingering scent trapped in the collar. Dropping on to the chaise longue, she glanced out of the window.

No sign of Joss's car—just neat parallel lines in the gravel leading away from where he had parked it yesterday. A shadow. A reminder that he had been there.

Eva shook her head, trying to shake off the gloom that had settled over her since she had woken in an empty bed. Was she overreacting? She hadn't even checked her phone. Her thoughts had flown straight to her parents—the way they had left her, as they always had. Her fears that anyone else she loved would do the same. She was going to feel pretty bloody stupid if there were half a dozen messages from Joss, explaining what was going on.

She crossed to the bedside table and picked up her phone, checking the screen. Nothing.

Well, she had never sat around waiting for a guy to call before, and she didn't much fancy starting now. She dialled Joss's number and felt her heart-rate jump when it started ringing. Once, twice—and then the voice-mail kicked in.

She frowned. It hadn't rung long enough for it to have redirected automatically. But the fact it had rung at all meant it was turned on. Which meant that he had to have rejected her call. He had seen her name flash up on the screen, known that she had woken without him, and then rejected her call rather than explain himself.

Nausea rose in her belly as she realised that he had really meant to abandon her. To leave her with no explanation at all. She fought the sickness down, forcing herself up from the chaise longue and formulating a plan for what to do next. She found her suitcase in the bottom of the wardrobe and started throwing things into it. If Joss didn't want her here—and he couldn't have made that much clearer—then fine. She would go.

She had tried and tried with her parents, had carried on loving them when they'd left her time and time again. And she had ended up with her heart broken. She had learnt her lesson—there was no point sticking around to let Joss do it to her again. She would get away and make a head start on building those walls she would need in place next time she had to face him in the office.

Eva jerked upright at the sound of footsteps on the landing, but it took only a split second for her to realise they were too light to belong to Joss. The gentle knock at the door confirmed her suspicions.

'Come in,' she called out, and knew before the head poked around the door that it must be Maria on the other side.

'I thought you might like some coffee,' Maria said, shoving the door open with a tray and setting it down on the table beside the chaise longue. 'And Joss asked me to fill you in on what happened last night.'

Mortification spread through Eva's veins. What on earth had Joss said to her? Had he told her what had happened? That they had slept together for the first time?

Then the reality of her situation started to sink in. No, Maria wasn't here to talk about what had happened between them in bed; she was here to make Joss's excuses for him.

Eva had fallen asleep last night, satisfied and safe in his arms. And at some point, when she had been reliving their passion in her dreams, he had sneaked away and arranged for Maria to do his dirty work.

'He didn't want to wake you or worry you,' Maria said.

From the hesitation in her voice, Eva guessed she wasn't any happier about the position Joss had put her in than Eva was.

Maria didn't know the half of it, she thought. Leaving unannounced was ungentlemanly at the best of times. In the middle of the night, following the first time they'd made love, when Joss knew exactly how big a risk she was taking on him... She didn't want to say it was unforgivable, but that was certainly how it felt right now.

'Edward was taken ill,' Maria said. 'We called the out-of-hours doctor and he called an ambulance. He's going to be in hospital for a few days.'

Eva nodded slowly, taking this news in. Perhaps she should have guessed that something like this had happened. She tried to get her head around the news and work out where this left her and Joss. So he had had a good reason for leaving. But none, she could see, for doing it without saying goodbye. Without a quick kiss and an explanation.

Had it not occurred to him that she would want to support him? That she would want to be there for him and Edward—especially when things were tough?

And it didn't explain why he'd rejected her call. Why

he'd not found the time in the last however many hours to drop her a quick message, letting her know what had happened. It seemed he had found time to keep Maria informed, after all.

Her heart ached for Edward, and for Joss watching his father fade. But it ached for herself as well. For the trust she had finally managed to put in Joss, only to see it trampled. To find herself abandoned, with her worst fears coming true.

She went to the tray to pour some coffee, wanting something to focus on.

'I'll leave you to your breakfast,' Maria said, her voice kind, and Eva guessed she had picked up on her distress even if she didn't know the cause.

As Eva sat and drank her coffee she wondered whether she was overreacting. Joss was at the hospital. Perhaps it had just been an inconvenient moment for her to call.

She watched the screen of her phone, wondering if he would call back, and then remembered that she was far too old to be playing those sorts of games.

CHAPTER TWELVE

JOSS REACHED INTO his pocket for his phone, and guessed before he looked at the screen that it was Eva calling. He was tempted to fire it off to voicemail again, as he had the last time, but knew that there were only so many times he could do something so cowardly.

As he had sat by his father's bedside last night he had gone over and over his decision to leave without waking her. He had taken his phone out of his pocket and replaced it again, wondering what he could say that would lessen the blow of her waking up alone in the morning, knowing he had left without a word.

It couldn't be undone now. He could apologise, explain that it had been an emergency, he hadn't wanted to worry her.

But he didn't want to lie.

The truth was he hadn't been thinking at all. He had been acting completely on instinct—looking after his father, looking after himself. And that was what worried him the most. Because in a time of crisis his selfish instincts had led to Eva getting hurt.

He'd not taken the time last night to think about how

his actions might affect her. It was what he had been afraid of all along—his selfishness. His instinct to look after his own needs was evidently incompatible with a relationship. They had only tried it for one night, and already Eva was paying the price. He had to put a stop to this before he did any more damage.

'Eva?' he said, hitting the green button on the screen.

'Hey,' she said, her voice neutral, flat. 'How's your dad?'

'Better, thanks.'

So Maria must have let her know what had happened. At least she had opened with a topic that he knew how to talk about. He could give her the facts, repeat what the doctors had said.

'They've made his breathing more comfortable. He'll be discharged in a couple of days. Maybe even tomorrow.'

'That's good news.'

He waited as the silence between them grew awkward.

'Can I come by and visit?' she asked.

The question was inevitable, but his answer had to be more than that. It had to protect her, to show her that they had got too close last night and needed to find some safe space between them again.

'That's not a good idea,' Joss said. 'He's still very tired. He's been asleep most of the time.'

'Okay,' Eva said, and they fell into silence again.

He thought back to being in bed with her, how they had moved and sighed and breathed as one body, and wondered how it was that intimacy like that could be lost. Easily, he realised, when one of you had walked away with no care for the damage they were causing. This wasn't something that had happened *to* them. It was something *he* had done.

'I'm sorry I had to leave in a hurry.' There—the apology was out. 'If you want to go back to London…' Joss continued, not sure whether or not he wanted her to take the hint, to be gone when he was eventually able to leave the hospital.

'I'll book a taxi to the station,' Eva said, and this time she couldn't hide the slight shake in her voice, that little tell of emotion.

He was doing it again. Being responsible for another person's emotions was too much. The people he loved were always going to be disappointed. Always going to get hurt. Even when he was trying to protect Eva, everything he did just meant she got hurt. It was better to end it now, like this, he told himself. The sooner he did it the better. He'd proved last night—to himself as much as to her—that he wasn't relationship material. If he didn't do this now, he was only going to end up hurting her more in the long run.

On Monday morning Joss pulled his car up to the front of his father's London house and rested his elbows on the steering wheel. Was it two days ago that he had done the same journey in reverse with Eva, or three? With the bright fluorescent lights and the constant noise of a busy hospital, it was hard to tell how much time had passed. Perhaps it was only two nights that he had spent sleeping uncomfortably in a straight-backed chair, aching to be home, to be back with Eva.

Except he'd known she wouldn't be waiting for him at the country house—not when he had all but told her to leave. And he couldn't go back to the mews. It wouldn't be fair to pick up as normal when he knew that they both needed to back off—for Eva's sake.

He'd not called her again. It was spineless, he knew, avoiding her hurt and recriminations like this, but what more was there to say? He didn't need her to tell him how badly he had acted. But now his father had been discharged, and they were back in London, he knew he couldn't put it off for ever.

He would have to see her at work. Tell her that they had to stop this. See if he could persuade her to keep up the pretence to his father, but forget that incredible night had ever happened. He wasn't sure how she was meant to do that—not when his own efforts had been so dismal. But they had to try.

He settled his father in bed and headed down to the kitchen to make them both a drink. When he returned, he eased open the door to his father's bedroom slowly, not wanting to wake him if he'd fallen asleep. But Edward was sitting up in bed.

'I thought you were going straight to the office?' Edward said, his eyebrows high with surprise.

'There's no hurry. I want to make sure you have everything you need first.'

Nothing to do with wanting to delay the inevitable confrontation, he told himself.

'From the way you crept in here, you thought I was sleeping—not likely to need much, in that case.'

So his father could see through him. Could see he wasn't telling him everything even if he didn't know the details of the evasion.

'It doesn't matter,' Joss said, refusing to engage with his father's probing. 'The office can manage without me for one morning.'

'And what does Eva think about this?' Edward asked.

Joss tried not to let his emotions show on his face, tried to keep his voice light. His dad was like a dog with a bone when he got an idea in his head. He wasn't going to be able to shrug his way out of this, he suspected.

'She didn't drive back with us.' Edward continued his line of questioning. 'I take it she left while I was in hospital?'

'One of us needed to be in the office,' Joss said. 'But she sends her love. I'm sure she'll visit soon.'

'Of course.' Joss could tell from the tone of his father's voice that he knew he had hit a fruitful line of questioning. 'Everything okay there?' he asked with fatherly concern. 'With you and Eva, I mean.'

'Of course it is,' Joss said, not wanting to worry his dad with the problems in his fake relationship.

He wished he could sound more convincing, but the truth was that things between him and Eva had never been worse. And their lie was meant to be making their father happy, not making him worry about them.

'I know all this must be putting a strain on things,' Edward said, reaching across to the chair beside his bed and patting the seat.

Joss sat down stiffly, recognising an order when he saw one.

'It's bound to. It's normal to have problems. Do you want to talk about them?'

'We're not having problems, Dad.'

He felt a wrench in his gut at lying to his father. Except he didn't even know at the moment what was a lie and what was true. He and Eva had started as something pretend, but this pain he was feeling—this was real. More real than anything he had felt through his actual marriage.

'And if you were you wouldn't talk to your old man about them anyway, isn't that right? I've been here before, Joss. Watching you struggle, keeping things to yourself. I don't want to do that again. I wished there was more I could do to help last time. I don't want to die wishing the same thing all over again.'

Joss dropped his head into his hands. 'I never knew you felt that way. I know I let you down with the divorce…'

Edward reached out and took his hand. 'Whatever gave you that idea? It broke my heart to see you struggling and not be able to do anything to help. But you have *never* let me down, son. You recovered, and now you have the opportunity to be happy. Please don't waste it.'

He couldn't lie to his father any more—even for his own good. He couldn't go on letting him think he was something that he wasn't. There had been too much unsaid between them over the years. Too many truths hidden.

'This is different, Dad. I'm sorry. Me and Eva—'

'You haven't told me everything about your relationship. I know that. I'm not simple, Joss. I don't need the details, because it's clear that you two care about each other very much. I think that was clear to me before it was to you. You love her, don't you?'

Joss didn't know what to say. He had tried so hard to convince himself he didn't—that it would be better for Eva if he didn't. But he couldn't lie to his father—not after what he had just told him.

'Yes. I do.'

'Then I want you to go to her and tell her that. And no matter what is happening with me, or what is happening with the business, I want you to remember to tell her that often. Okay? Nothing is more important.'

Joss wished it were that simple. That loving her would be enough.

CHAPTER THIRTEEN

EVA'S BACK AND cheeks ached with keeping her spine constantly straight and her expression neutral as she ghost-walked her way through Monday morning in the office, determined not to let memories of Joss break her perfect composure.

She'd been there since before the sun was up, and the streets were still quiet. If anyone had asked she would have chalked her early start up to commitment and professionalism, rather than the fact that she'd woken at five and been unable to bear the silence of her empty house any longer.

It was just the change back from the big, staffed country house to her little mews that had her spooked, she told herself. Nothing to do with the fact that the house didn't feel quite so much like a home now without Joss in it. Without knowing whether he had any intention of coming back to it.

She was completely in limbo. She hadn't spoken to him for three days, but as far as their colleagues were concerned they were still engaged. *Were* they still engaged? Or as much as they had ever been, anyway? She just didn't know. And it wasn't as if she could ask.

Under normal circumstances she would have no problem asking the man in her life what he thought was going on between them, but these were about as far from 'normal circumstances' as you could get.

As the last person left the office for lunch she let out a long breath and pulled in a lungful of air. It felt like the first she had taken in days. Her shoulders dropped from where they had been up by her ears, and as she tapped away at her keyboard she felt the rest of her body follow their lead and start to relax.

Which was why she jumped when she heard the all too familiar tread of his footsteps behind her, spookily loud in the silent office. She froze where she sat, fingers still on the keyboard. Taking a deep breath, she sent it to her shoulders again, forcing them into a state of relaxation that she didn't genuinely feel but she hoped would look convincing.

She turned slowly in her chair, delaying the moment when she would have to face Joss, lift her gaze to meet his. When she eventually did, anger and sympathy warred within her.

He looked like hell.

It was clear from the black bags under his eyes and the deep lines on his forehead that he hadn't slept properly since she'd seen him last, but worse than that was the expression of pain so clear in his features.

He'd obviously been going through hell. And he'd chosen to go through it alone rather than let her into his life and trust her to support him. To be there for him.

'We need to talk,' he said, his voice cold.

Her blood ran colder as she thought he must have terrible news about Edward. But she followed him through to his office and closed the door behind them.

'How's your dad?' she asked, bracing herself for the worst.

'Better,' Joss said. 'Home now.'

The air left her in a rush of relief, and she collapsed back into one of the chairs by his desk. 'Oh, thank God for that. From your face, I thought you were coming to tell me that he'd...gone.'

Joss sat beside her his expression still grim. 'No, he's home now. That's not what I need to talk to you about. It's us.'

All of a sudden she felt that chill again. The hairs on the back of her neck prickled, and she had a sudden premonition of where this conversation was going. Or where Joss thought it was going, at least.

'What happened on Friday night—it was a mistake, Eva. I should never have let it go that far.'

'Let it?' she asked, not able to keep the note of derision out of her voice. 'I don't think you were *letting* anything happen, Joss. I think you were making it happen. We both were.'

He leaned back against his desk and looked straight at her. She felt a shiver go through her at the emptiness in his expression.

'Then that was the mistake. However it happened, Eva, it was wrong.'

Surely he couldn't feel as blank as he looked about that night. She hadn't imagined the intimacy they had shared, or the ecstasy they had found together. And she wasn't going to let him repaint it all as flat and empty just because he had got scared.

'It felt right to me,' she countered. She knew she hadn't been alone in thinking that. Not at the time at least. 'It felt pretty good for you too, if I remember. I know you, Joss. You can't fake that with me.'

'How it felt isn't the point,' Joss said, refusing to engage with her. No eye contact. No acknowledgement that what she was saying was spot on the truth, whether he wanted to admit to it or not.

Eva stood and took a step towards him, planted her hands on her hips and forced herself into his line of sight. No hiding.

'It felt right, Joss, because it *was* right. There's something between us, and I know that you know it. Whatever it was that spooked you, that has you scared and running from this connection, we can talk about that. But I will not stand here and listen to you talk about it like it meant nothing. Like I mean nothing to you.'

'I want it to be nothing, Eva. It shouldn't have happened. I wish it never had.'

The words were so unpolished, so simple, it was impossible to hide from their blow. Eva felt the blunt impact square in her chest, and had to fight not to look defeated.

'And that's why you left me—even though you knew how much that would hurt me? This is because of your divorce, isn't it?' she said, deciding that nothing short of tackling this head-on was going to get through to him. 'Your depression.'

'This is because of *you*. Because I don't want you to get hurt.'

Oh, so noble while he was breaking her heart.

'Then don't hurt me again.'

It was as simple as that. He could give up on them now, walk away as if this connection didn't mean anything to him. Or he could try again, face his past and his fears, and vow to make his future different. He could accept that this depression might return, but that if it did this time he'd find support in a relationship, rather than seeing it as a burden.

'I'm trying, here, Eva. I'm not standing here saying this because it feels good. Or because I've somehow forgotten everything that happened on Friday night. It's burnt into my memories and my retinas and my skin and I'll never be rid of it. I'm doing this for *you*. Because I want to protect you.'

'And I'm meant to stand here and take it? While you push me away when we both know that we can make each other happy? I'm sorry, Joss, but no deal. You're going to have to try harder than that.'

She didn't know where it was coming from, this fire inside her. When she had woken to that empty bed, that empty room, that empty heart, she had been sure that this was over. That nothing Joss could say to her would make up for what he had done.

But as the days had passed she'd realised she was angrier about what he was doing to their future than what he had actually done the other day. If she'd had another chance with her mother she knew she would have jumped at it. She wouldn't walk away just because she had been hurt once. She would keep trying, keep fighting to keep the ones she loved in her life.

'I didn't want to hurt my ex-wife, Eva, and look what happened,' Joss said. 'I don't want the same thing happening to you.'

'I *know* what happened.' She took a step away from him now, raising her voice and throwing her arms up— anything to try and get through to him. 'You got ill, and your behaviour while you were unwell was a symptom of the disease. When you recognised that you saw a doctor and you got better. It's sad—of course it is—that by the time you realised what was happening it was too late for your marriage. But last time I checked permanent celibacy wasn't prescribed for depression.'

'There isn't a cure.'

Joss's voice was still infuriatingly flat and she stilled for a moment, studying him, looking for any sign of the man she had spent that incredible night with.

'Perhaps not. But there's treatment. There's hard work. There's support, if you'll accept it. Most importantly, Joss, there are second chances, and they're generally not to be sniffed at. I want to be with you. I want to try loving you. Believe me, I'm going into this with my eyes wide open.'

Joss met those eyes now, staring her down. Maybe using the L word had finally got through to him.

'The last few days—'

'Have been pretty terrible. It's taken a while for me to feel ready to have this conversation. To forgive you. Believe me, if you'd asked these questions on Saturday you would have got a very different reaction.'

'The one I deserved?'

'Probably. But this is the one you're getting now. I'm not letting you off the hook, Joss. I'm not going to be complicit in you walking away. If you want to break this relationship you're going to have to try harder.'

'I'll end up hurting you again. You know it's true.'

'Would you stop talking in prophecies, Joss?'

Ugh! If she didn't feel so frustrated she'd be close to giving up on him and his fatalism right about now. There were only so many rejections her ego could take, and whatever that number was they were getting dangerously close to it. She was going to walk out of this office with dignity, whatever Joss decided. So this was it. All her cards on the table. Then Joss could take it or leave it.

'Yes, you might do things that hurt me,' she started. 'You'd be a saint if you got through any sort of relationship without occasionally doing that. I'm pretty sure I'll hurt you too. Soon, actually, if you don't start listening to me rather than talking at me. A relationship comes from moving past that. Recognising that you've done something wrong, apologising for it and trying harder next time. If you're willing to do that, Joss, then I'm still game. Because, quite frankly, I can't imagine how I could walk away from this—from you—now.'

She stood watching him as he remained leaning against his desk, still scowling, still silent. Then he looked up and met her gaze.

It was clear to see how conflicted he was. There was something about the expression around his eyes that reminded her of how passionate he'd been that night, when he'd had her beneath him in his arms, ready and wanting him. But there was a tension in his jaw that she knew meant he was still fighting it. That her words hadn't had the effect she'd wanted. He was still afraid—of himself, not of her.

'This is a lot to take in,' she said, her voice hard but not angry. 'I cleared your diary for the day. I didn't expect you to be in the office at all. Why don't you go back to the house? Rest. You look like you've not slept for days. We can talk again later.'

He ran a hand through his hair and glanced at his watch, as if it held magical answers. 'You're right. I need to sleep.'

He stood upright and took a couple of paces towards her. He was about to step past her when he stopped, laid a hand on her cheek, and she drew in a breath, wondering if everything had changed in that last fraction of a second. But when she looked up she saw from his expression that he was still holding back.

He stroked her cheek with his thumb, and Eva had to resist the urge to turn her face into the warmth of his hand. She had made her position perfectly clear; it was up to him to come closer if that was what he wanted.

'I'm sorry for hurting you,' he said.

His voice trailed off and she knew he wasn't ready yet. He didn't understand his own feelings enough to share them with her.

She pressed her lips gently to his, cutting him off before he could undo what he had just said.

'That's a start.'

CHAPTER FOURTEEN

Joss watched Eva leave his office with the touch of her lips still burning on his mouth.

She made it sound so simple. As if everything they had felt the night they'd slept together was enough to base a relationship on. As if that were enough to cancel out what he had done afterwards.

It wasn't just that he'd left. It was that he'd cut her out completely. He hadn't been able to bring himself to talk to her on the phone, knowing that just the sound of her voice would make his resolve crumble. He'd kept it up for three days, falling back into old habits and isolating himself.

When he'd walked into the office and seen her sitting there, clearly aware of his presence, his breath had frozen in his chest. Waiting for her to turn around and look at him, he had felt every emotion he had been trying to bury over the last few days flood back, hitting him with a tidal wave of longing.

And then she'd been so angry, so fierce, and so sure of what she had been saying it had been impossible to argue with her. He'd walked into the office convinced that the best thing he could do for her was get as far away as possible—emotionally, at least, even if they couldn't manage it physically. It had never occurred to him what *she* might want. That she might be prepared to give him another chance.

He thought back to the dark days of his marriage. All the times his wife had tried to offer support and he'd thrown it back at her. Retreated more and more into himself, telling himself it was for the best, that he was protecting her. And where had that led them? She'd been hurt, and he'd had to carry the guilt of that. Was he just repeating himself now?

He turned the corner to Eva's mews and looked up at the big picture window of her apartment. He'd been looking forward to getting back here, he realised. It wasn't his own home he had been wishing for when he'd been trying to sleep in that crippling hospital chair. It had been Eva's. And he wasn't so stupid to think it was the bricks and mortar he'd been missing.

Nor was it her delicious body in his bed, because a sturdy wall separated them in this house. No, it was just *her*. Being close to her. Sharing his life with her. That was what had made this feel like his home.

He traipsed up the stairs and into the bedroom, shedding his jacket and shirt as he went. By the time he reached his bed he was down to his underwear and he collapsed onto the duvet, letting his muscles relax, finally, into the bed.

As his eyes drifted closed moments from his conversation with Eva back at the office drifted through his mind until one caught at him—*I want to try loving you.*

Not the first time he'd heard that word today. He'd told his father that he loved her, but he hadn't told Eva.

And in the moment when she'd all but told him she loved him too, he'd been so intent on telling Eva what he thought she needed to know that he hadn't listened to her. Her words hadn't reached him somehow. But he was listening now. *Did* she love him? Was that what she had been trying to say?

He couldn't stop the broad smile that crossed his lips as that thought sank home. It should have been scary. It should have set off warning beacons and alarms and flashing lights. Instead it filled him with warmth, a feeling of fullness that he couldn't remember ever having before. It filled him with hope.

And as he drifted into sleep he suspected that his world had changed.

He awoke to the sun low in the window, and creases from the pillow on his face. He'd fallen quickly and easily into sleep—something that had been a trial ever since his father had given him the news of his illness. His body felt refreshed and his mind was energised, full of Eva—still going over everything she had said to him at the office. Every retort to his omens of doom. Every argument against his careful reasons why they shouldn't be together.

She actually wanted to do this. She knew the risks. She knew who he had been before. She knew that the situation with his father could only ever get worse. And she still wanted to try.

The smile that had formed on his face before he had fallen asleep was fixed in place now, because he knew what he needed to do. He couldn't let her go. Not when he felt like this. She had put everything on the line for him, told him exactly how she felt, and he owed her the same in return.

He pulled on some clothes and went through to the kitchen, pulling open the fridge and glancing in cupboards. He was certain Eva would be able to create something from what he could see, but it was definitely not his forte.

He pulled out his phone and placed a call to one of his favourite restaurants, and arranged for them to deliver something worthy of Eva's palate. With glasses and cutlery and a nice bottle of red in hand he went through to the other room and laid the table, and then dug around in drawers to find candles for every surface. If he was doing this, he was going to do it properly.

She deserved that.

She deserved everything from him.

She had shown faith in him when he had deserved it least. When he hadn't even had faith in himself. And for once he believed her more than he believed the voices of self-doubt in his head. The voices that told him he was better off alone. That no woman deserved to have to put up with him again.

He was curious too. She had seemed so strong when she was talking to him back in the office. But he knew she feared being abandoned. That it was something that had haunted her life. And then, when he had gone and done it—had left her as she had feared—she'd seemed to come out of it stronger, rather than more shaken.

A knock at the door told him the food had arrived,

and he jogged down the stairs, returning a few moments later laden with foil containers. He placed them in the oven, as instructed, and then glanced at the clock. Quarter to seven. She could be home any minute.

He had barely sat down when he heard her key in the door downstairs. He jumped up and glanced around the room to make sure he had got it right. Candles flickered, reflected and refracted in the glass of the windows. The music was low and atmospheric. And the smells coming from the kitchen rivalled anything that Maria or Eva had rustled up for him.

There was nothing more he could do to prepare. It was time for them to talk.

'Something smells good,' he heard Eva call as she reached the top of the stairs and her footsteps turned towards the kitchen. She appeared in the doorway, and he stood completely still as her eyes widened when she took in the table and the candles.

'You've been busy,' she said, and he could tell from the careful modulation of her voice that she was taking care to keep her tone even. She wasn't going to give anything away, then. Wasn't going to make this easy for him.

'I might not cook, but I can order as well as anyone,' he said, trying out a smile, wanting to break the tension between them.

This afternoon he had been so sure this was right that he had forgotten how the tension in the atmosphere ratcheted up when he and Eva were in a room together. It was never going to be the case that they could sit and have a detached, impersonal conversation about where their relationship was headed. He shook his head: what would be the point of detached and impersonal? That was the last thing he wanted. It had taken Eva to show him how stunted that had left his life. How much he was missing out on.

He wanted this to be personal, and he didn't care if it got messy. He didn't care if he got hurt. He just wanted it to be real.

'Have a seat. I'll get us a drink,' he said, heading for the kitchen and buying himself a couple of minutes to decide what he wanted to say first.

He thought back to what his dad had said to him about how he should tell her what he felt. How he had been able to see through the complications of their relationship to the fact that they cared about each other. And he was right. Whatever else was fake about their relationship, the feelings he had for her—the strength he felt from knowing he had her support—that was real.

He hoped it was for her too.

He brought two gin and tonics through and set them on the table, taking a seat opposite Eva, noticing how the shine of the waves in her hair caught and played in the candlelight.

'Did you sleep?' Eva asked. 'You look better.'

'Yeah, I did, thanks. I feel it. Everything okay in the office?'

She looked slightly disappointed at the question, and he could understand why. He was disappointed in himself for asking it. He didn't want small talk. He wanted more than that. He wanted to talk about them: what they were to each other and where they were going.

'Everything's fine. Any news from your dad?'

'He's fine too. Look, Eva, this afternoon you asked me to think. And I have. Since I left the office I've done nothing *but* think. About you.'

She gave a small nod and lifted her brows, encouraging him to go on.

'And you're right. I've been scared. Scared of history repeating itself. Scared of hurting you. When I left you alone the other night I knew what I was doing. I don't think I get a free pass on that just because Dad is sick.'

'I didn't say anything about a free pass,' Eva said, her voice steadier than his. 'Yes, you hurt me. I expect you to learn from that. And to try extremely hard not to do it again.'

'Did it make you think of your parents?' Joss asked.

It wasn't where he'd planned on this conversation going, but he was curious. Something about her had changed in the days that he'd been at the hospital with his dad, and he wanted to understand her better.

Eva nodded. 'Of course it did. But knowing what you were going through with your dad also made me think harder about them than I have before. When I was a teenager the "poor abandoned me" routine was easier to maintain. But I'm an adult now, and I don't expect the world to revolve around me. There are other things going on, and lots of interests that compete with mine. I want to be with someone who makes me a priority. But I'd rather be alone than with someone who doesn't put the needs of their sick parent above mine. My parents did what they thought was right: they lived trying to balance all of the lives they felt were their responsibility. And for them the lives of people caught up in conflict were just as important as mine. They protected me from the effects of that as much as they could, and I never gave them credit for it. I think they genuinely did the best they could, and it wouldn't be fair of me to expect more than that of them.'

Joss leaned back in his chair and took a sip of his drink. So *that* was what had changed. 'That's quite a realisation to come to after so many years.'

'Yeah, well, I had a bit of a push.' She gave him a meaningful look. 'And a weekend with nothing to do but think.'

He leaned forward and reached across the table for Eva's hand. When she turned her palm to meet his and threaded their fingers together he couldn't hold back the smile that spread across his features.

'Eva, you said earlier that you want to try loving me. Well, I want that too. I want you to try desperately hard—because I'm already so in love with you. I want to be with you, here, every day for the rest of our lives. I want to feel *this* ring...' he turned their hands over and kissed the diamonds they had chosen together '...every time I hold your hand, and remember how I felt the day we chose it. How I feel right this second.'

He paused, and looked up from her hand to meet her gaze.

'I want to hear you say I love you in every language you know. I want you to teach me to say it back, so that I'm never lost for a way to tell you exactly how I feel. I want you to be my wife, Eva.'

Her hand gripped his a little harder, and he knew he

had taken her by surprise. Well, no wonder. He'd surprised himself. He already knew he wanted to be with her, but he hadn't planned to ask that question just yet. Now that it was out there, he realised how desperate he was for her to feel the same. He looked into her eyes, tried to read her answer from the shape of her mouth, the expression in her eyes.

'Yes,' she said eventually, a smile breaking her features at last. 'Yes,' she said again as she rose from the table and took a step towards him. *'Oui.'*

At the sight of her pursed lips and the sound of those breathy vowels, he ached to pull her into his lap, but she wasn't done yet.

'Sí, sì, naí, ja,' she added as she reached him, and placed a hand on each of his cheeks.

She leaned in close, so close he could have met her lips with the tiniest movement. But this moment was all hers, and he wanted to hear her tell him yes in every language she could.

'Ano, tak, ie, na'am. I love you, Joss. Of course I'll marry you.'

At last her lips met his, and heat swept through him as he pulled her into his lap, threaded his fingers through her hair and kissed her with all the passion he'd been holding back for weeks. Part of him—no surprise which part—wanted to pick her up, carry her to the bedroom and never let her go. But there was more to this than just wanting her.

'I love you,' he told her again as he wrapped his arms tight around her waist, holding her hard against him.

'I've never wanted anything more than I want to make you happy and to deserve you.'

She smiled down at him, and he felt the connection that ran between them pull at him deep inside.

'We're going to work so hard to deserve each other,' she said with a smile. 'Every day. For the rest of our lives.'

He tipped her face down to his, and poured his whole heart into their kiss.

* * * * *

SECRETS OF A
RUTHLESS TYCOON

CATHY WILLIAMS

CHAPTER ONE

IN THE DIMINISHING light, Leo Spencer was beginning to question his decision to make this trip. He looked up briefly from the report blinking at him on his laptop and frowned at the sprawling acres of countryside reaching out on either side to distant horizons which had now been swallowed up by the gathering dusk.

It was on the tip of his tongue to tell his driver to put his foot down, but what would be the point? How much speed would Harry be able to pick up on these winding, unlit country roads, still hazardous from the recent bout of snow which was only now beginning to melt? The last thing he needed was to end up in a ditch somewhere. The last car they had passed had been several miles back. God only knew where the nearest town was.

He concluded that February was, possibly, the very worst month in which to have undertaken this trip to the outer reaches of Ireland. He had failed to foresee the length of time it would take to get to his destination and he now cursed the contorted reasoning that had made him reject the option of flying there on the company plane.

The flight to Dublin had been straightforward enough but, the minute he had met his driver outside the airport, the trip had evolved into a nightmare of traffic, diversions and, as they'd appeared to leave all traces of civilisation behind, a network of bleak, perilous roads made all the more threatening by the constant threat of snow. It hung in the air like a death shroud, biding its time for just the right unsuspecting mug to come along.

Giving up on all hope of getting anything useful done, Leo snapped shut his laptop and stared at the gloomy scenery.

The rolling hills were dark contours rising ominously up from flat fields in which lurked a honeycomb network of lakes, meandering streams and rivers, none of which was visible at this time of the late afternoon. Leo was accustomed to the almost constant artificial light of London. He had never had much time for the joys of the countryside and his indifference to it was rapidly being cemented with each passing mile.

But this was a trip that had to be undertaken.

When he reflected on the narrative of his life, he knew that it was an essential journey. The death of his mother eight months previously—following so shortly after his father's own unexpected demise from a heart attack whilst, of all things, he had been playing golf with his friends—had left him with no excuses for avoidance. He had to find out where he really came from, who his real birth parents were. He would never have disrespected his adoptive parents when they were alive by searching out his birth family but the time had come.

He closed his eyes and the image of his own life flickered in front of him like an old-fashioned movie reel: adopted at birth by a successful and wealthy couple in their late thirties who had been unable to have children of their own; brought up with all the advantages a solid, middle-class background had to offer; private school and holidays abroad. A brilliant academic career followed by a stint at an investment bank which had been the springboard for a meteoric rise through the financial world until, at the ripe old age of thirty-two, he now had more money than he could ever hope to spend in a lifetime and the freedom to use it in the more creative arena of acquisitions.

He seemed to possess the golden touch. None of his acquisitions to date had failed. Additionally, he had been bequeathed a sizeable fortune by his parents. All told, the only grey area in a life that had been blessed with success was the murky blur of his true heritage. Like a pernicious weed, it had never been completely uprooted. Curiosity had always been there, hovering on the edges of his consciousness, and he knew that it would always be there unless he took active measures to put it to rest once and for all.

Not given to introspection of any sort, there were moments when he suspected that it had left a far-reaching legacy, despite all the advantages his wonderful adoptive parents had given him. His relationships with women had all been short-lived. He enjoyed a varied love life with some of the most beautiful and eligible women on the London scene, yet the thought of committing to any of them had always left him cold. He always used the excuse of being the kind of man whose commitment to work left little fertile ground on which a successful relationship could flourish. But there lurked the nagging suspicion that the notion of his own feckless parents dumping him on whatever passing strangers they could had fostered a deep-seated mistrust of any form of permanence, despite the sterling example his adoptive parents had set for him.

He had known for several years where he could locate his mother. He had no idea if his natural father was still on the scene—quite possibly not. The whereabouts of his mother was information that had sat, untouched, in his locked office drawer until now.

He had taken a week off work, informing his secretary

that he would be contactable at all times by email or on his mobile phone. He would find his mother, make his own judgements and he would leave, putting to rest the curiosity that had plagued him over the years. He had a good idea of what he would find but it would be useful having his suspicions confirmed. He wasn't looking for answers or touching reconciliations. He was looking for closure.

And, naturally, he had no intention of letting her know his identity. He was sinfully rich and there was nothing like money to engender all the wrong responses. There was no way he intended to have some irresponsible deadbeat who had given him up for adoption holding out a begging bowl and suddenly claiming parental love—not to mention whatever half- siblings he had who would feel free to board the gravy train.

His mouth curled derisively at the mere thought of it.

'Any chance we could actually get this car into fifth gear?' he asked Harry, who caught his eye in the rear-view mirror and raised his eyebrows.

'Aren't you appreciating the wonderful scenery, sir?'

'You've been with me for eight years, Harry. Have I ever given any indication that I like the countryside?' Harry, strangely, was the only one in whom Leo had confided. They shared an uncommonly strong bond. Leo would have trusted his driver with his life. He certainly trusted him with thoughts he never would have shared with another living soul.

'There's always a first, sir,' Harry suggested calmly. 'And, no, there is no way I can drive any faster. Not on these roads. And have you noticed the sky?'

'In passing.'

'Snow's on the way, sir.'

'And I'm hoping that it will delay its arrival until I'm through…doing what I have to do.' From where he was sitting, it was hard to see where the sky met the open land. It was all just a black, formless density around them. Aside from the sound of the powerful engine of the car, the silence was so complete that, with eyes closed, anyone could be forgiven for thinking that they were suffering sensory deprivation.

'The weather is seldom obedient, sir. Even for a man like yourself who is accustomed to having his orders obeyed.'

Leo grinned. 'You talk too much, Harry.'

'So my better half often tells me, sir. Are you certain you don't require my services when we reach Ballybay?'

'Quite certain. You can get a cab driver to deliver the car back to London and the company plane will return you to your better half. I've alerted my secretary to have it on standby; she'll text you where. Make sure you tell my people to have it ready and waiting for when I need to return to London. I have no intention of repeating this journey by car any time soon.'

'Of course, sir.'

Leo flipped back open the laptop and consigned all wayward thoughts of what he would find when he finally arrived to the furthermost outer reaches of his mind. Losing yourself in pointless speculation was a waste of time.

It was two hours by the time he was informed that they were in Ballybay. Either he had missed the main part of the town or else there was nothing much to it. He could just about make out the vast stillness of a lake and then a scattering of houses and shops nestling amidst the hills and dales.

'Is this it?' he asked Harry, who tut-tutted in response.

'Were you expecting Oxford Street, sir?'

'I was expecting a little more by way of life. Is there even a hotel?' He frowned and thought that allowing a week off work might have been over- estimating the time he would need. A couple of days at most should see him conclude his business.

'There's a pub, sir.'

Leo followed his driver's pointing finger and made out an ancient pub that optimistically boasted 'vacancies'. He wondered what the passing tourist trade could possibly be in a town that time appeared to have forgotten.

'Drop me off here, Harry, and you can head off.' He was travelling light: one holdall, suitably battered, into which he now stuffed his slim laptop.

Already, he was making comparisons between what appeared to be this tiny town of splendid isolation and the completely different backdrop to life with his adoptive parents. The busy Surrey village in which he had been brought up buzzed with a veritable treasure trove of trendy gastropubs and designer shops. The landscape was confined and neatly manicured. The commuter links to London were excellent and that was reflected in the high-end property market. Gated mansions were hidden from prying eyes by long drives. On Saturdays, the high street was bursting with expensive people who lived in the expensive houses and drove the expensive cars.

He stepped out of the Range Rover to a gusty wind and freezing cold.

The ancient pub looked decidedly more inviting given the temperatures outside and he strode towards it without hesitation.

Inside the pub, Brianna Sullivan was nursing an incipient headache. Even in the depths of winter, Friday nights brought in the crowds and, whilst she was grateful for their patronage, she yearned for peace and quiet. Both seemed about as elusive as finding gold dust in the kitchen sink. She had inherited this pub from her father nearly six years ago and there were no allowances made for time out. There was just her, and it was her livelihood. Choice didn't feature heavily on the menu.

'Tell Pat he can come and get his own drinks at the bar,' she hissed to Shannon. 'We're busy enough here without you carrying trays of drinks over to him because he broke his leg six months ago. He's perfectly capable of getting them himself, or else he can send that brother of his over to get them.' At one end of the bar, Aidan and two of his friends were beginning to sing a rousing love song to grab her attention.

'I'll have to chuck you out for unruly behaviour,' she snapped at Aidan as she slid refills for them along the counter.

'You know you love me, darling.'

Brianna shot him an exasperated look and told him that he either settled his tab in full, right here and right now, or else that was the last pint he was going to get.

She needed more people behind the bar but what on earth would she do with them on the week days, when the place was less rowdy and busy? How could she justify the expenditure? And yet, she barely had enough time to function properly. Between the bookkeeping, the stock taking, the ordering and the actual standing behind the bar every night, time—the one thing she didn't have—was galloping past. She was twenty-seven years old and in the blink of an eye she would be thirty, then forty, then fifty, and still doing the things she was doing now, still struggling to kick back. She was young but, hell, she felt old a lot of the time.

Aidan continued to try his banter on her but she blocked him out. Now that she had begun feeling sorry for herself, she was barely aware of what was going on around her.

Surely her years at university had not equipped her to spend the rest of her life running this pub? She loved her friends and the tight-knit community but surely she was entitled to just have some *fun*? Six months of fun was all she had had when she had finished university, then it had been back here to help look after her father who had managed to drink himself into a premature grave.

Not a day went by when she didn't miss him. For twelve years after her mother had died it had been just the two of them, and she missed his easy laughter, his support, his corny jokes. She wondered how he would feel if he knew that she was still here, at the pub. He had always wanted her to fly away and develop a career in art, but then little had he known that he would not be around to make that possible.

She only became aware that something was different when, still absorbed in her own thoughts, it dawned on her that the bar had grown silent.

In the act of pulling a pint, she raised her eyes and there, framed in the doorway, was one of the most startlingly beautiful men she had ever seen in her life. Tall, wind-swept dark hair raked back from a face that was shamefully good-looking. He didn't seem in the slightest taken aback by the fact that all eyes were on him as he looked around, his midnight-black eyes finally coming to rest on her.

Brianna felt her cheeks burn at the casual inspection, then she returned to what she was doing and so did everyone else. The noise levels once again rose and the jokes resumed; old Connor did his usual and began singing lustily and drunkenly until he was laughed down.

She ignored the stranger, yet was all too aware of his presence, and not at all surprised that when she next glanced up it was to find him standing right in front of her.

'The sign outside says that there are vacancies.' Leo practically had to shout to make himself heard above the noise. The entire town seemed to have congregated in this small pub. Most of the green leather stools assembled along the bar were filled, as were the tables. Behind the bar, two girls were trying hard to keep up with the demands—a small, busty brunette and the one in front of whom he was now standing. A tall, slender girl with copper-coloured hair which she had swept up into a rough pony tail and, as she looked at him, the clearest, greenest eyes he had ever seen.

'Why do you want to know?' Brianna asked.

His voice matched the rest of him. It was deep and lazy and induced an annoying, fluttery feeling in the pit of her stomach. 'Why do you think? I need to rent a room and I take it this is the only place in the village that rents rooms…?'

'Is it not good enough for you?'

'Where's the owner?'

'You're looking at her.'

He did, much more thoroughly this time. Bare of any make-up, her skin was satin-smooth and creamy white. There was not a freckle in sight, despite the vibrant colour of her hair. She was wearing a pair of faded jeans and a long-sleeved jumper but neither detracted from her looks.

'Right. I need a room.'

'I will show you up to one just as soon as I get a free moment. In the meantime, would you like something to drink?' What on earth was this man doing here? He certainly wasn't from around these parts, nor did he know anyone around here. She would know. It was a tiny community; they all knew each other in some way, shape or form.

'What I'd like is a hot shower and a good night's sleep.'

'Both will have to wait, Mr…?'

'My name is Leo and, if you give me a key and point me in the right direction, I'll make my own way upstairs. And, by the way, is there anywhere to eat around here?'

Not only was the man a stranger but he was an obnoxious one. Brianna could feel her hackles rising. Memories of another good-looking, well-spoken stranger rose unbidden to the foreground. As learning curves went, she had been taught well what sort of men to avoid.

'You'll have to go into Monaghan for that,' she informed him shortly. 'I can fix you a sandwich but—'

'Yes—but I'll have to wait because you're too busy behind the bar. Forget the food. If you need a deposit, tell me how much and then you can give me the key.'

Brianna shot him an impatient glance and called over to Aidan. 'Take the reins,' she told him. 'And no free drinks. I've got to show this man to a room. I'll be back down in five minutes, and if I find out that you've helped yourself to so much as a thimble of free beer I'll ban you for a week.'

'Love you too, Brianna.'

'How long would you be wanting the room for?' was the first thing she asked him as soon as they were out of the bar area and heading upstairs. She was very much aware of him following her and she could feel the hairs on the back of her neck rising. Had she lived so long in this place that the mere sight of a halfway decent guy was enough to bring her out in a cold sweat?

'A few days.' She was as graceful as a dancer and he was tempted to ask why a girl with her looks was running a pub in the middle of nowhere. Certainly not for the stress-free existence. She looked hassled and he could understand that if it was as busy every night of the week.

'And might I ask what brings you to this lovely part of Ireland?' She pushed open the door to one of the four rooms she rented out and stood back, allowing him to brush past her.

Leo took his time looking around him. It was small but clean. He would have to be sharp-witted when it came to avoiding the beams but it would do. He turned round to her and began removing his coat which he tossed onto the high-backed wooden chair by the dressing table.

Brianna took a step back. The room was small and he seemed to over-power it with his presence. She was treated to a full view of his muscular body now he was without his coat: black jeans, a black jumper and the sort of olive-brown complexion that told her that, somewhere along the line, there was a strain of exotic blood running through him.

'You can ask,' Leo agreed. Billionaire searching for his long-lost, feckless parent wasn't going to cut it. One hint of that and it would be round the grapevine faster than he could pay her the deposit on the room; of that he was convinced. Checking his mother out was going to be an incognito exercise and he certainly wasn't going to be ambushed by a pub owner with a loose tongue, however pretty she was.

'But you're not going to tell me. Fair enough.' She shrugged. 'If you want breakfast, it's served between seven and eight. I run this place single-handed so I don't have a great deal of time to wait on guests.'

'Such a warm welcome.'

Brianna flushed and belatedly remembered that he was a paying guest and not another of the lads downstairs to whom she was allowed to give as good as she got. 'I apologise if I seem rude, Mr...'

'Leo.'

'But I'm rushed off my feet at the moment and not in the best of moods. The bathroom is through there...' She pointed in the direction of a white-washed door. 'And there are tea- and coffee-making facilities.' She backed towards the door, although she was finding it hard to tear her eyes away from his face.

If he brought to mind unhappy memories of Daniel Fluke, then it could be said that he was a decidedly more threatening version: bigger, better looking and without the readily charming patter, and that in itself somehow felt more dangerous. And she still had no idea what he was doing in this part of the world.

'If you could settle the deposit on the room...' She cleared her throat and watched in silence as he extracted a wad of notes from his wallet and handed her the required amount.

'And tell me, what is there to do here?' he asked, shoving his hands in his pockets and tilting his head to one side. 'I guess you must know everything...and everyone?'

'You've picked a poor time of year for sightseeing, Mr... eh...Leo. I'm afraid walking might be a little challenging, especially as snow is predicted, and you can forget about the fishing.'

'Perhaps I'll just explore the town,' he murmured. Truly amazing eyes, he thought. Eyelashes long and dark and in striking contrast to the paleness of her skin. 'I hope I'm not making you nervous... Sorry, you didn't tell me your name, although I gather it's Brianna...?'

'We don't get very many strangers in this part of town, certainly not in the depths of winter.'

'And now you're renting a room to one and you don't know what he does or why he's here in the first place. Understandable if you feel a little edgy...' He shot her a crooked smile and waited for it to take effect; waited to see her loosen up, smile back in return, look him up and down covertly; waited for the impact he knew he had on women to register. Nothing. She frowned and looked at him coolly, clearly assessing him.

'That's right.' Brianna folded her arms and leaned against the doorframe.

'I…' He realised that he hadn't banked on this. He actually hadn't expected the place to be so small. Whilst he had acknowledged that he couldn't just show up on his mother's doorstep and do his character assessment on the spot, he was now realising that the other option of extracting information from random drinkers at some faceless, characterless bar close to where the woman lived was quite likely also out of the question.

'Yes?' Brianna continued to look at him. She might be grateful for the money—it wasn't as though people were falling over themselves to rent a room in the depths of winter—but on the other hand she *was* a single woman, here on her own, and what if he turned out to be a homicidal maniac?

Granted it was unlikely that a homicidal maniac would announce his intentions because she happened to ask, but if he seemed too shifty, just too untrustworthy, then she would send him on his way, money or not.

'I'm not proud of this.' Leo glanced around him. His gaze settled on an exquisite watercolour painting above the bed and moved to the row of books neatly stacked on the shelf just alongside it. 'But I jacked in a perfectly good job a fortnight ago.'

'A perfectly good job doing what?' Brianna knew that she was giving him the third degree; that he was under no obligation to explain himself to her; that she could lose trade should he choose to spread the word that the landlady at the Angler's Catch was the sort who gave her customers a hard time. She also knew that there was a fair to middling chance that Aidan had already had a couple of free whiskies at her expense, and that Shannon would be running around like a headless chicken trying to fill orders, but her feet refused to budge. She was riveted by the sight of his dark, handsome face, glued to the spot by that lazy, mesmerising drawl.

'Working at one of those big, soulless companies...' Which was not, strictly speaking, a complete lie, although it had to be said that his company was less soulless than most. 'Decided that I would try my luck at something else. I've always wanted to...write, so I'm in the process of taking a little time out to try my hand at it; see where that takes me...' He strolled towards the window and peered out. 'I thought a good place to start would be Ireland. It's noted for its inspiring scenery, isn't it? Thought I would get a flavour of the country...the bits most people don't see; thought I would set my book here...'

He glanced over his shoulder to her before resuming his thoughtful contemplation of the very little he could actually see in the almost complete, abysmal darkness outside. 'The weather has knocked my progress off a little, hence—' he raised his shoulders in a rueful, elegant shrug '—here I am.'

A budding author? Surely not. He certainly didn't *look* like one, yet why on earth would he lie? The fact that he had held down a conventional job no doubt accounted for that hint of *sophistication* she was getting; something intangible that emanated from him, an air of unspoken authority that she found difficult to quite define but...

Brianna felt herself thaw. 'It gets a little quieter towards the end of the evening,' she offered. 'If you haven't fallen asleep, I can make you something to eat.'

'That's very kind of you,' Leo murmured. The passing guilt he had felt at having to concoct a lie was rationalised, justified and consigned to oblivion. He had responded creatively to an unexpected development.

Getting her onside could also work in his favour. Publicans knew everything about everyone and were seldom averse to a bit of healthy gossip. Doubtless he would be able to extract some background information on his mother and, when he had that information, he would pay her a visit in the guise of someone doing business in the area—maybe interviewing her for the fictitious book he had supposedly jacked his job in for. He would add whatever he learnt to whatever he saw and would get a complete picture of the woman who had abandoned him at birth. He would get his closure. The unfinished mosaic of his life would finally have all the pieces welded together.

'Right, then…' Brianna dithered awkwardly. 'Is there anything you need to know about…the room? How the television works? How you can get an outside line?'

'I think I can figure both out,' Leo responded dryly. 'You can get back to your rowdy crew in the bar.'

'They are, aren't they?' She laughed softly and hooked her thumbs into the pockets of her jeans.

Without warning, Leo felt a jolt of unexpected arousal at the sight. She was very slender. Her figure was almost boyish, not at all like the women he was routinely attracted to, whose assets were always far more prominent and much more aggressively advertised; beautiful, overtly sexy women who had no time for downplaying what they possessed.

He frowned at his body's unexpected lapse in self-control. 'You should employ more people to help you out,' he told her abruptly.

'Perhaps I should.' Just like that she felt the change in the atmosphere and she reminded herself that, writer or not, guys who were too sexy for their own good spelled trouble. She reminded herself of how easy it was to be taken in by what was on the outside, only to completely miss the ugly stuff that was buried underneath.

She coolly excused herself and returned to find that, just

as expected, Aidan was knocking back a glass of whisky which he hurriedly banged on the counter the second he spotted her approaching.

Shannon appeared to be on the verge of tears and, despite what Brianna had told her, was scuttling over with a tray of drinks to the group of high-spirited men at the corner table, most of whom they had gone to school with, which Brianna thought was no reason for them to think they could get waitress service. Old Connor, with several more drinks inside him, was once again attempting to be a crooner but could scarcely enunciate the words to the song he was trying to belt out.

It was the same old same old, and she felt every day of her twenty-seven years by the time they all began drifting off into an unwelcoming night. Twenty-seven years old and she felt like forty-seven. The snow which had thankfully disappeared for the past week had returned to pay them another visit, and outside the flakes were big and fat under the street lights.

Shannon was the last to leave and Brianna had to chivvy her along. For a young girl of nineteen, she had a highly developed mothering instinct and worried incessantly about her friend living above the pub on her own.

'Although at least there's a strapping man there with you tonight!' She laughed, wrapping her scarf around her neck and winking.

'From my experience of the opposite sex...' Brianna grinned back and shouted into the darkness with a wave '...they're the first to dive for cover if there's any chance of danger—and that includes the strapping ones!'

'Then you've just met the wrong men.'

She spun round to see Leo standing by the bar, arms folded, his dark eyes amused. He had showered and changed and was in a pair of jeans and a cream, thickly knitted jumper which did dramatic things for his colouring.

'You've come for your sandwich.' She tore her eyes away from him and quickly and efficiently began clearing the tables, getting the brunt of the work done before she had to get up at seven the following morning.

'I gathered that the crowd was beginning to disperse. The singing had stopped.' He began giving her a hand.

Clearing tables was a novel experience. When he happened to be in the country, he ate out. On the rare occasions when he chose to eat in, he ate food specially prepared for him by his housekeeper, who was also an excellent chef. She cooked for him, discreetly waited until he was finished and then cleared the table. Once a month, she cooked for both him and Harry and these meals were usually preplanned to coincide with a football game. They would eat, enjoy a couple of beers and watch the football. It was his most perfect down time.

He wondered when and how that small slice of normality, the normality of clearing a table, had vanished—but then was it so surprising? He ran multi-million-pound companies that stretched across the world. Normality, as most people understood it, was in scarce supply.

'You really don't have to help,' Brianna told him as she began to fetch the components for a sandwich. 'You're a paying guest.'

'With a curious mind. Tell me about the wannabe opera singer...'

He watched as she worked, making him a sandwich that could have fed four, tidying away the beer mugs and glasses into the industrial-sized dishwasher. He listened keenly as she chatted, awkwardly at first, but then fluently, about all the regulars—laughing at their idiosyncrasies; relating little anecdotes of angry wives showing up to drag their other halves back home when they had abused the freedom pass they had been given for a couple of hours.

'Terrific sandwich, by the way.' It had been. Surprisingly so, bearing in mind that the sandwiches he occasionally ate were usually ornate affairs with intricate fillings prepared by top chefs in expensive restaurants. He lifted the plate as she wiped clean the counter underneath. 'I'm guessing that you pretty much know everyone who lives around here…'

'You guess correctly.'

'One of the upsides of living in a small place?' He could think of nothing worse. He thoroughly enjoyed the anonymity of big-city life.

'It's nice knowing who your neighbours are. It's a small population here. 'Course, some of them have gone to live in other parts of Ireland, and a few really daring ones have moved to your part of the world, but on the whole, yes, we all know each other.'

She met his steady gaze and again felt that hectic bloom of colour invade her cheeks. 'Nearly everyone here tonight were regulars. They've been coming here since my dad owned the place.'

'And your dad is…?'

'Dead,' Brianna said shortly. 'Hence this is now my place.'

'I'm sorry. Tough work.'

'I can handle it.' She took his plate, stuck it into the sink then washed her hands.

'And, of course, you have all your friends around you for support… Siblings as well? What about your mother?'

'Why are you asking me all these questions?'

'Aren't we always curious about people we've never met and places we've never seen? As a…writer you could say that I'm more curious than most.' He stood up and began walking towards the door through which lay the stairs up to his bedroom. 'If you think I'm being too nosy then tell me.'

Brianna half-opened her mouth with a cool retort, something that would restore the balance between paying guest and landlady, but the temptation to chat to a new face, a new person, someone who didn't know her from time immemorial, was too persuasive.

A writer! How wonderful to meet someone on the same wavelength as her! What would it hurt to drop her guard for a couple of days and give him the benefit of the doubt? He might be good-looking but he wasn't Danny Fluke.

'You're not nosy.' She smiled tentatively. 'I just don't understand why you're interested. We're a pretty run-of-the-mill lot here; I can't imagine you would get anything useful for your book.' She couldn't quite make him out. He was in shadow, lounging indolently against the wall as he looked at her. She squashed the uneasy feeling that there was more to him than met the eye.

'People's stories interest me.' He pushed himself away from the wall and smiled. 'You'd be surprised what you can pick up; what you can find...useful.' There was something defiant yet vulnerable about her. It was an appealing mix and a refreshing change from the women he normally met.

'Tomorrow,' he said, 'Point me in the direction of what to do and you can relax. Tell me about the people who live here.'

'Don't be crazy. You're a guest. You're paying for your bed and board and, much as I'd love to swap the room for your labour, I just can't afford it.'

'And I wouldn't dream of asking.' He wondered how she would react if she knew that he could buy this pub a hundred times over and it would still only be loose change to him. He wondered what she would say if she knew that, in between the stories she had to tell, there would be that vital one he wanted to hear. 'No, you'd be helping me out, giving me one or two ideas. Plus you look as though you could use a day off…'

The thought of putting her feet up for a couple of hours dangled in front of her like the promise of a banquet to a starving man. 'I can work and chat at the same time,' she conceded. 'And it'll be nice to have someone lend a hand.'

CHAPTER TWO

BRIANNA WOKE AT six the following morning to furious snowfall. Outside, it was as still as a tomb. On days like this, her enjoyment of the peace and quiet was marred by the reality that she would have next to no customers, but then she thought of the stranger lying in the room down from hers on the middle floor. Leo. He hadn't baulked at the cost of the room and, the evening before, had insisted on paying her generously for an evening meal. Some of her lost income would be recovered.

And then…the unexpected, passing companionship of a fellow artiste. She knew most of the guys her age in the village and it had to be said that there wasn't a creative streak to be found among the pack of them.

She closed her eyes and luxuriated for a few stolen minutes, just thinking about him. When she thought about the way his dark eyes had followed her as she had tidied and chatted, wiped the bar counter and straightened the stools, she could feel the heat rush all through her body until it felt as though it was on fire.

She hadn't had a boyfriend in years.

The appearance of the stranger was a stark reminder of how her emotional life had ground to a standstill after her disastrous relationship with Daniel Fluke at university. All those years ago, she had fancied herself in love.

Daniel had been the complete package: gorgeous, with chestnut-brown hair, laughing blue eyes and an abundance of pure charm that had won him a lot of admirers. But he had only had eyes for her. They had been an item for nearly two years. He had met her father; had sat at the very bar downstairs, nursing a pint with him. He had been studying law and had possessed that peculiar surety of someone who has always known what road they intended to go down. His father was a retired judge, his mother a key barrister in London. They were all originally from Dublin, one of those families with textbook, aristocratic genealogy. They still kept a fabulous apartment in Dublin, but he had lived in London since he had been a child.

Looking back, Brianna could see that there had always been the unspoken assumption that she should consider herself lucky to have nabbed him, that a guy like him could have had any pretty girl on campus. At the time, though, she had walked around with her head in the clouds. She had actually thought that their relationship was built to last. Even now, years after the event, she could still taste the bitterness in her mouth when she remembered how it had all ended.

She had been swept off her feet on a post-graduation holiday in New Zealand, all expenses paid. She shuddered now when she thought back to the ease with which she had accepted his generosity. She had returned to Ireland only to discover that her father was seriously ill and, at that point, she had made the mistake of showing her hand. She had made the fatal error of assuming that Daniel would be right there by her side, supporting her through tough times.

'Of course,' he had told her, 'There's no way I can stay there with you. I have an internship due to start in London...'

She had understood. She had hoped for weekends. Her

father would recover, she had insisted, choosing to misread the very clear messages the doctors had been giving her about his prognosis. And, when he did, she would join him in London. There would be loads of opportunities for her in the city and they would easily be able to afford a place to rent. There would be no need to rush to buy... not until they were ready really to seal their relationship. Plus, it would be a wonderful time for her finally to meet his family: the brother he spoke so much about, who did clever things in banking, and his kid sister who was at a boarding school in Gloucester. And of course his parents, who never seemed to be in one place for very long.

She had stupidly made assumptions about a future that had never been on the cards. They had been at university together and, hell, it had been a lot of fun. She was by far the fittest girl there. But a future together...?

The look of embarrassed, dawning horror on his face had said it all but still, like the young fool she had been, she had clung on and asked for explanations. The more he had been forced to explain, the cooler his voice had become. They were worlds apart; how could she seriously have thought that they would end up *married*? Wasn't it enough that she had had an all-expenses-paid farewell holiday? He was expected to marry a certain type of woman... that was just the way it was...she should just stop clinging and move on...

She'd moved on but still a part of her had remained rooted to that moment in time. Why else had she made no effort to get her love life back on track?

The stranger's unexpected arrival on the scene had opened Pandora's box in her head and, much as she wanted to slam the lid back down, she remained lying in bed for far longer than she should, just thinking.

It was after eight by the time she made it down to the

bar, belatedly remembering the strict times during which her guest could have his breakfast. As landladies went, she would definitely not be in the running for a five-star rating.

She came to a halt by the kitchen door when she discovered that Leo was already there, appearing to make himself at home. There was a cup of coffee in front of him, and his laptop, which he instantly closed the second he looked up and spied her hovering in the doorway, a bit like a guest on her own premises.

'I hope you don't mind me making myself at home,' Leo said, pushing his chair back and folding his hands behind his head to look at her. 'I'm an early riser and staying in bed wasn't a tempting thought.' He had been up since six, in fact, and had already accomplished a great deal of work, although less than he had anticipated, because for once he had found his mind wandering to the girl now dithering in front of him. Was it because he was so completely removed from his comfort zone that his brain was not functioning with the rigid discipline to which it was accustomed? Was that why he had fallen asleep thinking of those startling green eyes and had awakened less than five hours later with a painful erection?

He might be willing to exploit whatever she knew about his mother, if she knew anything at all, but he certainly wasn't interested in progressing beyond that.

'You've been working.' Brianna smiled hesitantly. His impact on all her senses seemed as powerful in the clear light of day as it had been the night before. She galvanised herself into action and began unloading the dishwasher, stacking all the glasses to be returned to the bar outside; fetching things from the fridge so that she could make him the breakfast which was included in the money he had paid her.

'I have. I find that I work best in the mornings.'

'Have you managed to get anything down? I guess it must be quite an ordeal trying to get your imagination to do what you want it to do. Can I ask you what your book is going to be about? Or would you rather keep that to yourself?'

'People and the way they interact.' Leo hastened to get away from a topic in which he had no intention of becoming mired. The last time he had written anything that required the sort of imagination she was talking about had been at secondary school. 'Do you usually get up this early?'

'Earlier.' She refilled his mug and began cracking eggs, only pausing when he told her to sit down and talk to him for a few minutes rather than rushing into making breakfast.

Brianna blushed and obeyed. Nerves threatened to overwhelm her. She sneaked a glance at him and all over again was rendered breathless by the sheer force of his good looks and peculiar magnetism. 'There's a lot to do when you run a pub.' She launched into hurried speech to fill the silence. 'And, like I said, I'm doing it all on my own, so I have no one to share the responsibility with.'

Leo, never one to indulge his curiosity when it came to women—and knowing very well that, whatever information he was interested in gathering, certainly had nothing to do with *her* so why waste time hearing her out?—was reluctantly intrigued. 'A curious life you chose for yourself,' he murmured.

'I didn't choose it. *It* chose *me*.'

'Explain.'

'Are you really interested?'

'I wouldn't ask if I wasn't,' Leo said with a shrug. He had wondered whether she was really as pretty as he had imagined her to be. Subdued lighting in a pub could do flattering things to an average woman. He was discovering that his first impressions had been spot on. In fact, they had failed to do her justice. She had an ethereal, angelic beauty about her that drew the eye and compelled him to keep on staring. His eyes drifted slightly down to her breasts, small buds causing just the tiniest indentations in her unflattering, masculine jumper, which he guessed had belonged at one point to her father.

'My dad died unexpectedly. Well, maybe there were signs before. I didn't see them. I was at university, not getting back home as often as I knew I should, and Dad was never one to make a fuss when it came to his health.' She was startled at the ease with which she confessed to the guilt that had haunted her ever since her father had died. She could feel the full brunt of Leo's attention on her and it was as flattering as it was unnerving, not at all what she was accustomed to.

'He left a lot of debts.' She cleared her throat and blinked back the urge to cry. 'I think things must have slipped as he became ill and he never told me. The bank manager was very understanding but I had to keep running the pub so that I could repay the debts. I couldn't sell it, even though I tried for a while. There's a good summer trade here. Lots of fantastic scenery. Fishing. Brilliant walks. But the trade is a little seasonal and, well, the economy isn't great. I guess you'd know. You probably have to keep a firm rein on your finances if you've packed your job in...'

Leo flushed darkly and skirted around that ingenuous observation. 'So you've been here ever since,' he murmured. 'And no partner around to share the burden?'

'No.' Brianna looked down quickly and then stood up. 'I should get going with my chores. It's snowing outside and it looks like it's going to get worse, which usually means that the pub loses business, but just in case any hardy souls show up I can't have it looking a mess.'

So, he thought, there *had* been a man and it had ended badly. He wondered who the guy was. Some losers only stuck by their women when the times were good. The second the winds of change began blowing, they ran for the hills. He felt an unexpected spurt of anger towards this mystery person who had consigned her to a life on her own of drudgery, running a pub to make ends meet and pay off bills. He reined back his unruly mind and reminded himself that his primary purpose wasn't as counsellor but as information gatherer.

'If you really meant it about helping—and I promise I won't take advantage of your kind offer— you could try and clear a path through the snow, just in case it stops; at least my customers would be able to get to the door. It doesn't look promising...' She moved to one of the windows and frowned at the strengthening blizzard. 'What do you intend to do if the weather doesn't let up?' She turned to face him.

'It'll let up. I can't afford to stay here for very long.'

'You could always incorporate a snow storm in your book.'

'It's a thought.' He moved to stand next to her and at once he breathed in the fragrant, flowery smell of her hair which was, again, tied back in a pony tail. His fingers itched to release it, just to see how long it was, how thick. He noticed how she edged away slightly from him. 'I'll go see what I can do about the snow. You'll have to show me where the equipment is.'

'The equipment consists of a shovel and some bags of sand for gritting.' She laughed, putting a little more distance between them, because just for a second there she had felt short of breath with him standing so close to her.

'You do this yourself whenever it snows?' he asked, once the shovel was in his hand and the door to the pub thrown open to the elements. He thought of his last girl-friend, a model who didn't possess a pair of wellies to her name, and would only have gone near snow if it happened to be falling on a ski slope in Val d'Isere.

'Only if it looks as though it would make a difference. There've been times when I've wasted two hours trying to clear a path, only to stand back and watch the snow cover it all up in two minutes. You can't go out in those... er...jeans; you'll be soaked through. I don't suppose you brought any, um, waterproof clothing with you?'

Leo burst out laughing. 'Believe it or not, I didn't pack for a snow storm. The jeans will have to do. If they get soaked, they'll dry in front of that open fire in the lounge area.'

He worked out. He was strong. And yet he found that battling with the elements was exercise of a completely different sort. This was not the sanitised comfort of his expensive gym, with perfectly oiled machinery that was supposed to test the body to its limits. This was raw na-ture and, by the time he looked at his handiwork, a mea-gre path already filling up with fast falling snow, an hour and a half had flown past.

He had no gloves. His hands were freezing. But hell, it was invigorating. In fact, he had completely forgotten the reason why he was in this Godforsaken village in the first place. His thoughts were purely and utterly focused on try-ing to outsmart and out-shovel the falling snow.

The landscape had turned completely white. The pub was set a distance from the main part of the village and was surrounded by open fields. Pausing to stand back, his arm resting heavily on the shovel which he had planted firmly in the ground, he felt that he was looking at infinity. It evoked the strangest sensation of peace and awe, quite different from the irritation he had felt the day before when he had stared moodily out of the window at the tedium of never-ending fields and cursed his decision to get there by car.

He stayed out another hour, determined not to be beaten, but in the end he admitted defeat and returned to the warmth of the pub, to find the fire blazing and the smell of food wafting from the kitchen.

'I fought the snow…' God, he felt like a caveman returning from a hard day out hunting. 'And the snow won. Don't bank on any customers today. Something smells good.'

'I don't normally do lunch for guests.'

'You'll be royally paid for your efforts.' He stifled a surge of irritation that the one thing most women would have given their eye teeth to do for him was something she clearly had done because she had had no choice. She was stuck with him. She could hardly expect him to starve because lunch wasn't included in the price of the room. 'You were going to fill me in on the people who live around here.' He reminded her coolly of the deal they had struck.

'It's not very exciting.' She looked at him and her heart-beat quickened. 'You're going to have to change. You're soaked through. If you give me your damp clothes, I can put them in front of the fire in the snug.'

'The snug?'

'My part of the house.' She leaned back against the kitchen counter, hands behind her. 'Self-contained quarters. Only small—two bedrooms, a little snug, a kitchen, bathroom and a study where Dad used to do all the accounts for the pub. It's where I grew up. I can remember loving it when the place was full and I could roam through the guest quarters bringing them cups of tea and coffee. It used to get a lot busier in the boom days.'

She certainly looked happy recounting those jolly times but, as far as Leo was concerned, it sounded like just the sort of restricted life that would have driven him crazy.

And yet, this could have been his fate—living in this tiny place where everyone knew everyone else. In fact, he wouldn't even have had the relative comforts of a village pub. He would probably have been dragged up in a hovel somewhere by the town junkie, because what other sort of loser gave away their own child? It was a sobering thought.

'I could rustle up some of Dad's old shirts for you. I kept quite a few for myself. I'll leave them outside your bedroom door and you can hand me the jeans so that I can launder them.'

She hadn't realised how lonely it was living above the pub on her own, making every single decision on her own, until she was rummaging through her wardrobe, picking out shirts and enjoying the thought of having someone to lend them to, someone sharing her space, even if it was only in the guise of a guest who had been temporarily blown off-path by inclement weather.

She warmed at the thought of him trying and failing to clear the path to the pub of snow. When she gently knocked on his bedroom door ten minutes later, she was carrying a bundle of flannel shirts and thermal long-sleeved vests. She would leave them outside the door, and indeed she was bending down to do just that when the door opened.

She looked sideways and blinked rapidly at the sight of bare ankles. Bare ankles and strong calves, with dark hair... Her eyes drifted further upwards to bare thighs... lean, muscular bare thighs. Her mouth went dry. She was still clutching the clothes to her chest, as if shielding herself from the visual invasion of his body on her senses. His *semi-clad* body.

'Are these for me?'

Brianna snapped out of her trance and stared at him wordlessly.

'The clothes?' Leo arched an amused eyebrow as he took in her bright-red face and parted lips. 'They'll come in very handy. Naturally, you can put them on the tab.'

He was wearing boxers and nothing else. Brianna's brain registered that as a belated postscript. Most of her brain was wrapped up with stunned, shocked appreciation of his body. Broad shoulders and powerful arms tapered down to a flat stomach and lean hips. He had had a quick shower, evidently, and one of the cheap, white hand towels was slung around his neck and hung over his shoulders. She felt faint.

'I thought I'd get rid of the shirt as well,' he said. 'If you wouldn't mind laundering the lot, I would be extremely grateful. I failed to make provisions for clearing snow.'

Brianna blinked, as gauche and confused as a teenager. She saw that he was dangling the laundry bag on one finger while looking at her with amusement.

Well of course he would be, she thought, bristling. Writer or not, he came from a big city and, yes, was ever so patronising about the *smallness* of their town. And here she was, playing into his hands, gaping as though she had never seen a naked man in her life before, as though he was the most interesting thing to have landed on her doorstep in a hundred years.

'Well, perhaps you should have,' she said tartly. 'Only a fool would travel to this part of the world in the depths of winter and *not* come prepared for heavy snow.' She snatched the laundry bag from him and thrust the armful of clothes at his chest in return.

'Come again?' *Had she just called him a fool?*

'I haven't got the time or the energy to launder your clothes every two seconds because you didn't anticipate bad weather. In February. Here.' Her eyes skirted nervously away from the aggressive width of his chest. 'And I suggest,' she continued tightly, 'That you cover up. If I don't have the time to launder your clothes, then I most certainly do not have the time to play nursemaid when you go down with flu!'

Leo was trying to think of the last time a woman had raised her voice in his presence. Or, come to think of it, said anything that was in any way inflammatory. It just didn't happen. He didn't know whether to be irritated, enraged or entertained.

'Message understood loud and clear.' He grinned and leaned against the doorframe. However serious the implications of this visit to the land that time forgot, he realised that he was enjoying himself. Right now, at this very moment, with this beautiful Irish girl standing in front of him, glaring and uncomfortable. 'Fortunately, I'm as healthy as a horse. Can't remember the last time I succumbed to flu. So you won't have to pull out your nurse's uniform and tend to me.' Interesting notion, though... His dark eyes drifted over her lazily. 'I'll be down shortly. And my thanks once again for the clothes.'

Brianna was still hot and flustered when, half an hour later, he sauntered down to the kitchen. One of the tables in the bar area had been neatly set for one. 'I hope you're not expecting me to have lunch on my own,' were his opening words, and she spun around from where she had been frowning into the pot of homemade soup.

Without giving her a chance to answer, he began searching for the crockery, giving a little grunt of satisfaction when he hit upon the right cupboard. 'Remember we were going to...talk? You were going to tell me all about the people who live here so that I can get some useful fodder for my book.' It seemed inconceivable that a budding author would simply up sticks and go on a rambling tour of Ireland in the hope of inspiration but, as excuses went, it had served its purpose, which was all that mattered. 'And then, I'll do whatever you want me to do. I'm a man of my word.'

'There won't be much to do,' Brianna admitted. 'The snow's not letting up. I've phoned Aidan and told him that the place will be closed until the weather improves.'

'Aidan?'

'One of my friends. He can be relied on to spread the word. Only my absolute regulars would even contemplate trudging out here in this weather.'

'So…is Aidan the old would-be opera singer?'

'Aidan is my age. We used to go to school together.' She dished him out some soup, added some bread and offered him a glass of wine, which he rejected in favour of water.

'And he's the guy who broke your heart? No. He wouldn't be. The guy who broke your heart has long since disappeared, hasn't he?'

Brianna stiffened. She reminded herself that she was not having a cosy chat with a friend over lunch. This was a guest in her pub, a stranger who was passing through, no more. Confiding details of her private life was beyond the pale, quite different from chatting about all the amusing things that happened in a village where nearly everyone knew everyone else. Her personal life was not going to be fodder for a short story on life in a quaint Irish village.

'I don't recall telling you anything about my heart being broken, and I don't think my private life is any of your business. I hope the soup is satisfactory.'

So that was a sore topic; there was no point in a follow-up. It was irrelevant to his business here. If he happened to be curious, then it was simply because he was in the unique situation of being pub-bound and snowed in with just her for company. In the absence of anyone else, it was only natural that she would spark an interest.

'Why don't you serve food? It would add a lot to the profits of a place like this. You'd be surprised how remote places can become packed if the food is good enough...' He doubted the place had seen any changes in a very long time. Again, not his concern, he thought. 'So, if you don't want to talk about yourself, then that's fair enough.'

'Why don't *you* talk about yourself? Are you married? Do you have children?'

'If I were married and had children, I wouldn't be doing what I'm doing.' Marriage? Children? He had never contemplated either. He pushed the empty soup bowl aside and sprawled on the chair, angling it so that he could stretch his legs out to one side. 'Tell me about the old guy who likes to sing.'

'What made you suddenly decide to pack in your job and write? It must have been a big deal, giving up steady work in favour of a gamble that might or might not pay off.'

Leo shrugged and told himself that, certainly in this instance, the ends would more than justify the means—and at any rate, there was no chance that she would discover his little lie. He would forever remain the enigmatic stranger who had passed through and collected a few amusing anecdotes on the way. She would be regaling her friends with this in a week's time.

'Sometimes life is all about taking chances,' he murmured softly.

Brianna hadn't taken a chance in such a long time that she had forgotten what it felt like. The last chance she had taken had been with Danny, and hadn't *that* backfired spectacularly in her face? She had settled into a groove and had firmly convinced herself that it suited her. 'Some people are braver than others when it comes to that sort of thing,' she found herself muttering under her breath.

Leading remark, Leo thought. He had vast experience of women dangling titbits of information about themselves, offering them to him in the hope of securing his interest, an attempt to reel him in through his curiosity. However, for once his cynicism was absent. This woman knew nothing about him. He did not represent a rich, eligible bachelor. He was a struggling writer with no job. He had a glimpse of what it must feel like to communicate with a woman without undercurrents of suspicion that, whatever they wanted, at least part of it had to do with his limitless bank balance. He might have been adopted into a life of extreme privilege, and that privilege might have been his spring board to the dizzying heights of his success, but with that privilege and with that success had come drawbacks—one of which was an inborn mistrust of women and their motivations.

Right now, he was just communicating with a very beautiful and undeniably sexy woman and, hell, she was clueless about him. He smiled, enjoying the rare sense of freedom.

'And you're not one of the brave ones?'

Brianna stood up to clear the table. She had no idea where this sudden urge to confide was coming from. Was she bonding with him because, underneath those disconcerting good looks, he was a fellow artist? Because, on some weird level, he *understood* her? Or was she just one of those sad women, too young to be living a life of relative solitude, willing to confide in anyone who showed an interest?

Her head was buzzing. She felt hot and bothered and, when he reached out and circled her wrist with his hand, she froze in shock. The feel of his warm fingers on her skin was electrifying. She hadn't had a response like this to a man in a very long time. It was a feeling of coming alive. She wanted to snatch her hand away from his and rub away where he had touched her… Yet she also wanted him to keep his fingers on her wrist; she wanted to prolong the warm, physical connection between them. She abruptly sat back down, because her legs felt like jelly, and he released her.

'It's hard to take chances when you have commitments,' she muttered unsteadily. She couldn't tear her eyes away from his face. She literally felt as though he held her spellbound. 'You're on your own. You probably had sufficient money saved to just take off and do your own thing. I'm only now beginning to see the light financially and, even so, I still couldn't just up and leave.' She was leaning forward in the chair, leaning towards him as though he was the source of her energy. 'I should get this place tidied up,' she said agitatedly.

'Why? I thought you said that the pub would be closed until further notice.'

'Yes, but…'

'You must get lonely here on your own.'

'Of course I'm not lonely! I have too many friends to count!'

'But I don't suppose you have a lot of time to actually go out with them…'

Hot colour invaded her cheeks. No time to go out with them; no time even to pursue her art as a hobby. She hated the picture he was painting of her life. She was being made to feel as though she had sleepwalked into an existence of living from one day to the next, with each day being exactly the same. She dragged herself back to reality, back to the fact that he was just a budding writer on the hunt for some interesting material for his book. He wasn't interested in *her*.

'Will I be the sad spinster in your book?' She laughed shakily and gathered herself together. 'I think you're better off with some of the more colourful characters who live here.' She managed to get to her feet, driven by a need to put some distance between them. How could she let this one passing stranger get to her with such breath-taking speed? Lots of guys had come on to her over the years. Some of them she had known for ever, others had been friends of friends of friends. She had laughed and joked with all of them but she had never, not once, felt like *this*. Felt as though the air was being sucked out of her lungs every time she took a peek...as though she was being injected with adrenaline every time she came too close.

She busied herself tidying, urging him to sit rather than help. Her flustered brain screeched to a halt when she imagined them standing side by side at the kitchen sink.

She launched into nervous conversation, chattering mindlessly about the last time a snow storm had hit the village, forcing herself to relax as she recounted stories of all the things that could happen to people who were snow bound for days on end, occasionally as long as a fortnight: the baby delivered by one panicked father; the rowdy rugby group who had been forced to spend two nights in the pub; the community spirit when they had all had to help each other out; the food that Seamus Riley had had to lift by rope into his bedroom because he hadn't been able to get past his front door.

Leo listened politely. He really ought to be paying a bit more attention, but he was captivated by the graceful movement of her tall, slender body as she moved from counter to counter, picking things up, putting things away, making sure not to look at him.

'In fact, we all do our bit when the weather turns really bad,' she was saying now as she turned briefly in his direction. 'I don't suppose you have much of that in London.'

'None,' Leo murmured absently. Her little breasts pointed against the jumper and he wondered whether she was wearing a bra; a sensible, white cotton bra. He never imagined the thought of a sensible, white cotton bra could be such an illicit turn-on.

He was so absorbed in the surprising disobedience of his imagination that he almost missed the name that briefly passed her lips and, when it registered, he stiffened and felt his pulses quicken.

'Sorry,' he grated, straightening. 'I missed that…particular anecdote.' He kept his voice as casual as possible but he was tense and vigilant as he waited for her to repeat what she had been saying, what he had stupidly missed because he had been too busy getting distracted, too busy missing the point of why he was stuck here in the first place.

'I was just telling you about what it's like here—we help each other out. I was telling you about my friend who lives in the village. Bridget McGuire…'

CHAPTER THREE

So HIS MOTHER wasn't the drunk or the junkie that he had anticipated, if his landlady was to be believed...

Leo flexed his muscles and wandered restlessly through the lounge where he had been sitting in front of his computer working for the past hour and a half.

Circumstance had forced him into a routine of sorts, as his optimistic plan of clearing off within a few days had faded into impossibility.

After three days, the snow was still falling steadily. It fluctuated between virtual white-out and gentle flakes that could lull you into thinking that it was all picture-postcard perfect. Until you opened the front door and clocked that the snow you'd cleared moments previously had already been replaced by a fresh fall.

He strolled towards the window and stared out at a pitch-black vista, illuminated only by the outside lights which Brianna kept on overnight.

It was not yet seven in the morning. He had never needed much sleep and here, more than ever, he couldn't afford to lie in. Not when he had to keep communicating with his office, sending emails, reviewing reports, without her knowing exactly what was going on. At precisely seven-thirty, he would shut his computer and head outside to see what he could do about beating back some of the snow so that it didn't completely bank up against the door.

It was, he had to admit to himself, a fairly unique take on winter sport. When he had mentioned that to Brianna the day before, she had burst out laughing and told him that he could try building himself a sledge and having fun outside, getting in touch with his inner child.

He made himself a cup of coffee and reined in the temptation to let his mind meander, which was what it seemed to want to do whenever he thought of her.

His mother was in hospital recovering from a mild heart attack.

'She should have been out last week,' Brianna had confided, 'But they've decided to keep her in because the weather's so horrendous and she has no one to take care of her.'

Where was the down-and-out junkie he had been anticipating? Of course, there was every chance that she *had* been a deadbeat, a down and out. It would be a past she would have wanted to keep to herself, especially with Brianna who, from the sounds of it, saw her as something of a surrogate mother. The woman hadn't lived her whole life in the village. Who knew what sort of person she had been once upon a time?

But certainly, the stories he had heard did not tally with his expectations.

And the bottom line was that his hands were tied at the moment. He had come to see for himself what his past held. He wasn't about to abandon that quest on the say-so of a girl he'd known for five minutes. On the other hand, he was now on indefinite leave. One week, he had told his secretary, but who was to say that this enforced stay would not last longer?

The snow showed no sign of abating. When it *did* abate,

there was still the question of engineering a meeting with his mother. She was in hospital and when she came out she would presumably be fairly weak. However, without anyone to act as full-time carer, at least for a while, what was the likelihood of her being released from hospital? He was now playing a waiting game.

And throughout all this, there was still the matter of his fictitious occupation. Surely Brianna would start asking him questions about this so-called book he was busily writing? Would he have to fabricate a plot?

In retrospect, out of all the occupations he could have picked, he concluded that he had managed to hit on the single worst one of them all. God knew, he hadn't read a book in years. His reading was strictly of the utilitarian variety: legal tomes, books on the movements of financial markets, detailed backgrounds to companies he was planning to take over.

The fairly straightforward agenda he had set out for himself was turning into something far more complex.

He turned round at the sound of her footsteps on the wooden floor.

And that, he thought, frowning, was an added complication. She was beginning to occupy far too much space in his head. Familiarity was not breeding contempt. He caught himself watching her, thinking about her, fantasising about her. His appreciation of her natural beauty was growing like an unrestrained weed, stifling the disciplined part of his brain that told him that he should not go there.

Not only was she ignorant of his real identity but whatever the hell had happened to her—whoever had broken her heart, the mystery guy she could not be persuaded to discuss—had left her vulnerable. On the surface, she was capable, feisty, strong-willed and stubbornly proud. But he sensed her vulnerability underneath and the rational part of him acknowledged that a vulnerable woman was a woman best left well alone.

But his libido was refusing to listen to reason and seemed to have developed a will of its own.

'You're working too hard.' She greeted him cheerfully. Having told him that she would not be doing his laundry, she had been doing his laundry. Today he was wearing the jeans she had washed the day before and one of her father's checked flannel shirts, the sleeves of which he had rolled to the elbows. In a few seconds, she took in the dark hair just visible where the top couple of buttons of the shirt were undone; the low-slung jeans that emphasised the leanness of his hips; the strong, muscular forearms.

Leo knew what he had been working on and it hadn't been the novel she imagined: legal technicalities that had to be sorted out with one small IT company he was in the process of buying; emails to the human resources department so that they reached a mutually agreeable deal with employees of yet another company he was acquiring. He had the grace to flush.

'Believe me, I've worked harder,' he said with utmost truth. She was in some baggy grey jogging bottoms, which made her look even slimmer than she was, and a baggy grey sweatshirt. For the first time, her hair wasn't tied back, but instead fell over her shoulders and down her back in a cascade of rich auburn.

'I guess maybe in that company of yours—'

'Company of mine?' Leo asked sharply and then realised that guilt had laced the question with unnecessary asperity when she smiled and explained that she was talking about whatever big firm he had worked for before quitting.

She had noticed that he never talked about the job he had done, and Brianna had made sure to steer clear of the subject. It was a big enough deal getting away from the rat race without being reminded of what you'd left behind, because the rat race from which he had escaped was the very same rat race that was now funding his exploits into the world of writing.

'You still haven't told me much about your book,' she said tentatively. 'I know I'm being horribly nosy, and I know how hard it is to let someone have a whiff of what you're working on before it's finished, but you must be very far in. You start work so early and I know you keep it up, off and on during the day. You never seem to lack inspiration.'

Leo considered what level of inspiration was needed to review due diligence on a company: none. 'You know how it goes,' he said vaguely. 'You can write two...er... chapters and then immediately delete them, although...' He considered the massive deal he had just signed off on. 'I must admit I've been reasonably productive. To change the subject, have you any books I could borrow? I had no idea I would be in one place for so long...'

When had his life become so blinkered? he wondered. Sure, he played; he enjoyed the company of beautiful women, but they were a secondary consideration to his work. The notion of any of them becoming a permanent fixture in his life had never crossed his mind. And, yes, he relaxed at the gym but, hell, he hadn't picked up a novel in years; hadn't been to a movie in years; rarely watched television for pleasure, aside from the occasional football match; went to the theatre occasionally, usually when it was an arranged company event, but even then he was always restless, always thinking of what needed to be done with his companies or clients or mergers or buyouts.

He impatiently swept aside the downward spiral of introspection and surfaced to find her telling him that there were books in her study.

'And there's something I want to show you,' she said hesitantly. She disappeared for a few minutes and in that time he strolled around the lounge, distractedly looking at the fire and wondering whether the log basket would have to be topped up. He wondered how much money she was losing with this enforced closure of the pub and then debated the pros and cons of asking her if he could have a look at her books.

'Okay...'

Leo turned around and walked slowly towards her. 'What do you have behind your back?'

Brianna took a deep breath and revealed one of the small paintings she had done a few months back, when she had managed to squeeze in some down-time during the summer. It was a painting of the lake and in the foreground an angler sat, back to the spectator, his head bent, his body leaning forward, as if listening for the sound of fish.

'I don't like showing my work to anyone either,' she confided as he took the picture from her and held it at a distance in his hands. 'So I fully understand why you don't want to talk about your book.'

'*You* painted this?'

'What do you think?'

'I think you're wasted running a pub here.' Leo was temporarily lost for words. Of course he had masterpieces in his house, as well as some very expensive investment art, but this was charming and unique enough to find a lucrative market of its own. 'Why don't you try selling them?'

'Oh, I could never produce enough.' She sighed regretfully. She moved to stand next to him so that they were both looking at the painting. When he rested it on the table, she didn't move, and suddenly her throat constricted as their eyes tangled and, for a few seconds, she found that she was holding her breath.

Leo sifted his fingers through her hair and the door slammed shut on all his good intentions not to let his wayward libido do the thinking for him. He just knew that he wanted this woman, more than he had ever wanted any woman in his life before, and for the hell of him he had no idea why. He had stopped trying to work that one out. He was not a man who was accustomed to holding out. Desire was always accompanied by possession. In fact, as he looked down at her flushed, upturned face, he marvelled that he had managed to restrain himself for so long because hadn't he known, almost from the very start, that she was attracted to him? Hadn't he seen it there in those hot, stolen looks and her nervous, jumpy reactions when he got fractionally too close to her?

He perched on the edge of the table and drew her closer to him.

Brianna released her breath in a long shudder. She was burning up where he touched her. Never in a million years would she have imagined that she could do this, that she could *feel* this way, feel so connected to a guy that she wanted him to touch her after only a few days. Showing him that painting, had he only known it, had been a measure of how much she trusted him. She felt *easy* in his company. Gone were the feelings of suspicion which had been there when she had first laid eyes on him, when she had wondered what such a dramatic looking stranger was doing in their midst, standing there at the door of the pub and looking around him with guarded coolness.

She had let down her defences, had thawed. Being cooped up had blurred the lines between paying guest and a guy who was as amusing as he was intelligent; as witty and dry as he was focused and disciplined. He might have worked in a company and done boring stuff but you would never guess that by the breadth of his conversation. He knew a great deal about art, about world affairs, and he had travelled extensively. He had vaguely told her that it was all in connection with his job, and really not very exciting at all because he did nothing but work when he got to his destination, but he could still captivate her with descriptions of the places he had been and the things he had seen there.

In short, he was nothing at all like any of the men she had ever met in her entire life, and that included Danny Fluke.

'What are you doing?' she asked weakly.

'I'm touching you. Do you want me to stop?'

'This is crazy.'

'This is taking a chance.'

'I don't even…know you.'

No, she certainly didn't. And yet, strangely, she knew more about him than any other woman did. Not that there was any point in getting tied down with semantics. 'What does that have to do with wanting someone?' His voice was a low murmur in her ear and, as he slid his hand underneath the jumper to caress her waist, she could feel all rational thought disappearing like dew in the summer sun.

So, she thought, fighting down the temptation to moan as his fingers continued to stroke her bare skin, he wasn't going to be sticking around. He was as nomadic as she was rooted to this place. But wasn't that what taking chances was all about?

She reached up and trembled as she linked her fingers behind his neck and pulled him down towards her.

His kiss was soft, exploratory. His tongue mingled against hers and was mind-blowingly erotic. He angled his long legs open and she edged her body between them so that now she was pushed up against him and could feel the hardness of his erection against her.

'You can still tell me to stop...' And, if she did, he didn't know what he would do. Have a sub-zero shower? Even then, he wasn't sure that it would be enough to cool him down. 'Taking a chance can sometimes be a dangerous indulgence...'

And yet there was a part of her that knew that *not* taking this chance would be a source of eternal regret. Besides, why on earth should she let one miserable experience that was now in the past determine her present?

'Maybe I want to live dangerously for once...'

His hand had crept further up her jumper and he unhooked her bra strap with practised ease.

Brianna's breath caught in her throat and she stilled as he inched his way towards one small breast. She quivered at the feel of his thumb rubbing over it. She wanted him so badly that she was shaking with desire.

Leo marvelled that something he knew they just shouldn't be doing could feel so damned *right*. Had he been going stir crazy here without even realising it? Was that why he had been so useless at disciplining his libido? The lie that had taken him so far, that had started life as just something he had been inspired to do because he had needed an excuse for being there in the first place, hung around his neck with the deadly weight of an albatross.

He shied away from the thought that she might find out, and then laughed at the possibility of that happening.

'I won't be around for much longer.' He felt compelled to warn her off involvement even though he knew that the safest route he could take if he really didn't want to court unwanted involvement would be to walk away. 'Sure you want to take a chance with someone who's just passing through?' He spoke against her mouth and he could feel her warm breath mingling with his.

Brianna feverishly thought of the last guy she had become involved with—the guy she had thought wasn't passing through, the guy she had thought she might end up spending the rest of her life with but who, in fact, had always known that he would be moving on. This time, there would be no illusions. A fling: it was something she had never done in her life before. Danny had been her first and only relationship.

'I'm not looking for permanence,' she whispered. 'I thought I had that once and it turned out to be the biggest mistake I ever made. Stop talking.'

'Happy to oblige,' Leo growled, his conscience relieved. 'I think I wanted this within hours of meeting you.' He circled her waist with his hands and then pushed the jumper up, taking the bra with it as well.

For a split second, Brianna was overwhelmed by shyness. She closed her eyes and arched back, every nerve and pore straining towards a closeness she hadn't felt in such a long time. When she felt the wetness of his mouth surround her nipple, she groaned and half-collapsed. Her hands coiled into his thick, dark hair as he continued sucking and teasing the stiffened peaks until she wanted to faint from the pleasure of it. When he drew back, she groaned in frustration and looked at him drowsily from under her lashes, her heartbeat quickening to a frantic beat as she watched him inspecting her breasts with the same considered thoroughness with which he had earlier inspected her painting.

'I want to see you,' Leo said roughly. He was surprised at the speed with which his body was reacting, racing towards release. His erection was uncomfortable against his jeans, bulging painfully. Yet he didn't want to rush this. He had to close his eyes briefly and breathe deeply so that he wouldn't be thrown off-balance by the sight of her bare breasts, small and crested with large, pink nipples that were still glistening from where he had sucked them.

In response, Brianna traced the contours of his shoulders, broad and powerful. It was driving her crazy just thinking about touching his chest, the bronzed, muscled chest that had sent her imagination into overdrive on that first day when he had stood half-naked in front of her, waiting for the shirts she had brought for him.

'I don't want to make love to you here...' He swung her off her feet as though she weighed nothing and carried her up the stairs towards his bedroom, and then, pausing briefly, up the further flight of stairs that led to her bedroom. He didn't dare look down at her soft, small breasts or he would deposit her on the stairs and take her right there. His urgency to have her lying underneath him was shocking. Not cool; definitely not his style.

He found her bedroom, barely taking time to look around him as he placed her on the bed and ordered her to stay put.

'Where do you think I'm going to go?' She laughed with nervous excitement and levered herself onto one elbow, watching with unconcealed fascination as he began to strip off. With each discarded item of clothing, her heart rate picked up speed until she had to close her eyes and take deep breaths.

Her response was so wonderfully, naturally open and unconcealed that Leo experienced a raw, primitive thrill that magnified his burning lust a thousand-fold.

He took his time removing the jeans because he was enjoying watching her watching him. Most of all he enjoyed her gasp as he stepped out of his boxers and moved towards her, his erection thick, heavy and impressively telling of just how aroused he was.

Brianna scrabbled to sit up, pulses racing, the blood pumping in her veins hot with desire.

She couldn't believe she was doing this, behaving in a way that was so out of character. She sighed and moaned as the mattress depressed under his weight; the feel of his hands tucking into the waistband of the jogging bottoms, sliding them down, signalled the final nail in her crumbling defences

'You're beautiful.' He straddled her and kissed her with intimate, exquisite thoroughness, tracing her mouth with his tongue, then trailing his lips against her neck so that she whimpered and tilted her head to prolong the kiss.

Every small noise she made, every tiny movement, bore witness to how much she was turned on and it gave him an unbelievable kick to know that she had allowed herself to be pulled along by an irresistible force even though it went against the grain.

Her skin was supple and smooth, her breasts perfect, dainty orbs that barely fitted his large hand.

He teased the tip of her nipple with his tongue and then submerged himself in the pleasure of suckling on it, loving the way she writhed under him; the way her fingers bit into his shoulder blades; the way she arched back, eyes closed, mouth parted, her whole body trembling.

He let his hand drift over her flat stomach to circle the indentation of her belly button with one finger while he continued to plunder her breasts, moving between them, sucking, liking the way he could draw them into his mouth. He was hungry for more but determined not to take things fast. He wanted to savour every second of tasting her body.

He parted her legs gently with his hand and eased the momentary tension he could feel as she stilled against him.

'Shh,' he whispered huskily, as though she had spoken. 'Relax.'

'It's...been a long time.' Brianna gave a half- stifled, nervous laugh. He raised his head and their eyes tangled, black clashing with apple-green.

'When you say *long*...'

'I haven't slept with anyone since... Well, it's been years...' She twisted away, embarrassed by the admission. Where had the time gone? It seemed as though one minute she had been nursing heartbreak, dealing with her father's death, caught up in a jumble of financial worries, her life thrown utterly off course, and the next minute she was here, still running the pub, though with the financial worries more or less behind her. She was hardly sinking but definitely not swimming and living a life that seemed far too responsible for someone her age.

Leo tilted her face to his, kissed her on the side of her mouth and banked down his momentary discomfort at thinking that he might be taking advantage of her.

Yet she was perfectly aware of the situation, perfectly aware that he wasn't going to be hanging around. Naturally, she was not in possession of the true facts regulating his departure, but weren't those just details? Looking at the bigger picture, she knew where she stood, that this was just a fling—not even that.

'I'll be gentle.'

'I guess you...you've had a lot of girlfriends?'

'I haven't espoused a life of celibacy.' He slipped his finger into the wet groove of her femininity and felt whatever further questions she wanted to ask become stifled under her heated response. She moved against his finger and groaned.

He could have played with her body all day, all night. Right now, he couldn't get enough of her and he moved downwards. She sucked in her breath sharply and he rested the palm of his hand flat on her stomach, then he nuzzled the soft hair covering the apex between her thighs. He breathed in the musky, honeyed scent of her and dipped his tongue to taste her. How did he know that this was something she was experiencing for the first time? And why was that such a turn on?

He teased the throbbing bud of her clitoris and, when she moaned and squirmed, he flattened his hands on her thighs so that her legs were spread wide open for his delectation.

Brianna had never known anything like this before. There wasn't a single part of her body that wasn't consumed with an overpowering craving. She wanted him to continue doing what he was doing, yet she wanted him in her, deep inside. She weakly tugged at his hair but was powerless to pull him up. When she looked down and saw his dark head between her legs, and his strong, bronzed hands against the paleness of her thighs, she almost passed out.

Could years of living in icy isolation have made her so vulnerable to his touch? Had her body been so deprived of human contact that it was now overwhelmed? It felt like it.

When he rose, she was so close to tipping over the edge that she had to squeeze her eyes shut and grit her teeth together to maintain self-control.

'Enjoying yourself?' Leo raised some hair from her flushed face to whisper in her ear. He rubbed his stiff erection against her belly and felt sensation lick through his body at frightening speed.

Brianna blushed and nodded, then raised herself up so that she could kiss him on the mouth, draw him down over her so that their bodies were pressed together, fused with slick perspiration. She reached down and took him in her hand and he angled himself slightly away to accommodate her. His breathing thickened as she continued to work her movements into a deep rhythm.

He was impressively big and she shivered with heady anticipation.

'A condom... Wait; in my wallet...'

Already he was groping in the pocket of his jeans for his wallet and fumbling to fetch a condom, his eyes still pinned to her flushed, reclining body. How on earth could he be thinking of *anything* at a time like this? She just couldn't wait for him to be inside her, filling her with his bigness.

'You're well prepared.' She sighed and thought that of course he would be; he was a man of the world after all.

She groaned and felt the slippery, cool sheath guarding his arousal; her hands impatiently guided him to her, longing for the moment when he would fill her completely. She flipped onto him and arched up, her hands on his broad chest, her small breasts tipping teasingly towards him. 'I know you're moving on and I like it that way.' Did she? Yes, she did! 'I *need* this.' She leaned forward, bottom sticking up provocatively, and covered her mouth with his. 'The last thing I would take a gamble on is with a pregnancy.'

'You wouldn't want to be stuck with a loser like me?' Leo grinned, because those words had never passed his lips before. 'A travelling writer hoping to make his fortune?' He curved his hands on her rear and inserted himself into her. He drove into her and Brianna felt a surge of splintering pleasure as he moved deep inside her. Her head was flung back and he could feel the ends of her long hair on his thighs, brushing against them.

'A guy could feel insulted.'

She was on her back before she knew it and he was rear-ing up over her, big, powerful and oh, so breathtakingly beautiful, one-hundred per cent alpha male.

She came with such intensity that she had to squeeze her eyes shut on the gathering tears. She knew her fingers were digging in to the small of his back and they dug harder as she felt him swell and reach his orgasm inside her.

God, nothing had ever felt *that* good. Years of celibacy, running the pub and coping with all the day-to-day worries had obviously had the effect of making her respond like a wanton to being touched. She had never been like that before. But then, she had been so much younger when she had met Danny. Had the years and the tough times released some sort of pent-up capacity for passion that she had never known about?

'So...' Leo drawled, rolling onto his side then pulling her to face him so that their naked bodies were front to front and still touching, almost as though neither of them wanted to break the physical contact. 'You were telling me all about how you were using me to get you out of a dry patch.' He inserted his thigh between her legs and felt her wetness slippery against his skin.

'I never said that,' Brianna murmured.

'You didn't have to. The word "need" gave it away.'

'Maybe you're right. It's been a slog for the past few years. Don't get me wrong, there have been times when I've enjoyed running this place. It's just not how I expected my life to turn out.'

'What had you expected?'

'I expected to be married with a couple of kids, pursuing the art career that never took off, as it happens.'

'Ah. And the couple of kids and the wedding ring would have been courtesy of the heartbreaker?'

'He dumped me.' It had haunted her, had been responsible for all the precautions she had taken to protect herself. Yet lying here, with his thigh doing wonderful things between her legs, stirring up all the excitement that had only just faded, she could barely remember Danny's face. He had stopped being a human being and had become just a vague, disturbing recollection of a past mistake. She couldn't care less what had become of him, so how on earth had he carried on having such an influence on her behaviour?

'I wasn't good enough,' she said, anger replacing the humiliation that usually accompanied this thought. 'We went out for ages; when I thought that we really were destined to be together, he broke it to me that I had just been a good time at university. Dad was ill and I had discovered that the guy I thought I was in love with had been using me all along for a bit of fun. At least *you've* been honest and up-front.'

'Honest and up-front?'

'You're moving on. You're not here to stay. No illusions. I like that.'

'Before you start putting me on a pedestal and getting out the feather brush to dust my halo, I should tell you that you know very little about me.'

'I know enough.'

'You have little to compare me with. I'm a pretty ruthless bastard, if you want the truth.'

Brianna laughed, a clear, tinkling sound of pure amusement. She sifted her fingers through his dark hair and curled up closer to him which kick-started a whole lot of very pleasurable sensations that had him hardening in record time.

He edged her back from him and looked at her, unsmiling. 'You've been hurt once. You've spent years buried here, working beyond the call of duty to keep the wolves from the door. You've had no boyfriends, no distractions to occupy your time. Hell, you haven't even been able to wring out an hour or two to do your painting. And then along I come. I'm not your knight in shining armour.'

'I never said that you were!' Brianna pulled back, hurt and confused at a sudden glimpse of ruthlessness she wouldn't have imagined possible.

'It's been my experience that what women say is often at variance to what they think. I won't be hanging around—and even if I lived next door to you, Brianna, I don't do long-term relationships.'

'What do you mean, you *don't do long-term relationships*?'

'Just what I say, so be warned. Don't make the mistake of investing anything in me. What we have is sexual attraction, pure and simple.' He softened and gentled his voice. 'We have something that works at this precise moment in time.'

But it was more than that. What about the conversations they had had; the moments of sharing generated by close proximity? Some sixth sense stopped her from pointing that out. She was finding it difficult to recognise the cool, dark eyes of this stranger looking at her.

'And stop treating me as though I'm a stupid kid,' she bit out tightly, disentangling herself from him. 'I was one of those once.' Her voice was equally cool. 'I don't intend to repeat the same mistake twice. And, if you think that I would ever let myself get emotionally wrapped up with someone who doesn't want to spend his life in one place, then you're crazy. I value security. When I fall for someone, it will be someone who wants to settle down and isn't scared of commitment. I'm thankful that you've been honest enough to tell me as it is, but you have nothing to fear. Your precious independence isn't at risk.'

'If that's the case, why are you pulling away from me?'

'I don't like your tone of voice.'

'Just so long as it's not what I say but how I'm saying it,' he murmured softly. He tugged her back towards him and Brianna placed her hand on his shoulder but it was a pathetically weak attempt to stave off the fierce urgings of her body.

As his hand swept erotically along her thigh, she shimmied back towards him, the coolness in his eyes forgotten, the jarring hardness of his voice consigned to oblivion.

They made love slowly, touching each other everywhere, absorbing each other's pleasurable groans. She tasted him with as much hunger as he tasted her. She just couldn't get enough of him—at her breasts, between her thighs, urging her to tell him what she wanted him to do and telling her in explicit detail what he wanted her to do to him.

Eventually, just as she was falling into a light, utterly contented doze, she heard the insistent buzz of her mobile phone next to the bed where she had left it charging. She was almost too sleepy to pick up but, when she did, she instantly sat up, drawing the covers around her.

Leo watched her, his keen antennae picking up her sudden tension, although from this end of the phone he could only hear monosyllabic replies to whatever was being said.

'Remember I told you about my friend? Bridget McGuire?' Brianna ended the call thoughtfully but remained holding the mobile, caressing it absently.

Leo was immediately on red-hot alert, although he kept his expression mildly interested and utterly expressionless. 'The name rings a bell...'

'They need to release her from hospital. There's been an accident on the motorway and they need all the beds they can get. So she's leaving tomorrow. The snow is predicted to stop. She's coming here...'

CHAPTER FOUR

'WHEN?' HE SLID out of the bed, strolled towards the window and stared down to a snowy, grey landscape. The sun had barely risen but, yes, the snow appeared to be lessening.

This was the reason he was here, pretending to be someone he wasn't. When he had first arrived, he had wondered how a meeting with his mother could possibly be engineered in a town where everyone seemed to know everyone else. Several lies down and his quarry would be delivered right to his doorstep. Didn't fate work in mysterious ways?

Brianna, sitting up, wondered what was going through his head.

'For the moment, they're going to transfer her to another ward and then, provided the snow doesn't get worse, they're going to bring her here tomorrow. You're making me nervous, standing by the window like that. What are you thinking? I have room here at the pub. It won't make any difference to you. You won't have to vacate your room—in fact, you probably won't even notice that she's here. I shall have her in the spare room next to my bedroom so that I can keep a constant eye on her, and of course I doubt she'll be able to climb up and down stairs.'

Leo smiled and pushed himself away from the window

ledge. When he tried to analyse what he felt about his birth mother, the most he could come up with was a scathing contempt which he realised he would have to attempt to conceal for what remained of his time here. Brianna might have painted a different picture, but years of preconceived notions were impossible to put to bed.

'So...' He slipped back under the covers and pulled her towards him. 'If we're going to have an unexpected visitor, then maybe you should start telling me the sort of person I can look forward to meeting and throw me a few more details...'

Brianna began plating their breakfast. Was it her imagination or was he abnormally interested in finding out about Bridget? He had returned to the bed earlier and she had thrown him a few sketchy details about her friend yet, off and on, he seemed to return to the subject. His questions were in no way pressing; in fact, he barely seemed to care about the answer.

A sudden thought occurred to her.

Was he really worried that their wonderful one-on-one time might be interrupted? He had made it perfectly clear that he was just passing through, and had given her a stern warning that she was not to make the mistake of investing in him, yet was he becoming possessive of her company without even realising it himself?

For reasons best known to himself, he was a commitment-phobe, but did he respond out of habit? Had he warned her off because distancing himself was an automatic response?

He might not want to admit it, but over the past few days they had got to know one another in a way she would never have thought possible. He worked while she busied herself with the accounts and the bookkeeping but, for a lot of the time, they had communicated. He had even looked at her ledgers, leading her to think that he might have been an accountant in a previous life. He had suggested ways to improve her finances. He had persuaded her to show him all the paintings she had ever done, which she kept in portfolios under the bed, and had urged her to design a website to showcase them. She had caught herself telling him so much more than she had ever told anyone in her life before, even her close friends. He made a very good listener.

His own life, he had confided, had been as uneventful as it came: middle class, middle of the road. Both of them were single children, both without parents. They laughed at the same things; they bickered over the remote control for the television in the little private lounge which was set aside for the guests, on those rare occasions she had some. With the pub closed, they had had lots of quality time during which to get to know one another.

So was he *scared* that the arrival of Bridget would signal the end of what they had?

With a sigh, she acknowledged that if the ambulance could make it up the lane to the pub to deliver their patient then her loyal customers could certainly make it as well. The pub would once again reopen and their time together would certainly be curtailed.

'I've been thinking,' she said slowly, handing him a plate of bacon, eggs and toast and sitting down. 'I might just keep the pub closed for a couple of weeks. Until the snow is well and truly over and the path outside the pub is completely safe.'

She told herself that this was something that made perfect sense. And why shouldn't she have a little break? The last break she had had was over summer when she had grabbed a long weekend to go to Dublin with her friends. At other times, while they'd been off having lovely warm holidays in sunny Spain or Portugal, she had always been holed up at the pub, unable to take the time off because she couldn't afford to lose the revenue.

So why shouldn't she have time off now? A couple of weeks wouldn't break the bank—at least, not completely. And she would make up for it later in the year. Leo had suggested a website to promote the pub and she would take him up on that. He had intimated that she could really take off with only minimal changes, a few things to bring the place up to date.

And, if she closed the pub for a couple of weeks, they would continue to have their quality time until he disappeared.

'It would be better for Bridget as well,' she hurried on, not wanting to analyse how much of this idea was down to her desire to keep him to herself for a little longer. 'She's going to need looking after, at least in the beginning, and it would give me the opportunity to really take care of her without having to worry about running the pub as well.'

'Makes sense, I suppose...'

'You won't be affected at all.'

'I know. You've already told me.'

'And I don't want you to think that your needs are going to be overlooked. I mean, what I'm trying to say is...'

Leo tilted his head to one side. She blushed very easily. Especially when you considered the hard life she had had and the financial worries she had faced. No one would ever be able to accuse her of not being a fighter.

'Is that you'll carry on making my breakfast for me? Fixing me sandwiches for lunch? Slaving over a recipe book for something to cook for dinner? Making sure my bed is...warm and that you're in it?'

'I'm not part of a package deal.' Brianna bristled, suddenly offended at the picture he painted of her. 'You haven't paid for me along with the breakfast, lunch and dinner.' She stood up and began clearing the dishes, only pausing when she felt his arms around her at the sink. When she looked straight ahead, she could see their dim reflection in the window pane, his head downbent, buried in her hair. He didn't like it when she tied it back so she had left it loose the past couple of days and now he wound one of the long, auburn strands around his finger.

His other hand reached underneath the sweater and she watched their hazy reflection, the movement of his hand caressing her breast, playing with her nipple, rubbing the pad of his thumb over it. Liquid pooled between her legs, dampening her underwear and making her squirm and shift in his embrace.

She could feel his hard arousal nudging her from behind and, when she half-closed her eyes, her imagination took flight, dwelling on the image of her touching him there, licking and sucking with his fingers tangled in her hair. She wanted to do the same now. She pictured him kneeling like a penitent at her feet, her body pressing against the wall in her bedroom, her legs parted as he tasted her.

He seemed to have the ability to make her stop thinking the second he laid a finger on her and he did it as easily as someone switching a tap off.

She watched, eyes smoky with desire, as he pushed the jumper up; now she could see the pale skin of her stomach and his much darker hands on her breasts, massaging them, teasing them, playing with her swollen, sensitive nipples.

She shuddered and angled her neck so that he could kiss her.

'I know you're not part of the package,' he murmured. 'And, just to set the record straight, I enjoy you a hell of a lot more than I enjoy the meals you prepare.'

'Are you implying that I'm a bad cook?' He had undone

the top button of her jeans and she wriggled as he did the same with the zip, easing the jeans down over her slim hips, exposing her pale pink briefs.

'You're a fantastic cook. One of the best.' He stood back slightly so that she could swivel to face him.

'You're a terrible liar.'

Leo flushed guiltily at this unwittingly inaccurate swipe, said in jest.

'Don't bank on that,' he murmured into her ear. 'You forget that I've already warned you that I'm a ruthless bastard.'

'If you really *were* a ruthless bastard, then you wouldn't have to warn me. I'd see all the giveaway signs.' She tiptoed and drew his head down so that she could kiss him. Her body was heating up, impatiently anticipating the moment when it could unite with his.

In the heat of passion, it was always him who thought about protection. So he was scrupulous when it came to taking no chances—that didn't mean that he wasn't becoming more attached to her, did it? The fact he didn't want an unwanted pregnancy any more than she did, didn't indicate that his nomadic lifestyle wasn't undergoing a subtle ground-change…

'Touch me,' he commanded roughly and he rested his hands on her hips and half-closed his eyes as she burrowed underneath his jumper, her hands feathering across his chest, pausing to do wonderful things to his nipples. He was breathing quickly, every sinew and muscle stretched to a point of yearning that made a nonsense of his legendary self-control.

He yanked his jumper off and heard her sigh with pleasure, a little, soft sigh that was uniquely hers. His eyes were still half-closed and he inhaled slightly to accommodate her fumbling fingers as they travelled downwards to un-button and unzip his jeans.

Outside a watery sun was making itself known, pushing through the blanket of leaden grey of the past few days. Like an unfamiliar visitor, it threaded its way tentatively into the kitchen, picking up the rich hues of her hair and the smooth, creamy whiteness of her skin.

He stilled as she lowered herself to begin pulling down his jeans, taking his boxers with them until they were at his ankles and he stepped out of them and kicked them to one side.

He couldn't withhold his grunt of intense satisfaction as she began delicately to lick the tip of his erection. He was so aroused that it was painful and as he looked down at the crown of her head, and her pink, darting tongue as it continued to tease him, he became even more aroused.

'You're driving me crazy, woman…' His voice was un-steady, as were his hands as he coiled his fingers into her hair.

Brianna didn't say anything. His nakedness had her firing on all cylinders and his vulnerability, glimpses of which she only caught when they were making love, was the most powerful of aphrodisiacs. She took him in her mouth, loving the way every atom of pleasure seemed to be transmitted from him to her via invisible, powerful pathways. As she sucked and teased, her hands caressed, and she was aware of his big, strong body shaking ever so slightly. How could he make her feel so powerful and so helpless at the same time?

She was so damp, her body so urgent for his, that she itched to rip off her clothes. Her jumper was back in place and it felt heavy and uncomfortable against her sensitised skin. She gasped as he pulled her up, and she obediently lifted her arms so that he could remove the offending jumper. The cool air hit her heated breasts like a sooth-ing balm.

'I can't make it to the bedroom…' He breathed heav-ily as she wriggled out of the jeans and then he hoisted her onto the kitchen table, shoving aside the remnants of their breakfast—the jar of marmalade, the little ceramic butter dish, the striped jug with milk. Surprisingly, noth-ing crashed to the ground in the process.

When he stood back, he marvelled at the sight of her naked beauty: her arms outstretched, her eyes heavy with the same lust that was coursing through his bloodstream like an unstoppable virus.

Her vibrant hair streamed out around her, formed a tangle over one breast, and the glimpse of a pink nipple peeping out was like something from an erotic X-rated magazine. Her parted legs were an invitation he couldn't refuse, nor was his body allowing him the luxury of fore-play. As she raised her knees, he embedded himself into her in one hard, forceful thrust and then he lifted her up and drove again into her, building a furious rhythm and somehow ending up with her pressed against the kitchen wall, her legs wrapped around him.

Her hair trailed over her shoulder, down her back, a silky mass of rich auburn. He felt her in every part of him in a way that had never happened with any woman before. He didn't get it, but he liked it. He was holding her under-neath her sexy, rounded bottom and as he thrust long and deep into her he looked down at her little breasts bounc-ing in time to their bodies. The tips of her nipples were stiff and swollen, the big, flattened pink discs encircling them swollen and puffy. Every square inch of her body was an unbelievable turn-on and, even as he felt the satiny tightness of her sheath around him, he would have liked to close his mouth over one of those succulent nipples so that he could feast on its honeyed sweetness.

They came as one, their bodies fused, their breathing mirroring each other.

'That was…indescribable.' He eased her down and they stood facing one another, completely naked. Sanity began restoring itself, seeping through the haze of his hot, replete satisfaction. He swore under his breath and turned away. 'The condom…it seems to have split…'

Brianna's eyes widened with shock. She went over to her bundle of clothes and began getting dressed. He looked horrified. There was a heavy, laden silence as he likewise began getting dressed.

'It's okay. It takes more than one mistake for a person to get pregnant! If you read any magazine there are always stories of women trying for months, *years,* to conceive…' Her menstrual cycle had always been erratic so it was easy to believe that.

Leo shook his head and raked his fingers through his hair. 'This is a nightmare.'

'I won't get pregnant! I'm one-hundred per cent sure about that! I know my body. You don't have to look as though…as though the sky has fallen in!'

Yes, he was a nomad. Yes, he had just jacked in his job to embark on a precarious and unpredictable career. But did he have to look so damned *appalled*? And then, hard on the heels of that thought, came wrenching dismay at the insanity of thinking that a pregnancy wouldn't be the end of the world. God, what was she *thinking*? Had she gone completely *mad*?

She snatched the various bits and pieces left on the kitchen table and began slamming them into cupboards.

'God knows, you're probably right,' he gritted, catching her by the arm and pulling her round to face him. 'But

I've had sufficient experience of the fairer sex to know that they—'

'*What* experience? What are you talking about?'

Leo paused. Money bred suspicion and he had always been suspicious enough to know that it was a mistake to trust contraception to the opposite sex.

Except, how could he say that when he was supposed to be a struggling writer existing on the remnants of his savings from whatever two-bit job he had been in? How could he confess that five years previously he had had a scare with a woman in the dying stages of their relationship. The Pill she claimed to have been on, which she then later denied... Two weeks of hell cursing himself for having been a trusting idiot and, in the end, thankfully there had been no pregnancy. There was nothing he could have done in the circumstances, but a split condom was still bad news.

But how could he concede that his vast financial reserves made him a natural target for potential gold-diggers?

'You must really think that you're such a desirable catch that women just can't help wanting to tie you down by falling pregnant!'

'So you're telling me that I'm *not* a desirable catch?' Crisis over. Deception, even as an acceptable means to an end, was proving unsavoury. He smiled a sexy half-smile, clearing his head of any shade of guilt, telling himself that a chance in a million did not constitute anything to get worked up about.

'There are better options...' The tension slowly seeped out of her although she was tempted to pry further, to find out who these determined women were—the ones he had bedded, the ones who had wanted more.

She tried to picture him in his other life, sitting in a cubicle behind a desk somewhere with a computer in front of him. She couldn't. He seemed so at home in casual clothes; dealing with the snow; making sure the fireplace was well supplied with logs; doing little handyman jobs around the place, the sort she usually ended up having to pay someone to do for her. He now had a stubbly six o'clock shadow on his jawline because he told her that he saw no point in shaving twice a day. He was a man made for the great outdoor life. And yet...

'You were going to tell me about Bridget,' Leo said casually, moving to sit at the table and shoving his chair out so that he could stretch his legs in front of him. 'Before you rudely decided to interrupt the conversation by demanding sex.'

Brianna laughed. Just like that, whatever mood had swept over her like an ugly, freak wave looming unexpectedly from calm waters dissolved and disappeared.

'As I said, you'll like her.' She began unloading the dishwasher, her mind only half-focused on what she was saying; she was looking ahead to the technicalities of keeping the pub shut, wondering how long she could afford the luxury, trying to figure out whether her battered four-wheel drive could make it to the village so that she could stock up on food...

Leo's lips twisted with disdain. 'Funnily enough, whenever someone has said that to me in the past I'm guaranteed to dislike the person in question.' For the first time, he thought of his birth mother in a way that wasn't exclusively abstract, wasn't merely a jigsaw piece that had to be located and slotted in for the completed picture.

What did she look like? Tall, short, fat, thin...? And from whom had he inherited his non-Irish looks? His adoptive parents had both been small, neat and fair-haired. He had towered above them, dark-haired, dark-eyed, olive-skinned…as physically different from them as chalk from cheese.

He stamped down his surge of curiosity and reminded himself that he wasn't here to form any kind of relationship with the woman but merely finally to lay an uncertain past to rest. Anger, curiosity and confusion were unhappy life companions and the faster he dispensed with them, the better.

'You're very suspicious, Leo.' Brianna thought back to his vehement declaration that women couldn't be trusted when it came to contraception. 'Everyone loves Bridget.'

'You mentioned that she didn't have a…partner.' A passing remark on which Brianna had not elaborated. Now, Leo was determined to prise as much information out of her as he could, information that would be a useful backdrop for when he met the woman the following day. It was a given, he recognised, that some people might think him heartless to extract information from the woman he was sleeping with, but he decided to view that as a necessity—something that couldn't be helped, something to be completely disassociated from the fact that they were lovers, and extremely passionate lovers at that.

Life, generally speaking, was all about people using people. If he hadn't learned that directly from his adoptive parents, then he certainly must have had it cemented somewhere deep within his consciousness. Perhaps, and in spite of his remarkably stable background, the fact that he was adopted had allowed a seed of cynicism to run rampant over the years.

'She doesn't talk much about that.'

'No? Why not? You're her…what would you say…confidante? I would have thought that she would find it a comfort to talk to you about whatever happened. I mean, you've known each other how long? Were your parents friends with the woman?'

Brianna laughed. 'Oh, gosh, no!' She glanced round the kitchen, making sure that all her jobs were done. 'Bridget is a relative newcomer to this area.'

'Really…' Leo murmured. 'I was under the impression that she was a valued, long-standing member of the community.' He almost laughed at the thought of that. Valued member of the community? Whilst jettisoning an unwanted child like an item of disposable garbage? Only in a community of jailbirds would someone like that have been up for consideration as a valued member.

'But now you tell me that she's a newcomer. How long has she been living in the area?'

'Eight years tops.'

'And before that?'

Brianna shot him a look of mild curiosity but, when he smiled that smile at her, that crooked, sexy half-smile, she felt any niggling questions hovering on the tip of her tongue disappear.

'You're asking a lot of questions,' she murmured breathlessly. He signalled for her to come closer and she did, until he could wrap his arms around her and hold her close.

'Like I said, I have a curious mind.' He breathed in the clean floral scent of her hair and for a few seconds forgot everything. 'You shouldn't have put your jumper back on,' he remarked in a voice that thrilled her to the core. 'I like looking at your breasts. Just the perfect mouthful…'

'And I have calls to make if I'm to keep the pub shut!' She slapped away his wandering hand, even though she would have liked nothing more than to drag him up to the bedroom to lay claim to him. 'And you have a book to work on!'

'I'd rather work on you…'

'Thank goodness Bridget isn't here. She'd be horrified.'

Leo nearly burst out laughing. 'And is this because she's the soul of prurience? You still haven't told me where she came from. Maybe she was a nun in her former life?' He began strolling out of the kitchen towards the sitting room with the open fire which he had requisitioned as his working space. His computer was shut and there was a stack of novels by the side of it, books he had picked from her collection. He had already started two, abandoned them both and was reaching the conclusion that soul-searching novels with complicated themes were not for him.

'There's no need to be sarcastic.' Brianna hovered by the table as he sat down. She knew that he demanded complete privacy when he was writing, sectioning off a corner of the sitting area, his back to the window. Yet somehow it felt as though their conversation was not quite at an end, even though he wasn't asking any further questions.

'Was I?'

His cool, dark eyes rested on her and she flushed and traced an invisible pattern with her finger on the table. Was there something she was missing? Some important link she was failing to connect?

'You've known this woman for a few years…'

'Nearly seven. She came to the pub one evening on her own.'

'In other words, she has a drinking habit?'

'No! She'd moved to the area and she thought it might be a way of meeting people! We have quiz nights here once a month. She used to come for the quiz nights, and after a while we got chatting.'

'Chatting about where she had come from? Oh no; of course, you know nothing about that. And I'm guessing not many clues as to what she was doing here either? It's a small place for a woman who wants to meet people…'

'It's a community. We make outsiders feel welcome.' She blushed at her unwitting choice of words. 'I felt sorry for her,' Brianna continued hurriedly. 'I started an over-forties' quiz night, ladies only, so that she could get talking to some of them.'

Leo was mentally joining the dots and was arriving at a picture not dissimilar to the one he had always had of the woman who had given birth to him—with a few extra trimmings thrown in for good measure.

A new life and a new start for someone with a dubious past to conceal. Tellingly, no one knew about this past life, including the girl who had supposedly become her anchor in the community.

It didn't take a genius to figure out that, where there were secrets that required concealment, those secrets were dirty little ones. He had received half a picture from Brianna, he was certain of it—the rosy half, the half that didn't conform to his expectations.

'And you did all this without having a clue as to this woman's past?'

'I don't need to know every single detail about someone's past to recognise a good person when I see one!' She folded her arms tightly around her and glared down at him. She should have let him carry on with his writing. Instead, she had somehow found herself embroiled in an argument she hadn't courted and was dismayed at how sick it made her feel. 'I don't want to argue with you about this, Leo.'

'You're young. You're generous and trusting. You're about to give house room to someone whose past is a mystery.' He drew an uneasy parallel with his own circumstance, here at the pub under a very dubious cloud of deceit indeed, and dismissed any similarities. He was, after all, as upstanding and law-abiding as they came. No shady past here.

On the very point of tipping over into anger that he was in the process of dismissing her as the sort of gullible fool who might be taken in by someone who was up to no good, another thought lodged in the back of her mind. It took up residence next to the pernicious feel-good seed that had been planted when she had considered the possibility that he might not be welcoming Bridget because he cherished their one-to-one solitude.

Was he seriously *worried* about her? And if he was... That thought joined the other links in the chain that seemed to represent the nebulous beginnings of a commitment...

She knew that she was treading on very dangerous ground even having these crazy day dreams but she couldn't push them away. With her heart beating like a jack hammer, she attempted to squash the thrilling notion that he was concerned about her welfare.

'Do you think that my friend might be a homicidal maniac in the guise of a friendly and rather lonely woman?'

Leo frowned darkly. Brianna's thoughts about Bridget were frankly none of his concern, and irrelevant to the matter in hand, but he couldn't contain a surge of sudden, disorienting protectiveness.

Brianna had had to put her dreams and ambitions on hold to take charge of her father's failing business, whilst at the same time trying to deal with the double heartbreak of her father's death and her lover's abandonment. It should have been enough to turn her into an embittered shrew. Yet there was a transparent openness and natural honesty about her that had surfaced through the challenging debris of her past. She laughed a lot, she seldom complained and she was the sort of girl who would never spare an act of kindness.

'When people remove themselves for no apparent reason to start a new beginning, it's usually because they're running away from something.'

'You mean the police?'

Leo shrugged and tugged her towards him so that she collapsed on his lap with a stifled laugh. 'What if she turns into an unwanted pub guest who overstays her welcome?' He angled her so that she was straddling him on his lap and delicately pushed up the jumper.

'Don't be silly,' Brianna contradicted him breathlessly. 'You should get down to your writing. I should continue with my stock taking...'

In response to that, Leo eased the jumper off and gazed at her small, pert breasts with rampant satisfaction. He began licking one of her nipples, a lazy, light, teasing with the tip of his tongue, a connoisseur sampling an exquisite and irresistible offering.

'She has a perfectly nice little house of her own.' There was something wonderfully decadent about doing this, sitting on his lap in the middle of the empty pub, watching him as he nuzzled her breast as if he had all the time in the world and was in no hurry to take things to the next level.

'But—' Leo broke off. 'Here...' he flicked his tongue against her other nipple '...she would have...' he suckled for a few seconds, drawing her breast into his mouth '...you...' a few kisses on the soft roundness until he could feel her shiver and shudder '...to take care of her; cook her food...'

He held one of her breasts in his hand so that it was pushed up to him, the nipple engorged and throbbing, and he delicately sucked it. 'Brianna, she might seem perfectly harmless to you.' With a sigh, he leaned back in the chair and gave her tingling breasts a momentary reprieve. 'But what do you do if she decides that a cosy room in a pub, surrounded by people and hands-on waitress service, is more appealing than an empty house and the exertion of having to cook her own food?'

At no point was he inclined to give the woman the benefit of the doubt. In his experience, people rarely deserved that luxury, and certainly not someone with her particular shady history.

Never one ever to have been possessive or protective about the women in his life, he was a little shaken by the fierce streak suddenly racing through him that was repelled by the thought of someone taking advantage of the girl sitting on his lap with the easy smile, the flushed face and tousled hair.

'You need to exercise caution,' he muttered grimly. He raked his fingers through his hair and scowled, as though she had decided to disagree with him even though she hadn't uttered a word.

'Then maybe,' Brianna teased him lightly, 'you should stick around and make sure I don't end up becoming a patsy...'

The journey here should have taken no time at all; his stay should have been over in a matter of a couple of days. There were meetings waiting for him and urgent trips abroad that could only be deferred for so long. It had never been his intention to turn this simple fact-finding exercise into a drama in three parts.

'Maybe I should,' he heard himself say softly. 'For a while...'

'And you can chase her away if she turns out to be an unscrupulous squatter who wants to take advantage of me.' She laughed as though nothing could be more ridiculous and raised her hand to caress his cheek.

Leo circled her slim wrist with his fingers in a vice-like grip. 'Oh, if she tries that,' he said in a voice that made her shiver, 'she'll discover just what a ruthless opponent I could prove to be—and just how regrettable it can be to cross my path.'

CHAPTER FIVE

THE SNOW HAD stopped. As grey and leaden as the skies had been for a seemingly unstoppable length of time, the sun now emerged, turning a bleak winter landscape into a scene from a movie: bright-blue skies and fields of purest white.

Bridget's arrival had been delayed by a day, during which time Leo had allowed the subject of her dubious, unknown past to be dropped. No more hassle warning Brianna about accepting the cuckoo in the nest. No more words of caution that the person she might have considered a friend and surrogate mother might very well turn out to be someone all set to take full advantage of her generous nature and hospitality. There would be fallout from this gesture of putting the woman up while she recuperated; he was certain of that and he would be the man to deal with it. So he might never have specialised in the role of 'knight in shining armour' in his life before, but he was happy with his decision.

London would have to take a little back seat for a while. He was managing to keep on top of things just fine via his computer, tablet and smartphone and, if anything dramatic arose, then he could always shoot down to sort it out.

All told, the prospect of being holed up in the middle of nowhere was not nearly as tedious as he might have imagined. In fact, all things considered, he was in tremendously high spirits.

Of course, Brianna was a hell of a long way responsible for that. He glanced up lazily from his computer to the sofa where she was sitting amidst piles of paperwork. Her hair was a rich tumble over her shoulders and she was cross-legged, leaning forward and chewing her lip as she stared at her way-past-its-sell-by-date computer which was on the low coffee table in front of her.

In a couple of hours the ambulance would be bringing his destiny towards him. For the moment, he intended to enjoy his woman. He closed the report in front of him and stood up, stretching, flexing his muscles.

From across the small, cosy room, Brianna looked up and, as always happened, her eyes lingered, absorbing the beautiful sight of his long, lean body; the way his jeans rode low on his hips; the way he filled out her father's checked flannel shirt in just the right way. He had loosely rolled the sleeves to his elbow and his strong, brown forearms, liberally sprinkled with dark hair, sent a little shiver of pleasurable awareness rippling through her.

'You should get a new computer.' Leo strolled towards her and then stood so that he was looking down at the columns of numbers flickering on the screen at him. 'Something faster, more up-to-date.'

'And I should have a holiday, somewhere warm and far away… And I'll do both just as soon as I have the money.' Brianna sighed and sat back, keenly aware of him looking over her. 'I just want to get all this stuff out of the way before Bridget gets here. I want to be able to devote some quality time to her.'

Leo massaged her neck from behind. Her hair, newly washed, was soft and silky. The baggy, faded pink jumper was the most unrevealing garment she could have worn but he had fast discovered that there was no need for her to wear anything that outlined her figure. His imagination was well supplied with all the necessary tools for providing graphic images of her body that kept him in a state of semi-permanent arousal.

'Was the urgent trip to the local supermarket part of the quality-service package?' He moved round to sit next to her, shoving some of the papers out of the way and wondering how on earth she could keep track of her paperwork when there seemed to be no discernible order to any of it.

'I know you don't agree with what I'm doing; I know you think I should just leave her to get on with things on her own but—'

'This conversational road is guaranteed to lead to a dead end,' he drawled smoothly. 'Let's do ourselves a favour and not travel down it.'

'You enjoyed the supermarket experience.' Brianna changed the subject immediately. She didn't want an argument. She didn't even want a mild disagreement, and she knew what his feelings were on the subject of their soon-to-be visitor, even though he had backed off from making any further disparaging remarks about her naïvety in taking in someone whose entire life hadn't been laid out on a plate for her perusal.

'It was…novel.' Actually, Leo couldn't recall the last time he had set foot in a supermarket. He paid someone to deal with the hassle of all that.

'Margaret Connelly has only just opened up that place. Actually, it's not a supermarket as such.'

'I'd noticed.'

'More of a…a…'

'Cosy space filled to overflowing with all manner of things, of which food is only one component? Brussels sprouts nestling next to fishing tackle…?'

'The lay out can seem a bit eccentric but the food's all fresh and locally sourced.'

Leo grinned, swivelled her so that she had her back to him and began massaging her shoulders. 'You sound like an advertisement for a food magazine. I'm going to have to put my foot down if you're thinking of slaving over a hot stove preparing dishes on this woman's whim.'

Brianna relaxed into the massage and smiled with contentment. She felt a thrill of pleasure at the possessive edge to his voice. 'She has to be on a bland diet—doctor's orders.'

'That's irrelevant. You're not going to be running up and down those stairs because someone rings a bell and wants a cup of tea immediately.'

'*You* could always do the running for me if you think I'm too fragile to cope.'

Leo's lips curled with derision and he fought down the impulse to burst into sardonic laughter. 'Running and doing errands for people isn't something I do.'

'Especially not in this instance,' Brianna said, remembering that he *was*, after all, a paying guest despite their unusual arrangement. He had given her a shocking amount of money for his stay thus far, way too much, and had informed her that it was something to do with company expenses owed to him before he'd quit his job. She hadn't quite understood his explanation. Nor had he backed down when she refused to take the full amount.

'Take it,' he had ordered, 'Or I'll just have to find another establishment that will accommodate what I want to pay. And I shall end up having to take taxis here to see you. You wouldn't want to add that further cost to a poor, struggling writer, would you?'

'What do you mean?' Leo stilled now.

'I mean you're a customer. Running up and down stairs

isn't something I would ask you to do. That would be ridiculous. I would never take advantage of you like that.'

'But you *would* take advantage of me in other ways... because I happen to enjoy you taking advantage of me in all those other imaginative ways of yours...'

'Is *sex* all you ever think about?' she murmured, settling back against him and sighing as he slipped his hands underneath her jumper to fondle her breasts.

No. Sex most certainly had never been *all* he thought about. In fact, Leo contemplated with some bemusement, although he had always enjoyed an exceptionally varied and active sex life it had never been at the top of his priorities. Sex, and likewise women, had always taken a back seat to the more important driving force in his life, which was his work.

'You bring out the primitive in me,' he said softly into her ear. 'Is it my fault that your body drives me insane?' He relaxed into the sprawling sofa so that he had Brianna half-lying on top of him, her back pressed against his torso, her hair tangled against his chest. He removed one hand to brush some of her hair from his cheek and returned his hand to her jeans to rest it lightly on her hip. A stray sheet of paper wafted to the ground, joining a disconcerting bundle already there.

Brianna's body was responding as it always did, with galloping excitement and sweet anticipation. She might very well joke that sex was the only thing on his mind, but it certainly seemed to have taken over all her responses as well. Even the problem supplier she knew she had to deal with urgently was forgotten as she undid the button and zip of her jeans.

'Tut, tut, tut; you're going to have to do better than that, my darling. How am I expected to get my hand where it wants to be?'

Brianna giggled softly. He had no hang-ups about where they made love. His lack of inhibition was liberating and it worked in tandem with her own period of celibacy to release an explosion of passion she had never experienced in her life before. She couldn't seem to get enough of him.

She wriggled out of her jeans and he chuckled.

'For someone with a body like yours, I'm always amazed that you've stuck to the functional underwear...' He thought about seeing her in something small, lacy and sexy, lying in his super-king-sized bed in his penthouse apartment in Chelsea.

The thought was random, springing from nowhere and establishing itself with such graphic clarity that he drew in his breath sharply with shock.

Hell, where was his mind going? This was a situation that was intensely enjoyable but it only functioned within very definite parameters. Like it or not, they were operating within a box, a box of his own making, and freedom from that box in any way, shape or form was a possibility that was not to be entertained.

With that in mind, he cleared his head of any inappropriate, wandering thoughts about her being in his apartment. Crazy.

'Is that how you like your women?' Brianna asked casually. He never spoke about his love life. A sudden thought occurred to her and, although this hardly seemed the time for a deep, meaningful conversation, she had to carry on regardless. 'Is that why you're here?'

'What are you talking about?'

Brianna wriggled so that she was on her side, still nestled between his legs, and she looked up at him, breathing in that clean, tangy scent that always seemed to scramble all her thoughts. His hand was curved on her hip, fingers dipping against her stomach. Even that small, casual contact did devastating things to her already hot, aroused body. She was slippery and wet, and it was mad, because she had to get things together before Bridget arrived.

'You know, all the way from London.'

'No clue as to what you're talking about.'

'Never mind. We need to start tidying up.' She sighed. 'Bridget's going to be here soon.'

'Didn't they say that they would telephone you before they left the hospital?'

'Yes, but...'

'No phone call yet.' After the disturbing tangent his thoughts had taken only moments before when he had imagined her in his apartment, the last thing Leo wanted was a heart-to-heart. He wanted to touch her; touching her was like a magic antidote to thinking. Hell, he had worked while he had been here, but his mind had not been on the cut and thrust of business deals with its customary focus. This was as close to a holiday as he had had in years, and the last thing he had expected when he had started on this journey of discovery.

He reached under her knickers, a dull beige with not a scrap of lace in sight, and slid his finger against the wet crease, seeking out the little nub of her clitoris. This was so much better than talking and a damn sight more worthwhile than the sudden chaos of thoughts that had earlier afflicted him.

Brianna moaned softly as he continued to rub. She squirmed and sighed and half-closed her eyes, her nostrils flaring and her breathing thickening the closer she came to a point of no return.

Questions still hovered at the back of her mind like pesky insects nipping at her conscience, refusing to go away, but right now she couldn't focus on any of that. Right now, as the movement of his strong, sure hand picked up speed, she moaned and arched her body and wave upon wave of pleasure surged through her. Lying with her back to him, she couldn't see his face, only his one hand moving inside her while the other was flattened against her thigh and his legs, spread to accommodate her body between them. But she knew that he was watching her body as he brought her to orgasm and the thought of that was wantonly exciting.

She was aware of her uneven, shaky breathing as she lay back and let her heated body return to planet Earth.

For a few seconds, there was silence. Leo linked his fingers on her stomach and absently noted the way they glistened with her honeyed wetness.

'I'm going to start clearing all my paperwork away,' she said eventually. 'I don't seem to have made much progress with our snack supplier. I'm going to have a shower.' She eased herself over his legs and off the sofa, and began tidying the papers which were strewn everywhere. She didn't bother to put on her jeans, instead choosing to scoop them up and drape them over one arm.

It all came down to sex. She knew that she was being silly for objecting to that because this was a situation that was never going to last longer than two minutes. It was something she had jumped into, eyes wide open, throwing caution to the winds and accepting it for what it was, and there was no excuse now for wanting more than what had been laid on the table.

Except…had she thought that this perfect stranger would possess the sort of complex personality that she would end up finding strangely compulsive?

Could she ever have imagined that an unexpected, astounding, elemental physical attraction would turn into something that seemed to have her in its hold? That taking a walk on the wild side, breaking out of the box for just a little while, would have repercussions that struck a chord of fear into her?

She wanted more. She couldn't even begin to think of him leaving, carrying on with his travels. He had entered her life, and what had previously been bland, dull and grey was now Technicolor-bright. She alternated between reading all sorts of things behind his words and actions and then telling herself that she really shouldn't.

'You never said…' Brianna begin heading up the stairs, carrying as much with her as she could: files, her jeans and her trainers, which she didn't bother to stick on completely.

Behind her, Leo scooped up the remainder of the files and began following her.

'Never said what?'

'All those women you're so cynical about…' She paused to look at him over her shoulder. 'The ones who wear lacy underwear…'

'Did I ever say that? I don't recall.'

'You didn't have to. I can read between the lines.' She spun back round and headed towards her suite of rooms, straight to the study, where she dumped all the files she had been carrying. She stood back and watched as he deposited the remainder of them, including her computer, which was as heavy as a barrow full of bricks, and—yes, he was right—in desperate need of updating.

Brianna took in his guarded, shuttered expression and knew instinctively that she was treading on quicksand, even though he hadn't rushed in with any angry words telling her to mind her own business. She could see it on his face. Her heart was beating so fiercely that she could almost hear it in the still quiet of the room.

'I'm going to have a shower,' she mumbled, backing out of the little office. 'On my own, if you don't mind.'

Leo frowned and raked his fingers through his hair, but he didn't move a muscle.

She wanted to *talk*. Talk about what? His exes? What was the point of that? When it came to women and meaningful conversations, they invariably led down the same road: a dead end. He wasn't entirely sure where his aversion to commitment came from and he knew, if he were honest, that his parents would have wanted to see him travel down the traditional route of marriage and kids by thirty—but there it was; he hadn't. He had never felt the inclination. Perhaps a feeling of security was something that developed in a mother's womb and having been given up for adoption, by definition, had wiped that out and the security of making money, something tangible he could control, had taken its place.

At any rate, the minute any woman started showing signs of crossing the barriers he had firmly erected around himself, they were relegated to history.

He told himself that there should be no difficulty in this particular relationship following the same course because he could see, from the look in her eyes, that whatever chat she wanted to have was not going to begin and end with the choice of underwear his women were accustomed to wearing.

He told himself that in fact it would be *easier* to end this relationship because, in essence, it had never really functioned in his real life. It had functioned as something sweet and satisfying within a bubble. And within a day or two, once he had met his birth mother and put any unanswered questions to rest, he would be gone.

So there definitely was *no* point to a lengthy heart-to-,heart. He strolled into the bedroom and glanced down at the snow which was already beginning to thaw.

She emerged minutes later from the shower with a towel

wrapped round her, her long hair piled up on top of her head and held in place with a hair grip. Tendrils had escaped and framed her heart-shaped face. She looked impossibly young and vulnerable.

'What are you doing in my bedroom?'

'Okay. So I go out with women who seem to spend a lot of money on fancy underwear.' He glowered at her. 'I don't know what that has to do with anything.' He watched as she rummaged in her drawers in silence and fetched out some faded jogging bottoms and a rugby-style jumper, likewise faded.

Brianna knew that a few passing remarks had escalated into something that she found unsettling. She didn't want to pry into his life. She wanted to be the adult who took this on board, no questions asked and no strings attached. Unfortunately...

She disappeared back into the bathroom, changed and returned to find him still standing in an attitude of challenging defensiveness by the bedroom window.

'You wanted to talk...' he prompted, in defiance of common sense. 'Are you jealous that I've had lovers? That they've been the sort of women who—?'

'Don't run pubs, live on a shoestring and wear functional underwear from department stores? No, I'm not jealous. Why would I be?'

'Good. Because, personally, I don't do jealousy.' It occurred to Leo that there were a number of things he didn't do when it came to his personal relationships and yet, here he was, doing one of them right now: having a *talk*.

'Have we ended up in bed because you think I make a change?' She took a deep breath and looked him squarely in the face. He was so beautiful. He literally took her breath away. 'From all those women you went out with?' If *she* found him beautiful, if he blew *her* mind away, then why wouldn't he have had the same effect on hordes of other women?

'No! That's an absurd question.'

'Is it?' She turned on her heel and began back down the stairs to the bar area where she proceeded to do some unnecessary tidying. He lounged against the bar, hands in his pockets, and watched her as she worked. She appeared to be in no hurry to proceed with the conversation she had initiated. The longer the silence stretched between them, the more disgruntled Leo became.

Moving to stand directly in front of her, so that she was forced to stop arranging the beer mats in straight lines on the counter, he said, 'If there's any comparison to be done, then you win hands down.'

Brianna felt a stupid surge of pleasure. 'I'm guessing you *would* say that, considering we're sleeping together and you're pretty much stuck here.'

'Am I? The snow seems to be on its way out.' They weren't touching each other, but he could feel her as forcibly as if they had been lying naked on her bed.

'How long do you intend to stay?' She flushed and glanced down at her feet before taking a deep breath and looking at him without flinching. 'I'm going to keep the pub closed for another fortnight but just in case, er, bookings come in for the rooms, it would be helpful for me to know when yours might be free to, er, rent out...'

And this, Leo thought, was the perfect opportunity to put a date in the calendar. It was as obvious as the nose on his face that her reason for wanting to find out when he would be leaving had nothing to do with a possible mystery surge in bookings for the rooms. He didn't like being put in a position of feeling trapped.

'I told you I'd stick around, make sure you didn't get ripped off or taken advantage of by this so-called best buddy of yours,' he said roughly. 'I won't be going any-where until I'm satisfied that you're okay on that score. Satisfied? No; you're not. What else is on your mind, Bri-anna? Spit it out and then I can disappear for a shower and some work and leave you to get on with your female bonding in peace.'

Brianna shrugged. Everything about his body language suggested that he was in no mood to stand here, answer-ing questions. Perhaps, she thought, answering questions was something else he *didn't do* when it came to women. Like jealousy. And yet he wasn't moving. 'Did you end up here on the back of a bad relationship?' she asked bluntly. She shot him a defiant look from under her lashes. 'I know you don't want me to ask lots of questions...'

'Did I ever say that?'

'You don't have to.'

'Because, let me guess, you seem to have a hot line to my thoughts!' He scowled. Far from backing away from an interrogation he didn't want and certainly didn't need, his feet appeared to be disobeying the express orders of his brain. Against all odds, he wanted to wipe that defensive, guarded expression from her face. 'And no, I did not end up here on the back of a bad relationship.' He had ended up here because...

Leo flushed darkly, uncomfortable with where his thoughts were drifting.

'I'm sleeping with you, and I know it's going to end soon, but I still want to know that you're not using me as some sort of sticking plaster while you try to recover from a broken heart.'

'I've never suffered from a broken heart, Brianna.' Leo smiled crookedly at her and stroked the side of her face with his finger.

Just then her mobile buzzed and after only a few seconds on the phone she said to him, 'Bridget's had her final check-up with the consultant and they're going to be setting off in about half an hour. They'll probably be here in about an hour and a half or so. Depends on the roads, but the main roads will all be gritted. It's only the country lanes around here that are still a little snowed up.'

An hour and a half. Leo's lips thinned but, despite the impending meeting with his mother, one which he had quietly anticipated for a number of years ever since he had tracked down her whereabouts, his focus remained exclusively on the girl standing in front of him.

'Everyone has suffered from a broken heart at some point.' She reverted to her original topic.

'I'm the exception to the rule.'

'You've never been in love?'

'You say that as though it's inconceivable. No. Never. And stop looking at me as though I've suddenly turned into an alien life-form. Are you telling me that, after your experience with the guy you thought you would be spending your life with, you're still glad to have *been in love*?'

He lounged against the bar and stared down at her. He had become so accustomed to wearing jeans and an assortment of her father's old plaid flannel shirts, a vast array of which she seemed to have kept, that he idly wondered what it would feel like returning to his snappy handmade suits, his Italian shoes, the silk ties, driving one of his three cars or having Harry chauffeur him. He would return to the reality of high- powered meetings, life in the fast lane, private planes and first-class travel to all four corners of the globe.

Here, he could be a million miles away, living on another planet. Was that why he now found himself inclined to have this type of conversation? The sort of touchy-feely conversation that he had always made a point of steering well clear from? Really, since when had he ever been into probing any woman about her thoughts and feelings about past loves?

'Of course I am,' Brianna exclaimed stoutly. 'It may have crashed and burned, but there were moments of real happiness.'

Leo frowned. Real happiness? What did she mean by that? Good sex? He didn't care much for a trip down happiness lane with her. If she felt inclined to reminisce over the good old days, conveniently forgetting the misery that had been dished up to her in the end, then he was not the man with the listening ear.

'How salutary that you can ignore the fact that you were taken for a ride for years... Are you still in touch with the creep?'

Brianna frowned and tried to remember what the creep looked like. 'No,' she said honestly. 'I haven't got a clue what he's up to. The last I heard from one of my friends from uni, he had gone abroad to work for some important law firm in New York. He's disappeared completely. I was heartbroken at the time, but it doesn't mean that I'm not glad I met him, and it doesn't mean that I don't hope to meet that someone special at some point in the future.'

And as she said that a very clear picture of Mr Special floated into her mind. He was approximately six-two with bronzed skin, nearly black hair and lazy, midnight-dark eyes that could send shivers racing up and down her spine. He came in a package that had carried very clear health warnings but still she had fallen for him like a stupid teenager with more hormones than common sense.

Fallen *in lust* with him, she thought with feverish panic. She hadn't had a relationship with a guy for years! And then he had come along, drop-dead gorgeous, with all the seductive anonymity of a stranger—a writer, no less. Was it any wonder that she had fallen *in lust* with him?

Was that why she could now feel herself becoming *clingy*? Not wanting him to go? Losing all sense of perspective?

'And no one special is on the scene here?' Leo drawled lazily. 'Surely the lads must be queuing up for you...'

Of course there had been nibbles, but Brianna had never been interested. She had reasoned to herself that she just didn't have the time; that her big, broken love affair had irreparably damaged something inside her; that, just as soon as the pub really began paying its way, she would jump back into the dating world.

All lies. She could have had all the time in the world, a fully paid-up functioning heart and a pub that turned over a million pounds a year in profit and she still wouldn't have been drawn to anyone—because she had been waiting for just the moment when Leo Spencer walked through the door, tall, dark and dangerous, like a gunslinger in a Western movie.

'I'm not interested in anything serious at the moment,' she said faintly. 'I have loads of time. Bridget should be arriving any minute now.'

'At least an hour left to go...' How was it possible to shove all thoughts of his so-called mother out of his head? He had almost forgotten that the woman was on her way.

'I need to go and get her room ready.'

'Haven't you already done that? The potpourri and the new throw from the jack-of-all-trades supermarket?'

She had. But suddenly she wanted nothing more than to escape his suffocating masculine presence, find a spot where she could straighten out her tangled thoughts.

'Well, I want to make sure that it's just right,' she said sharply.

Leo stepped aside. 'And I think I'll go and have a shower and do something productive with my time in my room.'

'You don't have to disappear! You're a paying guest, Leo. You can come down and do your writing in your usual place. Bridget and I won't make any noise at all. She'll probably just want to rest.'

'I'll let the two of you do your bonding in peace,' he murmured. 'I'll come down for dinner. I take it you'll be cooking for three?'

'You know I will, and please don't start on the business of me being a mug.'

Leo held up both hands in a gesture of mock-indignation that she could even contemplate such a thing.

Brianna shot him a reluctant smile. 'You wait and see. You'll end up loving her as much as I do.'

'Yes. We'll certainly wait and see,' Leo delivered with a coolness that Brianna felt rather than saw, because his expression was mildly amused. She wondered if she had perhaps imagined it.

Leo remained where he was while she disappeared upstairs to do her last check of the bedroom where Bridget would be staying, doubtless making sure that the sheets were in place with hospital precision, corners tucked in just so.

His mouth curled with derision. The thought of her being taken advantage of filled him with disgust. The thought of her putting her trust in a woman who would inevitably turn out not to be the person she thought she was made his stomach turn. He could think of no other woman whose trusting nature should be allowed to remain intact.

He slammed his clenched fist against the wall and gritted his teeth. He had come here predisposed to dislike the woman who had given birth to him and then given him away. He was even more predisposed to dislike her as the woman who, in the final analysis, would reveal her true colours to the girl who had had the kindness to take her under her wing.

The force of his feelings on this subject surprised him. It was like the powerful impact of a depth charge, rumbling down deep in the very core of him.

He didn't wait for the ambulance bearing his destiny towards him to arrive, instead pushing himself away from the wall and heading up to his bedroom. His focus on work had been alarmingly casual and now, having had a shower, he buried himself in reports, numbers, figures and all the things that usually had the ability to fully engage his attention.

Not now. His brain refused to obey the commands being issued to it. What would the woman look like? Years ago, he could have had pictures taken of her when he had set his man on her trail, but he hadn't bothered because she had been just a missing slot in his life he had wanted to fill. He hadn't given a damn what she looked like. Now, he had to fight the temptation to stroll over to the window and peer out to the courtyard which his room overlooked.

He stiffened when he eventually heard the sound of the ambulance pulling up and the muffled rise and fall of voices which carried up to his room.

Deliberately he tuned out and exerted every ounce of will power to rein in his exasperating, wandering mind.

At a little after five, he got a text from Brianna: a light early supper would be served at six. If he wanted to join them, then he was more than welcome. Sorry she couldn't come up to his room but she had barely had time to draw breath since Bridget had arrived.

She had concluded her text with a smiley face. Who

did that? He smiled and texted back: yes, he'd be down promptly at six.

He sat back and stared at the wall. In an hour he would meet his past. He would put that to bed and then, when that was done, he would move on, back to the life from which he had taken this brief respite.

He had an image of Brianna's face gazing at him, of her lithe, slim body, of the way she had of humming under her breath when she was occupied doing something, and the way she looked when she was curled up on the sofa trying to make sense of her accounts.

But of course, he thought grimly, that was fine. Sure, she would be on his mind. They might not have spent a long time in each other's company but it had been concentrated time. Plenty long enough for images of her to get stuck in his head.

But she was not part of his reality. He would check out the woman who had given birth to him, put his curiosity to bed and, yes, move on...

CHAPTER SIX

LEO WASN'T QUITE sure when the snow had stopped, when the furious blizzards had turned to tamer snowfall, and when that tamer snowfall had given way to a fine, steady drizzle that wiped clean the white horizon and returned it to its original, snow-free state.

He couldn't quite believe that he was still here. Of course, he returned to London sporadically mid-week and was uncomfortably aware of his conscience every time he vaguely intimated that there were things to do with the job he had ditched: paperwork that needed sorting out; problems with his accommodation that needed seeing to; social engagements that had to be fulfilled because he should have returned to London by now.

The lie he had blithely concocted before his game plan had been derailed did not sit quite so easily now. But what the hell was he to do?

He rose to move towards the window and stared distractedly down at the open fields that backed the pub. It was nearly three. In three hours, the pub would be alive with the usual Friday evening crowd, most of whom he knew by sight if not by name.

How had something so straightforward become so tangled in grey areas?

Of course, he knew. In fact, he could track the path

as clearly as if it was signposted. His simple plan—go in, confirm all the suspicions he had harboured about his birth mother, close the book and leave—had slipped out of place the second he had been confronted with Brianna.

She was everything the women he had dated in the past were not. Was that why he had not been able to kill his ill-advised temptation to take her to bed? And had her natural, open personality, once sampled, become an addiction he found impossible to jettison? He couldn't seem to see her without wanting her. She turned him on in ways that were unimaginable. For once in his life, he experienced a complete loss of self-control when they made love; it was a drug too powerful to resist.

And then…his mother. The woman he had prejudged, had seen as no more than a distasteful curiosity that had to be boxed and filed away, had not slotted neatly into the box he had prepared.

With a sigh, he raked his fingers through his hair and glanced over his shoulder to the reports blinking at him, demanding urgent attention, yet failing to focus it.

He thought back to when he had met her, that very first impression: smaller than he'd imagined, clearly younger, although her face was worn, very frail after hospital. He had expected someone brash, someone who fitted the image of a woman willing to give away a baby. He had realised, after only an hour in her company, that his preconceived notions were simplistic. That was an eventuality he had not taken into account. He lived his life with clean lines, no room for all those grey areas that could turn stark reality into a sludgy mess. But he had heard her gentle voice and, hard as he had tried not to be swayed, he had found himself hovering on the brink of needing to know more before he made his final judgement.

Not that anything she had said had been of any importance. The three of them had sat on that first evening and had dinner while Brianna had fussed and clucked and his mother had smiled with warm sympathy and complained about her garden and the winter vegetables which would sadly be suffering from neglect.

She had asked him about himself. He had looked at her and wondered where his dark eyes and colouring came from. She was slight and blonde with green eyes. At one point, she had murmured with a faraway expression that he reminded her of someone, someone she used to know, but he had killed that tangent and moved the conversation along.

Seeing her, meeting her, had made him feel weird, confused, uncomfortable in his own skin. A thousand questions had reared their ugly heads and he had killed them all by grimly holding on to his anger. But underneath that anger he had known only too well that the foundations on which he had relied were beginning to feel shaky. He had no longer known what he should be feeling.

Since that first day, he had seen her, though, only in brief interludes and always with Brianna around. Much of the time she spent in her bedroom. She was an avid reader. He had had to reacquaint himself with literature in an attempt to keep his so-called writer occupation as credible as possible. He had caught himself wondering what books she enjoyed reading.

On his last trip to London, he had brought with him a stack of books and had been surprised to discover that, after a diet of work-related reading, the fiction and non-fiction he had begun delving into had not been the hard work he had expected. And at least he could make a halfway decent job of sounding articulate on matters non-financial.

Where this was going to lead, he had no idea.

He headed downstairs and pulled up short at the sight

of Bridget sitting in the small lounge set aside from the bar area, which Brianna had turned into her private place if she didn't want to remain in her bedroom.

Because of Bridget, the pub now had slightly restricted opening and closing hours. He assumed that that was something that could only be achieved in a small town where all the regulars knew what was going on and would not be motivated to take their trade elsewhere—something that would have been quite tedious, as 'elsewhere' was not exactly conveniently located to get to by foot or on a bike.

'Leo!'

Leo paused, suddenly indecisive at being confronted by his mother without Brianna around as an intermediary. She was sitting by the large bay window that overlooked the back garden and the fields behind the pub. Her fair hair was tied back and the thin, gaunt lines of her face were accentuated so that she resembled a wraith.

'Brianna's still out.' She patted the chair facing hers and motioned to him to join her. 'We haven't chatted very much at all. Why don't you have a cup of tea with me?'

Leo frowned, exasperated at his inability to take control of the situation. Did he want to talk to his mother on a one-to-one basis? Why did he suddenly feel so...*vulnerable* and at odds with himself at the prospect? Wasn't this why he had descended on this back-of-nowhere town in the first place? So things had not turned out quite as he had anticipated, but wasn't it still on his agenda to find out what the woman was like?

He was struck by the unexpectedly fierce urge to find out what had possessed her to throw him to the wolves.

He thought that perhaps the facade she portrayed now was a far cry from the real person lurking underneath, and he hardened himself against the weak temptation to be swept along into thinking that she was innocent, pathetic and deserving of sympathy. Could it be that, without Brianna there to impress, her true colours would be revealed?

'I think I'll have black coffee myself. Would you like to switch to coffee?'

'No, my dear, my pot of tea will be fine, although perhaps you could refresh the hot water. I feel exhausted if I'm on my feet for too long and I've been far too active today for my own good.'

He was back with a mug of coffee and the newly refreshed pot of tea which he rested on the table by her, next to the plate of biscuits which were untouched.

'I'm so glad I've caught you on your own,' she murmured as soon as he had taken a seat next to her. 'I feel I barely know you and yet Brianna is so taken with you after such a short space of time.'

'When you say "taken with me"...' He had told Brianna that he saw it as his duty to keep an eye on her houseguest, to scope her out, because a houseguest with a mysteriously absent past was not a houseguest to be trusted. Was the houseguest doing the same with him? He almost laughed out loud at the thought. As always when he was in her company, he had to try not to stare, not to try and find similarities...

'She's, well, I suppose you know about...'

'About the guy who broke her heart when she was at university?'

'She's locked herself away for years, has expressed no interest in any kind of love life at all. I've always thought it sad for someone so young and caring and beautiful, that she wouldn't be able to share those qualities with a soul mate.'

Leo said something and nothing. He looked at the cane leaning against the chair and wondered what it must feel like to be relatively young and yet require the assistance of a walking stick.

'If you don't mind my asking, how old are you, Bridget?'
Bridget looked at him in surprise. 'Why do you ask?'
Leo shrugged and sipped his coffee.

'Not yet fifty,' Bridget said quietly. 'Although I know I look much, much older.' She glanced away to stare through the window and he could see the shine of unshed tears filming her eyes.

In his head, he was doing the maths.

'But we weren't talking about me,' she said softly.

Leo felt a surge of healthy cynicism and thought that if she figured she could disappear behind a veil of anonymity then she was in for a surprise. There were things he wanted to find out, things he *needed* to find out, and he knew himself well—what he wanted, he got, be it money, women or, in this case, answers. The unsettling hesitancy that had afflicted him off and on, the hesitancy he hated because he just wasn't a hesitant person, thankfully disappeared beneath the weight of this new resolve.

'Indulge me,' he said smoothly. 'I hate one-sided conversations. I especially hate long chats about myself... I'm a man, after all. Self-expression is a luxury I don't tend to indulge very often. So, let's talk about you for a minute. I'm curious. You're not yet fifty, you tell me? Seems very young to have abandoned the lure of city lights for a quiet place like this.' He still could not quite believe that she was as young as she said. She looked like a woman in her sixties.

'What you may call "quiet", by which I take it you mean "dull", is what I see as peace.'

'Brianna said that you've been here a while—quite a few years; you must have been even younger when you decided that you wanted "peace".' He couldn't help thinking that, although their colouring was different, he had her eyes, the shape of them. He looked away with a frown.

She blushed and for the first time he could see her relative youth peep out from behind the care-worn features.

'My life's been…complicated. Not quite the life I ever expected, matter of fact.'

Curiosity was gnawing at him but he kept his features perfectly schooled, the disinterested bystander in whom he hoped she would confide. He could feel in his bones that the questions he wanted answering were about to be answered.

'Why don't you talk about it?' he murmured, resting the cup on the table and leaning towards her, his forearms resting on his thighs. 'You probably feel constrained talking to Brianna. In such a small, close-knit community perhaps you didn't want your private life to be thrown into the public arena?' He could see her hesitate. Secrets were always burdensome. 'Not that Brianna would ever be one to reveal a confidence, but one can never be too sure, I suppose.'

'And who knows how long I have left?' Bridget said quietly. She plucked distractedly at the loose gown she was wearing and stared off through the window as though it might offer up some inspiration. 'My health isn't good: stress, built up over the years. The doctor says I could have another heart attack at any time. They can't promise that the next time round won't be fatal.' She looked at him pensively. 'And I suppose I wouldn't want to burden Brianna with my life story. She's a sweet girl but I would never want to put her in a position of having to express a sympathy she couldn't feel.'

Or pass judgement which would certainly mean the end of your happy times with her, Leo thought with another spurt of that healthy cynicism, cynicism he knew he had to work at.

'But I don't come from here...' he encouraged in a low voice.

'I grew up in a place not dissimilar to this,' she murmured. 'Well, bigger, but not by a lot. Everybody knew everybody else. All the girls knew the boys they would end up marrying. I was destined for Jimmy O'Connor; lived two doors away. His parents were my parents' best friends. In fact, we were practically born on the same day, but that all went up the spout when I met Robbie Cabrera. *Roberto* Cabrera.'

Leo stilled. 'He was Spanish?'

'Yes. His father had come over for a temporary job on a building site ten miles out of town. Six months. He was put into our school and all the girls went mad for him. I used to be pretty once, when I was a young girl of fifteen...you might not guess it now.' She sighed and looked at him with a girlish smile which, like that blush, brought her buried youth back up to the surface.

'And what happened?' Leo was surprised he could talk so naturally, as though he was listening to someone else's story rather than his own.

'We fell madly in love. In the way that you do when you're young and innocent.' She shot him a concerned looked and he hastened to assure her that whatever she told him would stay with him. Adrenaline was pumping through him. He hadn't experienced this edge-of-the-precipice feeling in a very long time. If ever. This was why he was here. The only reason he was here.

From nowhere, he had a vision of Brianna laughing and telling him that there was nothing more satisfying than growing your own tomatoes in summer, and teasing him that he probably wouldn't understand because he probably lived in one of those horrible apartment blocks where you wouldn't be able to grow a tomato if your life depended on it.

He thought of himself, picking her up then and hauling her off to his bedroom at a ridiculous hour after the pub had finally been closed. Thought of her curving, feline smile as she lay on his bed, half-naked, her small, perfect breasts turning him on until his erection felt painful and he couldn't get his clothes off fast enough.

'Sorry?' He leaned in closer. 'You were saying…?'

'I know. You're shocked. And I don't mean to shock you but it's a relief to talk about this; I haven't with anyone. I fell pregnant. At fifteen. My family were distraught, and of course there was no question of abortion, not that we would have got rid of it. No, Robbie and I were committed to one another.'

'Pregnant…'

'I was still a child myself. We both were. We wanted to keep it but my parents wouldn't allow it. I was shipped off to a convent to give birth.'

'You wanted to keep it?'

'I never even held it. Never knew if it was a boy or a girl. I returned to Ireland, went back to school, but from that moment on my parents were lost to me. I had three younger siblings and they never knew what had happened. Still don't. Family life was never the same again.'

'And the father of the child?'

Bridget smiled. 'We ran away. His father ended up on a two-year contract. We skipped town when we were sixteen and headed south. I kept my parents informed of my whereabouts but I couldn't see them and they never lived down the shame of what I'd done. I don't think they cared one way or the other. Robbie always kept in touch with his parents and in fact, when they moved to London, we stayed with them for several months before they returned to Spain.'

'You…ran away…' For some reason, his normally agile mind seemed to be lagging behind.

'We were very happy, Robbie and me, for over twenty years until he died in a hit-and-run accident and then I went back to Ireland. Not back to where I grew up, but to another little town, and then eventually I came here.'

'Hit and run…' The tidal rush of emotions was so intense that he stood up and paced like a wounded bear, before dropping back into the chair.

'We never had any more children. Out of respect for the one I was forced to give up for adoption.'

Suddenly the room felt too small. He felt himself break out in a fine perspiration. Restless energy poured through him, driving him back onto his feet. His cool, logical mind willed him to stay put and utter one or two platitudes to bring the conversation to a satisfactory conclusion. But the chaotic jumble of thoughts filling every corner of his brain was forcing him to pace the room, his movements uncoordinated and strangely jerky.

He was aware of Bridget saying something, murmuring, her face now turned to the window, lost in her thoughts.

There was so much to process that he wasn't sure where to start. So this was the story he had been waiting for and the ending had not been anticipated. She hadn't been the convenient stereotype he had envisaged: she wasn't the irresponsible no-hoper who had given him away without a backward glance. And, now that he knew that, what the hell happened next?

He turned to her, saw that she had nodded off and almost immediately heard the sound of Brianna returning.

'What's wrong?' About to shut the door, Brianna stood still and looked at him with a concerned frown. She had been out shopping and had had to force herself to take her time, not to hurry back, because she just wanted to *see* him, to *be* with him. 'Is…is Bridget all right?' She walked towards him and he automatically reached out to help her with the bags of shopping. Brianna stifled the warm thrill that little slice of pretend domesticity gave her.

'Bridget is fine. She appears to have fallen asleep. Have you ever…?' Leo murmured, reaching to cup the nape of her neck so that he could pull her towards him. 'Thought that you were going in one direction, only to find that the signposts had been switched somewhere along the way and the destination you were heading to turned out to be as substantial as a mirage?'

Brianna's heart skipped a beat. Was he talking about *her*? she wondered with heightened excitement. Was he trying to tell her that meeting her had derailed him? She placed her hand flat on his chest and then slipped it between two buttons to feel his roughened hair.

'What are you saying?' she whispered, wriggling her fingers and undoing the buttons so that she could now see the hard chest against which her fingers were splayed.

'I'm saying I want to have sex with you.' And right at that moment it really was exactly what he wanted. He wanted to drown the clamour of discordant voices in his head and just make love to her. With the bags of shopping in just one hand, he nudged her towards the kitchen.

'We can't!' But her hands were scrabbling over him, hurrying to undo the buttons of his shirt, and her breasts were aching in anticipation of being touched by him. 'Bridget…'

'Asleep.' He shut down the associated thoughts that came with mention of her name.

'I've got to start getting ready to open up.'

'But not for another half-hour. I assure you…' They

were in the kitchen now and he kicked the door shut behind him and pushed her towards the wall until she was backed up against it. 'A lot can be accomplished in half an hour.'

The low drawl of intent sent delicious shivers racing up and down her spine and she groaned as he unzipped her jeans and pushed his hand underneath her panties. Frustrated because his big hand couldn't do what it wanted to do thanks to the tightness of her jeans, he yanked them down, and Brianna quickly stepped out of them.

Bridget, she thought wildly, would have another heart attack if she decided to pop into the kitchen for something. But fortunately her energy levels were still very low and if she was asleep then she would remain asleep at least for another hour or so.

Her fingers dug into his shoulders and she uttered a low, wrenching groan as he pulled the crotch of her panties to one side and began rubbing her throbbing clitoris with his finger.

Her panties were damp with her arousal. She gave a broken sigh and her eyelids fluttered. She could feel him clumsily undoing his trousers and then his thick hardness pushing against her jumper.

This was fast and furious sex.

Where was his cool? Leo was catapulted right back to his days of being a horny teenager lacking in finesse, except he couldn't remember, even as a horny teenager, being as wildly out of control as he was now. He didn't even bother with taking off her jumper, far less his. He hooked his finger under her knickers and she completed the job of disposing of them. He could barely get it together to don protection. His hand was shaking and he swore in frustration as he ripped open the packet.

Then he took her. He hoisted her onto him and thrust into her with a grunt of pleasurable release. Hands under her buttocks, he pushed hard and heard her little cry of pleasure with intense satisfaction.

They came together, their bodies utterly united, both of them oblivious to their surroundings.

He dropped her to the ground, his breathing heavy and uncontrolled. 'Not usually my style.' But, as he watched her wriggle back into her underwear and jeans, he figured it could well become part of his repertoire without a great deal of trouble.

'You look a little hot and flustered.' He gently smoothed some tendrils of hair away from her face and Brianna added that tender gesture to the stockpile she was mentally constructing. She felt another zing of excitement when she thought back to what he had said about his plans not going quite as he had anticipated. She would have loved nothing more than to quiz him further on the subject, but she would let it rest for the moment. One thing she had learnt about him was that he was not a man who could be prodded into saying anything or doing anything unless he wanted to.

'Right—the bar. I need to get going. I need to check on Bridget.'

Plus a million and one other things that needed doing, including sticking away the stuff she had bought. All that was running through her head as a byline to the pleasurable thought of the big guy behind her admitting to wanting more than a passing fling. A nomad would one day find a place to stay put, wouldn't he? That was how it worked. And, if he didn't want to stay put *here*, then she would be prepared to follow him. She knew she would.

Her mind was a thousand miles away, so it took her a few minutes to realise that something was wrong when she entered the little lounge to check on Bridget.

She should have been in the chair by the window. It was where she always sat, looking out or reading her book. But she wasn't there. Her mind moved sluggishly as she quickly scanned the room and she saw the limp body huddled behind the chair about the same time as Leo did.

It felt like hours but in fact it could only have been a matter of seconds, and Leo was on it before her brain had really had time to crank into gear. She was aware of him gently inspecting Bridget while barking orders to her at the same time: make sure the pub was shut; fetch some water; get a blanket; bring him the telephone because his mobile phone was in his bedroom, then amending that for her to fetch his mobile phone after all.

'I'll call an ambulance!'

'Leave that to me.'

Such was his unspoken strength that it didn't occur to her to do anything but as he said. She shut the pub. Then it was upstairs to fetch his mobile phone, along with one of the spare guest blankets which she kept in the airing cupboard, only stopping en route to grab a glass of water from the kitchen.

'She's breathing,' was the first thing he said when she returned. 'So don't look so panicked.' He gestured to his phone, scrolled down and began dialling a number. She couldn't quite catch what he was saying because he had walked over to the window and was talking in a low, urgent voice, his back to her. Not that she was paying any attention. She was loosely holding Bridget, talking to her in soft murmurs while trying to assess what the damage was. It looked as though she had fallen, banged her head against the table and passed out. But, in her condition, what could be the ramifications of that?

'Right.' Leo turned to her and slipped the mobile phone into his jeans pocket. 'It's taken care of.'

'Sorry?'

'It's under control. The main thing is to keep her still. We don't know what she's broken with that fall.'

'I'm glad you said that it was a fall. That's what I thought. Surely that must be less serious than another heart attack. Is the ambulance on its way? I've made sure the "closed" sign's on the front door. When I get a chance, I'll ring round a couple of the regulars and explain the situation.'

Leo hesitated. 'No ambulance.'

Brianna looked at him, startled. 'But she's got to go to hospital!'

'Trust me when I tell you that I have things under control.' He squatted alongside them both. The time of reckoning had come and how on earth had he ever played with the thought that it wouldn't? How had he imagined that he would be able to walk away without a backward glance when the time came?

Of course, he certainly hadn't reckoned on the time coming in this fashion. He certainly hadn't thought that he would be the one rescuing his mother because it now seemed that there was more conversation left between them.

'You have things under control?' Brianna looked at him dubiously. 'And yet there's no ambulance on the way?'

'I've arranged to have her air-lifted to the Cromwell Hospital in London,' Leo said bluntly.

'I beg your pardon?'

'It should be here any minute soon. In terms of timing, it will probably get here faster than an ambulance would, even an ambulance with its sirens going.'

In the midst of trying to process what sounded like complete gibberish to her, Brianna heard the distant sound of an overhead aircraft. Landing would be no problem. In fact, there couldn't have been a better spot for an air ambulance to land. The noise grew louder and louder until it felt as though it would take the roof off the pub, and then there was a flurry of activity while she stood back, confused.

She became a mystified bystander as the professionals took over, their movements hurried and urgent, ferrying Bridget to the aircraft.

Then Leo turned to her. 'You should come.'

Brianna looked at him in complete silence. 'Leo... what's going on?' How had he managed to do *that*? Who on earth could arrange for someone to be airlifted to a hospital hundreds of, miles away? She had thought that maybe he had been in computers, but had he been in the medical field? Surely not. She was uneasily aware that there were great, big gaps in her knowledge about him but there was little time to think as she nodded and was hurried along to the waiting aircraft.

'I don't have any clothes.'

'It's not a problem.'

'What do you mean, it's *not a problem*?'

'We haven't got time to debate this. Let's go.'

Brianna's head was full of so many questions, yet something in her resisted asking any of them. Instead she said weakly, as they were lifted noisily into the air and the aircraft swung sharply away, leaving the pub behind, 'Do you think she'll be all right?' And then, with a tremulous laugh, because the detachment on his dark face filled her with a dreadful apprehension, 'I guess this would make a fantastic scene in your book...'

Leo looked at her. She was huddled against him and her open, trusting face was shadowed with anxiety.

This was a relationship that was never going to last. They had both been aware of that from the very start. He had made the position perfectly clear. So, in terms of conscience, he was surely justified in thinking that his was completely clear? But it still took a great deal of effort to grit his teeth and not succumb to a wave of unedited, pure regret for what he knew now lay on the horizon. But this wasn't the time to talk about any of this so he chose to ignore her quip about the book that was as fictitious as the Easter Bunny.

'I think she'll be fine but why take chances?'

'Leo…'

'We'll be at the hospital very shortly, Brianna.' He sighed deeply, pressed his thumbs against his eyes and then rested his head against the upright, uncomfortable seat. 'We'll talk once Bridget's settled in hospital.'

Brianna shivered as he looked away to stare out of the window but she remained silent; then there wasn't much time to do any thinking at all as everything seemed to happen at once and with impressive speed.

Once again she stood helplessly on the sidelines and watched as the machinery of the medical world took over. She had never seen anything like it and she was even more impressed at Leo's handling of the situation, the way he just seemed to take charge, the way he knew exactly what to do and the way people appeared to listen to him in a way she instinctively knew they wouldn't have to anyone else.

Like a spare part, she followed him into the hospital, which was more like a hotel than anything else, a hotel filled with doctors and nurses, somewhere designed to inspire confidence. The smallness of her life crowded her as she watched, nervously torn between wanting to get nearer to Bridget, who had now been established in a room of her own, and wanting to stay out of the way just in case she got mown down by the crisp efficiency of everyone bustling around their new patient.

It felt like ages until Bridget was examined, wheeled off for tests and examined again. Leo was in the thick of it. She, on the other hand, kept her distance and at one point was firmly ushered to a plush waiting room, gently encouraged to sit, handed a cappuccino and informed that she would help matters enormously if she just relaxed, that everything was going to be perfectly fine.

How on earth was she supposed to relax? she wondered. Not only was she worried sick, but alongside all her concerns about her friend other, more unsettling ideas were jostling in her head like pernicious, stinging insects trying to get a hold.

She was dead on her feet by the time Leo finally made an appearance and he, too, looked haggard. Brianna half-rose and he waved her back down, pulled one the chairs across and sat opposite her, legs apart, his arms resting loosely on his thighs.

More than anything else, she wanted to reach out and smooth away the tired lines around his eyes and she sat on her hands to avoid giving in to the temptation which here, and now, seemed horribly inappropriate.

'Leo, what's going on?'

'The main thing is that Bridget is going to be okay. It seems she stood up and fell as she was reaching for her cane. She banged her head against the edge of the table and knocked herself out. They've done tests to make sure that she suffered no brain damage and to ascertain that the shock didn't affect her heart.' He looked at her upturned face and flushed darkly.

'I'm amazed you rushed into action like that when she could have just gone to the local hospital.' She reached out tentatively to touch his arm and he vaulted upright and prowled through the shiny, expensive waiting room of which they were the only occupants.

'Brianna…' He paused to stare down at her and all of a sudden there was no justification whatsoever for any of the lies he had told. It didn't matter whether they had been told in good faith, whether the consequences had been unforeseen. Nor did the rights and wrongs of sleeping with the girl, now staring up at him, come into play.

'It's late. You need to get some rest. But more importantly we have to talk…'

'Yes.' Why was she so reluctant to hear what he had to say? Where was that gut reaction coming from?

'I'm going to take you back to my place.'

'I beg your pardon? You still have a place in London? What place? I thought you might have sold that—you know?—to do your travelling.'

Leo shook his head and raked his fingers through his dishevelled hair. 'I think when we get there,' he said on a heavy sigh, 'some of the questions you're asking yourself might begin to fall into place.

CHAPTER SEVEN

BRIANNA'S FIRST SHOCK was when they emerged from the hospital and Leo immediately made a call on his mobile which resulted, five minutes later, in the appearance of a top-of-the range black Range Rover. It paused and he opened the back door for her and stood aside to allow her to slide into the luxurious leather seat.

Suddenly she was seeing him in a whole new light. He was still wearing the jeans in which he had travelled, a long-sleeved jumper and one of the old coats which he had found in a cupboard at the back of the pub and which he had adopted because it was well lined. But even with this casual clothing he now seemed a different person. He was no longer the outdoor guy with that slow, sexy smile that dragged on her senses. There was a harshness to his face that she was picking up for the first time and it sent a shiver of apprehension racing up and down her spine.

The silence stretched on and on as the car slowly pulled away from the kerb and began heading into central London.

When she looked over to him, it was to quail inwardly at the sight of the forbidding cast of his features, so she pretended to be absorbed in the monotonous, crowded London landscape of pavements and buildings.

It was very late but, whereas in Ireland the night sky

would be dense and black at this hour and the countryside barely visible, here the streetlights illuminated everything. And there were people around: little groups shivering on the pavements, the odd business man in a suit and, the further towards the centre of London the car went, the busier the streets were.

Where one earth were they going? So he had a house in London. Why had he never mentioned that? Her mind scrabbled frantically to come up with some logical reason why he might have kept it a secret. Perhaps he was in the process of selling it. Everyone knew that it could take for ever to sell a property and, if he *was* selling it, then maybe he thought that there was no point mentioning it at all. But when she glanced surreptitiously at his forbidding profile, all the excuses she tried to formulate in her head withered and died.

'Where are we going? I know you said your house, but where exactly is that?'

Leo shifted and angled his body so that he was facing her. Hell, this was a total mess; he could only lay one-hundred per cent of the blame for that at his own door. He had behaved like a stupid fool and now he was about to be stuck handling the fallout.

Brianna was a simple country girl. He had known that the second he had seen her. She might have had the grit and courage to single-handedly run a pub, but emotionally she was a baby, despite her heartbreak. She was just the sort of woman he should have steered clear from, yet had he? No. He had found that curious blend of street-wise savvy and trusting naivety irresistible. He had wanted her and so he had taken her. Of course, she had jumped in to the relationship eyes wide open, yet he couldn't help but feel that the blame still lay entirely on his shoulders. He had been arrogant and selfish and those qualities, neither of which had caused him a moment's concern in the past, now disgusted him.

He harked back to his conversation with Bridget. Before it had turned to the illuminating matter of her past, she had wanted to talk to him about Brianna, had opened the subject by letting on that Brianna hadn't been involved with anyone since her loser boyfriend from university had dumped her. Leo now followed the path of that conversation which had never got off the starting blocks as it turned out.

Had she been on the brink of confiding just how deeply Brianna was involved with him?

Of course she had been! Why kid himself? He might have laid down his ground rules and told her that he was not in the market for involvement, but then he had proceeded to demonstrate quite the opposite in a hundred and one ways. He couldn't quite figure out how this had happened, but it had, and the time had come to set the matter straight.

'Knightsbridge,' he told her, already disliking himself for the explanation he would be forced to give. Less than twenty-four hours ago they had been making love, fast, furious love, her legs wrapped around him, as primitive and driven as two wild animals in heat. The memory of it threatened to sideswipe him and, totally inexplicably, he felt himself harden, felt his erection push painfully against his zip so that he had to shift a little to alleviate the ache.

'Knightsbridge. Knightsbridge as in *Harrods,* Knightsbridge?' The last time Brianna had been to London had been three years ago, and before that when she had been going out with Daniel. She would have had to be living on another planet not to know that Knightsbridge was one of the most expensive parts of London, if not the most expensive.

'That's right.' On cue, the gleaming glass building in which his duplex apartment was located rose upwards, arrogantly demanding notice, not that anyone could fail to pay attention and salute its magnificence.

He nodded towards it, a slight inclination of his head, and Brianna, following his eyes, gasped in shock.

'My apartment's there,' he told her and he watched as the colour drained away from her face and her eyes widened to huge, green saucers.

Before she could think of anything to say, the chauffeur-driven Range Rover was pulling smoothly up in front of the building and she was being ushered out of the car, as limp as a rag doll.

She barely noticed the whoosh of the lift as it carried them upwards. Nor did she take in any of her surroundings until she was finally standing in his apartment, a massive, sprawling testimony to the very best money could buy.

With her back pressed to the door, she watched as he switched on lights with a remote control and dropped blinds with another remote before turning to her with his thumbs hooked into the pockets of his jeans.

They stared at each other in silence and he finally said, the first to turn away, 'So this is where I live. There are five bedrooms. It's late; you can hit the sack now in one of them, or we can talk'

'You actually *own* this place?' Her gaze roamed from the slate flooring in the expansive hall to the white walls, the dark wood that replaced the slate and the edge of a massive canvas she could glimpse in what she assumed would be another grand space—maybe his living room.

'I own it.' He strolled through into the living area, which had been signposted by that glimpse of wall art. Following behind him, Brianna saw that it was a massive piece of abstract art and that there were several others on the walls. They provided the only glimpse of colour against a palette that was uniformly white: white walls, white rug against the dark wooden floor, white leather furniture.

'I thought you were broke.' Brianna dubiously eyed the chair to which she was being directed. She yawned and he instantly told her that she should get some rest.

'I'd prefer to find out what's going on.'

'In which case, you might need a drink.' He strolled towards a cabinet and she looked around her, only to refocus as he thrust a glass with some amber liquid into her hand.

He sat down next to her and leaned forward, cradling his drink while he took in her flushed face. He noticed that she couldn't meet his eyes and he had to steel himself against a wave of sickening emotion.

'We should never have slept together,' he delivered abruptly and Brianna's eyes shot to his.

'What do you mean?'

'I mean…' He swirled his drink round and then swallowed a long mouthful. Never had he needed a swig of alcohol more. 'When I arrived in Ballybay, it was not my intention to get involved with anyone. It was something that just seemed to happen, but it could have and should have been prevented. I blame myself entirely for that, Brianna.'

Hurt lanced through Brianna. Was this the same guy about whom she had been nurturing silly, girlish daydreams involving an improbable future? One where he stuck his hat on the door and decided to stay put, so that they could explore what they had? She felt her colour rise as mortification kicked in with a vengeance.

'And why is that?'

'Because I knew you for what you were, despite what you said. You told me that you were tough, that you weren't looking for anything committed, that you wanted nothing more from me than sex, pure and simple. I chose to believe you because I was attracted to you. I chose to ignore the voice of reason telling me that you weren't half as tough as you claimed to be.' Even now—and he could see her stiffening as she absorbed what he was saying—there was still a softness to her mouth that belied anything hard.

He found that he just couldn't remain sitting next to her. He couldn't feel the warmth she was radiating without all his thoughts going into a tailspin.

'I'm pretty tough, Leo. I've been on my own for a long time and I've managed fine.'

Leo prowled through the room, barely taking in the exquisite, breathtakingly expensive minimalist décor, and not paying a scrap of attention to the Serpentine glittering hundreds of metres in the distance, a black, broad stripe beyond the bank of trees.

'You've taken over your father's pub,' he said heavily, finishing the rest of his drink in one long gulp and dumping the glass on the low, squat table between the sofa and the chairs. It was of beaten metal and had cost the earth. 'You know how to handle hard work, but that's not what I'm talking about and we both know that. I told you from the start that I was just passing through and that hasn't changed. Not for me. I'm…I'm sorry.'

'I understood the rules, Leo.' Her cheeks were stinging and her hands didn't want to keep still. She had to grip the glass tightly to stop them from shaking. 'I just don't get…' she waved her hand to encompass the room in which they were sitting, with its floor-to-ceiling glass windows, its expensive abstract art and weirdly soulless, uncomfortable furniture '…all of this. What sort of job did you have before?'

Leo sighed and rubbed his eyes. It was late to begin this conversation. It didn't feel like the right time, but then what *would* be the right time? In the morning? The following afternoon? A not-so-distant point in the future? There *was* no right time.

'No past tense, Brianna.'

'Sorry?'

'There's no past tense. I never gave my job up.' He laughed mirthlessly at the notion of any such thing ever happening. He was defined by his work, always had been. Apart from the past few weeks, when he had played truant for the first time in his life.

'You never gave your job up…but…?'

'I run a very large and very complex network of companies, Brianna. I'm the boss. I own them. My employees report to me. That's why I can afford all of this, as well as a house in the Caribbean, an apartment in New York and another in Hong Kong. Have another sip of that drink. It'll steady your nerves. It's a lot to take in, and I'm sorry about that, but like I said I never anticipated getting in so deep… I never thought that I would have to sit here and have this conversation with you, or anyone else, for that matter.'

Brianna took a swig of the brandy he had poured for her and felt it burn her throat. She had a thousand angry questions running through her head but they were all silenced by the one, very big realisation—he had lied to her. She didn't know why, and she wasn't even sure that it mattered, because nothing could change the simple truth that he had lied. She felt numb just thinking about it.

'So you're not a writer.'

'Brianna, I'm sorry. No. The last time I did any kind of creative writing was when I was in school, and even then it had never been one of my stronger subjects.' She wasn't crying and somehow that made it all the harder. He had fired a lot of people in his time, had told aspiring employees that their aspirations were misplaced, but nothing had prepared him for what he was feeling now.

'Right.'

Unable to keep still, he sprang to his feet and began pacing the room. His thoughts veered irrationally, comparing the cold, elegant beauty of his sitting room and the warm, untidy cosiness of the tiny lounge at the back of her pub, and he was instantly angry with himself for allowing that small loss of self-control.

He had had numerous girlfriends in the past. He had always told them that commitment wasn't an option and, although quite a few had made the mistake of getting it into their heads that he might have been lying, he had never felt a moment's regret in telling the deluded ones goodbye.

'So what were you doing in Ballybay?' she asked. 'Did you just decide on the spur of the moment that you needed a break from…from the big apartment with the fancy paintings and all those companies you own? Did you think that you needed to get up close and personal with how the other half lives?'

She laughed bitterly. 'Poor Leo. What a blow to have ended up stuck in my pub with no mod cons, having to clear snow and help with the washing up. How you must have missed your flash car and designer clothes! I bet you didn't bank on having to stick around for as long as you did.'

'Sarcasm doesn't suit you.'

But he had flushed darkly and was finding it difficult to meet her fierce, accusatory green-eyed stare. 'I'm sorry,' Brianna apologised with saccharine insincerity. 'I find it really hard to be sweet and smiling when I've just discovered that the guy I've been sleeping with is a liar.'

'Which never made our passion any less incendiary.'

Her eyes tangled with his and she felt the hot, slow burn

of an unwitting arousal that made her ball her hands into angry fists. Unbelievable: her body responding to some primitive vibe that was still running between them like a live current that couldn't be switched off.

'Why did you bother to make up some stupid story about being a writer?' she flung at him. 'Why didn't you say that you were just another rich businessman who wanted to spend a few days slumming it and winding down? Why the fairy story? Was that all part of the *let's adopt a different persona*?' She kept her eyes firmly focused on his face but she was still taking in the perfection of the whole, the amazing body, the strong arms, the length of his legs. Knowing exactly what he looked like underneath the clothes didn't help. 'Well?' she persisted in the face of his silence.

'The story is a little more complex than a bid to take time out from my life here...'

'What do you mean?' She was overwhelmed by a wave of giddiness. She couldn't tear her eyes away from his face and she found that she was sitting ramrod erect, as rigid as a plank of wood, her hands positioned squarely on her knees.

'There was a reason I came to Ballybay.' Always in control of all situations, Leo scowled at the unpleasant and uncustomary sensation of finding himself on the back foot. Suddenly the clinical, expensive sophistication of his surroundings irritated the hell out of him. It was an unsuitable environment in which to be having this sort of highly personal conversation. But would 'warm and cosy' have made any difference? He had to do what he had to do. That was just the way life was. She would be hurt, but she was young and she would get over it. It wasn't as though he had made her promises he had had no intention of keeping!

He unrealistically told himself that she might even *ben-*

efit from the experience. She had not had a lover for years. He had crashed through that icy barrier and reintroduced her to normal, physical interaction between two people; had opened the door for her to move forward and get back out there in the real world, find herself a guy to settle down with...

That thought seemed spectacularly unappealing and he jettisoned it immediately. No point losing track of the moment and getting wrapped up in useless speculation and hypotheses.

'A reason?'

'I was looking for someone.' He sat heavily on the chair facing hers and, as her posture was tense and upright, so his was the exact opposite as he leaned towards her, legs wide apart, his strong forearms resting on his thighs. He could feel her hurt withdrawal from him and it did weird things to his state of mind.

'Who?'

'It might help if I told you a little bit about myself, Brianna.'

'You mean aside from the lies you've already told me?'

'The lies were necessary, or at least it seemed so at the time.'

'Lies are never necessary.'

'And that's a point we can possibly debate at a later date. For now, let me start by telling you that I was adopted at birth. It's nothing that is a state secret, but the reason I came to Ballybay is because I traced my birth mother a few years ago and I concluded that finding her was something I had to do. Not while my adoptive parents were still alive. I loved them very much; I would never have wanted to hurt them in any way.'

Brianna stared at him open-mouthed. It felt as though the connections in her brain were all backfiring so that nothing made sense any more. What on earth was he going on about? And how could he just *sit there* as though this was the most normal conversation in the world?

'You're adopted?' was all she could say weakly, because she just couldn't seem to join the dots in the conversation.

'I grew up in leafy, affluent suburbia, the only child of a couple who couldn't have children of their own. I knew from the beginning that I was adopted, and it has to be said that they gave me the sort of upbringing that most kids could only dream about.'

'But you didn't want to find your real mother until now?'

'*Real* mother is not a term I would use. And finding her would not have been appropriate had my adoptive parents still been alive. Like I said, I owe everything to them, and they would have been hurt had I announced that I was off on a journey of discovery.'

'But they're no longer alive. And so you decided to trace your...your...'

'I've had the information on the woman for years, Brianna. I simply bided my time.'

Brianna stared at him. He'd simply *bided his time*? There was something so deliberate and so controlled about that simple statement that her head reeled.

'And...and...you came to Ballybay and pretended to be someone you weren't because...?'

'Because it was smaller than I imagined,' he confessed truthfully. 'And I wanted to find out about the woman before I passed judgement.'

'You mean if you had announced yourself and told everyone why you were there...what? Your mother—sorry, your *birth* mother—would have tried to...to what?' She looked around her at the staggering, shameless testimony to his well-heeled life and then settled her eyes back on him. 'Did you think that you needed to keep your real identity a secret because if she knew how rich you were she would have tried to latch on to your money?'

Leo made an awkward, dismissive gesture with his hand. 'I don't allow people to latch on to my money,' he said flatly. 'No, I kept my identity a secret, as indeed my purpose in being there in the first place, because I wasn't sure what I would do with the information I gathered.'

'How can you talk about this with such a lack of emotion? I feel as though I'm seeing a stranger.'

Leo sat back and raked his fingers through his hair. He was being honest. In fact, he was sparing no detail when it came to telling the truth, yet he still felt like the guy wrecking Christmas by taking a gun to Santa Claus.

'A stranger you've made love to countless times,' he couldn't help but murmur in a driven undertone that belied his cool exterior. He took a deep breath and tried to fight the intrusive memory of his hands over her smooth, slender body, tracing the light sprinkling of freckles on her collarbone, the circular discs of her nipples and the soft, downy hair between her legs. She was the most naturally, openly responsive lover he had ever had. When he parted her legs to cup the moisture between them, he felt her responding one-hundred per cent to his touch. She didn't play games. She hadn't hidden how he had made her feel.

'And I wish I hadn't.' Brianna was momentarily distracted from the direction of their conversation.

'You don't mean that. Whatever you think of me now, your body was always on fire for mine!'

Again she felt that treacherous lick of desire speed along her nerve endings like an unwanted intruder bypassing all her fortifications. This was not a road she wanted to travel down, not at all. Not when everything was collapsing around her ears.

'And did you find her?' she asked tightly.

'I did,' he answered after only the briefest of hesitations.

'Who is she?'

'At the moment, she's lying in the Cromwell Hospital.'

Brianna half-stood and then fell back onto the chair as though the air had been knocked out of her lungs.

His mother was Bridget. Bridget McGuire. And all of a sudden everything began falling into place with sickening impact. Perhaps not immediately, but very quickly, he had ascertained that she knew Bridget, that she considered Bridget one of her closest friends. Try as she might, Brianna couldn't reference the time scale of this conversation. Had it happened *before* he'd decided to prolong his stay? Surely it would have?

That realisation was like a physical blow because with it came the inevitable conclusion that he had used her. He had wanted to find out about his mother and she had been an umbilical cord to information he felt he might have needed; to soften her up and raise no suspicions, he had assumed the spurious identity of a writer. When he had been sitting in front of his computer, she'd assumed that he had been working on his book. Now, as head of whatever vast empire he ran, she realised he would have been working, communicating with the outside world from the dreary isolation of a small town in Ireland he would never have deigned to visit had he not needed to.

How could she have been so stupid, so naive? She had swooned like a foolish sixteen-year-old the second she had clapped eyes on him and had had no qualms about justifying her decision to leap into bed with him.

She had been his satisfying bonus for being stuck in the boondocks.

'I didn't even know that Bridget had ever had children…

Does she know?' Her voice was flat and devoid of any expression.

That, without the tears, told him all he needed to know about her state of mind. He had brought this on himself and he wasn't going to flinch from this difficult conversation. He told himself that there had never been any notion of a long-lasting relationship with her, yet the repetition of that mantra failed to do its job, failed to make him feel any better.

'No. She doesn't.'

'And when will you tell her?'

'When I feel the time is right.'

'If you wanted to find your mother and announce yourself—if you weren't suspicious that she would try and con money out of you—then why the secrecy? Why didn't you just do us all a favour: show up in your fancy car and present yourself as the long-lost prodigal son?'

'Because I didn't know what I was going to find, but I suspected that what I found would—how shall I put this?— not be to my liking.'

'Hence all your warnings about her when I told you that she was going to be coming to the pub to stay after her bout in hospital…' Brianna said slowly, feeling the thrust of yet another dagger deep down inside her. 'You knew she was hiding a past and you assumed she was a lowlife who would end up taking advantage of me, stealing from me, even. What changed?'

Leo shrugged and Brianna rose to her feet and managed to put distance between them. For a few seconds she stared down at the eerily lit landscape below her, devoid of people, just patches of light interspersed with darkness. Then she returned to the chair and this time she forced herself to try and relax, to give him no opportunity to see just how badly she was affected by what he had said to her.

'So you were using me all along,' she said matter-of-factly. 'You came to Ballybay with a purpose, found out that it wasn't going to be as straightforward as you anticipated—because it's the kind of small place where everybody knows everybody else, so you wouldn't be able to pass unnoticed, without comment—you adopted an identity and the second you found out that I knew your mother...sorry, your *birth mother*...you decided that it would be an idea to get to know me better.'

Leo's jaw hardened. Her inexorable conclusions left a bitter taste in his mouth but he wasn't going to rail against them. What was needed here was a clean break. If she had become too involved, then what was the point in encouraging further involvement by entering into a debate on what he had meant or not meant to do?

His failure to deny or confirm her statement was almost more than Brianna could bear but she kept her voice cool and level and willed herself just to try and detach from the situation. At least here, now; later, she would release the emotion that was building inside her, piling up like water constrained by paper-thin walls, ready to burst its banks and destroy everything in its path.

She could read nothing from his expression. Where was the guy she had laughed with? Made love to? Teased? Who was this implacable stranger sitting in front of her?

How, even more fatally, could she have made such a colossal mistake again? Misjudged someone so utterly that their withdrawal came as complete shock? Except this time it was all so much worse. She had known him for a fraction of the time she had known Daniel. Yet she knew, without a shadow of a doubt, that the impact Daniel had made on her all those years ago was nothing in comparison to what she would feel when she walked away from this. How was that possible? And yet she knew that what Leo had generated inside her had reached deeper and faster and was more profound in a million ways.

'I guess you decided that sleeping with me would be a good way to get background information on Bridget. Or maybe it was just something that was given to you on a silver platter.' Bitterness crept into her voice because she knew very well that what she said was the absolute truth. He hadn't had to energise himself into trying to get her into bed. She had leapt in before he had even finished asking the question.

'We enjoyed one another, Brianna. God, never have I apologised so much and so sincerely.'

'Except I wasn't using you.' She chose to ignore his apology because, in the big picture, it was just stupid and meaningless.

'I...' *Wasn't using you?* How much of that statement could he truthfully deny? 'That doesn't detract from the fact that what we had was real.'

'Don't you mean that the *sex* we had was real? Because beyond that we didn't have anything. You were supposed to be a writer travelling through, getting inspiration.' The conversation seemed to be going round and round in circles and she couldn't see a way of leading it towards anything that could resemble a conclusion. It felt like being in a labyrinth and she began walking on wooden legs towards her coat which she had earlier dumped on one of the chairs.

'Where are you going?'

'Where do you think, Leo? I'm leaving.'

'To go where? For God's sake, Brianna, there are guest rooms galore in this apartment. Pick whichever one you want to use! This is all a shock, I get that, but you can't just run out of here with nowhere to go!' Frustration laced his words with a savage urgency that made him darken and he sprang up, took a couple of steps towards her and then stopped.

They stood staring at one another. Her open transparency, which was so much part and parcel of her personality, had been replaced by a frozen aloofness that was doing all sorts of crazy, unexpected things to his head. He was overcome with an uncontrollable desire to smash things. He turned sharply away. His head was telling him that if she wanted to go, then he should let her go, but his body was already missing the feel of hers and he was enraged with himself for being sidestepped by an emotion over which he appeared to have no control.

Brianna could sense the shift of his body away from her, even though she was trying hard not to actually look at him, and that was just a further strike of the hammer. He couldn't even look at her. She was now disposable, however much he had wanted her. He had found his mother, had had whatever conversation with her that had changed his mind about her, and now he had no further use for the woman he had taken and used.

'Well?' he demanded roughly. 'Where are you going to go at this hour? Brianna, please...'

She wanted to tell him that the last thing she could do was sleep in one of his guest bedrooms. Just the thought of him being under the same roof would have kept her up all night.

She backed towards the door. 'I'm going to go to the hospital.'

'And do *what* there, Brianna? Visiting hours are well and truly over and I don't think they'll allow overnight guests in the common area.' He felt as though he was being ripped apart. 'You have my word that I won't come near you,' he said, attempting to soften his tone. 'I'll leave the apartment, if you want. Go stay in a hotel.'

Did he think that she was scared that he might try and break down her bedroom door so that he could ravish her? Did he honestly imagine that she was foolish enough to fear any such thing after what he had said?

'You can leave or you can stay, Leo.' She gave a jerky shake of her shoulder. 'I don't honestly care. I'm going to the hospital and, no, I won't be trying to cadge a night's sleep on the sofa in the common area. I'm going to leave a letter for one of the nurses to hand to Bridget in the morning, explaining that I've had to get back to the pub.'

'And the reason for that being...?' There were shadows under her eyes. He didn't feel proud to acknowledge the fact that he had put them there. His guilty conscience refused to be reined in. 'What reason could you have for needing to rush back to the pub? Or do you intend to tell Bridget the truth about who I am?'

'I would never do that, Leo, and the fact that you would think that I might just shows how little you know me. As little, as it turns out, I know you. We were just a couple of strangers having fun for a few weeks.' Her heart constricted painfully when she said that. 'I know you think that I'm all wrapped up in you, but I'm not. I'm upset because I didn't take you for a liar and, now that I know what you are, I'm glad this is all over. Next to you, Daniel was a walk in the park!'

For several reasons, none of which she intended to divulge, this was closer to the truth than he could ever imagine and she could see from his dark flush that she had hit home. He had been fond of referring to her distant ex as one of life's great losers.

She stuck her chin up and looked him squarely in the eyes without flinching. 'After I've been to the hospital, I shall find somewhere cheap to stay until I can catch the first train out of London.'

'This isn't Ballybay! London isn't safe at night to be wandering around in search of cheap hotels!'

'I'll take my chances!' Of course he would see no problem with her sleeping in his apartment, she thought with punishing reality. She meant nothing to him, so why on earth would he be affected by her presence? And, if that were the case, then wouldn't it be the same for her? 'And when I leave here I never, ever want to see you again.'

CHAPTER EIGHT

'DIDN'T THIS OCCUR to you at all, Miss Sullivan?'

Her doctor looked at her with the sort of expression that implied this was a conversation he had had many times before. Possibly, however, not with someone who was unmarried. Unmarried and pregnant in these parts was a rare occurrence.

Her head was swimming. It had been over a month since she had walked out of Leo's life for ever and in the interim she had heard not a word from him, although she had heard *about* him, thanks to Bridget, who emailed her regularly with updates on the joys of finding her long-lost son.

Bridget had remained in London in his apartment, where she had all the benefits of round-the-clock care and help courtesy of a man who had limitless funds. She hadn't even needed to fetch any of her clothes, as she was now the fortunate recipient of a brand-new wardrobe.

On all fronts, he was the golden child she thought she had lost for ever.

In between these golden tributes, Brianna never managed to get any answers to the questions she *really* wanted to ask, such as did he ever talk about her? Was he missing her? Was there someone else in his life?

And now *this*.

'No, not really.' Brianna found that she could barely

enunciate the words. Pregnant. They had been so careful. Aside from that one time... She resisted the temptation to put her hand on her still flat stomach. 'I...I didn't even notice that I'd skipped a period...' Because she had been so wrapped up thinking about him, missing him, wishing he was still around. So busy functioning on autopilot that she had missed the really big, life-altering thing happening.

'And what will you do now, Brianna?

Brianna looked at the kindly old man who had delivered her and pretty much everyone her age in Ballybay and beyond.

'I'm going to have this baby, Dr Fallow, and I shall be a very proud, single mother.' She stuck her chin up defiantly and he smiled at her.

'I would have expected nothing less from Annie Sullivan's daughter. And the father?'

And the father...?

The question plagued her over the next few days. He deserved to know. Or did he? He had used her and then dispatched her once her usefulness was at an end. Did a man like that deserve to know that she was having his baby? He had been ultra-careful with precautions. How ironic that despite the best laid plans—because of a split condom, a one-in-a-million chance—here she was, the exception to the rule. And a cruel exception, because having a baby was not on his agenda, least of all with a woman he had used. So what would be his reaction should she show up on his doorstep with the happy news that he was going to be a daddy? She shuddered when she thought of it: horror, rage, shock. And, although there was no way he could blame her, he would still be upset and enraged that fate had dealt him a blow he couldn't deal with.

Yet, how could she *not* tell him? Especially given the circumstances of his adoption? Would he appreciate being left in the dark about his own flesh and blood? Perhaps finding out at some much later date down the road, and being destined forever to imagine that his son or daughter had grown up thinking of him as someone who had not taken enough interest to make contact? Being left in the awful position of wondering whether his own life story had been repeated, except without him even being aware of it?

The pros and cons ran through her head like a constant refrain, although beneath that refrain the one consolation was that she was in no doubt that she was happy about the pregnancy, however much it would disrupt her way of life. In fact, she was ecstatic. She had not thought about babies, having had no guy in her life with whom to have them. And, although she couldn't have chosen a less suitable candidate for the role of father, she was filled with a sense of joyous wonder at the life slowly growing inside her.

A life which would soon become apparent; pregnancy was not a condition that could be kept secret. Within a month or two, she would be the talk of the town, and of course Bridget would know. How could she fail to?

Which pretty much concluded her agonising. Leo would find out and she would have to be the one to tell him before he heard it second-hand.

It seemed the sort of conversation to be held in the evening and, before the bustle of the pub could begin, sweeping her off her feet, she got on the phone and dialled his mobile.

Around her, the pub lacked its usual shine and polish. She would have to start thinking about getting someone in to cover for her on a fairly permanent basis. There was no way she and Shannon could cope but there was also no way she could afford to close the pub, far less find a buyer for it.

Money, she foresaw, was going to be a headache and she

gritted her teeth together because she knew what Leo's solution would be: fling money at the problem. Which would leave her continually indebted to him and that was not a situation that filled her with joy.

But then, she would never, ever be able to break contact with him from here on in, would she?

Even if he just paid the occasional visit in between running those companies of his, he would still be a permanent cloud on her horizon. She would have to look forward to seeing him moving on, finding other women, other women to whom he hadn't fabricated a convoluted story about himself. Eventually, she would have to witness his happiness as he found his soul mate, married her, had children with her. It didn't bear thinking about.

His disembodied voice, deep, dark and lazy, jolted her out of her daydreaming and fired up every nerve in her body. All at once, she could picture him in every vivid, unsettling detail: the way he used to look at her, half-brooding, full of sexy promise; the way he used to laugh whenever she teased him; the way the muscles of his amazing body rippled and flexed when he moved...

'It's me,' she said a little breathlessly, before clearing her throat and telling herself to get a grip.

'I know who it is, Brianna,' Leo drawled. He rose to shut his office door. She had caught him as he had been about to leave. Ever since his mother had arrived on the scene and was recuperating happily at his apartment, he had been leaving work earlier than normal. It was a change of pattern he could not have foreseen in a million years, but he was strangely energised by getting to know his mother a little better. She could never replace the couple who had adopted him, but she was a person in her own right, and one he found he wanted to get to know. It seemed that a genetic link was far more powerful a bond than he could ever have conceived possible.

He thought back to that moment when he had sat next to her at her hospital bed and taken her hand in his. An awkward moment and one he had never envisaged but as she had lain there, frail and bewildered at her expensive private room, it had seemed right.

And he had told her—haltingly at first, trying to find the words to span over thirty years. He had watched her eyes fill up and had felt the way her hand had trembled. He had never expected his journey to take him there and he had been shocked at how much it had changed his way of thinking, had made him see the shades of grey between the black and white. No one could ever replace the wonderful parents he had had, but a new road had opened up—not better, but different—and he had felt a soaring sense of fulfilment at what lay ahead. He had known that they both did.

For a man who had always known the way ahead, he had discovered the wonder of finding himself on a path with no signposts, just his feelings to guide him, and as he had opened up to his mother, asked her questions, replied to the hundreds she had asked him in return, he had turned a corner. The unknown had become something to be embraced.

'How's Bridget?'

'I thought you spoke and emailed daily?' He sat back down at his desk and swivelled his chair so that it was facing the broad floor-to-ceiling glass panes that overlooked the city.

'Why are you calling?' It had been more of a struggle putting her behind him than he could ever have believed possible. Was it because Bridget was staying with him? Because her presence kept alive memories he wanted to bury? He didn't know. Whilst his head did all the right things and told him that she no longer had a place in his life—that what they'd had had been good but it had never been destined to last—some irrational part of him insisted on singing a different tune.

He had found his concentration inexplicably flagging in the middle of meetings. On more than one occasion, he had awoken from a dream-filled sleep to find himself with an erection. Cold showers were becoming the rule rather than the exception. All told, he felt as though he was in unchartered territory. He was taking new steps with his mother and discovering that old ways of dealing with exes did not apply to Brianna.

He knew that she and Bridget were in touch by phone daily and it took every ounce of willpower not to indulge his rampant curiosity and try to prise information out of his house guest. What was she up to? Had she found a replacement for him in her bed? There was no denying that she was hot; what man wouldn't want to try his luck? And she was no longer cocooned within those glacial walls of celibacy. She had stepped out from behind them and released all the unbelievable passion he knew her to be capable of. There was no way that she could ever return to living life like a nun. And, however much she had or hadn't been wrapped up in him, she was ripe for a rebound relationship.

Was that what she was doing right now—engaging in wild sex with some loser from the town or another passing stranger?

He had never considered himself someone who was prone to flights of fancy, but he was making up for lost time now.

All of this introduced a level of coolness to his voice as he stared out of the window and waited for her to come up with an answer.

She damn well wasn't phoning for an update on Bridget, so why was she?

Brianna picked up the unwelcoming indifference in his voice and it stung. Had he *completely* detached from her? How was that possible? And how was he going to greet what she had to tell him, were that the case?

'I…I…need to talk to you.'

'I'm listening. But make it quick. I was on my way out.'

'I need to see you…to discuss what I have to say.'

'Why?'

'Can't you be just a little more polite, Leo? I know you have no further use for me, but the least you can do is not treat me as though I'm something the cat dragged in.'

'Is it money?' His anger at himself for continuing to let her infiltrate his head and ambush his thoughts transferred into a healthy anger towards her and, although he knew he was being unfair, there was no way he was going to allow himself to be dragged down the apology route.

'I beg your pardon?'

'You know how rich I am now. You must know the life-style Bridget's enjoying—I'm sure she's told you so. Have you decided that you'd like me to throw some money in your direction for old times' sake?' God, was this *him*? He barely recognised the person behind the words.

Brianna clutched the phone so tightly that she thought she might break it in two. Did he know how insulting he was being right now? Did he care? How could she have misread someone so utterly? Was there some crazy missing connection in her head that allowed her to give everyone the benefit of the doubt, including people who were just bad for her health?

'You mentioned more than once that the place needed updating: new bar stools, new paint job on the outside, less tatty sofas in front of the fire…' The sofas had been damn near perfect, he seemed to recall. The sort of sofas a person could sink into and remain sunk in for hours, remain sunk in for a lifetime. 'Consider it done. On me. Call it thanks for, well, everything'

'How generous of you, Leo.' She reined in her explosive rage and kept her voice as neutral as she possibly could. 'And I suppose this might eventually have something to do with money. But I really need to see you face to face to talk about it.'

Perversely, Leo was disappointed that he had hit the nail on the head. Other women played the money angle. Other women assessed his wealth and expected a good time at his expense. It had never bothered him because, after all, fair's fair. But Brianna... She wasn't like other women. Apparently, however, she was.

'Name the figure,' he said curtly.

'I'd rather not. If you could just make an appointment to see me. I could come to London and take the opportunity to look in on Bridget as well...'

'I have no free time during the day. I could see you tomorrow some time after six thirty, and I'm doing you a favour because that would involve cancelling a conference call.'

'Er...' Money she knew she didn't have disappeared through the window at the prospect of finding somewhere to stay, because there was no way she would be staying at his apartment, especially after she had dropped her bombshell.

'Take it or leave it.' He cut into her indecisive silence. 'I can meet you at seven at a bistro near my office.' He named it and then, from nowhere, pictured her sitting there at one of the tables, waiting for him. He pictured her face, her startling prettiness; he pictured her body, which would doubtless be concealed underneath something truly unappealing—that waterproof coat of hers of indeterminate green which she seemed to wear everywhere.

On cue, his body jerked into life, sourly reminding him of the way just thinking of her could manage to turn him on.

Tomorrow, he resolved, he would rifle through his address book and see whether there wasn't someone he could date, if only as a distraction. Bridget, oddly, had not referred back to that aborted conversation she had had with him at the pub, had made no mention of Brianna at all. She would think there was nothing amiss were he to start dating. In fact, she would think something was amiss if he *didn't*.

'Well?' he said impatiently. 'Will you be there? This is a going, going, gone situation.'

'I'll be there. See you tomorrow.'

Brianna barely slept through the night. She was having a baby! Unplanned, unexpected, but certainly not unwanted.

She was on edge as she finally landed on English soil. The weather had taken a turn for the better but, to be on the safe side, she had still decided to wear her faithful old coat just in case. The deeper into the city she got, the more ridiculously out of place she felt in her clothing. Even at nearly seven in the evening, the streets were packed. Everyone appeared to be dressed in suits, carrying briefcases and in a massive rush.

She had given the address of the bistro to the taxi driver but, when she was dropped off, she remained outside on the pavement, her battered pull-along in one hand, her other hand shoved into the capacious pocket of her coat. Nerves threatened to overwhelm her. In fact, she wanted nothing more than to hop into the nearest taxi and ask it to deliver her right back to the airport.

There were people coming and going from the bistro. She stood to one side, shaking like a leaf, aware of the pathetic figure she cut, and then she took a deep breath and entered with all the trepidation of someone entering a lion's den.

The noise was deafening, exaggerated by the starkness of the surroundings and the wooden floor. It was teeming with people, all young, all beautiful. A young woman clacking along in her high heels, with a leather case clutched to her side, tripped over her pull-along and swore profusely before giving her the once-over with contempt.

'Oh God, darling, are you lost? In case you haven't noticed, this isn't the bus station. If you and your luggage take a left out of the door and keep walking, you both should hit the nearest bus stop and they can deliver you wherever you're going.'

Brianna backed away, speechless, and looked around desperately for Leo. Right now, he felt like the only safe port in a storm and she spotted him tucked away towards the back of the room, sitting at a table and nursing a drink. A wave of relief washed over her as she began threading her way towards him, her pull-along bumping into ankles and calves and incurring a trail of oaths on the way.

Leo watched her zig-zag approach with brooding intensity. Amongst the city folk, snappily dressed and all braying in loud voices that competed to be heard, she was as natural and as beautiful as a wild flower. He couldn't fail to notice the sidelong looks she garnered from some of the men and he quickly knocked back the remainder of his whisky in one gulp.

So she had come here on her begging mission. He would have to do a bit better than stare at her and make favourable comparisons between her and the rest of the overpaid, over-confident, over-arrogant crowd on show. He signalled to a waiter to bring him another drink. It was a perk of this bar that he was the only one to receive waiter service, but then again, had it not been for his injection of cash years previously, the place would have been run into the ground. Now he owned a stake in it and, as soon as he clicked his fingers, the staff jumped to attention. It certainly saved the tedium of queuing at the bar trying to vie for attention. It also secured him the best table in the house, marginally away from the crowds.

'I'm sorry I'm a little late.' Brianna found that she could barely look at him without her entire nervous system gathering pace and going into overdrive. How had she managed to forget the impact he had on her senses? The way those dark, dark eyes could make her head swim and scramble her thoughts until she could barely speak?

'Sit.' He motioned to the chair facing him with a curt nod and she sank onto it and pulled her little bag alongside her. 'So…' He leant back and folded his arms. She was pink and her hair, which had obviously started the trip as a single braid down her back, was in the process of unravelling.

'I hadn't expected so much noise.' Her eyes skittered away from his face but then returned to look at him with resolve. She had to forget about being out of her depth. She had come here for one reason and one reason only and she wasn't going to let an attack of nerves stand in her way. How much more could he hurt her?

Leo cast a cursory glance around him and asked her what she wanted to drink: a glass of water. He would have expected something a little more stiff to get her through her 'begging bowl' speech, but to each their own. He ordered some mineral water and another stiff drink for himself then settled back with an air of palpable boredom.

Something in him railed against believing the worst of

her, knowing her to be the person that she was, yet he refused to give house room to that voice. He felt he needed to be black and white or else forever be lost. Let it not be forgotten that she had refused to listen to him when he had attempted to explain the reason for his fabrications. She had turned her back and stalked off and for the past month he had seen and heard nothing from her.

She had taken off her coat, the gruesome coat which he was annoyed to discover made inroads into his indifference, because he could remember teasing her that she needed something a little less worn, that waterproof coats like that were never fashion statements.

'What's it like?' Brianna opened the conversation with something as far removed from what she actually needed to say as she could get, and Leo shot her a perplexed glance.

'What's what like? What are you talking about?'

'Having your… Having Bridget in your life. It must be very satisfying for you.'

Leo flushed. No one knew about Bridget, aside from Harry. He had never been the sort of man who spilled his guts to all and sundry and there had been absolutely no temptation to tell anyone about his mother living with him. He had not been dating, so there had been no women coming to his apartment, asking questions. Even if there had been, it was debatable whether he would have confided in any of them or not. He looked at her open, upturned face and found it hard to resurrect his cynicism.

'It's working for me,' he said gruffly. Working for them both. The years had dropped off his mother. She had been to the hairdresser, had her hair styled, had her nails done… She bore little resemblance to the fragile creature he had first set eyes on.

Drinks were brought and he sat back to allow the waiter to fuss as he put them on the table, along with a plate of appetisers which had not been ordered. 'But you didn't come here to talk about my relationship with Bridget.'

'No, I didn't, but I'm interested.' She just couldn't launch into her real reason for coming to London without some sort of preamble.

And, an inner voice whispered, didn't she just want to prolong being in his company, like a thief stealing time that didn't belong to them? Didn't she just want to breathe him in, that clean, masculine scent, and slide her eyes over a body she knew so well even when, as now, it was sheathed in the finest tailored suit money could buy?

'Just tell me why you're here, Brianna. You said something about money. How much are you looking for?'

'It's a bit more complicated than that.'

'What's more complicated than asking for a hand-out?'

Brianna looked down and fiddled with the bottle of water before pouring a little more into her glass. She envied him his stiff drink. She felt that under different circumstances, without this baby inside her, she could have done with a little Dutch courage.

'Leo…' She looked him directly in the eye and felt that this was the last time that she would be seeing him like this: a free man who could do whatever he wanted to do. She could even appreciate that, however dismissive he was of her now, it was an emotion that would soon be overtaken by far more overwhelming ones. Perhaps, thinking about it, it was just as well that they were having this conversation somewhere noisy and crowded.

'I'm pregnant.'

For a few seconds, Leo thought that he might have misheard her, but even as his mind was absorbing her body language—taking in the way she now couldn't meet his eyes, the hectic flush on her cheeks, the way her hand was trembling on the glass—he still couldn't put two and two together.

'Come again?' He leaned forward, straining to catch her every word. There was a buzzing in his ears that was growing louder by the second.

'I'm having a baby, Leo. Your baby. I'm sorry. I do realise that this is probably the last thing in the world you expected to hear, and the last thing you *wanted* to hear, but I felt you ought to know. I did think about keeping it to myself but that would have been impossible. Well, you know how small the place is, and sooner or later Bridget would have found out. In fact, there's no way that I would have wanted to keep it from her.'

Why wasn't he saying anything? She had expected more of an immediate and explosive reaction, but then he was probably still in a state of shock.

'You're telling me that you're having my baby.' The words felt odd as they passed his lips. The thought had taken root now with blinding clarity and he looked down at her stomach. She was as slender as she had always been. He heard himself asking questions: how pregnant was she? Was she absolutely certain? Had it been verified by a doctor? He knew home tests existed but any test that could be done at home would always be open to error...

'I'm not expecting anything from you,' Brianna ended. 'I just thought that you ought to know.'

'You thought that *I ought to know*?' Leo shot her a look of utter incredulity. The impersonal bistro he had chosen now seemed inappropriate. Restless energy was pouring through his body and, as fast as he tried to decipher a pattern to what he was thinking, his thoughts came unstuck, leaving him with just the explosive realisation that in a matter of months he was going to be a father.

'I realise that you might want to have some input...'

'You have got to be kidding me, Brianna. You come here, drop this bombshell on me, and the only two things you can find to say are that you felt I *ought to know* and you realise that I *might want some input*? We have to get out of here.'

'And go where?' she cried.

'Somewhere a little less *full of chattering morons.*'

'I'm not going to your apartment,' she said, refusing to budge and clutching the sides of her chair as though fearful that at any moment he might just get it into his head to bodily pick her up and haul her over his shoulder to the front door, caveman style.

'I haven't said anything to Bridget yet and I'd rather not just at the moment. I...I need time to absorb it all myself so, if you don't mind, I'd quite like to stay here. Not that there's much more for me to bring to the table.'

'And another classic line from you. God, I just don't believe this.'

Brianna watched as he dropped his head to his hands. 'I'm so sorry to be the bearer of unexpected tidings. Like I said, though...'

'Spare me whatever pearls of wisdom are going to emerge from your mouth, Brianna.' He raised his head to stare at her. 'It is as it is, and now we're going to have to decide how we deal with this situation.' He rubbed his eyes and continued holding her gaze with his.

'Perhaps you should go away and think about this. It's a lot to take on board. We could fix a time to meet again.'

'I don't think so.' He straightened and sat back. 'Waiting for another day isn't going to alter this problem.'

Brianna stiffened. 'This isn't your problem, it's mine, and I don't see it as a *problem*. I'm going to be the one having the baby and I shall be the one looking after it. I recognise that you'll want to contribute in some way, but let me assure you that I expect nothing from you.'

'Do you honestly believe that you can dump this on me and I'm going to walk away from it?'

'I don't know. A few weeks ago I would have said that the guy at the pub who helped clear snow wouldn't, but then you weren't that guy at all, were you? So, honestly? I have no idea.' She sat on her hands and leaned towards him. 'If you want to contribute financially, then that would be fine and much appreciated. I don't expect you to give anything to me, but helping to meet the needs of the baby would be okay. They may be small, but they can be very expensive, and you know all too well what the finances at the pub are like. Especially with all the closures of late.'

'I know what you think of me, Brianna, but I'm not a man to run away from my responsibilities—and in this instance my responsibilities don't stop at sending you a monthly cheque to cover baby food.'

'They don't?' Brianna queried uneasily. She wondered what else he had in mind. 'Naturally you would be free to see your child whenever you wanted, but it might be difficult, considering you live in London...' She quailed inwardly at the prospect of him turning up at the front door. She wondered whether the onslaught of times remembered, before she had discovered who he really was, would be just too much for her. Not that she would have any choice. It would be his right to visit his child, whether it made her uncomfortable or not.

'Visiting rights? No, I don't think so.'

'I won't let you take custody of my baby.'

'*Our* baby,' he corrected.

Brianna blanched as her worst imaginings went into free fall. She hadn't even thought that he might want to take the baby away from her, yet, why hadn't that occurred to her? He was adopted. He would have very strong feelings about being on hand as a father because his own real father had not been on hand. And, whatever concoctions he had come up with to disguise his true identity, she knew instinctively that he possessed a core of inner integrity.

And those concoctions, she was reluctantly forced to conclude, had not been fabricated for the sheer hell of it. They had been done for a reason and, once he had embarked on that road, it would have been difficult to get off it.

Would that core of integrity propel him to try and fight her for custody of the baby? He was rolling in money whilst she was borderline broke and, when it came to getting results, the guy who was rolling in money was always going to win hands down over the woman who was borderline broke. You didn't need a degree in quantum physics to work that one out.

'You can stop looking as though you're about to pass out, Brianna. I have no intention of indulging in a protracted battle with you to take custody of our baby.' He was slightly surprised at how naturally the words 'our baby' rolled off his tongue. The shock appeared to have worn off far more quickly than might have been expected, but then he prided himself as being the sort of guy who could roll with the punches and come up with solutions in the tightest of spots.

Brianna breathed a sigh of relief. 'So what are you proposing?'

'We get married. Obvious solution.'

'You have got to be joking.'

'Do I look like someone about to burst into laughter?'

'That's a crazy idea.'

'Explain why.'

'Because it's not a solution, Leo. Two people don't just

get married because, accidentally, there's a baby on the way. Two people who *broke up*. Two people who wouldn't have laid eyes on one another again were it not for the fact that the girl in question happens to find herself pregnant.'

'Brianna, I'm not prepared to take a backseat in the upbringing of my child. I'm not prepared for any child of mine to ever think that they got less of me than they might have wanted.'

'I'm not asking you to take a back seat in anything.'

'Nor,' Leo continued, overriding her interruption as though it hadn't registered, 'am I willing to watch on the sidelines as you find yourself another man who decides to take over the upbringing of my child.'

'That's not likely to happen! I think I've had enough of men to last a lifetime.'

'Of course, you'll have to move to London, but in all events that won't depend on the sale of the pub. In fact, you can hand it over to someone else to run on your behalf.'

'Are you listening to a *word* I'm saying?'

'Are you listening to what *I'm* saying?' he said softly. 'I hope so, because the proposal I've put on the table is the only solution at hand.'

'This isn't a maths problem that needs a solution. This is something completely different.'

'I'm failing to see your objections, aside from a selfish need to put yourself ahead of our child.'

'I could never live in London. And I could never marry someone for the wrong reasons. We would end up resenting one another and that would be the worst possible atmosphere in which to raise a child. Don't you see that?'

'Before you knew who I was,' Leo said tautly, his dark eyes fixed intently on her face, 'did you hope that our relationship would go further?'

He sat forward and all of a sudden her space was invaded and she could barely breathe. 'I knew that you weren't intending on hanging around,' she said and she could hear the choked breathlessness in her voice. 'You said so. You made that perfectly clear.'

'Which doesn't answer my question. Were you hoping for more?'

'I didn't think it would end the way it did,' she threw back at him with bristling defiance.

'But it did, and you may not have liked the way it ended, but what we had...' He watched the slow colour creep up her cheeks and a rush of satisfaction poured through him, because behind those lowered eyes he could *smell* the impact he still had on her.

'This wouldn't be a marriage in name only for the sake of a child. This would be a marriage in every sense of the word because—let's not kid each other—what we had was good.' Her naked, pale body flashed through his mind, as did the memory of all those little whimpering noises she made when he touched her, the way her nostrils flared and her eyelids quivered as her body gathered pace and hurtled towards orgasm. He already felt himself harden at the thought and this time he didn't try to kill it at source because it was inappropriate given she was no longer part of his life. She was a part of his life now, once again, and the freedom to think of her without restraint was a powerful kick to his system.

'What we had was...was...'

'Was good and you know it. Shall I remind you how good it was?' He didn't give her time to move or time even to think about what was coming. He leant across the small table, cupped his hand on the nape of her neck and pulled her towards him.

Brianna's body responded with the knee-jerk response of immediate reaction, as though responding with learned behaviour. Her mouth parted and the feel his tongue thrusting against her was as heady as the most powerful drug. Her mind emptied and she kissed him back, and she felt as though she never wanted the kiss to end. The coolness of his withdrawal, leaving her with her mouth still slightly parted and her eyes half-closed, was a horrifying return to reality.

'Point proven,' he murmured softly. 'So, when I tell you that you need to look outside the box and start seeing the upsides to my proposal, you know what I'm talking about. This won't be a union without one or two definite bonuses.'

'I'll never move to London and I'll never marry you.' Her breathing was only now returning to normal and the mortification of what she had done, of how her treacherous body had *betrayed* her, felt like acid running through her veins. 'I'm going now but I'll give you a call in a couple of days. When you're ready to accept what I've said, then we'll talk again.' She stood up on wobbly legs and turned her back. The urge to run away as fast as she could was overpowering, and she did. Out to the pavement, where she hailed the nearest taxi and instructed him to drive her to a hotel—something cheap, something close to the airport.

She wouldn't marry him. He didn't love her and there was no way that she would ever accept sacrificing both their lives for the wrong reason, whatever he said about the bonus of good sex. Good sex would die and then where would they be?

But she had to get away because she knew that there was something craven and weak in the very deepest part of her that might *just* play with the idea.

And there was no way she was going to give that weak, craven part of her a voice.

CHAPTER NINE

LEO LOOKED AT the sprawling house facing him and immediately wondered whether he had gone for the wrong thing. Too big, maybe? Too ostentatious? Too much land?

He shook his head with frustration and fired a couple of questions at the estate agent without bothering to glance in her direction.

In the space of six weeks, this was the eighth property he had personally seen out in the rolling Berkshire countryside, sufficiently far away from London to promote the idea of clean air, whilst being within easy commuting distance from the city.

Brianna had no idea that he was even hunting down a house. As far as she was concerned, he was the guy she'd refused to commit to who seemed intent on pursuing her even though she had already given him her answer—again and again and again, in varying formats, but all conveying the same message.

No thank you, I won't be getting married to you.

On the upside, he had managed to persuade her temporarily to move to London, although that in itself had been a task of no small order. She had refused to budge, had informed him that he was wasting his time, that they weren't living in the Victorian ages. She had folded her arms, given him a gimlet stare of pure stubbornness. He had been reduced to deviating from his intention to get what he wanted—what was *needed*, at all costs—in favour of thinking creatively.

For starters, he had had to pursue her to Ireland because she'd refused to continue her conversation with him in London. And then, he had had to travel to the pub to see her, because she didn't want him staying under her roof, not given the circumstances. He had refrained from pointing out the saying about horses bolting and stable doors. He had initiated his process of getting what he wanted by pointing out that it made sense.

He had done that over the finest meal to be had in a really very good restaurant not a million miles away from the pub. He had used every argument in the book and had got precisely nowhere. Then he had returned, this time to try and persuade her to see his point of view during a bracing walk by one of the lakes with the wind whipping his hair into disarray and his mega-expensive coat proving no match for the cold. He had tried to remind her of the sexual chemistry that was still there between them, but had cut short that line of argument when she'd threatened to walk back to the pub without him.

He had informed her that there wasn't a single woman alive who wouldn't have chewed off his arm to accept an offer of marriage from him, which had been another tactical error.

He had dropped all talk of anything and concentrated on just making her feel comfortable in his presence, whilst marvelling that she could carry on keeping him at arm's length, considering how close they had been. But by this point he had been clued up enough to make sure that he didn't hark back to the past. Nothing to remind her about how much she clearly loathed him, having found out about his lies.

Never in his life had Leo put this much effort into one woman.

And never in his life had he had so many cold showers. From having given no thought whatsoever to settling down, far less having a child, he now seemed fixated by the baby growing inside her and, the more fixated he became, the more determined he was that she would marry him. He was turned on by everything about her. Turned on by the way she moved, the way she looked at him, by all her little gestures that seemed ingrained inside his head so that, even when she wasn't around, he was thinking about her constantly.

Was it a case of the inaccessible becoming more and more desirable? Was it because she was now carrying his baby that his body seemed to be on fire for her all the time? Or was it just that he hadn't stopped wanting her because it had been a highly physical relationship that had not been given the opportunity of dying a natural death?

He didn't know and he didn't bother analysing it. He just knew that he still wanted her more than he could remember wanting anyone. He wanted her to be his. The thought of some other man stepping into his shoes, doing clever things behind the bar of the pub and having a say in his child's welfare, made him grit his teeth together in impotent rage.

The estate agent, a simpering woman in her thirties, was saying something about the number of bedrooms and Leo scowled.

'How many?'

'Eight! Perfect for having the family over!'

'Too many. And I can look at it from here and see straight away that it would be far too big for the person I have in mind.'

'Perhaps the lucky lady would like to pop along and have a look for herself? It's really rather grand inside...'

Leo flinched at the word 'grand'. He pictured Brianna wiping the bar with a cloth, standing back in her old jeans and sloppy jumper to survey her handiwork, before retiring to the comfy sofa in the lounge which had been with her practically since she'd been a kid. She wouldn't have a clue what to do with 'grand' and he had a gut feeling that if he settled on anything like this she would end up blaming him.

How, he thought as house number nine bit the dust, had he managed to end up with the one woman in the world to whom a marriage proposal was an insult and who was determined to fight him every inch of the way? Even though the air sizzled between them with a raw, elemental electricity that neither of them could deny.

But at least he had managed to get her to London. It was a comforting thought as his Ferrari ate up the miles back to the city centre and his penthouse apartment.

He had appealed to her sense of fairness. He wanted to be there while she was pregnant and what better way than for her to move to London? No need to live in his apartment. He would find somewhere else for her, somewhere less central. It would be great for Bridget as well. Indeed, it would be a blessing in disguise, for Bridget was tiring of the concrete jungle of inner London. She was back on her feet, albeit in a restricted way, and the constant crowds terrified her. They could share something small but cosy in West London. He would personally see to it that a manager was located for the pub...

She had acquiesced. That had been ten days ago and, although he had made sure to visit them both every evening after work, he had ostensibly dropped all mention of marriage.

That aggressive need to conquer had been forced into retreat and he was now playing a waiting game. He wasn't sure what would happen if that waiting game didn't work and he preferred not to dwell on that. Instead, he phoned his secretary and found out what other gems were available on the property market in picturesque Berkshire.

'Too impressive,' he told her about his last failed viewing. It was added to all the other too 'something or other' that had characterised the last eight viewings, all of which had come to nothing. He laughed when she suggested that he send someone in his place to at least narrow the possibilities.

He couldn't imagine anyone he knew having the slightest idea as to what to look for when it came to Brianna. They were people who only knew a London crowd, socialites for whom there could be nothing that could ever be too grand.

'Find me some more properties.' He concluded his conversation with his long-suffering PA. 'And forget about the marble bathrooms and indoor swimming pools. Go smaller.'

He hung up. It wasn't yet two-thirty in the afternoon. He had never taken this much time off work in his life before. Except for when he had voluntarily marooned himself at Brianna's pub. And yet, he was driven to continue his search. Work, meetings and deals would just have to take a back seat.

His secretary called him on his mobile just as he was leaving the M25, heading into London.

'It's a small village near, er, Sunningdale. Er, shall I read you the details? It's just on the market. Today, in fact. Thank goodness for estate agents who remember we exist…'

Leo thought that most estate agents would remember

any client for whom money was no object. 'I'll check that out now.' He was already halfway back to London but he manoeuvred his car off the motorway and back out. 'Cancel my five o'clock meeting.'

'You've already cancelled Sir Hawkes twice.'

'In that case, let Reynolds cover. He's paid enough; a little delegation in his direction will do him the world of good.'

He made it to the small village in good time and, the very second he saw the picture-postcard cottage with the sprawling garden in the back and the white picket fence at the front, he knew he had hit the jackpot.

He didn't bother with an offer. He would pay the full asking price and came with cash in hand. The estate agent couldn't believe his luck. Leo waved aside the man's ingratiating and frankly irritating bowing and scraping and elicited all the pertinent details he needed for an immediate purchase.

'And if the occupants need time to find somewhere else, you can tell them that they'll be generously compensated over and beyond what they want for the house to leave immediately.' He named a figure and the estate agent practically swooned. 'Here's my card. Call me in an hour and we'll get the ball rolling. Oh, and I'll be bringing someone round tomorrow, if not sooner, to look at it. Make sure it's available.' He was at his car and the rotund estate agent was dithering behind him, clutching the business card as though it were a gold ingot.

'What if…?' He cleared his throat anxiously as he was forced to contemplate a possible hitch in clinching his commission. 'What if the sellers want to wait and see if a better offer comes along?'

About to slide into the driving seat, Leo paused and

looked at the much shorter man with a wry expression. 'Oh, trust me, that won't be happening.'

'Sir...'

'Call me——and I'll be expecting a conversation that I want to hear.' He left the man staring at him red-faced, perspiring and doubtless contemplating the sickening prospect of sellers who might prove too greedy to accept the quick sale.

Leo knew better. They simply wouldn't be able to believe their luck.

He could easily have made it back to the office to catch the tail end of the meeting he had cancelled at the last minute. Instead, he headed directly to Brianna's house, which was an effortless drive off the motorway and into London suburbia.

Brianna heard the low growl of the Ferrari as it pulled up outside the house. It seemed her ears were attuned to the sound. She immediately schooled her expression into one of polite aloofness. In the kitchen Bridget was making them both a cup of tea, fussing as she always seemed to do now, clucking around her like a mother hen because she was pregnant, even though Brianna constantly told her that pregnancy wasn't an illness and that Bridget was the one in need of looking after.

'He's early this evening!' Bridget exclaimed with pleasure. 'I wonder why? I think I'll give you two a little time together and have a nice, long bath. The doctor says that I should take it easy. You know that.'

Brianna raised her eyebrows wryly and stood up. 'I don't think chatting counts as not taking it easy,' she pointed out. 'Besides, you know Leo enjoys seeing you when he gets here.' Every time she saw them together, she felt a lump of emotion gather at the back of her throat. However cut-throat and ruthless he might be, and however much of a lying bastard he had been, he was always gentle with Bridget. He didn't call her 'Mum' but he treated her with the respect and consideration any mother would expect from her child. And they spoke of all the inconsequential things that happened on a daily basis. Perhaps they had explored the past already and neither wanted to revisit it.

At any rate, Bridget was a changed person. She looked healthier, more *vibrant*. The sort of woman who was actually only middle-aged, who could easily get out there and find herself another guy but who seemed perfectly content to age gracefully by herself.

She quelled the urge to insist to Bridget that she stay put as the older woman began heading to her bedroom on the ground floor—a timely coincidence because the owners of the house from whom they were renting had had to cater for an ageing relative of their own.

Her stomach clenched as she heard the key being inserted into the front door.

She still wondered how he had managed to talk her into moving to London, a city she hated because it was too fast, too crowded and too noisy for her tastes.

But move to London she had, admittedly to a quieter part of the city, and now that she was here she was in danger of becoming just a little too accustomed to having Leo around. Okay, so he didn't show up *every* evening, and he never stayed the night, but his presence was becoming an addiction she knew she ought to fight.

He had dropped all talk of marriage and yet she still felt on red alert the second he walked through the door. Her eyes still feasted surreptitiously on him and, even though she knew that she should be thanking her lucky stars that he was no longer pursuing the whole marriage thing—because he had 'come to his senses' and 'seen the foolishness of hitching his wagon to a woman he didn't love'—she was oddly deflated by the ease with which he had jettisoned the subject.

As always, her first sight of him as he strode into the small hallway, with its charming flagstone floor and tiny stained-glass window to one side, was one of intense *awareness.* She literally felt her mouth go dry.

'You're here earlier than…um…normal.' She watched as he dealt her a slashing smile, one that made her legs go to jelly, one that made her want to hurl herself at him and wrap her arms around his neck. Every time she felt like this, she recalled what he had said about any marriage between them having upsides, having the distinct bonus of very good sex…

Leo's eyes swept over her in an appraisal that was almost unconscious. He took in the loose trousers, because there was just a hint of a stomach beginning to show; the baggy clothes that would have rendered any woman drab and unappealing but which seemed unbelievably sexy when she was wearing them.

'Is Bridget around?' He had to drag his eyes away from her. Hell, she had told him in no uncertain terms that mutual sexual attraction just wasn't enough on which to base a marriage, so how was it that she still turned him on? Even more so, now that she was carrying his baby.

'She's upstairs resting.'

'There's something I want to show you.' He had no doubt that he would be able to view the property at this hour. He was, after all, in the driving seat. 'So…why don't you get your coat on? It's a drive away.'

'What do you want to show me?'

'It's a surprise.'

'You know I hate surprises.' She blushed when he raised one eyebrow, amused at that titbit of shared confidence between them.

'This won't be the sort of surprise you got two years ago when you returned from a weekend away to find the pub flooded.'

'I'm not dressed for a meal out.' Nor was she equipped for him to resume his erosion of her defences and produce more arguments for having his way...although she killed the little thrill at the prospect of having him try and convince her to marry him.

'You look absolutely fine.' He looked her over with a thoroughness that brought hectic colour to her cheeks. And, while he disappeared to have a few quick words with Bridget, Brianna took the opportunity—cursing herself, because why on earth did it matter, really?—to dab on a little bit of make-up and do something with her hair. She also took off the sloppy clothes and, although her jeans were no longer a perfect fit, she extracted the roomiest of them from the wardrobe and twinned them with a brightly coloured thick jumper that at least did flattering things for her complexion.

'So, where are we going?' They had cleared some of the traffic and were heading out towards the motorway. 'Why are we leaving London?'

Leo thought of the perfect cottage nestled in the perfect grounds with all those perfect features and his face relaxed into a smile. 'And you're smiling.' For some reason that crooked half-smile disarmed her. Here in the car, as they swept out of London on a remarkably fine afternoon, she felt infected with a holiday spirit, a reaction to the stress she had been under for the past few weeks. 'A man's allowed to smile, isn't he?' He flashed her a sideways glance that warmed her face. 'We're having a baby, Brianna. Being cold towards one another is not an option.'

Except, she thought, *he* hadn't been cold towards *her*. He had done his damnedest to engage her in conversation and, thus far, he had remained undeterred by her lack of enthusiasm for engagement. She chatted because Bridget was usually there with them and he, annoyingly, ignored her cagey responses and acted as though everything was perfectly fine between them. He cheerfully indulged his mother's obvious delight in the situation and, although neither of them had mentioned the marriage proposal, they both knew that Bridget was contemplating that outcome with barely contained glee.

'I hadn't realised that I was being cold,' she said stiffly. Her eyes drifted to his strong forearms on the steering wheel. He had tossed his jacket in the back seat and rolled up the sleeves of his shirt to his elbows. She couldn't look even at that slither of bare skin, the sprinkling of dark hair on his arms, without her mind racing backwards in time to when they were lovers and those hands were exploring every inch of her body.

'No, sometimes you're not,' he murmured in a low voice and Brianna looked at him narrowly.

'Meaning?'

'Meaning that there are many times when your voice is cool but the glances you give me are anything but...' He switched the radio on to soft classical music, leaving her to ponder that remark in silence. Did he expect her to say something in answer to that? And what could she say? She *knew* that he had an effect on her; she *knew* that she just couldn't stop herself from sliding those sidelong glances at him, absorbing the way he moved, the curve of his mouth, the lazy dark eyes. Of course he would have noticed! What *didn't* he notice?

She was so wrapped up in her thoughts that she only noticed that they had completely left London behind when fields, scattered villages and towns replaced the hard strip of the motorway, and then she turned to him with confusion.

'We're in the countryside.' She frowned and then her breath caught in her throat as he glanced across to her with amusement.

'Well spotted.'

'It's a bit far to go for a meal out.' Perhaps he wanted to talk to her about something big, something important. Maybe he was going to tell her that he had listened to everything she had said and had come to the conclusion that he could survive with her returning to Ireland whilst he popped up occasionally to see his offspring. Perhaps he thought that a destination far away would be suitable for that kind of conversation, because it would allow her time to absorb it on the return trip back into London.

Had having her at close quarters reminded him of how little he wanted any kind of committed relationship? Had familiarity bred the proverbial contempt? For maybe the first time in his life, he had been tied to a routine of having to curtail his work life to accommodate both her and Bridget. Had he seen that as a dire warning of what might be expected should he pursue his intention of marrying her, and had it put him off?

The more she thought about it, the more convinced she was that whatever he had to say over a charming pub dinner in the middle of nowhere would be...

Something she wouldn't want to hear.

Yet she knew that that was the wrong reaction. She needed to be strong and determined in the road she wanted to follow. She didn't want a half-baked marriage with a guy who felt himself trapped, for whom the only option looming was to saddle himself with her for the rest of his life. No way!

But her heart was beating fast and there was a ball of misery unfurling inside her with each passing signpost.

When the car turned off the deserted road, heading up a charming avenue bordered by trees not yet in leaf, she lay back and half-closed her eyes.

She opened them as they drew up outside one of the prettiest houses she had ever seen.

'Where are we?'

'This is what I wanted to show you.' Leo could barely contain the satisfaction in his voice. He had been sold on first sight. On second sight, he was pleased to find that there was no let-down. It practically had her name written all over it.

'You wanted to show me a *house*?'

'Come on.' He swung out of the car and circled round to hold her door open for her, resisting the urge to help her out, because she had already told him that she hadn't suddenly morphed into a piece of delicate china simply because she was pregnant.

Brianna dawdled behind him as he strode towards the front door and stooped to recover a key which had been placed underneath one of the flower pots at the side of the front step. What the hell was going on? She took a deep breath and realised that, although they were only a matter of forty-five minutes out of West London, the air smelled different. Cleaner.

'This isn't just any house.' He turned to look at her and was pleased at the expression on her face, which was one of rapt appreciation. 'Bar the technicalities, I've bought this house.'

'You've *bought* this house?'

'Come in and tell me what you think.'

'But...'

'Shh...' He placed a finger gently over her parted lips

and the feel of his warm skin against hers made her tremble. 'You can ask all the questions you want after you've had a look around.'

Despite the fact that he had only looked around the place once, Leo had no hesitation on acting as tour guide for the house, particularly pointing out all the quaint features he was certain she would find delightful. There was a real fire in both the sitting room and the snug, an Aga in the kitchen, bottle-green bedrooms that overlooked an orchard, which he hadn't actually noticed on first viewing, but which he now felt qualified to show her with some pride. He watched as she dawdled in the rooms, staring out of the windows, touching the curtains and trailing her finger along the polished oak banister as they returned downstairs, ending up in the kitchen, which had a splendid view of the extensive back gardens.

The owners had clearly been as bowled over by his over-the-top, generous offer as he had anticipated. There was a bottle of champagne on the central island and two champagne glasses.

'Well? What do you think?'

'It's wonderful,' Brianna murmured. 'I'd never have thought that you could find somewhere like this so close to London. Is it going to be a second home for you?'

'It's going to be a first home for us.'

Brianna felt as though the breath had temporarily been knocked out of her. Elation zipped through her at the thought of this—a house, the perfect house, shared with the man she loved and their child. In the space of a few seconds, she projected into the future where she saw their son or daughter enjoying the open space, running through the garden with a dog trailing behind, while she watched from the kitchen window with Leo right there behind her, sitting by the big pine table, chatting about his day.

The illusion disappeared almost as fast as it had sur-faced because that was never going to be reality. The re-ality would be her, stuck out here on her own, while Leo carried on working all hours in the city, eventually bored by the woman he was stuck with. He would do his duty for his child but the image of cosy domesticity was an il-lusion and she had to face that.

'It's not going to work,' she said abruptly, turning away and blinking back stupid tears. 'Nothing's changed, Leo, and you can't bribe me into marrying you with a nice house and a nice garden.'

For a few seconds, Leo wasn't sure that he had heard her correctly. He had been so confident of winning her over with the house that he was lost for words as what she had said gradually sank in.

'I didn't realise that I was trying to bribe you,' he mut-tered in a driven undertone. He raked his fingers through his hair and grappled with an inability to get his thoughts in order. 'You liked the house; you said so.'

'I do, but a house isn't enough, just like sex isn't enough. That glue would never keep us together.' The words felt as though they had been ripped out of her and she had to turn away because she just couldn't bear to see his face.

'Right.' And still he couldn't quite get it through his head that she had turned him down, that any notion of marriage was over. He hesitated and stared at the stubborn angle of her profile then he strode towards the door. He was filled with a surge of restlessness, a keen desire to be outside, as if the open air might clear his head and point him towards a suitably logical way forward.

It was a mild evening and he circled the house, barely taking in the glorious scenery he had earlier made a great show of pointing out to her.

Inside, Brianna heard the slam of the front door and

spun around, shaking like a leaf. The void he had left behind felt like a physical, tangible weight in the room, filling it up until she thought she would suffocate.

Where had he gone? Surely he wouldn't just drive off and leave her alone here in the middle of nowhere? She contemplated the awkward drive back into London and wondered whether it wouldn't be better to be stuck out here. But, when she dashed out of the front door, it was to find his car parked exactly where it had been when they had first arrived. And he was nowhere to be seen.

He was a grown man, fully capable of taking care of himself, and yet as she dashed down the drive to the main road and peered up and down, failing to spot him, she couldn't stop a surge of panic rising inside her.

What if he had been run over by a car? It was very quiet here, she sternly told herself; what called itself the main road was hardly a thoroughfare. . In fact, no more than a tractor or two and the occasional passing car, so there was no need to get into a flap. But, like a runaway train, she saw in her mind's eyes his crumpled body lying at the kerbside, and she felt giddy and nauseous at the thought of it.

She circled the house at a trot, circled it again and then…she saw him sitting on the ground under one of the trees, his back towards the house. Sitting on the *muddy* ground in his hand-tailored Italian suit.

'What are you doing?' She approached him cautiously because for the life of her she had never seen him like this—silent, his head lowered, his body language so redolent of vulnerability that she felt her breath catch painfully in her throat.

He looked up at her and her mouth went dry. 'You have no intention of ever forgiving me for the lie I told you, have you?' he asked so quietly that she had to bend a little to hear what he was saying. 'Even though you know that I had no intention of engineering a lie when I first arrived. Even though you know, or you *should* know, that what appeared harmless to me at the time was simply a means towards an end. I was thinking on my feet. I never expected to end up painting myself into the box of pathological liar.'

'I know you're not that,' Brianna said tentatively. She settled on the ground next to him. 'Your suit's going to be ruined.'

'So will your jeans.'

'My jeans cost considerably less than your suit.' She ventured a small smile and met with nothing in response, just those dark, dark eyes boring into her. More than anything else she wanted to bridge the small gap between them and reach for his hand, hold it in hers, but she knew that that was just love, her love for him, and it wouldn't change anything. She had to stand firm, however tough it was. She had to project ahead and not listen to the little voice in her head telling her that his gesture, his magnificent gesture of buying this perfect house for her, was a sign of something more significant.

'You were right,' he admitted in the same sort of careful voice that was so disconcerting.

'Right about what?'

'I was trying to bribe you with this house. The garden. Anything that would induce you to give us a chance. But nothing will ever be enough for you to do that because you can't forgive me for my deception, even though it was a deception that was never intended to hurt you.'

'I felt like I didn't know who you were, Leo,' Brianna said quietly. 'One minute you were the man helping out at the pub, mucking in, presumably writing your book when you were closeted away in the corner of the bar…and then the next minute you're some high-flying millionaire with a penthouse apartment and a bunch of companies, and the book you were writing was never a book at all. It was just loads of work and emails so that you could keep your businesses ticking over while you stayed at the pub and used me to get information about Bridget.'

'God, Brianna it wasn't like that...' But she had spelt out the basic facts and strung them together in a way that made sense, yet made no sense whatsoever. He felt like a man with one foot off the edge of a precipice he hadn't even known existed. All his years of control, of always being able to manage whatever situation was thrown at him, evaporated, replaced by a confusing surge of emotions that rushed through him like a tsunami.

He pressed his thumbs against his eyes and fought off the craven urge to cry. Hell, he hadn't cried since his father had died!

'But it was,' she said gently. 'And even if I did forgive you...' *and she had* '...the ingredients for a good marriage just aren't there.'

'For you, maybe' He raised his head to stare solemnly at her. 'But for me, the ingredients are all there.'

CHAPTER TEN

HE LOOKED AT her solemnly and then looked away, not because he couldn't hold her stare, but because he was afraid of what he might see there, a decision made, a mind closed off to what he had to say.

'When I came to search out my mother, I had already presumed to know what sort of person she was: irresponsible, a lowlife, someone without any kind of moral code... In retrospect, it was a facile assumption, but still it was the assumption I had already made.'

'Then why on earth did you bother coming?'

'Curiosity,' Leo said heavily. Rarely given to long explanations for his behaviour, he knew that he had to take his time now and, funnily enough, talking to her was easy. But then, he had talked to her, really talked to her, a lot more than he had ever talked to any other woman in his life before. That should have been a clue to the direction his heart was taking, but it had been a clue he had failed to pick up on.

Now he had a painful, desperate feeling that everything he should have said had been left too late. In his whole life, he had never taken his eye off the ball, had never missed connections. He had got where he had not simply because he was incredibly smart and incredibly proactive but because he could read situations with the same ease with which he could read people. He always knew when to strike and when to hold back.

That talent seemed to have deserted him now. He felt that if he said one wrong word she would take flight, and then where would he be?

'I had a wonderful upbringing, exemplary, but there was always something at the back of my mind, something that needed to fill in the missing blanks.'

'I can get that.'

'I always assumed that...' He inhaled deeply and then sat back with his eyes closed. This was definitely not the best spot to be having this conversation but somehow it felt right, being outside with her. She was such an incredibly outdoors person.

'That?'

'That there must be something in me that ruled my emotions. My adoptive parents were very much in love. I had the best example anyone could have had of two people who actually made the institution of marriage work for them. And yet, commitment was something I had always instinctively rejected. At the back of my mind, I wondered whether this had something to do with the fact that I was adopted; maybe being given away as a baby had left a lasting legacy of impermanence, or maybe it was just some rogue gene that had found its way into my bloodstream; some crazy connection to the woman who gave birth to me, something that couldn't be eradicated.'

Brianna let the conversation wander. She wanted to reassure him that no such rogue gene existed in anyone, that whatever reasons he might have had in the past for not committing it was entirely within his power to alter that.

Except, she didn't want him to leap to the conclusion that any altering should be done on her behalf. She was still clinging to a thread of common sense that was telling her not to drop all her defences because he seemed so vulnerable. He might be one-hundred per cent sincere in wanting her to marry him, but without the right emotions she would have to stick fast to her decision. But it was difficult when her heart wanted to reach out to him and just assure him that she would do whatever it took to smooth that agonised expression from his face.

'As you know, I've been biding my time until I made this trip to find her. I had always promised myself that hunting down my past would be something I would do when my parents were no longer around.'

'I'm surprised you could have held out so long,' Brianna murmured. 'I would have wanted to find out straight away.'

'But then that's only one big difference between us, isn't it?' He gave her a half-smile that made her toes curl and threatened to permanently dislodge that fragile thread of common sense to which she was clinging for dear life. 'And I didn't appreciate just how *good* those differences between us were.'

'Really?' Brianna asked breathlessly. The fragile thread of common sense took a serious knocking at that remark.

'Really.' Another of those smiles did all sorts of things to her nervous system. 'I think it was what drew me to you in the first place. I saw you, Brianna, and I did a double take. It never occurred to me that I would find myself entering a situation over which I had no control. Yes, I lied about who I was, but there was no intention to hurt you. I would never have done that...*would* never do that.'

'You wouldn't?'

'Never,' he said with urgent sincerity. 'I was just passing through then we slept together and I ended up staying on.'

'To find out as much as you could about Bridget.'

'To be with you.'

Hope fluttered into life and Brianna found that she was holding her breath.

'I didn't even realise that I was sinking deeper and deeper. I was so accustomed to not committing when it came to relationships that I didn't recognise the signs. I told myself that I was just having time out, that you were a novelty I was temporarily enjoying but that, yes, I'd still be moving on.'

'And then you met her.'

'I met her and all my easy black-and-white notions flew through the window. This wasn't the lowlife who had jettisoned a baby without any conscience. This was a living, breathing human being with complexities I had never banked on, who overturned all the boxes I had been prepared to stick her in. I wanted to get to know her more. At the back of my mind—no, scratch that, at the forefront of my mind—I knew that I had dug a hole for myself with that innocuous lie I had told in the very beginning—and you know something? I couldn't have chosen a more inappropriate occupation for myself. Reading fiction is not my thing, never mind writing it. I didn't like myself for what I was doing, but I squashed that guilty, sickening feeling. It wasn't easy.'

'And then Bridget had that fall and...'

'And my cover was blown. It's strange, but most women would have been delighted to have discovered that the guy they thought was broke actually was a billionaire; they would happily have overlooked the "starving writer" facade and climbed aboard the "rich businessman" bandwagon. I'm sorry I lied to you, and I'm sorry I wasn't smart enough to come clean when I had the chance. I guess I knew that, if there was one woman on the planet who would rather the struggling writer than the rich businessman, it was you...'

Brianna shrugged.

'And, God, I'm sorry that I continued to stick to my facade long after it had become redundant... I seem to be apologising a heck of a lot.' His beautiful mouth curved into a rueful, self-deprecatory smile.

'And you don't do apologies.'

'Bingo.'

'What do you mean about sticking to your facade after it had become redundant?'

'I mean you laid into me like an avenging angel when you found out the truth about my identity and what did I do? I decided that nothing was going to change; that you might be upset, and we might have had a good thing going, but it didn't change the fact that I wasn't going to get wrapped up in justifying myself. Old habits die hard.'

He sighed and said, half to himself, 'When you walked out of my life, I let you go and it was the biggest mistake I ever made but pride wouldn't allow me to change my mind.'

'Biggest mistake?' Brianna said encouragingly.

'You're enjoying this, aren't you?' He slanted a glance at her that held lingering amusement.

'Err...'

'I can't say I blame you. We should go inside.'

'We can't sit on anything, Leo. We're both filthy. I don't think the owners would like it if we destroyed their lovely furniture with our muddy clothes.'

'My car, then. I assure you that that particular owner won't mind if the seats get dirty.' He stood up, flexed his muscles and then held out his hand for her to take.

She took it and felt that powerful current pass between them, fast, strong and invisible, uniting them. He pulled her up as though she weighed nothing and together they walked towards his car, making sure that the house was firmly locked before they left and the key returned to its original hiding place.

'No one living in London would ever dare to be so trusting,' he said, still holding her hand. She hadn't pulled away and he was weak enough to read that as a good sign.

'And no one where I live would ever be suspicious.'

He wanted to tell her that that was good, that if she chose to marry him, to share her life with him, she would be living somewhere safe, a place where neighbours trusted one another. If he could have disassociated himself from his extravagantly expensive penthouse apartment, he would have.

She insisted that they put something on the seats and he obliged by fetching a rug from the trunk, one of the many things which Harry had insisted would come in handy some day but for which he had never before had any use. Then he opened the back door of the car so that he wasn't annoyed by a gear box separating them.

Brianna stepped in and said something frivolous about back seats of cars, which she instantly regretted, because didn't everyone know what the back seats of cars were used for?

'But you liked the house; you said so.' Had he mentioned that before? Was he dredging up an old, tired argument which she had already rejected? 'It's more than just the house, Brianna, and it's more than just marriage because it makes sense. It's even bigger than my past, bigger than me wanting to do right by this child because of what happened to me when I was a baby.' He rested back and sought out her hand without looking at her.

Brianna squeezed his fingers tentatively and was reassured when he returned the gesture.

'If you hadn't shown up, if you hadn't sought me out to tell me about the pregnancy, I would have eventually come for you because you were more than just a passing relationship. I may have wanted to keep you in that box, but you climbed out of it and I couldn't stuff you back in and, hell, I tried.' He laughed ruefully. 'Like I said, old habits die hard.'

'It means a lot for you to say that you would have come for me,' Brianna said huskily. They weren't looking at one another but the connection was still thrumming between their clasped fingers.

'I wouldn't have had a choice, Brianna. Because I need you, and I love you, and I can't imagine any kind of life without you in it. I think I've known that for a long time, but I just didn't admit it to myself. I've never been in love with any one before, so what were my points of comparison? Without a shred of vanity, I will admit that life's been good to me. Everything I touched turned to gold, but I finally realised that none of the gold was worth a damn when the only woman I've ever loved turned her back on me.'

Brianna had soared from ground level to cloud nine in the space of a heartbeat.

'You *love* me?'

'Which is why marriage may not make sense to you, but it makes sense to me. Which is why all the ingredients are there…for me.'

'Why didn't you say?' She twisted to face him and flung her arms around his neck, which was an awkward position, because they were sitting alongside one another. But as she adjusted her body, so did he, until they were face to face, chest to chest, body pressed tightly against body. Now she was sure that she could feel his heart beating, matching hers.

'I love you so much,' she whispered shakily. 'When you proposed, all I could think was that you were doing it because it was the sensible option, and I didn't want us to be married because it was a sensible option. If I hadn't loved you so much, Leo, maybe I would have jumped at the chance—but I knew that if you didn't love me back that road would only end up leading to heartbreak.'

His mouth found hers and they kissed urgently and passionately, holding on to one another as if their lives depended on it.

'I've never felt anything like this before...' The feel of her against him was like a minor miracle. He wanted just to keep holding her for ever. 'And I didn't have the vocabulary to tell you how I felt. The only thing I could do was hope that my actions spoke on my behalf and, when they didn't, when I thought that I was going to lose everything...'

'You came out there...' She reached up and sighed with pleasure as their mouths met yet again, this time with lingering tenderness. She smoothed her fingers over his face and then through his hair, enjoying the familiarity of the sensation.

'So...' he said gravely. Even though he was ninety-nine per cent certain of the answer she would give him, he still feared that one per cent response he might hear. This, he thought, was what love felt like. It made you open and vulnerable to another person. It turned wanting into needing and self-control into a roller-coaster ride. He could think of nowhere he would rather have been.

'Yes. Yes, yes, yes! I'll marry you.'

'When?' Leo demanded and Brianna laughed with pleasure.

'When do you think? A girl needs time to plan these things, you know...'

'Would two weeks be time enough?'

She laughed again and looked at him tenderly. 'More than enough time!'

* * *

But in the end, it was six long weeks before they tied the knot in the little local church not a million miles away from her pub. The entire community turned out for the bash and, with typical Irish exuberance, the extremely happily wedded couple were not allowed to leave until for their honeymoon until the following morning.

They left a very proud Bridget behind to oversee the running of the pub because Ireland was her home in the end and she had been reluctant to leave it behind for good.

'But expect a very frequent visitor,' she had said to Brianna.

Brianna didn't doubt it. The older woman had redis-covered a joy for living ever since Leo had appeared on the scene, ever since she had rediscovered the baby, now a man, whom she had been compelled to give away at such a young age. She had spent her life existing under a dark cloud from which there had been no escape, she had con-fided to Brianna,. The cloud had now gone. Being asked to do the job of overseeing the pub, which had been signed over to her, was the icing on the cake.

Now, nearly two days after their wedding, Brianna sat on the veranda of their exquisite beach villa, a glass of orange juice in her hand and her baby bump a little big-ger than when she had first headed down to London with a madly beating heart to break the news of her pregnancy to the man who she could hear padding out to join her.

The past few weeks had been the happiest of her life. By the time they returned to England, the house which she had loved on sight would be theirs and what lay ahead glit-tered like a pathway paved in precious jewels: a life with the man she adored; a man who never tired of telling her how much he loved her; a baby which would be the perfect celebration of their love. And not forgetting Bridget, a true member of their family.

'What are you thinking?'

Brianna smiled and looked up at him. The sun had already set and the sea was a dark, still mass lapping against the sand. It was warm and the sound of myriad insects was harmonious background music: the Caribbean at its most perfect.

'I'm thinking that this must be what paradise is like.'

'Sun, sand and sea but without the alcoholic cocktails?' Leo teased, swinging round so that he could sit next to her and place his hand on her swollen stomach. He marvelled that he never seemed to tire of feeling the baby move. He was awestruck that he was so besotted with her, that he hated her being out of sight, that work, which had hitherto been his driving force, had taken a back seat.

'That's exactly right.' Brianna laughed and then her eyes flared as he slipped his hand under the loose cotton dress so that now it rested directly on her stomach, dipping below the swell to cup her between her legs.

'Have I told you how sexy I find your pregnant body?' he murmured into her ear.

'You may have once or twice, or more!' She lay back, as languorous as a cat, and smiled when he gave a low grunt of pleasure.

'And now...' he kissed the lobe of her ear and felt her smile broaden '...I think there are more pressing things for us to do than watch the sea, don't you?'

He could have added that he too now knew what paradise felt like.

* * * * *

MILLS & BOON
True Love
Romance from the Heart

Celebrate true love with tender stories of
heartfelt romance, from the rush of falling
in love to the joy a new baby can bring,
and a focus on the emotional
heart of a relationship.

LET'S TALK
Romance

For exclusive extracts, competitions
and special offers, find us online:

f   facebook.com/millsandboon

🐦   @MillsandBoon

📷   @MillsandBoonUK

Get in touch on 01413 063232

For all the latest titles coming soon, visit
millsandboon.co.uk/nextmonth